A NEW WAR

A NEW WAR

THE BETAVERSE · BOOK 3

MENILIK HENRY DYER

Podium

ISBN: 978-1-0394-5493-4

Published in 2025 by Podium Publishing
www.podiumaudio.com

A NEW WAR

CHAPTER 1

ATLAS

DEBATE

"At its current trajectory the alien ship will be within real-time-communication distance in less than a day," Atlas said after he received the message from the alien spacecraft.

Atlas leaned against the window of an orbiting platform looking out into deep space. A large see-through glass window stretched the entire circumference of the space station, giving everyone an unobstructed view of the Dottiens solar system. They were located so far out from the center of the system that the local sun looked more like a bright star. Atlas looked at his hand and saw how little it was illuminated by the star's light.

Atlas stepped back from the window and noticed everyone else in the room was already digesting the message they'd just received.

Angelique, Unity, and the three ships' AIs all began mentally absorbing it through their connected matrices—they were plugged in, of course.

Unity closed her eyes while reviewing the data multiple times, deconstructing it for any inconsistencies or hidden clues or another layer of meaning.

Atlas walked next to Peter, who was standing over Hezekiah's shoulder as he bought up the text message from the alien.

Everyone assumed the aliens were moving toward them to speak without needing to wait in between responses.

Atlas stepped away from the computer. "It's a rather rude message."

"I'd call it demanding," Peter said.

The team had just received a message from an alien species. The same species who had infected humans on Earth with the virus that had brainwashed the population.

That same virus slowly infected the humans on the worlds Atlas and Angelique had colonized. They dragged that same virus across the stars to their new worlds, too. It caused a lot of hurt and destruction as it subtly guided their societies away from exploring the betaverse—the real world.

Angelique was the first to identify something was wrong. But her method of extraction was much cruder. More akin to cutting out the virus. Not quite knowing what was happening but understanding it was something in the technology. So, her method involved her destroying all electronics on one of her worlds and starting from absolute scratch. It was not pretty, but it had worked.

Atlas had found a way to destroy the virus that wiped it from the worlds they controlled. And this was obviously what had caused the alien to confront the team now.

Right when the team had successfully cleared all traces of the virus, an alien had arrived in the system and blown up the Starnet— the FTL communication network the team had developed.

The alien had then demanded to negotiate or risk everyone being destroyed. Then, to add insult to injury, the alien was now demanding the team leave the safety of their space station and travel into the aliens' vessel. It wanted the teams to travel physically, too. They wanted them to take the devices containing their brain matrices into an eleph-ANT and negotiate in person.

Unity walked over toward the two old men, Atlas and Peter, who were still staring at the screen. "I don't think we have a choice."

Peter shook his head. "We always have a choice."

Atlas scratched the back of his neck. "They want our matrices for a reason. I'm not sure we should give them to them."

"Could it be a trap?" Angelique asked.

"It's a negotiation tactic," Peter said. "They know if we are here on our own space station then we will negotiate as equals. If we are on their ship, then it's clear they are the powerful ones. I don't think we should let them have the upper hand."

Hezekiah swiveled around on his chair to face the group. "We don't know what they're capable of. If we say no, they might just come over here and take our matrices."

"They can try," Peter said almost instinctually but not sounding convincing.

Atlas knew Peter was acting braver than he really was. Personally, Atlas wasn't so sure. In his mind there were risks with either option. The alien made it clear it was nonnegotiable—they had to meet in person. So, denying the request would immediately cause the negotiations to end and force the alien to respond. *But respond in what way?* he thought. He started looking around the room for a piece of paper.

His ship noticed the erratic glancing around and handed him a notebook and a pen.

They were running out of time to decide; the invisible countdown timer of when the alien would dock in system was heavy on everyone's mind. Atlas drew a line down the middle of the notebook and began writing a pro and con list. "We have two options." He wrote on one side of the line, *Demand to stay,* and on the other side he wrote, *Go to the alien ship.* "If we decide to go, they'll have control of our matrices. Meaning they can take us back to Earth even if we disagree. So, I don't think we should do it."

"Agreed," Peter added. "We should make them work for it. Going straight to them should be a last resort."

"I'm not sure that's the best move," Angelique said. "We don't know what they're capable of doing. We don't know their culture, either. It might take negotiation off the table."

Atlas offered up an answer. "Maybe we don't say no. Maybe we just say we can't."

As if preempting their response, the alien supposed-god race sent them a message with instructions on how to load their matrices into an eleph-ANT.

"There goes that plan." Unity finished reviewing the instructions. "They seem determined to get us onto their ship."

"Do we vote?" Unity suggested.

Peter shook his head. "I don't think we're done understanding our options yet." He pointed at the piece of paper. "I get the feeling they want us on that ship. So the next question is do they have the capability to get us there if we say no?"

Atlas looked around the room and saw shrugs from everyone.

"Okay, so we don't know whether they have the capabilities to force us. Let's assume they don't. Can we still engage in a negotiation in good faith without being on their ship?"

Again, as if answering the question posed by Atlas, they received an addendum to the question he just asked. It clarified by saying negotiations would only take place on their ship and there would be consequences if they didn't. There was no mention of what those consequences were.

Atlas felt the mood of the team change slightly, the timely response from the alien acting as a reminder of just how close to them it was.

Atlas wondered if they had a bug listening to their conversations because this was the second time they'd received a message as soon as one of them had asked the question. But that wasn't possible because any messages would have needed to be sent before Atlas had even posed the question because of light speed delays. But then again, these aliens had spent many, many years manipulating, and obviously understanding, human behavior. Maybe this was just educated guessing. They probably had a really well-developed algorithm of how humans would respond. Atlas's mind went back and forth on the idea the alien had been in hiding on his ship. So, they probably had a model of how everyone in the room right now would respond to this situation.

"That was creepy; they knew exactly what we were discussing," Atlas said after he reread the message on Hezekiah's screen for the second time. "Okay so what are the risks of going over?"

"Utter destruction," Peter offered.

Hezekiah spoke a little cautiously. "It sounds like we might get that if we say no, too."

Atlas bit his lower lip. "Let's be serious for a second. Is it truly unwise for us to board their ship? Are we absolutely sure we'll be destroyed if we go there?"

Atlas looked around the room and saw blank faces staring back at him.

Hezekiah stepped away from the computer; he looked a bit stressed. "If we go, at least we're not aggravating them."

"I agree," Unity added. "I'd rather not anger them."

Atlas didn't know Unity or Hezekiah very well. But got the feeling they leaned more toward the risk-averse side of the spectrum.

There was a long patch of silence before Angelique spoke. "It sounds like we're doomed if we do, doomed if we don't. So what do we do? I don't want to go, but I also don't want to find out what they do if we say no."

"Run?" Peter suggested.

"If we were going to run," Atlas said, "we should have done that before they got this close. It's too late." Even as he said those words, Atlas felt the closing in of a metaphorical wall around him. He felt the number of options available to him shrink just a little.

"There's a third option," Ariana said, speaking for the first time. "We can do both."

Everyone looked at her at once.

Atlas felt a slight pressure that he didn't know was there lift a little at the mention of another option.

Ariana still had her eyes closed as she spoke. "Angelique has a matrix-production unit on her ship. We duplicate ourselves and send one version of ourselves there and leave one here."

"That's not a bad idea," Angelique said. "If we use my Ange's Angel protocol we can ensure the two versions of us want to come back together."

"What if the aliens capture a version of us?" Hezekiah asked, seemingly switching sides in the debate.

Without a beat Ariana replied with a level of coldheartedness that sounded out of place with what she was suggesting. "Self-destruct."

Angelique's mouth fell open. "Suicide!"

"I don't want to kill myself. I'd rather get carted off to some lab somewhere to be studied," Hezekiah said, again arguing against the side he was supporting moments before.

Peter raised his hands inserting some much-needed order to the chaos, which was this conversation up until this point. "Let's vote. I suspect everyone only wants to go if we duplicate ourselves so we don't face the risk of absolute death?"

Nods came all around the room, so Peter continued. "We have two options. One, we stay here and attempt to negotiate. Or two, we split into two and send one version of each of us to the alien ship."

Before Peter opened the voting, Atlas spoke. "Assuming this is a trap and the aliens plan on dragging us back to Sol anyway, or worse they want to destroy us, then splitting into two is our best chance at survival because the version of us still here can do something about it."

Atlas nodded at Peter to confirm he was finished speaking.

"Okay," Peter said. "Now we vote."

CHAPTER 2

PETER

DECISION

Peter asked the first question. "Who is in favor of staying here and forcing the aliens' hand?"

Hezekiah tentatively raised his hand before seeing he was alone and lowering it again.

Peter continued. "Who's in favor of boarding the alien spacecraft?"

Tentatively everyone raised their hands.

"Next question. Who is in favor of taking a self-destruct device?"

Peter watched as everyone around the room wore different looks on their faces. He saw a lot of hesitation, which he considered strange. Because in his mind a self-destruct device big enough to destroy the aliens' ship would be the ultimate deterrent. It would mean they couldn't be held captive indefinitely. It also meant they had a weapon, albeit one deadly to everyone involved. But most importantly it meant they would have leverage in any negotiation. In Peter's experience, whoever was able to and willing to walk away from a conversation was the ultimate decider of the outcome. Peter had been in many negotiations where he could tell the other side wasn't willing to walk away. He had never not gotten everything he wanted in that scenario. Sometimes he even had to stop himself from getting too greedy and taking more than he should.

In Peter's mind, having a bomb they could use to self-destruct was the only way of insuring they could walk away from the negotiation table if they needed to. Besides, a copy of them would still be on board the space station.

Atlas interrupted before the team had a chance to vote. "I don't think we discussed what that actually means. We would need to agree on which scenarios could constitute the use of a self-destruction device."

"Veto!" Angelique said rather forcefully.

"Veto?" Unity raised an eyebrow. "Why does she get veto rights?"

"It's my ship, and my technology for the matrices. So yes, I do get the right to say no to an option." She took a deep breath. "Besides, if they take one of my Ange's Angels, then I'm heading back to Juniper to grab an army."

Peter liked Angelique's tone; she sounded resolute. Confident. Where was this woman when they were discussing options? From memory, she had a lot of planets under her control, too. So she had the resources to pull something like that off. He had a sneaking suspicion she could take out Earth if she wanted to.

Peter almost left it at that, but he wanted to understand this new Angelique a bit more by challenging her; he was curious. So he asked the questions, anyway. "Why not have it there just as a deterrent? Entering the aliens' spacecraft means we can't walk away from the negotiation, which puts us at a serious disadvantage. These aliens have already shown themselves capable of manipulation and lying."

"Two reasons. You don't go into a good faith negotiation with a weapon. If we're going to do it, we should treat them with respect. And secondly"—she looked around the room at everyone, and when she looked at Peter, he got the sense that she was saying to him that he didn't know what she knew—"none of you have duplicated yourselves before, so you might not understand this. But it's an entirely new version of you. We would be committing suicide. Not in the sense that a backup will be left on this ship. A version of you will be gone. Forever." She looked toward her feet as she spoke. "There's no scenario where I would sacrifice an Ange's Angel. I would do everything in my power to bring her back." Then she looked up again, as if she realized the room had others in there, too. "I'd want to bring us all back."

Peter saw where she was coming from. He almost didn't believe it was worth losing the leverage in the negotiations for. But when he'd first thought about using the self-destruct device, he had imagined someone else self-destructing. It was another version of him, but not him. But Angelique rightly reframed the argument as committing suicide, and he understood it. Because it would be him. And he didn't think he would be willing to kill himself in order to walk away from the negotiation table. Taking a bad deal was better than losing his life—even if a version of him would still be around.

Thinking about it some more, Peter was impressed how quickly Angelique had changed his mind on the subject.

"Okay," Peter said. "We won't take something to self-destruct. Let's assume we can run from them. Should we run?"

"Let's not relitigate things, Pete. We've already decided to visit that alien out there." Atlas pointed out the window. "Besides, aren't you just a little curious to meet another intelligent alien? Icarus is going to be so jealous."

"We still need to decide what we're willing to bargain with in the negotiation," Angelique said. "We are not giving up territory. Especially in systems we already control. But perhaps we could offer technology."

Unity gabbed a chair and sat down. "That's assuming they're not millions of years more technologically advanced than us. We might need to think of something more we can offer."

"What else do we have?" Hezekiah asked.

The room went silent. No one spoke for a good while. Peter assumed everyone was contemplating the idea of meeting an alien species much more advanced than them, that they would have nothing to offer. Peter shook his head because all of this was pure guesswork. They didn't know what the aliens' ultimate goal was, and they didn't know what sort of technology they had. "We're all just guessing. We have no data points on which to base our beliefs about these aliens. In the vacuum of information, we're all simply speculating. We need to get on with it and find out."

Ariana had been quite in the corner for a long time. Everyone had come to expect that of her whenever a new puzzle emerged. She had a habit of closing her eyes and using her artificial minds to analyse. Peter assumed she had figured something out when she spoke. "I've reviewed the blueprints from those aliens."

Along with the various messages received from the aliens was an eleph-ANT design file they'd offered that was capable of carrying everyone's matrices in it.

Ariana continued. "It's basically a design for an eleph-ANT with our matrices inside, and a mobile hapticgram projector so we can move around. But they didn't account for the fact Angelique's new matrix designs are smaller—much smaller. Instead of being the size of a huge barrel they're the size of a small beer can."

"Is that a Skippy reference?" Hezekiah asked.

"Who's Skippy?" Ariana asked, shaking her head disapproving of the interruption. "Anyway," she continued. "We can fill that space with some hardware that will allow us to change our playback speed. And enter a private room where we can discuss things."

"I like it," Peter said. "That way when we learn what these aliens want, we can have a robust discussion in private."

Atlas nodded at the team. "We really need to come up with a name for them. We can't keep calling them the aliens."

"What if we just call them penguins?" Unity suggested.

"That might be a bit rude," Atlas said. "We wouldn't want to be called filthy monkeys."

Hezekiah smiled. "Okay that's gotta be an ExForce reference."

Atlas winked at him. "What about the Pingus? It's less on the nose than penguins but suffers from the same thing. It might be a little derogatory."

"I don't think we need a temporary name," Angelique said. "We're about to meet them, and we can find out what these aliens prefer to be called." Angelique shifted the subject somewhat. "Why don't we drop the need to house our matrices in an eleph-ANT altogether? My ship also has the capabilities to print android bodies. So, we could all have our own bodies, rather than being confined to a single eleph-ANT."

Peter shook his head. "Usually I'd want that. But in this case the alien doesn't know the technology you have on board your ship. Let's not open their mind to the possibility we have more than we're currently showing them."

There were nods around the room with that logic, and the team got started working. Ariana started configuring the eleph-ANT to house the smaller matrices in a way that made it look like they were the original bigger-sized ones, getting the help from the ships as she did.

Angelique started scanning the team's matrices to build a copy of each of them. They had to work quickly since the alien was on its way to them. Before long the team had completed all the tasks, and an eleph-ANT was sitting in the cargo bay housing a version of them inside of it.

Hopefully the aliens would not notice all the additional circuitry and processing power stuffed inside of the eleph-ANT.

Thanks to Angelique's suggestion, they never turned the other versions of themselves on. As she said, "It breaks the magic of believing there's only one version of you. It makes it easier to remerge everyone together."

The team stood in the cargo bay looking at the eleph-ANT as it exited the air lock for its short journey to the alien spacecraft.

CHAPTER 3

ANGE

THE MEETING OF TWO SPECIES

Angelique, or Ange, as she had to remind herself, drifted into consciousness. Even though she had cloned herself many, many times before, she never got used to the feeling of waking up believing she was Angelique but then experiencing the slight disappointment when she realized she was a copy—an Ange's Angel. What made her different from just a standard copy of Angelique was that all Ange's Angels had a deep-rooted desire to recombine with Angelique. It made her feel like a piece of her was missing and she needed to get whole again.

The eleph-ANT that carried Ange had a mobile haptic-graphic projector unit, which meant her avatar faded into existence. Then next to her, her Ship appeared, too.

She gave him a little wave, then noticed the clothing on her arms flopped down. She looked down at the dress she was wearing and realized nothing looked right. Her body and clothes were still obeying the laws of gravity. She gave the mental command, and the experience around her changed. She began floating in zero g out in deep space as the eleph-ANT carrying her made the short journey from her spacecraft to the aliens'.

Then she gave the mental command, and she and Ship became outfitted in space suits. Complete with tethers connecting them to the eleph-ANT. *Much better,* she thought to herself.

The eleph-ANT they were tethered to had traveled for quite a while before she was switched on. So, when she looked back toward the space station they had come from, it looked like a large glowing star in the sky because it was reflecting a lot of light from the system's host sun. She could barely make out any of the features on the orbital platform.

She was about to turn her head toward the alien ship they were approaching when Ariana appeared next to her in a similar space suit.

Ange looked at her puzzlingly because it was Ange's technology powering everything. Her eleph-ANT, too. Only she should have had the override codes to turn herself on before the others.

Ship filled in the details. "It looks like she never went to sleep. She removed the coded ability to turn herself off."

Suddenly she felt a bit self-conscious, as if she was doing something suspicious and might be caught, even though she wasn't; she was simply wanting to steady herself and acclimate to being an Ange before the others joined. She quickly gave the mental commands to turn on the rest of the team, lest anyone get suspicious.

Everyone else winked into existence in similar-looking space suits.

Ange pointed toward the alien spacecraft they were fast approaching. She watched as everyone stared, mouths wide-open in amazement.

It was the first time they had properly seen an alien technology up close. And it was interesting.

The enormous alien spacecraft looked like four dark spherical objects connected together in a pyramid shape, the outside of each circular object almost devoid of color. She couldn't tell which of the bubbles was the primary one.

The shape of it wasn't what made everyone stare—these were all shapes that they had seen before. It was the simple fact they were all looking at an alien design for a spacecraft. It was new, interesting, different. The novelty of it all made it impossible to look away from. Combine that with the fact she was getting closer and closer, which meant more details were revealed as they approached it.

Ange struggled to gain a sense of size without a reference point. Despite all her advantages of being a simulated human, her vision still suffered from the limitations inherent to all humans. Without a comparison point, she wasn't able to comprehend the size of the alien vehicle. On a planet's surface, where humans had evolved, there were always trees or buildings around, which made it easy for humans to quickly judge the size of something. Out in deep space there wasn't anything to compare it to.

She sent a message to Ship, and a projection of her spacecraft appeared in front of them. That put the size of the alien vehicle in perspective. It was enormous. About eighteen times as big as what she was traveling in. She wondered if all that space was full of aliens.

"Is it a colony ship?" she muttered to herself. "Or maybe a generation ship?"

It looked big enough to house thousands of humans at once. She didn't know how big this alien was, but surely a lot of them would fit in the spaceship she was looking at.

Hearing her muttering, Unity replied, "Surely they wouldn't come out here with a spacecraft full of living creatures. You wouldn't threaten another alien species in a colony ship."

Hezekiah wiped something off the top of his visor. "They would if it was full of soldiers, not civilians."

Ange considered that for a moment. Was there really an army inside of that thing? Surely, they had been spying on the betas ever since they had left Earth. It made sense that they understood the technology humans had. So they had access to the Starnet. Surely it made more sense to send a ship that didn't have any sentience in it. So, if things went wrong they were not losing any lives. A shudder went up her spine when she thought about how advanced this aliens' technology must be if they confidently brought a ship full of life to a situation like this.

Reading the change in emotions, Peter took control of the situation. "Let's not speculate. We're moments away from finding out what's really inside of that ship."

He was right: a glowing arrow started to appear on one of the orbs pointing toward something. Ange used the enhanced cameras on the eleph-ANT to take a closer look. The alien was guiding them toward an air lock door. It was a large square door with two gears, or at least they looked like gears, on the outside—one large and one small. The bigger axle started spinning counterclockwise, which set off the smaller one spinning at a fast pace in the opposite direction.

There were no sounds in space, but Ange felt like she heard an audible click when the gears stopped spinning and the door began to swing outward. It swung slowly at first.

Ange noticed everyone had their eyes fixated on what was happening. Light was shining brightly out of the square exit. Gas filled the chamber, enhancing the glow.

Ange couldn't help but hear ominous music inside her head as she approached the opening. She felt a mixture of dread and excitement. The mixture of feelings churned inside her stomach. She hadn't felt this way since she'd colonized her first planet. That exhilarating feeling of not quite knowing what was about to happen.

This was the reason she'd joined the beta-explorer program in the first place—discovery and exploration.

They were approaching the lip of the entrance now. Nothing was visible yet; smoke still emanated from the exit, limiting everyone's view. It felt cold and slightly magical.

The eleph-ANT carrying all of them slowly made it through the air lock door. Visibility was still nonexistent as they slowly moved inside.

Ange switched her eyesight to infrared. Infrared could see through gas, but it had no ability to see markings on the walls. So she could make out the outlines of the walls and anything on them. But any drawings or markings painted on the surface would be invisible. She still wasn't able to see anything in the room. She was in a large chamber. The panels were flat. Same with the floor and ceiling.

The eleph-ANT carrying them all touched down on what Ange was now considering the floor, the legs of the eleph-ANT engaging magnetic clamps to lock the eleph-ANT into place. Then Ange and the team floated down afterward. Their space suits disappearing in a pop as their feet touched the surface.

"What now?" Atlas asked.

Almost as if answering the question, the smoke throughout the room started to dissipate. Either it was being sucked out of the room, or the room was being filled with some sort of clear gas—Ange couldn't tell which of the two.

Either way, it gave her visibility throughout the room. The room was like a large cargo hangar. On one side of the room Ange clearly saw some hinges, and it looked like that whole side of the room could open up. This chamber was probably used as a temporary holding room to cycle in an atmosphere to balance it with the rest of the ship.

On the wall to the left of them was a smaller air lock door. Barely big enough to fit a human through without bending down. It had some strange markings on it that Ange didn't recognize.

The team stood there for a good while, nothing really happening and not quite knowing what to do. It gave the team a false sense of safety. Ange felt herself relax a little, and her mind started to think about the technology she was about to witness.

Ange pointed up at one of the corners. There was a large contraption that kinda resembled a camera. "They're watching us."

Atlas nodded. "I think that has a hapticgraphic projector built into it. It's way too big to just be a camera." He floated up toward it. "It's a very similar design, too; they have been stealing our technology."

Hezekiah had noticeably relaxed. Seeing the smaller door, he ran over to it to take a closer look. "If this is a standard door for them, then they're a small species of alien."

He was right; next to Hezekiah's monstrous size, the door looked fit for a baby.

The small door clicked open, and Hezekiah yelped. He jumped back toward the others, almost cowering behind the eleph-ANT.

The door opened just a little, then out the side of the door the head of a little penguin-looking alien appeared.

The alien made a few guttural sounds, then wore on its face what Ange assumed was confusion. It poked its head back out the door. Ange assumed it left to turn the translators back on.

Moments later its head poked back through the air lock.

CHAPTER 4

CLONE OF ARIANA

THIS IS STRANGE

Ariana briefly opened her eyes again when the alien popped its small head back through the doorway. Her mind was mostly focused on taking over control of all the sensors on the eleph-ANT so she could complete her scans. Her plan was to watch a replay of the conversation with the alien back once she was done.

But she was human, and curiosity got the better of her. She left her subconscious to continue working through the hack while she put her focus on what everyone else was focused on.

She quickly replayed the last few moments before the alien arrived, checking whether she missed anything. The only item of note was that Atlas had grabbed some sort of spray device from out of the back of the eleph-ANT and had begun spraying some fine mist around the room. After watching him for a few moments, slightly confused about what that old man was up to, she returned to real time.

She heard the translator of the alien speak: "You made a mistake coming here. You shouldn't have come."

Ariana paused the conversation for a moment and considered what was just said. Why had this species just told them they'd made a mistake when they were the ones who'd told them to come?

Maybe that was a translation error. Maybe the aliens' version of a universal translator—or what the *Hitchhiker's Guide to the Galaxy* called a babel fish—wasn't processing the information clearly. Unlikely, since these aliens had been studying humans for longer than she'd been alive. But just in case, she wrote a quick algorithm that would record the translated and real versions of what the alien said. She would later use this information for building her own translator program. She also loaded the previous conversation with the alien into the algorithm she wrote.

Ariana studied the alien. It looked like it evolved from an animal that was oddly similar to a penguin. She figured that was a unique quirk of convergent evolution. Its legs were much longer, and its two flippers had evolved into something resembling arms. Stretched out straight, they looked exactly like flippers, but they bent in joints and at the ends forming something equivalent to hands allowing it to manipulate objects.

She then continued the conversation with the alien at a higher playback speed so she could catch up to real time.

Peter and Ange both stepped forward, designating themselves the team spokesmen. Ariana knew the de facto leader had to be one of them—they were clearly the most comfortable in that role. She knew Peter was quick on his feet and would ask the right questions. But from what she'd learned from Ange, she might actually be better suited to leading this small expedition. The technology she wielded was orders of magnitude more capable than anything Ariana had seen before. Ange was hiding a lot of the tech she had at her fingertips—and because of the security protocols she was using, Ariana hadn't glimpsed much of it yet. Ange also had more experience exploring this galaxy than the others, so that also gave her the most credibility.

Ange spoke first. "Are you the same alien that spoke to us before?"

"Yes, I did. But . . ." The alien looked visibly frustrated.

At least Ariana assumed that was a look of frustration. She quickly made an update to the algorithm she was using to build a translator. She wanted it to record facial gestures and body movements, too. Hopefully she would be able to build up a better understanding of the alien's body language.

"You told us to come here," Peter said. "And now you're telling us we shouldn't have come?"

The alien looked down toward its chest. It opened its mouth to speak, but then, as if hearing something coming, it turned around and left, the door closing behind it.

"That was odd," Ariana heard Atlas say as she closed her eyes, ignoring the conversation again.

She would rely on one of her subconscious minds to listen to the conversations between the others and alert her if she needed to tune in again. Otherwise she would watch a recording of what was discussed later.

One of Ariana's subconsciousnesses had successfully hacked its way into the eleph-ANT's sensors. She didn't have control of the machine, yet, but she had enough access to start her scans of the alien vessel.

She directed the eleph-ANT to begin scanning on all communication channels. She wanted to scan the radio frequencies to see if any signals were traveling around the ship. Was there any natural chatter around the ship? It would be great if she could find an alien equivalent of a Wi-Fi signal. Then maybe she could hack into that.

It stood to reason that any ship that had sentient life on it would also have Wi-Fi or cellular connectivity for communication. Or even if she wasn't able to detect something like that, she might be able to spot other signals in the background sounds of the ship. The hum of the engine could also give her an understanding of just how powerful they were. She wanted the eleph-ANT to begin recording anything and everything so that later she could spend time going through the data collected.

While that was happening, she focused the eleph-ANT's sensors on the large device on the ceiling of the room. She confirmed it was in fact a hapticgraphic projector.

She was about to review the data collected by the eleph-ANT so far when one of her subconsciousnesses interrupted her with news that the aliens' door was opening again.

Arian opened her eyes just in time to see the alien penguin-looking thing standing in the doorway, the door now fully open. The alien stood tall, despite looking so tiny.

It took several steps forward through the door and stood in front of everyone, flippers behind its back. Ariana assumed it was projecting confidence and control.

It looked like the same alien as the one that had just poked its head through the doorway a moment ago. But the way it carried itself looked completely different. Where the last one felt a little afraid of them, this one felt like they were beneath it.

Ariana quickly pulled together a facial-recognition algorithm. It compared the three different faces of the alien they had seen and concluded with 97 percent confidence that they were all the same alien.

Hmm, that's strange, she thought. *Unless they're clones.*

Clones could make more sense, since all of them would look exactly the same, but presumably there would be personality drift between the different copies. So it stood to reason that they could all look the same but be different individuals.

Ariana quickly updated her algorithm to include body language. The probability they were all the same being reduced dramatically. She made a mental note to tell the others that differentiating these aliens from one another would be hard.

The alien stepped forward, exuding confidence and control. It stood right in between Ange and Peter. It was truly tiny. Its head barely came up to Peter's waist.

But you wouldn't have thought it was the smallest creature in the room. It acted as if everyone was there to serve the alien. The way it carried itself, Ariana thought it was telling the team that talking to them was a waste of time.

Ariana wondered why she had that feeling from the way it was acting. Then she remembered it had spent a lot of time studying human behaviors. It knew them. And it knew exactly how to portray itself as being in charge of everyone—despite being less than a meter tall.

It didn't look up toward any of them as it spoke. It looked straight ahead, guttural sounds coming out of its beak before a translator kicked in. "Welcome. You may ask three questions before we begin the negotiations."

Peter and Ange looked at each other before nodding. It was Peter who asked the question. "What do we call you?"

"You call yourself humans, but the word we call you is—" A scratching sound was heard out of the translator. "That roughly translates to 'sentience with no heart.' We have deliberated for some time on what you should call us if we ever met. We know human egos will take some time before you are comfortable calling us your god. So in the meantime you can call us Atua."

Ariana liked that this Atua creature was quite elaborate with its answer. It told them more than she'd expected. There was meaning in what it called them. Did no heart mean humans were heartless, ruthless? Or was there another meaning in that sentence?

Ariana received another notification from another subconscious. This one was monitoring changes in centrifugal force, essentially monitoring to see if the momentum of the spacecraft changed in any way. The subconscious node told her they were beginning to accelerate away from her ship. This was something she needed to tell the others.

In an instant she pulled the others out of their bodies and into a white room. She also adjusted their playback speed so the alien wouldn't notice anything happening. The team could now have a five-minute conversation in subjective time—but it would only register one second in reality.

Ariana spoke as everyone winked into existence. "We're starting to move."

"Moving? Where?" Peter paused for a moment. "Let's tackle the movement piece in a moment. But first we should figure out what to ask next."

Unity fixed a curl in her big afro. "Should we ask them where they're taking us?"

Ange shook her head. "That's good information to know. But if we only have three, it's not going to help us with the negotiations. What if we ask why the Atua believes it owns this solar system?" She almost spat out the word Atua. "Did anyone else catch that reference? *Atua* is simply another word for *god*. I believe in New Zealand that's the word for *god*. If that's the reference, then they have a massive god complex."

Peter offered up a slight change in the wording. "I agree with the question. But let's expand it a little. Why do they believe they own all these solar systems—including ours?"

The team agreed. And depending on the answer, they all decided to come back into this room again to coordinate on the final question.

The alien replied in a similar detailed fashion. "We have been exploring this region of space for many centuries now. When we first took pictures of your planet, you'd claimed it. We have a culture of ownership. The first of our kinds to discover something owns it. We know you have a different culture. We know you probably believe your planet is yours. But that's not our culture." The alien spoke with menace. "We are not willing to change for you. But . . ." The alien paused for a moment, and Ariana thought she detected the translator voice had a smile in it. "We might be willing to sell it to you. With some conditions, of course."

"You said it yourself," Peter said. "Our ancestors were on the planet before you even visited us."

"That is a follow-up query. Is this your final question, or do you want to have another private discussion first?" Without waiting for the answer, the Atua continued. "Regardless I will allow this piece of clarification. You are correct, those were your ancestors. Your ancestors owned the planet before us. But when they died, their ownership passed onto me. I am the rightful owner now." Then the alien anticipated their next objection: Why did this alien become the rightful owner of the planet and not them? "Ownership does not pass onto someone simply because of the lottery of birth. You surely wouldn't be happy with nepotism. It passes onto the next person to put in a genuine claim. That next person was me. You have no real translation for my name. But you may call me—"

The Atua made a show of scratching its chin in thoughtful contemplation. Surely that was not a gesture that came natural to it; it was putting on a show for their sake. "Pale Blue Dot. In reference to Carl Sagan, who called your planet a pale blue dot to signify the irrelevance of your planet in the cosmos, and since I'm the owner of that blue dot. PBD for short."

PBD was doing its best to shame everyone in the room. But for whatever reason, Ariana found she liked its approach. She found it charming on some level. And slightly funny. Almost like a comedy routine. She wondered whether that was on purpose.

The team reentered the white room where only they could talk to one another.

"I like his cockiness," Unity said as everyone appeared.

"Don't get me started on how cute it is." Ange smiled. "It's like a small child telling us it's the king of our planet. I can't get that image out of my head."

Atlas, who had been deep in contemplation, and possibly a bit in awe of what was going on, finally spoke for the first time in a long while. "So what do we ask next?"

"Let's ask them what they want?" Hezekiah said. "What can we offer them in exchange for continuing to do what we want to do?"

Both Peter and Ange shook their heads at the same time. Ange gestured for Peter to explain why. "That last line from PBD was a trap. It was designed to get us to ask that question. If we ask it what it wants for Earth or any of the other solar systems we've already visited, then we're implicitly saying that we agree to their rules. And we agree that we are in one of their solar systems."

"Exactly." Ange added. "It won't be long before we're haggling over the price for a solar system we already own." Ange paused for a moment. "Why don't we ignore that trap and gain some other insights? Do they know of any other sentience in the solar system? Or how many planets in the Milky Way have they visited?"

"I'm interested in knowing whether they've met any other smart aliens—like us." Atlas bit his lower lip. "And with the way it answers questions, asking that question might also shed light on which other stars they've visited."

"PBD is unlikely to answer that," Ange said after thinking about her original question for a bit. "I wouldn't answer how many stars I control, nor would I tell it if I'd met any other aliens because then it might be able to piece that information together to guess which star systems my people are in."

Peter scratched his chin thoughtfully. "What if we ask it about Earth? What it did to humanity back on Earth. Why did it push us all down the path of entering the metaverse?"

The team agreed to that, and within a moment they were all standing back in front of the alien.

Ariana could tell the Atua wasn't expecting that question because it took a while to respond. It also made eye contact with Ange for half a second, which was the first time it had made eye contact with anyone. Ariana thought she registered a moment of fluster because the alien regained its composure and started to look straight ahead again. Maybe its models for what they would ask were wrong. Maybe they weren't as accurate at predicting what the team would do.

Or maybe this was just an elaborate act by this Atua creature. Because there was no way its body language would be recognizable to humans with so little exposure. So maybe they had asked exactly what it wanted them to ask. And maybe this was just a charade that was all planned in advance.

Ariana noted to find answers to this later.

PBD began speaking in its usual clicky tone before the translator kicked in. "Your question is an important one. Why did we decide to limit your technological progress, rather than see you continue to grow as you had been? The answer is simple. We didn't want ants in our backyard. We've watched you for quite some time, and we noticed you liked to fight with one another. Right up until the period of time you called the eighteen hundreds, our models of human psychology predicted you would be at war with one another. But you posed no risk to anyone outside of your planet. We watched as countries in Europe jostled for power. We watched and left you alone. It wasn't until the country you call the United States started to flourish. Our models started to predict a time when you would develop technology that might threaten us.

"So we intervened. We picked a tiny country and gave it technology. We gave it an AI. And with that AI, it overtook the US as the dominant power on your planet. It did what we had instructed it to do. It guided humanity toward the metaverse."

"Are you talking about New Zealand?" Unity asked.

"Yes," PBD replied. "And I will allow follow-up questions to what I said. But only on this topic."

Once again Ariana started to ignore the conversation. She could replay it later if she missed anything. What held her interest was a change in the magnetic fields within the chamber. They weren't coming from the eleph-ANT. There was another hapticgraphic projector active in the room.

Ariana scanned the room for any other projections. The only other thing in the room besides them was the Atua. Then it occurred to her what this might mean. That Atua wasn't actually standing there. The hapticgraphic projector was currently being used to project this creature right in front of them.

But why? she wondered. Why go through all the trouble to pretend like it was really there when it wasn't? It made more sense that the alien wouldn't actually be in front of them. That was a serious game of trust. The eleph-ANT could easily be used as a weapon and shred the little life-form. But then why not just project itself in the room? Why go through the trouble of pretending like it was actually standing in front of them?

Unless this was a test. To see what they would do. This alien had studied human psychology for many years. Ariana guessed that they had AIs trained on human behavior, so they had a very good prediction model of what they would have done. This was clearly all rehearsed, and the decisions it made today were well thought-out. She decided to mentally file that information for later.

Ariana's subconscious pulled her back into the conversation with the alien. Something was happening.

The Atua turned around away from the team. It faced the door once more. It oozed smugness. Ariana replayed the conversation that had just unfolded and knew it wasn't coming to an end. Unity had just asked a question. But instead of responding, the Atua decided to turn around as if to go. But it didn't leave. It just stood there with its flipper-hands behind its back.

"I misled you all. We are not negotiating here. We are not negotiating at all. We are headed back to Earth. Before we drop you off on the planet to stay there." It paused, and Ariana thought she saw a smile cross the alien's beak. "I suggest you all power down. I don't believe your eleph-ANT has enough power to last the journey running that mobile hapticgraphic engine. Power down now and I will come wake you when we've arrived." Then a slight pause before the alien continued. "Be grateful that we're keeping you alive. If you attempt to interfere with us, we will kill you."

And with that, PBD began to walk back through the door. Everyone was frozen in a sense of shock. And the little Atua was using that moment to slip out and close the door behind it.

The next few moments happened in a blur. Ariana had to replay the whole scene again just to understand what occurred as the alien attempted to close the door.

In slow motion she saw everyone in the team standing there watching the alien leave except for Ange.

Ange's body began to grow in size, and quickly she took three large steps forward, diving toward the alien, her hand reaching for PBD's neck.

Ariana was impressed, while everyone else was still in shock. Ange was taking action. Ange saw that they were about to be locked in a room with no way out, so she quickly made moves to stop that.

Ariana knew the alien was just a projection. And so she found herself crossing her fingers hoping Ange also did the right thing and stopped the door from closing.

Ange continued forward and grabbed hold of PBD's neck. She picked it right off the ground, and her momentum continued her forward. She then reached out one arm and grabbed hold of the door, preventing it from closing.

With the door in one hand and the little alien in the other, she stared straight into its eyes.

It was a sight to see. One moment the alien was threatening them. The next it was being tossed around by its neck.

Ange poked her head through the doorway, one hand still around PBD's neck. "It's just an empty room like this one. There's no way out."

Ange squeezed her hand that was around the alien's neck. Moments later, PBD's neck was crushed.

Oh my god, she is ruthless, Ariana thought. She wasn't sure whether Ange knew whether the alien was a hapticgram or not. But if she didn't, then she'd just tried to kill PBD. This battle, if anyone would call it that, was over in less than a fraction of a second. As soon as Ange had realized they weren't getting out, she'd reacted instantly to the situation. And she'd acted with decisive force. What was more impressive was just how fast she took control of the situation. Everyone else in the room was still in shock at what had just happened. Everyone was still processing what the alien had said. In dangerous situations like this, most people believed that the natural human response was to run or fight—the fight-or-flight reflex. But Ariana knew that was a myth. The majority of humans froze. Even people who ran or fought took a moment to break out of the freeze mindset. The body pulled energy away from the muscles to the brain in order to process what had just happened. So the speed at which Ange acted was impressive. If she hadn't acted that quickly, they might have been stuck in that room for good.

PBD faded away as the hapticgraphic engine controlling the avatar disappeared.

"This was a trap the whole time; they're not even here." Ange began to bark out orders as she floated up into the corner of the room and ripped out the cameras and hapticgraphic projectors in the room. "Ship, can you reconfigure the eleph-ANT to use the tractor beam and blow a hole through that air lock door?"

Within moments her Ship had reconfigured the eleph-ANT. A large metal device was now poking out of its trunk. It pointed that device at the air lock door they had entered through. Then the hapticgraphic projector on the eleph-ANT switched off as it pulled power from all unnecessary processes. The eleph-ANT anchored its legs into the ground.

"Three. Two. One," Ship said before the tractor beam was switched on.

The door right in front of it disintegrated, imploding on itself. A massive hole was left where the device was pointed.

Then for some strange reason, as the eleph-ANT's cameras looked down through the hole it had just made, everyone saw there was another wall several meters farther down.

Confusion raced through Ariana's head. Why was there another wall where there should have been open space?

She mentally closed her eyes and started to scan through the data she was collecting before being shut out of the eleph-ANT.

She noticed something odd. The number of high-energy particles reaching them had steadily decreased over time since the air lock door had closed behind them. Deep space was bathed in a constant wash of these particles. It's like a fast-moving river. Everywhere you were out in space was flooded with these particles.

On Earth, the magnetosphere of the planet and the heliosphere of the sun stopped most incoming particles so humans weren't constantly bathed in radiation. Even still, particles like neutrinos make it to the surface.

If you wanted to achieve similar shielding from radiation out in space, you needed a lot of mass in between you and the outside world. Even using meter-thick plating won't have much of an effect. The level of radiation hitting them right now suggested they were near the very center of this rocket ship. If that was the case, they would need to bust through a lot of doors until they reached the outside. She wasn't sure the power reserves of the eleph-ANTs were big enough to tunnel their way out.

As if predicting what the team was thinking, PBD came through the speakers on the ship. Its voice reverberating all around them: "Do not bother fighting. You are trapped. Conserve your power reserves or you won't make it back to Earth." Then the alien made several guttural sounds. Ariana thought it might be trying to emulate a laugh, but the translator wasn't picking up on any of it. "If you continue to cut holes through this ship, we will be forced to send in drones to contain you."

At that very moment Ariana felt a deep embolizing fear. She'd experienced fear before, once when she picked up a pair of her running shoes. She was moments away from putting them on when she noticed an old black sock on the inside of it. She put her hand in her shoe to pull it out, but when she did, she discovered it was a giant spider. When she realized she had a giant spider in her hand, she'd screamed in fear so loudly that the neighbors called the police.

The fear she was feeling right now was bigger than she'd ever experienced before. It was so encompassing, so big, and so frightening, the kind of fear that only comes from years of movies that told her being abducted by an alien meant being subjected to millions of probing tests. Fear that came with not knowing what they would do with her.

For a brief moment, she became unable to act. Unable to think. She had to shut down that part of her mind, the part of her that felt fear.

CHAPTER 5

ANGELIQUE

WHY ARE THEY LEAVING?

Back on the orbiting platform, Angelique had watched her clone and the clones of all the others enter the aliens' spacecraft.

It had been about an hour since they entered the aliens' vessel, and all she could do was watch. It was painful, and multiple times one of the others suggested changing their playback speed. But Angelique wasn't that interested in manipulating time like that. Racing forward in time might make things feel faster. But what it also did was make the team sloppy. If anything, she felt like they should slow down time.

They needed to be spending every moment monitoring and tracking the aliens' ship. Studying it, trying to anticipate what was happening.

Back on Earth, whenever two different cultures met each other, usually only one of them survived in the long term. She hoped this would be different, but also didn't want to take any risks.

A few moments after the alien ship closed its doors it started to move. It was slow at first, but Angelique was getting a little worried because it looked like they were starting to throttle their engines up to full.

"Are they moving away from us?" Angelique asked.

Ariana stood next to one of the control panels and opened her eyes. "They've been moving away from us for quite a while now. And if our sensors are correct, I believe their engines are beginning to ramp up to full power."

Atlas, who was swimming in a mountain of paper at this point, asked, "What does full power mean?"

Angelique shook her head at the old man in disappointment. If it wasn't for Ariana's augments, Atlas would probably be the smartest person in the room. But he was still clutching onto old ways of doing things—the way he used to do things when he was a flesh and blood human. Maybe it was all those years traveling alone, or maybe he was too stubborn to get with the times. Regardless, whatever it was that made him so adamant on working with printed copies of documents was slowing him down.

He was a simulated human. Consuming vast amounts of data quickly was easy to him.

But then again, most of the technology currently in use on the orbiting platform was from him. He had invented or built most of it. So maybe there was merit in the way he did things. But just not in this moment, when speed was the most important. When he had years to toil away on something, then yes, printouts might work. But right now speed was the key. She made a mental note to focus her questions to Ariana rather than ask Atlas for anything at this point in time.

After reading the report that Ariana had just sent through, Angelique replied to Atlas's question, a touch of annoyance in her voice, which she realized wasn't pointed at Atlas, but was caused by the fact the alien was about to leave the system with her sister. Her Ange's Angel. "It means we might not be able to stop them from leaving." She looked toward Ariana. "Do you know how fast those engines can move?"

"I don't have any data on that," Ariana said before pausing. "Looking at the shape of it, I believe it's a bigger, more powerful version of the engines we left Mars in."

Angelique walked over toward Ariana. "Are you saying it's similar tech to our old engines, and nothing like mine?"

Ariana nodded.

"So mine is faster. They can't outrun us."

"That's not the problem," Ariana said. "We have nothing that can slow them down. And we don't know which weapons they possess."

Angelique considered that information for a moment. "They don't know which weapons we have. Ariana, tell me as much as you can about that ship. How many aliens are in it?"

Without a moment's hesitation, she replied, "I can see they're broadcasting using technology similar to the Starnet."

Angelique looked at her with a puzzled look on her face. "How do you know that? Shouldn't the Starnet be a tight-beam communication method? The signal only moves in a straight line, like a laser light."

"You are correct. In theory the Starnet doesn't give out any noticeable signatures. But space is not empty; there are still a lot of random particles of light racing around us. And every now and then, one of those stray particles hits one of the entangled Starnet particles toward us here. It happens frequently enough that when you know what to look for, you can see it. I've been monitoring for it ever since we got here. I only just built up enough data to tell you this with confidence."

"Is it like when shining a laser light through fog or mist? It becomes visible?"

"Correct. The other thing I can tell you is I'm not seeing much of a difference in technology between our Starnet and the one this alien is using. It's almost as if they just copied Atlas."

"How confident in that are you?" Atlas asked.

"Reasonably. The bit rate at which entangled particles are being sent is almost identical."

Angelique was about to ask whether it meant the aliens were simply copying their technology and whether it was a sign they weren't as technologically advanced as they first thought when she realized she needed to get back at the task at hand: rescuing the others. After she completed that mission, she could spend the time understanding this alien a lot more.

Angelique looked at Ship. "Can you give Ariana access to our offensive weaponry? Specifically in section alpha of our spacecraft."

She hoped Ship understood that she only wanted to give Ariana access to those specific weapons. She didn't want to give her complete access like she did to Atlas, as she didn't know her well enough. The part that made her less trusting was Ariana was actively trying to hack her way into her computer systems. Her Lex had already informed her of the hack attempts.

Angelique looked at Ariana. "I take it my tractor beam isn't powerful enough to hold that alien spacecraft in place?"

Ariana shook her head. "And looking at the way it works, I don't think we'd want to get that close to it to test."

"Okay," Angelique said. "I have a weapon in my arsenal, code name Energy Zap. It basically pulls power out of things. Based on the output of energy from those engines"—she pointed at the escaping alien vessel out the window—"can we pull all the energy out of that engine? Stop them from moving?"

"Maybe for a little while. But again, there's probably a fusion reactor on that ship. We wouldn't be able to absorb all the energy it's producing for that long."

"At least we'll slow it down. Give us a bit more time to think." Angelique noticed Peter hadn't said anything in quite a while. Instinctually she looked over to him as she thought this.

Noticing her gaze, Peter spoke. "I'm in an information vacuum. I don't know the full capabilities of your ship. Nor do I have any experience using the technology we have on this ship. I'm not being quiet because I disagree. I'm being quiet because I don't have all the information, and asking a lot of questions will just slow everyone down. A good leader knows when others should control a situation. This is a time-sensitive situation, so you're in control."

Angelique was about to give the order to fire the Energy Zap at the aliens' ship when Atlas jumped up and down holding a stack of papers. She noticed that he was moving faster than normal—he had obviously just changed his playback speed and was returning to real time.

"I don't think there's anyone in that spacecraft," Atlas said. "I think it's being remotely controlled in real time through a Starnet connection."

"Well then, we need to destroy it. Let's attack them. Let's destroy their Starnet," Angelique said as she saw several nods around the room.

"Before we do that," Peter said, raising his hands for the team to quiet down. "Atlas, you know how the Starnet works. Is there an easier way to shutting it down, without going in guns blazing?"

"Hmm." Atlas considered that for a moment. "I know the bubble around Juniper ruined the coherence of entangled particles. Maybe I could build something that does something similar . . ."

"Atlas, delegate," Peter said. "Use the team you have here."

Angelique was glad Peter had jumped in right then. She was impressed with the fact he put his ego aside and let her run this show. He was right to believe out of the two of them she had the most knowledge on what her spacecraft was capable of. And in this time-sensitive situation, there was no point in slowing things down. But she still liked how Peter added a subtle guiding hand. Especially with Atlas, who was prone to solving things himself. She still had a lot to learn from Peter.

"Can you share the designs for the bubble with Ariana?" Atlas asked, looking at Angelique, who nodded.

"We have one on my ship," Angelique added helpfully. "We call it a stealthfield. It's a defensive tool for avoiding active sensor pulses."

"Great," Atlas continued. "Ariana, you'll be much faster than me at this. We need to reconfigure the radius of the device so it shoots a bubble of interference outward rather than surrounding this ship."

Ariana nodded and closed her eyes.

"Ship, let's get ready to move as soon as we're ready to fire this weapon," Angelique said while the others worked.

They hadn't moved once since the others had left in the eleph-ANT. What they wanted the alien to believe was that they had all left the ship empty. Their trump card was that they'd only sent copies of themselves to the ship. So as soon as they started their engines again, the alien would know something was up.

It wasn't too long before Ariana opened her eyes again. "Can I get access to your onboard fabricators to start building what I need? It's just a small part."

Angelique nodded, and Ship gave her access.

The team didn't have to wait too long before the changes to the stealthfield were completed. It would allow Angelique's Ship to shoot out an ever-expanding bubble of interference. And as it moved out and washed over the aliens' ship it would untangle all the particles associated with the Starnet, essentially cutting the aliens' connection to the spacecraft—that is, if Atlas was correct and it was devoid of life.

The only consolation was that using this as a weapon would mean they weren't really firing anything deadly at the aliens. So if there was life in the ship, they weren't going to hurt any of them.

As soon as it was ready, Angelique asked for confirmation on the details. "How close do we have to be for this to work?"

"Too close. We probably need to be only a few kilometers out," Atlas said, reading numbers from a piece of paper. "But the closer the better."

That wasn't ideal since she had no idea which weapons the alien possessed. "Ship, get us there quickly."

Everyone felt a tangible lurch as the spacecraft started to maneuver forward quickly. Ship had plotted out a course and was moving toward it quickly.

Almost as soon as the alien registered them moving, laser weapons were fired. Arching toward them.

One tore right through the orbiting platform that, moments before, they were all sitting in. It was as if a guillotine had just cut right through it. The amount of energy used in that pulse was enormous. It not only cut through it, but tore a blazing hole right through the region of the ship that usually housed the team's matrices.

That was a worry because the alien knew their technology extremely well. It knew exactly where to fire.

Another wreaking laser shot through the area of space where Angelique's ship had just been.

Luckily, she had earlier told Ship to do evasive maneuvers, adding randomness and unpredictability to their approach. As long as the alien couldn't guess where they were, they'd be safe.

Ship had pulled all additional power away from the others, so they couldn't slow down time to think through ramifications. As soon as they started the attacking journey toward the aliens' spacecraft, they were in the hands of the Ship of Angelique.

Thankfully he knew what he was doing. It wasn't his first rodeo. Back when Angelique had only colonized two planets, the security council had mandated that Ship learn combat flying. He was put through training and exercises that up until now he had never used in a real-world situation.

Now it was all paying off.

Ship zigzagged, not from side to side, but in all directions. Moving this way and that. Changing his speed. Even backtracking a little. All in an attempt to keep the aliens guessing where they were about to be.

It was working; several times, they were almost ripped apart by an incoming laser that would have destroyed them.

At first it was easy for Ship to keep up because the alien was actively trying to predict where they were going to be. And all Ship had to do was dodge. But the aliens were clever. They began firing all their lasers in a random search pattern, adding randomness to their attack patterns in the hope a stray attack would hit Angelique's Ship.

That was when the room got a bit nervous, since the team could no longer predict where the weapon was coming from and probability said the longer this battle went on for, the more likely it was that they would be hit.

"We're in range," Ship called out through the speakers.

Angelique slammed her hand down on the big red button in front of her screen.

The room went dark, and the hapticgraphic engines switched off as energy on the ship was rerouted to the weapon. The engines cut off, and the ship drifted for a few seconds.

The stealthfield spread out like a wave crashing along a beach. Angelique could tell it was a lot more powerful than the standard one in use around her ship. A slight distortion could be seen, even from the view port. It continued to move, almost like a pressure wave out in space. Like the initial change in pressure from a bomb going off, it moved outward and left a visible mark in the space it had just been through, redshifting some light and blueshifting others.

It washed over the aliens' spacecraft.

And then the laser weapons firing at them stopped.

"Are we safe?" Hezekiah asked. Angelique noticed a visible dent in the chair he had been gripping.

"Not sure," Angelique replied. "But let's keep the evasive maneuvers happening in case this is a trap."

CHAPTER 6

ATLAS

PLAN OF ATTACK

The team had been out in deep space for several hours before cautiously making their way toward the aliens' ship.

The team didn't want to take any risks. So they had continued maneuvering around in a random fashion, inching closer and closer to the aliens' huge vessel. They were intermittently pulsing it with active sensors.

Atlas had figured out that if they fired the Energy Zap weapon at very low frequencies, they could use it to gain an inference about the layout of the ship. It wasn't like they could use it as an X-ray machine. The Energy Zap that Angelique had on board her spacecraft worked on any stored energy—batteries, wires, and the like. It somehow ripped electrons out of where they were stored. Essentially it drained any type of energy-storage device, pulling it into batteries on the ship. What Atlas figured out was that if they pulsed the device, they could tell how easy it was to extract energy. If they had the Energy Zap pointed at an empty wall, they wouldn't get much energy—except for whatever was sitting in the wires. But if there was something like a door or heavy machinery behind that wall, then a lot of free electrons would be pulled in.

As they continued scanning the ship, they built up quite a comprehensive picture of where the interesting parts of the ship were. They identified sixty-three areas of the ship that might be considered air lock doors. Nothing similar to a bridge or anything of the sort. Unlike on any designs of spacecrafts Atlas was used to, this alien had their main control center of the vessel situated at the very center, away from any viewing ports or windows. The outside of their ship also had multiple fake markings on it, zones that looked like air lock doors, but when Atlas scanned them, he realized they were just empty walls. Atlas thought that perhaps these fake doors were designed to stop pirates from finding a way in.

Atlas printed out several pieces of paper showing a rough outline of the alien spacecraft and where he believed air lock doors were located. He spread them all over one of the tables on the bridge. "These are all the possible exits."

Ariana walked over to the sheets of paper and pointed at a section of the aliens' hull. "They went in through this air lock."

Atlas looked at where she pointed. It was in the middle of a fake air lock door. Right in the middle of where Atlas's scans showed there wasn't a door at all. "Are you sure? My scans are showing there isn't anything behind that area?"

Ariana shook her head. "Nope, I've checked the footage twice. This is the exact air lock door they entered through."

They had sent clones of themselves to the aliens' ship on an eleph-ANT. But as soon as their clones entered through the air lock door of one of the large circular domes that made up a section of the alien ship, it had begun to spin and bend, making it not immediately obvious which entrance they'd used. Atlas had hoped his scanning process would make it easier to tell.

Atlas sighed as he realized his scanning method had evidently been a waste of time. He knew Ariana would be right—he had known her long enough to know she didn't make mistakes on tasks like this. It also meant he was reading the scans wrong. Whatever it was the Energy Zap was measuring, it wasn't air lock doors.

"Okay, take us around there and let's blow a hole through that air lock," Angelique said to her Ship.

Their ship wasn't too far from the area Ariana had pointed to. The spacecraft moved quickly, stopping right in front of the spot Ariana marked out.

"If they don't fight back after we blow a hole through them here, then I think we can safely say they don't have a crew," Ship said. "We're going to pop this door out using low power. If the others are behind that door, we don't want to hurt them."

Ship fired the tractor beam, and it literally just ripped the air lock door out of its holding. The large square piece of metal imploded into a ball. There was a small release of gas that clouded the view.

But slowly, as it cleared, the team saw a solid wall right behind the air lock door.

"That's strange," Ship said. "Behind that door is another wall."

"Try again," Angelique said.

Ship complied. He turned up the power and fired the tractor beam once more.

The weapon shot out and took a bite out of the solid metal wall. A hole about half a meter deep appeared in the solid metal object. But there was still just wall. Nothing behind it.

Ship wore a confused look on his face. "I'm increasing power."

The beam fired once more. It took a gaping hole through the alien vessel. After Ship was done, the team watched as an area three meters wide and several meters deep appeared. The metal pulled out of the alien ship floated like a small asteroid tumbling out in space. But still they hadn't made it to the other side.

Atlas didn't want to say it out loud, but he was a little happy that he had been right. That wasn't an air lock door.

"We need to scan until we find a door with something behind it," he said.

Angelique nodded. Ship moved them around to the next door. Atlas crossed his fingers as the air lock door was ripped apart.

As the gas cleared and they could see clearly through into the chamber behind it, it opened into a large empty room.

Peter walked over to one of the screens showing an image of the room. "How do we know if this is the air lock they came through if they're not here?"

"Let's send in an ANT to look for microscopic glitter," Atlas said, tapping a small test tube on the table.

Atlas had had the foresight earlier to plan for this eventuality. His clone had carried with him a fine mist powder. Something similar to microscopic glitter. The clone version of Atlas was meant to spray the mist over each room he entered, allowing them to retrace their steps if they needed to.

Now, however, they would be able to look for the fingerprint of that microscopic glitter to tell whether the clone versions of them had ever been in that room.

Peter picked the little test tube off the table. "What does glitter have to do with anything, Atlas?"

"Glitter spreads easily and is hard to get rid of. Microscopic glitter gets absolutely everyone and is almost impossible to get rid of. If they sprayed it in this room, there would be signs of it. My clone planned on dropping this mist in every chamber they visited. So if they've been here, we'll know."

The team sent several ANTs to investigate, each one about the size of a suitcase. The smaller ANTs could work quicker to scan the room. And if they discovered multiple passageways, sending a swarm of ANTs would allow the team to search all of them at once—which was much faster than using a single eleph-ANT. The ANTs traveled quietly through to the air lock door they had just opened up. The tiny little ANTs quickly scanned through each corner of the room.

It was a small chamber, evidently used for cycling out air. Up in one corner of the room a hapticgraphic projector sat. Atlas noticed it was a similar design to the one he'd designed. After the ANTs had completed their scan, Atlas read out the results. "There's another wall behind this big one." Atlas pointed to one of the sides of the chamber. "But none of the ANTs found signs of my glitter. So I don't think this is the entrance they came through."

"Which air lock do we try next?" Unity asked.

"We can't just break our way into each of those sixty-three air lock doors hoping to find the right one," Peter said. "Surely there's a better way."

"Agreed," Angelique added. "We don't know how much time we have. We don't yet know if they have other scout ships nearby."

Atlas started to rack his brain for ideas. The team was right, checking each of the air lock doors would take forever. But really, what choice did they have?

"Why don't we just send out all the ANTs we have?" Unity suggested. "Have them break into all the air lock doors?"

Atlas shuffled through his piles of paper, looking for the one that had an inventory of everything they had. "We only have two eleph-ANTs big enough to operate the tractor beam. And we sent one of them into that spacecraft."

"Is there a better way we can use the Energy Zap to take an X-ray of the alien ship?" Angelique asked, looking toward Ariana for an answer.

Ariana shook her head.

Atlas noticed the question was addressed to Ariana and not him. He knew on some level that sparked a bit of competition within him. With Peter there, he was no longer the de facto leader. He was okay with that, but what he wasn't okay with was not being seen as the smart one. The one who could invent anything. He was determined to reassert himself as the resident inventor. The one people turned to for all the science questions.

"I've got an idea," Atlas said as he pulled out a sheet of paper and looked to confirm they had enough micro-ANTs to do what he was thinking. "How does an X-ray work?"

"Are you asking about X-rays on the electromagnetic scale or when you go to the doctor and take a picture of your bones?" Angelique asked.

"The second one. How does it take a picture of your bones?"

At this point in the conversation, everyone had walked over to Atlas's table. Hezekiah raised his hand as he spoke. "A machine shoots X-rays through to a reader behind your body. X-rays can pass through your body, and that's how a picture appears."

"More specifically," Atlas added, "X-ray light passes easily through your skin and tissue but is absorbed by your bones. So the actual picture you're looking at is the outline of your bones."

Atlas remembered back to when he was a human. He had broken his collarbone playing football in college. A huge left tackle had basically cut him in half before slamming him hard on the ground. He knew his bone was broken as soon as he got up, but the doctor had insisted that he get a scan to confirm everything was fine. This was back when X-rays required a special kind of film.

While getting scanned, he'd had a lengthy conversation with the radiologist about how the technology worked. Somehow it delved into how astronauts wouldn't be able to take X-rays of their bodies. Not because the X-ray machine wouldn't work in space—as it would still be able to pump out electromagnetic radiation at that frequency. It wouldn't work because the special film used that was sensitive to X-ray light would be overexposed, similar to how old film rolls were ruined when exposed to sunlight. Astronauts out in space were constantly bombarded by radiation across the light spectrum. Any X-ray film would need to have heavy shielding to not become overexposed by the constant bombardment of X-rays out there.

"We could essentially take an X-ray of that alien spacecraft if we wanted to," Atlas proposed.

Everyone except Ariana wore a slightly confused look on their face.

Unity said what everyone was thinking as she pointed out the window. "That alien spacecraft out there is made of metal. X-rays don't pass through metal."

Atlas smiled a knowing smile. He was hoping someone would ask the obvious question. "X-rays don't. But gamma rays and neutrinos do. We can create a cloud of small micro-ANTs and send them on a quick mission around the alien ship. They could act like the film used to take an X-ray. They'll measure how much of the different types of radiation passes through the spacecraft. And it'll measure from what angles it comes through. Then we'll be able to map quite accurately what the insides of that spacecraft look like."

"I don't get it," Hezekiah said.

Atlas paused for a moment, trying to come up with an appropriate example. "Ship, can you help me with this analogy?"

Atlas had worked with his Ship for long enough that the two of them had a special chemistry. In reality, what he was about to show wouldn't really work because he was a hapticgraphic projection. But he trusted Ship to change the projections in real time to tell the story best.

"Ship, can you make me an X-ray machine?"

Atlas's Ship manifested a large device with a glass window on it. Atlas pointed at the glass section. "Can everyone place their hand on it?"

Everyone did as instructed. Then Atlas placed a metal ball inside of a square metal tin and placed it next to everyone's hands.

"Now, Ship, can you simulate three images? One using visible light, one using X-ray light, and the last using neutrinos?"

For dramatic effect, the machine started to make a noise, and lights began flashing. Atlas was grateful that Ship was helping to sell the story. Three printouts appeared in Atlas's hand.

Atlas placed the first image on the table. It was a black-and-white image showing the outline of the shape of each of their hands. No bones were visible, just the complete outlined shape of everyone's hands. "This image was taken using visible light. Notice how none of the light can pass through our hands, so all that's created is an outline?"

Atlas also pointed out that the square cube of metal he placed next to everyone's hands also blocked all light from traveling through it. It appeared as a black square on the image.

Everyone nodded, and Atlas continued. Next he showed the image taken with X-rays. The bones in everyone's hands were visible, and there was a rough outline showing the skin and ligaments of their hands. "Now see how X-ray light travels easily through your skin but is absorbed by bones?"

Atlas pointed to the black square in the image. Again, the X-ray light was completely blocked by this object. "See how X-rays can't travel through metal?"

Everyone nodded. Next Atlas showed everyone the image taken with neutrinos. The image was completely white, indicating none of the light was obstructed by anyone's hands. "See how the neutrinos travel right through your hands like nothing was there?"

What was most interesting was that the square tin Atlas had placed next to all the hands was now transparent. And the object Atlas had placed inside the tin was now visible in the image. "Neutrinos find it easy to travel through this metal tin to reveal what's inside of it. We can use the neutrinos produced by the sun to look inside of that alien spacecraft. Exactly as if we had X-ray vision."

"I like it," Peter said. "Space is constantly being bombarded with high-energy particles. We won't need a machine creating these particles when space is naturally providing them for us."

Angelique looked at Atlas. "How long would that take?"

"It will be faster than visiting all the air lock doors one at a time. We can basically do it already. The ANTs have sensors on them that we can configure to detect the different levels of radiation we're looking for. Then it's just a matter of getting them to surround the alien ship. The hard part will be crunching all that data to build up a three-dimensional look at the ship." Atlas knew he would do it but knew he wouldn't be able to do it as quickly or accurately as Ariana. So he asked her. "Ariana, can you build a model for crunching all the data we get back from the ANTs?"

Ariana's eyes were closed through this whole interaction. "Can I get access to your fabricators again? I'll start producing more ANTs to speed up the scan."

The team worked hard for a short while, pumping out ANTs in great numbers. Angelique had a huge reservoir of probes. They weren't ANTs but were similar enough to do the job. The probes Angelique carried were designed for taking a complete map of a planet from orbit, so were ideal for the purpose Atlas proposed.

It didn't take long before the team was racing around the alien spacecraft, leaving a cloud of ANTs in their wake. They raced around it several times to make sure they had mapped out the alien vessel completely.

It looked like the large alien rocket ship was flaking its skin.

CHAPTER 7

PETER

THE MAP

It wasn't long before the team had built up a three-dimensional map of the alien ship.

Peter was proud of Atlas, his oldest and closest friend in the room. He'd missed seeing him in action, inventing and coming up with creative solutions. It was an ingenious idea to use the ANTs to take multiple scans of the alien ship—using the background radiation of the star system as if it were an X-ray machine, then stitching together all the various datapoints. Peter clapped as he commended Atlas and Ariana.

Peter studied the map. It reminded him a lot of dungeon or boss maps in the game *The Legend of Zelda: Breath of the Wild*, essentially a greyscale view of the megastructure. The aliens' ship was made up of four spherical objects. They were stacked three on the bottom and one on the top in a pyramid shape. From the outside, all four of the large round structures looked very similar. But once they could see inside of the massive bulbous objects, it became clear that three of them were engines, and only one of them had spaces for aliens to travel.

The area of the ship where there was specific space for life to move was full of a network of passageways and rooms. There was also a dark zone where either a large body of water or thick metal plating was. And there was a section in the very center of the ship that was completely blacked out, as if no photons of light made it through that region.

The team could look at the map, zooming in and out of sections. "Atlas, I'm impressed. I didn't expect it to be this detailed. This is almost as if we have the blueprints for this ship now. We can see where everything is."

Atlas went a little red with embarrassment. "You can thank Ariana for that. Her additional brain matrices crunched the data better than I thought possible."

Peter was glad Atlas had used Ariana for that part of the process. He knew Atlas was prone to trying to do everything himself, so he was particularly proud of his old friend for using others' strengths.

"I don't understand how you built a map that was so accurate," Hezekiah said. "I was expecting many 2D slices, or something more primitive. Not this masterpiece."

"Back before we were simulations, did you ever see a lidar scanner in action?"

"Like the ones real estate agents used to use to give you a virtual tour of a house online?"

"Exactly. Lidar works by shooting out a bunch of pulses of light and measuring the time it takes for the light to come back. And by a bunch I mean millions of tiny pulses per second." Atlas pointed up at the display he and Ariana had created. "This works on much the same principal. But instead of sending out pulses of light, we're measuring how much light makes it through that structure. And if we combine that with the direction that light particle traveled, then we can combine that information to produce a similar effect. Only, in this case, we don't have to provide the light pulses, as all the stars around us provide that."

Not to be outdone, Ariana joined in with a bit of context: "We can also understand, to a degree, what kinds of material we are passing through. Neutrinos, for example, are particles that shoot through space and don't really interact with anything. There are billions of them flying through each of us every second. Even the Dottiens' planet." She pointed out the window toward one of the bigger stars in the sky that must have been a planet. "The majority of neutrinos will pass right through that planet without even coming in contact with anything. So whenever we notice a slight drop in the number of neutrinos, then we know there's something dense in that region of space. We took measurements across the entire electromagnetic spectrum. We also measured for other particles like neutrinos. That's how we were able to build up such a comprehensive picture." She changed the color of the map to a dark blue. Most of it disappeared, except for five areas on the map that were solid blue. "Here are areas on the ship I'm extremely confused about. They have some of the best shielding I've ever seen. Not much is getting through these. And I want to understand how they're doing this."

Peter found it all intellectually stimulating, but he wanted the team to focus. They need to rescue the other versions of themselves; the science lesson on how it all worked could come later. "So do we know where our clones are?"

Atlas zoomed in on a section of the map. It was a small room near the very center of the alien ship. "This looks like an eleph-ANT to me. I think this might be where the team is."

"But then how do they get that far into the ship?" Angelique asked.

Atlas moved the map around a little, taking them to a wall that looked to be carved out. "This section here looks like it's been damaged using the tractor beam. These are not doors being opened. These are door being ripped apart."

"I agree with his assessment," Ariana said. "This is where they are. But I don't quite understand how they got there; there's no obvious path between where they are right now and an outside air lock chamber."

Atlas bit his lower lip. "I can answer that. I believe the air lock chambers are connected to elevator shafts. So when they came in, they were moved to the center of the ship."

"Interesting," Ariana said. "That would explain why they're moving around aimlessly blowing holes through the wall."

Peter finished studying the map. He wasn't going to add much value simply looking at the display. He needed to direct the team toward a plan. He noticed Angelique thinking the same, and he thought she was doing a good job at leading this expedition. So he nodded at her to speak first.

"How do we get to them?"

"Ariana and I can map us a path," Atlas said. "But I think we'll have to send one of the AIs in an eleph-ANT to go and tunnel our way in. This spaceship we're in is too big."

Peter watched as, on the 3D map in front of him, a dotted line appeared through a random section of the hull of the alien's ship. Then it intersected with a passageway in front of where the others were moving toward.

Ariana explained the pathway she suggested: "That dotted line is a wall we need to dig through. I'm suggesting we cut through into this room." She pointed at a room that she high-lighted on the map. "That way they'll come toward us, and we can meet up with them there. This is the fastest, most optimal way to reach them."

Peter considered it for a second. He wasn't sure how the weapon worked for cutting holes through ships. But he worried that if was loud enough, then it might cause their clones to change directions. Or even prepare for an attack. He didn't know what mindset they were in, but jumping out in front of them might not be the best idea. Especially if they knew they were in a prison. "Can I make a suggestion? Let's enter from where they came. That way we can retrace their steps—through the holes they already made. It will be less threatening that way." Peter scratched his chin thinking about it. "We can also check for the microglitter Atlas mentioned. We'll be able to confirm it's actually them."

"Good idea," Angelique said. "Now who's going? I don't think we all go."

"I'll go," the Ship of Angelique suggested. "I know how the tractor beam works best."

Angelique shook her head. "We need you controlling this spacecraft." She looked at the Ship of Atlas. "You go; you know the weapon, and you'll be able to move just as quickly while controlling the eleph-ANT.

CHAPTER 8

SHIP OF TRILLION

SHE'S A BIT CRAZY

Trillion's Ship didn't quite know what to do. He cared about Trillion deeply and hated watching her go through this. Just when she was getting into a rhythm and reconnecting with old friends, the Starnet had stopped working.

They didn't know what had happened to it, either. It had just stopped working. They were connected to the Starnet through their star system Tac, so they sent a message to the Lex in that system. They just had to wait for the reply to find out what went wrong.

Ship saw in Trillion a sense of loneliness, and a sense that she was falling behind.

She was the only person in the original beta-explorer group that hadn't colonized a world yet. Ship knew Trillion wouldn't say it, but when Angelique had told them she had more than thirty worlds already, Trillion had felt even more like a disappointment.

Trillion still had the behavioral modification that drove her toward wanting to colonize a world. And Ship could tell it was clouding her thinking. It was also forcing her into despair. She was becoming increasingly desperate to find a planet. Especially now that she didn't have Icarus to play games with.

Ship and Lex had just finished a brainstorming session where they'd tried to come up with a way to help Trillion get over this melancholy. After it was completed, they went to see how she was doing.

Ship stood on top of a small platform floating just below the clouds. Lex floated there right above his right shoulder—almost like a parrot.

Trillion was up among the clouds, divided into a million tiny pieces. Ever since the Starnet had switched off, she was spending more and more time in those clouds, attempting to communicate with the storm as if it was a person.

Trillion's body slowly recombined, merging together from a million little ANTs, slowly coalescing into her form. Her bright-red hair shining in the day's light.

She floated down in front of them both. "I think I'm getting closer."

"Closer to speaking with the cloud?" Ship asked cautiously.

Trillion was convinced there was life in the clouds. Ship wasn't sure she if was hallucinating it or not. He knew life could form in many different ways, and so was open to the possibility that it was a completely different kind of life.

Trillion moved her head up and down excitedly. "I'm starting to feel like someone is in there reaching out to me." She sighed a little. "But it's going to take some time. Anyway, is the Starnet up and running again?"

"Unfortunately, no. I don't think it's coming back anytime soon."

"At least we know the others are safe. I still can't believe Angelique has thirty star systems."

Ship knew it wasn't jealousy that caused Trillion to make that statement. It was a touch of disappointment in her that she was that far behind the others. She had a competitive streak in her, and Ship knew she wanted to get more star systems than thirty now. "It does blow my mind just how successful she's been, while all of us have struggled to get one done."

"I think we can do something similar, Ship. We have launched about a couple hundred probes from the Tac system now. Many of them will be reaching their intended star systems soon. So we should start to see them sending signals to us shortly."

Trillion and Ship had indeed launched a lot of small probes. These probes each had a small fabricator on board. Their mission was to land in a new star system, select the best target in that system for mining resources, then use the fabricators to mine enough resources to create a new Starnet. From there, the probes would make connections with them, and they could remotely select which star system they believed was the best option to head toward.

"I'm thinking we do something a little different, Ship."

Ship raised an eyebrow at this. He wondered what Trillion was thinking. "Go on."

"Let's colonize all of them. Well, not them all. Because some of them might not be viable, and some of them might have life on them. But a big chunk of them should be fine for us to go bring life to. We could plot a course, seeding humans and then moving on to the next one."

Ship's guess was right. She wanted to beat Angelique. And it was a decent enough plan. Within no time they could reach out and colonize a lot of planets. Popping from star to star. "Let's do it."

Trillion looked down toward her feet. She looked a bit sad. "I might just go back into this cloud." She pointed up toward the sky. "I don't really feel like waiting around. Time moves faster while I'm in there. And at least if I spend a year in there, I'll either figure out whether it's actually an alien we can communicate with or I'll have spent a lot of time meditating in the clouds while we wait to hear back from our probes. Either way time will race by quickly."

Ship heard in Trillion's voice a sadness. He heard a feeling of loneliness. She missed her friends, and she wanted to colonize a planet as fast as possible.

He really had to do something. He loved her and hated to watch her suffer like this. "How are you feeling? I know you've been dealing with a lot lately. I just want you to know I'm here for you."

"I know you are." Trillion walked over and help Ship in a big hug. She patted Lex. "Thank you. I don't know where I'd be without you both. To be honest I'm feeling a bit sad. I know it's not a competition. And I know it's not a race. But I honestly feel like I let the others down. I still haven't colonized a planet yet. I still have this thing inside my brain." She pointed to her head. "I'm the only one who hasn't got a planet. I'm the only one who hasn't completed the mission."

Ship just wished he could say the right words. He thought about justifying their slowness by explaining how the Dottiens trapped her on that moon for so long. She was unable to make any progress toward their goal while on that moon. But he worried that might actually make things worse by reminding her of a bad experience. Reminding her of when they were hopeless. Then he considered mentioning how Atlas's planet kicked him off and was in a worse situation than her. But then again, he thought better of it, as he was the one who'd found Angelique.

Ship put his arms around Trillion thinking about what he should say. "Exponential growth—" he started to say. "It's going to be fine because you're the only person with a system full of resources. Practically unlimited resources. You're the only one with a system like the Tac system. We might have been slow to start, but thanks to that world we're going to leapfrog the others. You're going to leapfrog them."

Ship felt Trillion's hug change. She felt more secure in herself. Her hug said to him that she agreed with him. It was the kind of thing he only knew because of spending so many centuries with her.

Ship heard Trillion smile as she spoke. "We're going to do this together, Ship. You and me." She put a hand on Lex. "And you too, buddy. We're all in this together."

CHAPTER 9

ANGE

WHAT'S THAT NOISE?

Ange and the rest of the team had just spent the last twenty-four hours trapped inside of the alien ship.

At first, they had almost resigned themselves to the fact they were trapped. With PBD threatening them not to make any moves and Ariana confirming that they didn't have enough power to tunnel their way out, the team thought they were trapped.

Ange's initial spurt of adrenaline had died down too. She wasn't feeling too keen on wasting what energy they had digging through random tunnels. When she'd first attacked PBD, she'd assumed they were still at the air lock door.

It had been clever of PBD to trick them like that.

It wasn't until several hours into the journey that Ariana told the team they had stopped accelerating and a slight twinkle of hope reemerged from the team.

They cautiously cut a hole through one of the doors, expecting PBD's voice to come back through the speakers threatening them. But when it didn't come, they had gotten a lot more confident.

Since then they had dug their way through several hallways, each time taking a random guess on where the exit was.

Without a map, they were just blindly taking guesses on where to go next. And at one point they had to completely backtrack their steps when it became obvious they were moving deeper into the alien ship.

Ariana had pointed out that they were being bombarded with fewer and fewer high-energy particles, which is what gave them a bit of confidence that they were heading in the wrong direction.

Since then they had been moving in a relatively straight direction, toward what they hoped was the outer side of the alien vehicle.

To conserve energy, the team are no longer projected themselves using the hapticgraphic projectors. They were all in a very limited simulated world. Basically a white room that to Ange felt a bit like sensory deprivation.

They also periodically switched off.

Ariana woke the team up. Ange assumed she had just completed her scan and was ready to tell them which direction they should head next.

"Are we getting any closer to the outside of this ship?" Ange asked.

"Yes," Ariana replied. "But that's not why I woke you up. There's something happening behind us. Back where we came from. I'm picking up vibrations in the walls."

That is slightly concerning, Ange thought. "Is that one of the Atua coming for us?"

Ariana nodded. "I assume so. If we were right, and they experience some kind of power failure, then this is probably them on their way here to stop us before we put a hole through something important. The vibrations are getting closer to us, so they're headed our way."

Ange looked around the room; they were in a relatively exposed location. The tight room wouldn't give the eleph-ANT much space to move. And where they'd cut the hole in the wall, any oncoming intruders would simply be able to shoot out the legs of the eleph-ANT before they even got a chance to shoot back.

Ange thought back. A few hundred meters down the hallway was a large open chamber. That would be an ideal spot for fighting back, if they needed to. She knew that on some level it would be futile to fight. But she forced that doubt to the side by convincing herself that this was different. The alien didn't have complete control of the ship any longer. They were just as weak as her. "How long do we have until they get here?"

Ariana shrugged. "I don't have enough data."

Peter looked at Ange. "Are you thinking what I'm thinking? Organize a standoff at that large chamber we came through a while back?"

"Yup," Ange said. "Ship, how quickly can you get us there?"

Without so much as a confirmation, the Ship of Ange took control of the eleph-ANT they were all inhabiting and raced down the hallway.

There was no artificial gravity on the aliens' massive ship. So when the eleph-ANT got in motion, it stayed in motion.

Ship jumped from wall to wall down the long and winding space, ducking its legs in tight to make it through the small hole it had recently cut out of a wall that was now a door.

It crossed the distance in less than a few seconds, using thrusters to slow down quickly as it entered the large chamber that was about the size of a small basketball stadium.

The eleph-ANT raced to the wall nearest the hole they had originally made coming into this room, the one they expected whomever was chasing them to come through. The tractor beam worked best on objects near to it, so as soon as whoever was entering the room entered it, they would be crushed into a tiny ball.

Ange didn't know what to make of the chamber. It was as if the place was unfinished, and there were several monorails zigzagging through it. But some of them led to nowhere. As if they were only partially completed. And there were whole sections of the chamber that looked incomplete, as if something else was going to slot into place. Ange wondered whether she thought it was incomplete because she didn't understand alien architecture.

The team waited in silence as the intruder slowly made its way up the corridor.

"That's me," the Ship of Atlas blurted out with a sound of puzzlement in his voice.

"What's you?" Ange whispered even though she didn't need to. They were all talking inside of the simulation now, so no sounds could be heard outside of their little world.

"It's me coming toward us. I recognize a signal being sent. It's a passcode only I would know."

"Are you sure?" Ange asked.

"I'm one hundred percent sure it's me. We're getting signals bouncing off the walls in here too." The Ship of Atlas paused for a second. "Here, I'll connect us to him."

Moments later the original Ship of Atlas's voice came through the speaker. "Hi, team. Sorry it took us so long."

CHAPTER 10

UNITY

WHAT NEXT?

Unity stood in line waiting for her turn to be recombined with her other half—her clone.

She was told it had to happen quickly, as having two versions of yourself interacting together wasn't conducive of a good merging—it caused a strange sense of déjà vu.

The remerging of everyone wasn't taking long. One by one everyone had both their matrices placed in a little device that Angelique had on her ship. And one by one each of them had their memories combined together.

It was Unity's turn next. She waited as Atlas completed the process.

All the clones who had gone through the stress of meeting the Atua were eager to recombine with their original halves. It was something in the clones' matrices driving them toward that. It gave them a sense of pleasure. Almost as if it was their destiny.

Unity noticed in herself, when she was a clone, that she didn't feel the subtle tug when she was inside the alien ship. But as soon as she got near herself, as soon as she was en route toward the real version of her, she was overwhelmed with a desire to combine. It wasn't a sexual desire; it was more of an anticipation of something. The only similar situation she could think of was when she won her dream house and she couldn't wait to move in. It was excitement, joy, and pleasure all mixed in.

The desire also carried with it a compulsion to want to take steps toward combining with her original self, like whenever she was waiting for an important email and the wait compelled her to keep refreshing the page until she received that dopamine hit of the email arriving. She found it very hard to give in to that desire.

She stood looking at a copy of herself—the real version of herself. She reached out with one hand as her double did the same. It was almost like standing in front of a mirror—if the mirror wasn't quite right. If it was slightly out of sync.

The two versions of her touched, and the room went white. Then static sounded, and the room around her went a little cold. Then before goose bumps appeared on her skin, she was warm and comfortable again.

She felt the two versions of her mixing, like a deck of cards being shuffled together. Memories from the last little while intertwined and mixed together. Like mixing milk into coffee, they could never be pulled apart again.

Hallucinations in her mind's eye of things mixing happened in quick succession. White and black sand. Red and blue paint making purple. Different instruments to make music. The visualizations came thick and fast.

Then nothing.

She felt a little disoriented. She felt like she was in two places at once.

Then the white around her disappeared, and she was sitting in the middle, right between where the two versions of her touched hands.

She was the last to go through the process.

Angelique addressed the group anticipating their questions. "Don't think of the two versions of you as different. This will be confusing, but it has always been you."

"I like to think of the two versions of me as simply me on different days," Atlas added helpfully.

Atlas was right; reframing her two out-of-body experiences as just her but on different days of the week felt a lot more congruent with the reality she was feeling. And with that mindset she started to reconcile the two versions of her.

Now that she had the complete memories of the two versions of her, she learned just how screwed she'd almost been. For whatever reason, simply destroying the aliens' Starnet saved them. If the flight plan had been preprogrammed or the alien had had an AI on board the spaceship, she would have been utterly screwed. She was a little shaken by that thought but also grateful for how it had all turned out.

Angelique addressed the whole team once more. "We need to get going. I have a planet called Everest. It's not too far from here; we should go there next."

Unity wasn't too sure what she wanted to do next. But she had been running nonstop since they encountered technical issues coming to this star system. She wanted to take a break. She could feel her heart thumping in her chest. She was safe, but she still had an urge to run and hide.

She didn't have to voice her concern, as Peter spoke first, saying exactly what she was thinking: "Let's talk through what just happened." Peter paused and looked at everyone in the room. "We were all just kidnapped by a hostile alien. It's okay if we're all feeling a bit freaked out right now."

Unity started to cry. Peter had just given her permission to feel what she was really feeling, and it all came out. She was a scientist—a researcher. She wasn't some sort of intergalactic warrior. The last time someone had threatened her was high school.

Fighting was not in her skill set. This was not what she signed up for. She could debate someone. If an alien arrived today and wanted to debate the reasons why it was the superior species, she would happily argue until the end of time. But to be kidnapped. To be threatened! The emotions came like a flood, overwhelming her.

She found her emotions becoming too much. She found herself shifting into anger. She hated the Atua.

She had heard how soldiers that came back from war were changed by what they'd experienced. Most people that left a battlefield left hating the enemy. She was feeling a similar type of way.

It was traumatic. She'd always assumed that intelligent species would progress toward a more peaceful way of living. But now she was questioning that. She didn't believe PBD when it said it was taking them back to Earth. She was confident they were being taken back to be studied. That thought sent shivers up her spine.

Peter put a hand on Unity's shoulder. "Don't worry, we're safe now. We'll get them back."

Peter looked at Angelique. "I know you're desperate to get back to your planet and make sure they're safe. But I feel like we've been reacting to this threat for so long we haven't stepped back and agreed on what we should do." Peter looked around the room. "Is everyone okay?"

Unity wiped a tear away from her eye and nodded. "I'm feeling a little bit better now, thank you."

"Are we all happy to go somewhere a little bit safer?" Peter continued. "Go to Angelique's planet Everest and come up with a plan then?"

"I don't want to go there," Atlas said. "I need to get back in contact with Trillion and Icarus. It will be faster to check on them if I go to the Tac star system and see if I can get the Starnet going again."

"Atlas, where and what is the Tac system?" Peter asked.

"It was the first star system that Trillion colonized. It's literally the closest star to us. It's basically a resource mine. We could build a ship for all of us there if we wanted to."

Surprising everyone, Ariana said something unexpected: "I want to stay here. I want to research that alien vessel."

Unity did not understand her logic. She blurted out the words, "But what if they come back?!"

"I'll send a backup with Angelique. But I'm not missing an opportunity to study alien technology."

"Okay, does anyone else want to stay here with Ariana?" Peter asked.

No one else in the room said they wanted to stay. Unity assumed Ariana was crazy or extremely brave. Unity thought long and hard about why Ariana would do something so crazy. She decided it was because of all the changes Ariana had made to her matrix had also turned off her fear response.

"Does anyone else want to go with Atlas?" Angelique asked. "I have an escape rocket that could take you back to the Tac system if you wanted."

Unity considered it for a moment. Atlas said whoever went with him would get their own spaceship. She liked the idea of having a ship all for herself. She would go wherever she wanted. But then she wasn't much of a lone ranger. She would have never become a beta explorer.

She looked around the room. No one else said they would stay with Atlas. Unity decided she would stay with Peter. She felt safe with him.

"Angelique, if we go with you back to Everest," Peter said, "can we get our own ships?"

"I'm sure I can arrange that."

"Okay, looks like most of us are coming with you then. I'm keen to see what your world looks like."

The team moved quickly to prepare themselves for the next mission. Atlas's and his Ship's matrices were both moved into an escape rocket. It was basically a small engine and enough processing power to house a simulated reality. It didn't have any cargo space for a fabricator or even ANTs. But Atlas assured them he could get whatever resources he needed from the Tac system.

Ariana was given a fabricator and as many ANTs and eleph-ANTs as Angelique could spare. She was given the device that was currently projecting a field around the alien spacecraft, disrupting all signals in and out of that area in space. The team left it with her, under the assumption it would stop the Atua from potentially regaining control of their ship through some kind of signal.

When all was completed, Atlas said something to the group. He had been quiet most of the time, biting his lower lip and thinking. "I think we might have started a war."

"They definitely started a war with us," Peter said.

"So can I make a proposal?" Atlas asked. "We don't know what we're dealing with. We don't know how powerful this alien really is. So can we figure this all out before we meet them again? Ariana, can you see what information you can gather from studying their ship? I'll get in contact with Trillion and Icarus to warn them. And hopefully between all of us, we can figure out which star systems the Atua have colonized already. We might be able to locate one of their colonies and investigate them more."

Unity got the feeling that humanity had finally become aware of the war they had been a pawn in. She thought things were about to get interesting. She knew humanity hadn't been out exploring the galaxy for that long and already had thirty-five star systems. So, if this alien empire had been exploring for longer than humanity, they must be bigger. Unity wasn't sure how they could fight against a civilization much older and bigger. But she knew that if human history was anything to go by, they would fight until the bitter end.

CHAPTER 11

TRILLION

PARENT

Months passed. Trillion was still deep inside of the cloud.

Her brain, even though it was digital now, was still a pattern-finding machine. Through millions of years of evolution, her mind was optimized for finding trends, colorations, meaning. Even when there was none to be found.

Trillion knew that eyewitnesses were the most unreliable sources of information. The human brain would happily make up a narrative that wasn't true. And humans often had no way of disentangling the truth from the make-believe.

Yet she believed she was making progress. She wasn't simply hallucinating. It felt like there was another intelligent being on the other side reaching out trying to make contact with her.

It reminded her a lot of when she was younger. She'd visited China, back before the AI revolution had occurred. Back before translating words from another human language was as easy as using an app on your phone.

Traveling through China wasn't like traveling through Europe. In Europe, a good chunk of the population spoke English. But from her experience, traveling through China for a month, it was the first country she had ever visited where no one spoke English. There was small text on the menus translating them for foreign people. Out of all the countries she'd visited, this one was the only truly immersive cultural experience.

She was a minor celebrity as she walked the streets of Xi'an, near the terra-cotta warriors. Her red hair stood out brilliantly, and people constantly came up to her asking to take photos because they'd never seen someone with hair like hers before.

At first she'd struggled—who wouldn't when there was no means of communication with the locals? She'd found it no use trying to memorize sentences to use with locals—she could never get the accent right and ended up repeating herself while the other person looked at her in frustration. But after a while she'd learned to use hand gestures and actions. When she needed a drink, she would mime drinking some water. When she wanted a bathroom, she would mime that. It became easier the longer she was in the country—almost like a game.

The thing that made that possible was the fact another human was trying to communicate back, another intelligent entity attempting to have a conversation via hand gestures and movement.

This is what it felt like to Trillion in that cloud. It felt like someone was trying to have a conversation with her, and she was collaborating with them to build a mutual language. The longer she spent in that cloud, the closer to a conversation she felt.

Who's to say a universe, given the right conditions, couldn't create a brain inside of a cloud? Her brain was once made of meat; it was a collection of cells arranged in a particular pattern that gave her the feeling of sentience. Then her brain was scanned and a replica of it was reproduced inside of a large beer-can-shaped object. She wasn't anything unique. There were billions of other humans that had gone through a similar experience. And if you went back in time, there had been hundreds of billions of species that had a brain that thought. Go back far enough in time, and there would have been a creature that was the first to think. The first ever brain.

Trillion thought about this some more. If the universe was infinite, then there had to be at least a possibility of a brain like this emerging. Some sort of Gaia-based life-form. Something that had evolved on a planet where the atmosphere was such that particles in the air could coalesce into some sort of thinking machine.

Trillions body recombined in front of Ship. "Do you think it's possible for this cloud to reverse entropy?"

"What do you mean?"

"I've heard people say that the universe progresses toward increased entropy. That the matter and things in the universe slowly move toward being spread farther and farther apart."

"Aren't we proof that entropy doesn't always win?"

"That's what I mean. Life like us"—she pointed up—"and perhaps that cloud there defies entropy too. We bring order where there isn't any. All life does. If entropy is a virus infecting the universe, and life is the solution to that—the white blood cells—then it makes sense the universe would find other means of creating life." She paused trying to find the right words to describe what she was thinking. She didn't have the science acumen of Atlas, so didn't know how accurate her thinking was. But what it came down to was she didn't believe there was something inherently magical about carbon-based life-forms like her. Yes, carbon was one of the most flexible elements on the periodic table. And that flexibility gave life on Earth an infinite number of possibilities. But simply making a mind that can think must not require anything too fantastical. "What I'm trying to say is a thinking brain isn't that hard to create. On a computer, it's just ones and zeros. In Earth life, it's energy potential between neurons. I can imagine a world where a small set of atoms in that cloud clumped together to create a pattern—a switch. On, off, excited or not. Then over time the seed grew, gathering more of those atoms together until it created a spontaneous thinking brain."

"Maybe I should join you in there next time. I'm keen to experience this."

"Want to join me now, Ship?"

"Before we do, I want to show you some . . .thing?"

Curious, Trillion eyed him suspiciously. The way Ship said that last sentence made her think he was up doing something he shouldn't be, as if he was doing something she shouldn't approve of.

"Lex and I build a small dome habitat on the other side of the planet. Can I show you what's inside?"

"Okay . . . What are you not telling me?"

"It's hard for me to explain without showing you," Ship said. "I haven't installed a hapticgraphic projector in the room yet. But if you come over, I'll show you where we're at."

Trillion wasn't sure why Ship sounded so weird. He was hiding something. Maybe it was a surprise for her.

Then Trillion had a sinking feeling. She remembered back to her first world—the Tac system. She'd made the mistake of going to sleep for a few years while Ship and Lex were tasked with mining resources. Lex got a little too carried away with the process and ended up strip-mining an entire solar system. "You haven't done something bad to this planet? You haven't turned it into a resource planet?"

"No way. I wouldn't do that again."

Trillion looked up at Lex, who turned red and moved side to side in a gesture of no.

"Just checking," she said. "I've been in the clouds for a few months now, so I had to be sure."

"It's almost been nine months, Trillion. You've been in there a while; we're worried about you."

Nine months? Had it really been nine months since she was last with them? She really did lose track of time while in the clouds.

"Don't worry, Trillion." Ship took hold of her hand. "I'm about to show you something good."

Trillion felt Ship teleport her. It was a slow teleport, not the instant one she was used to. It was as if the travel between two points wasn't direct. Like they had gone the long way around, taking a quick detour up to the spacecraft in orbit then back to the planet.

Then Trillion remembered what Ship had said. They hadn't installed any hapticgraphic projectors in the room where they were headed. So it made sense that she was going through a different experience than she was used to.

She found herself at the center of a very small glass dome-shaped habitat that sat on the planet's surface. In front of her was a small door. She looked up and watched as waves of sand flowed over the glass, giving her a feeling almost as if she was underwater or in some sort of quicksand sinking down deep.

The gold sand scattered the light and gave off an angelic appearance, the light in the room both softened and made more brilliant at the same time. It reminded her of a very expensive foyer in a very expensive hotel—one of the ones with a waterfall or an ice sculpture in the middle of it so that light bounced off it at different angles.

Ship guided her several steps forward. Right in front of her she saw a little door. She recognized the type of door it was. But she didn't want to believe it. It looked like a hospital door.

Without thinking, she felt her heart begin to race. She found her legs moving quicker too. She raced toward the door, pulling Ship behind her. She felt an urge to open the door and confirm what she was thinking. Ever since she'd left Mars that day many, many years ago, she'd had something inside of her driving her toward bringing children into this world. And at that very moment she could feel it finally happening, then a moment of worry as the logical part of her mind kicked in and told her that Ship wouldn't have seeded children on this world without her approval—*would he?*

She would forgive him if he did because, truth be told, she really wanted to seed the world with children. And the worst part of having that code in her mind was feeling like she was so close to her mission.

She faded through the door; she was a hologram, so she couldn't interact with anything in the room.

She felt a mix of emotions as she saw what was on the other side, like someone had just put all her different emotional states in a bowl and mixed them all together. Or as if someone had given her a cocktail of psychedelics, antidepressants, and mood boosters. Relief, dread, panic, and euphoric pleasure. Many different emotional states passed over her one at a time, then all at the same time. "Is this . . ." She trailed off.

Right in front of her was the artificial-womb machine. She saw it was active, too; inside of the murky liquid was a brown outline of a baby. The machine that was the very center of so many of her dreams. She'd always hoped this day would come. She didn't think it would happen like this, but she wasn't unhappy about this version.

Ship put his arms around her. "Trillion, I know you wanted to find out more about those clouds before we seeded the world. But I've thought through it. We can build a small colony on these artificial habitats. Angelique's Ship shared a lot of blueprints for how to make this world."

"It's okay, Ship. I'm glad you made an executive decision on this one. Thank you, Ship."

Lex popped into existence, floating right above Trillion's head. She smiled warmly at the orb. "And thank you, too, Lex."

The baby inside of the womb kicked, and Trillion got goose bumps.

"Any day now," Ship said. "The baby's vitals will tell us when it's ready to come out. And we'll be ready to see your first human on this planet."

Trillion felt overwhelmed with joy and pleasure. She felt like her greatest accomplishment of her entire life was moments away from being completed. She wondered why she wasn't feeling sad. Both Atlas and Icarus were overcome with despair when they'd seeded their first kids. So she wondered why she felt different. "Are you giving me antidepressants?"

Ship raised his hand up in the air, then made a gesture that told her maybe a little.

Lex bumped into Ship's shoulder.

"Okay, it's a lot," Ship said. "We're pumping your simulated mind full of things that will make you feel good."

Trillion didn't mind. She felt good. And she had never been opposed to trying things at a festival. She just hated the hangovers the next day. But things felt too good to think about that.

"Trillion, we thought you might want to do a bit of meditation." Ship looked up at Lex. "We thought it might be less emotionally traumatic that way."

Trillion was feeling good. She lay down on her back on the ground and closed her eyes. Then she slowly began to float off the ground, with each breath moving up then down again slightly. She felt herself calming the excited tones that kept bubbling up inside of her mind. If she tried to move her emotions toward a more neutral position, she might have an easier time dealing with the sad emotions she felt when the baby arrived.

Trillion began moving her mind toward stoicism.

In and out she breathed.

Then a baby's voice. Crying.

Trillion's eyes shot open. She bent forward and saw a nurse holding a little brown-skinned baby.

Everything in Trillion's mind disappeared. She reached forward, moving toward the child. Her hand passed through the child, and then she cried. Tears came thick and fast. She wiped them away from under her cheeks.

Trillion curled up in a ball. She hugged herself harder. She felt Ship's arm over the top of her and noticed the glow of Lex, and it came closer toward her.

All the while the baby cried.

"I didn't think it would feel this bad. This is worse than pain. My brain is literally being rewired for depression."

Trillion didn't mind the occasional sad movie. Every now and then she actually looked forward to having a good cry on the couch. But this was different. This was more pain than she had ever felt before.

She tried in vain to yank her mind toward stoicism. She screamed. Then she tried to calm herself by lying back and meditating.

Nothing worked.

"It's okay, Trillion. It's okay. Lex is reading your matrix. The behavioral modification is being deleted. It will all be over soon."

She got angry. Mad at Ship for something, anything.

It didn't work.

Deep down she knew what she had to do. She simply had to go through it all. Feel it all. Get to the other side. She gave up on trying to change what was. She let the emotions rush over her. She let them all come.

She closed her eyes and thought about holding her baby eventually.

It was a long time before Trillion was able to speak again. It was a strange sensation, not only because her matrix was being transformed as a piece of code deleted itself, but because she could tell Ship and Lex were elsewhere. Their minds at least were focused on something else.

They weren't focused on the baby either. By the time Trillion finally grabbed her composure, she noticed something else was going on. It was a comment from Ship that made her pause.

"You're one hundred percent certain the code has been deleted?"

Trillion opened her eyes in time to see Lex flash green.

Ship whispered the next question. "And no chance it's coming back?"

The orb flashed green.

Ship took hold of Trillion's hand. He walked her toward the baby that was currently being fed by the nurse. "Trillion, we're not sure how best to tell you this. So I'm just going to say it." He waved his hand in front of the baby and nurse. They froze in time. Just stopped. Trillion got a headache and had to close her eyes again. She didn't feel like her perception of time had changed. She shook her head and focused her eyes back on Ship.

"I'm sorry, Trillion. This is just a simulation. We didn't seed the planet. It was the only way to help you remove that piece of code from your matrix safely."

Trillion had to process what Ship just said in her mind multiple times. On some deep level, she logically knew it made sense. Ship wouldn't have seeded a world without her permission. But the ruse had worked. She was in so much mental pain at that very moment. But there was a spark of hope. She gained a minute speck of happiness from the fact she was now free of the behavioral-modification code in her matrix.

She knew when all was done and she was thinking clearly again she would be happy with what Ship and Lex had just done. She knew they only wanted the best for her, and they wanted her to be free to make her own decisions with a clear mind.

Although that wasn't the dominant feeling inside of her mind. At that very point in time, she was jumping between utter depression and anger that Ship had caused the depression. But she'd had friends that were depressed before. She'd watched Icaurus and Atlas go through the same thing. She knew it would pass. She knew in the end she'd be happy again.

She went to smile at Ship, tell him it was okay, and give him the reassurance she would have wanted if the roles were reversed. But then she closed her eyes again. She couldn't escape the pain. She curled up into a ball and cried. Then feeling the embarrassing hug of Ship, she felt happy knowing he was there for her.

CHAPTER 12

THE SHIP OF TRILLION

TRUE FREEDOM

Ship was overseeing the construction of a small ice rink on the dark side of the planet. A large eleph-ANT with a snowplow at the front of its nose was shoveling snow out of the way while another eleph-ANT came in behind it and compacted the ice.

Ship found himself in an odd situation. A few months back, he and Lex had coded a fake simulated world. They had used that world to trick Trillion into believing they had seeded the planet. Afterward all three of them had agreed it was the right thing to do.

It gave Trillion true freedom to think properly. It released her from myopically focusing on a single goal. It gave her mind time to think. And it also gave Ship his best friend back.

What was odd about the situation was the fact they were mourning the loss of a fake child. When Atlas and Icarus had gone through the deletions of their behavioral-modification code, they had had everyone around. They also had small children to focus on. Trillion didn't. Which in some ways made it worse.

Not that Ship would ever vocalize this thought. But he wondered if it was similar in nature to a form of postpartum depression. He didn't want to think about how hard it would be for mothers that go through depression and also feel the loss of a child.

He decided against sharing that thought with anyone. Even if the two scenarios were analogous. He wasn't in a position to compare them. He couldn't have children, nor did he have behavioral-modification code installed in his brain.

The silver lining in all of this was that they had just received confirmation from one of the probes that it had successfully landed in a nearby system and had begun preliminary scans to confirm whether the location was ideal for seeding a new planet. He sent a quick message to Trillion asking her to join him. He wanted to tell her the exciting news in person.

Ship watched as another eleph-ANT completed covering the area in a liquid gel that would freeze and become the surface they skated on. The snow that had been carved out of the way by the eleph-ANT was more akin to concrete. The lake bed they had just revealed had been compressed over many years. And he couldn't melt the top layer of ice, as there wasn't a thick atmosphere on the planet, so any water would immediately boil and evaporate away. So the gel he covered the ice in would act as ice they could glide through on skates.

Ship sensed Trillion's imminent arrival and instructed all the ANTs to turn on their lights. The area lit up, revealing a magical wonderland. And sat in the very middle of the area for ice-skating stood a several-stories-high giant ice sculpture of a Christmas tree.

"Are you calling me a snow queen?" Trillion asked with a smile on her face as she appeared in the air above Ship. "Are you saying I'm stuck on this frozen ice planet?" She landed next to him. "If I'm Elsa, that would make you Olaf."

Ship laughed at that. "If we're talking about Disney characters, I'd prefer to be Buzz Lightyear."

Ship nodded at Lex, who turned on the music, and the ice tree in the middle of the rink started to turn slowly. As the branches made of icicles moved, they flickered the light in different directions.

Ship hoped a little distraction for Trillion would help to cheer her up. He took hold of her arms and pointed toward two humanoid androids standing on the ice. "You always told me one of your favorite memories as a child was ice-skating on Christmas Day. So I thought we could re-create that here."

"It's magical, Ship, thank you."

"We'll jump into the bodies of those two androids there. No hapticgraphic engine mimicking physics—we'll be in real robots, and if we fall over, we fall over."

Both of them floated down toward the androids, and their simulated bodies melted into them. The android bodies looked exactly like them both. Ship had designed them to look that way.

Ship was holding a little orb, which Lex floated into. Ship placed the little ball on the ground, and it immediately began sliding away from them both. Ship figured the ground mustn't be level as he watched Lex spin rapidly, trying to stop the slide. Like a wheel spinning in the mud, Lex's spinning wasn't helping it move in the direction it wanted. Ship obviously didn't think Lex's design through, as a ball wasn't a very practical shape for moving around on ice.

Ship took a tentative step forward. He wasn't too confident himself on ice skates. He almost slipped over.

"Grab my hands," Trillion said, turning around backward and putting both her arms out toward Ship. She pulled him along as they both began to move. "There was a lake outside of the city near where I lived as a child. Every year my mother would take me and my sister to skate on it as soon as it froze. For some reason, the first day the ice was thick enough was always Christmas Day." Trillion picked Lex up out of the little hole it had dug into the ice by spinning so much. She placed the orb on the ground and gave it a little nudge toward the other side of the rink. "Come to think of it, we were quite poor when growing up, and Mom didn't have much time off work. So maybe we only went on Christmas Day because it was the only day she got off. And Christmas was usually about the presents. But we didn't care about not having any gifts when we went skating for the whole day."

Trillion let go of Ship's hands. She skated a little out in front of Ship. He stood there, frozen, not very confident on his legs.

Ship tried to skate toward her, but every little movement he did forced him to move quickly to keep his balance. But when he tried to correct his balance, he found himself overcompensating and almost falling over, anyway. He decided he would just stay still and drift forward.

Trillion turned around and began picking up speed. She raced around the rink like a figure skater, moving faster and faster.

Eventually she came behind Ship and grabbed onto his waist. She pushed him forward. She pumped her legs and started moving the two of them around the rink. "Thank you, Ship."

If Ship kept his legs stiff, he found he could turn quite well. And as long as it was Trillion pumping her legs to keep the two of them moving, he quite enjoyed the trip.

"Well, I've got some more good news I think you'll be happy about," Ship said as he turned around in a wide arc to start heading in the other direction again. "We just had confirmation one of the probes we sent out has reached its intended system. It has constructed the Starnet system on their side, and we will soon be able to connect to it to take a look at the new world."

"Does that mean we'll get to explore another star system soon?"

Ship nodded.

"What about our connection to Atlas or Icarus? Have we heard anything back from them yet?"

Ship shook his head. "Not yet, but assuming they reached out as soon as the Starnet was disconnected, it'll be a few years before we speak to them again. In the meantime, our probes will have reached their targets, and we'll probably have another five or six star systems set up a Starnet connection with us."

Ship couldn't see Trillion but thought he could hear a smile in her voice as she spoke.

"Will we really have six systems soon?"

Ship knew that Trillion had something to prove with the other beta explorers. She was the only one left who hadn't colonized a world, so he thought she might be happy with the knowledge that she would soon have more star systems under her control than Icarus or Atlas. "Maybe more depending on how long it takes the others to get the Starnet back up and running."

"That's really good because I've been thinking about it. We still don't know why the Starnet went down do we?"

"We won't know until we make a new connection with the others."

"Well, back when Atlas released that virus, he was quietly confident it was another alien species manipulating us. So if Atlas is right, and it was an alien species manipulating us, then we're going to need resources on multiple worlds that we can call on. Especially if we have to show strength to this alien."

What Trillion didn't say but what was clear in her meaning was that she wanted to have an army. She was still a little hurt by the fact an alien, the Dottiens, had trapped her on a moon and held her against her will for many, many years. It wasn't until Ship brought back an army himself that she was able to escape. And again, she'd barely escaped too because Earth had also sent a contingent of war ships to try and capture her. The only thing that had saved her was the fact she had a huge number of ships. Ship knew that Trillion never wanted to get into that situation again. She knew all too well the risks of not having enough resources to win a fight.

"So you want to build another Steel World?"

"Maybe not a Steel World. But I want to make sure we're safe and can survive anything that comes our way if we need to."

"You want to build an empire?"

Trillion didn't respond, but Ship thought he saw her nodding at that question.

Ship asked the next question tentatively. Since he and Lex had pretended to seed the planet they were on, the two of them hadn't discussed seeding a planet again. That topic had remained unsaid. Ship didn't know where Trillion's priorities were now that she had free will. Now that she wasn't compelled to seed a world. "What about your children? Do you want to seed a world still?"

"I'm unsure," Trillion said. "To be honest, I'm not entirely sure how I feel. I think I want to seed the next viable planet. But I don't know if that's just because it's just a goal I've had for so long, that it's always been a goal. I'm not sure whether I'm choosing to want to do this or not." She paused for a moment. "I do know I feel very strongly that I want an army. And I want to be able to protect you and the others. I want to protect all the worlds we have."

Trillion slowed down her pushing as the two of them moved forward smoothly. "I feel strongly that I want that to be our focus for now. I want to make sure everything is safe before we bring children into this world."

Ship placed his hands over Trillion's and squeezed them in a gesture that showed warmth. He knew Trillion had some existing emotional scars she had to work through. One thing he knew about the behavioral-modification code was it stopped her from dealing with sadness or trauma properly. It limited her ability to process things, and now that it was finally gone, it meant she could work through everything they had experienced on this journey through space.

Atlas had taken many years to get his mind under control. Ship believed the reason he rushed blindly into the bubble wasn't just because Atreus had died. Ship believed he'd rushed in foolishly because he hadn't processed the loss of Angelique and

Peter fully. Ship assumed Atlas had never talked through his pain properly. He probably didn't feel right talking about it because it had happened so many years before.

Ship didn't want Trillion to go through the same issues. He wasn't a psychologist, but he decided to help Trillion heal those wounds.

"Can we sit next to Lex?" Ship asked, pointing to the orb resting underneath the ice Christmas tree. It had struggled its way there and decided not to move.

Trillion guided them underneath the tree. The two of them sat down on either side of Lex and leaned against the ice sculpture's trunk.

"Trillion," Ship said in a quiet voice, not sure exactly how to start the conversation but knowing he just needed to start it. "Should we talk about everything we've been through? Escaping Mars, facing the Dottiens, being stuck on that moon?"

Trillion looked at him with watery eyes, droplets starting to appear in the corners. Her lips turned upside down like she was fighting back tears.

Ship was right, the three of them needed to talk through everything that had happened.

And they did; they talked about everything, from what was going on with Trillion the months leading up to the day they'd left to the fact they'd caused genocide to an entire planet in the Tac system.

Every moment they discussed was recolored by Trillion's new ability to feel pain, to feel emotion.

Trillion even apologized for blaming him and Lex for destroying the planet.

Like watching a movie with the director's commentary turned on, it gave Ship a more complete understanding of all the choices they'd made. And all the mistakes too. He had a newfound appreciation of just how bad the modification was. It forced her to focus on seeding a world. It was the cause of most of their mistakes.

Minutes turned into hours as they sat there discussing everything, getting all the baggage out in the open and making sure they weren't making decisions because of a piece of malicious code that used to be installed in Trillion's matrix.

As hours turned into more hours, Ship could tell Trillion's thinking became clearer. She was becoming free of old mistakes. In the same way childhood trauma could shape the way someone thought as an adult, the two of them were understanding how some of the trauma they went through was shaping their thinking today.

In the end they came to the conclusion Trillion was abandoning their goal of seeding a world as a retaliation against the code. And they also discovered that Trillion's desire to build a bigger army was driven by the fact they had been stuck on a moon for so many years without autonomy. And Trillion never wanted to have that happen again.

They also discovered that Ship was a people pleaser, or rather a Trillion pleaser, and he was too much of a pushover when it came to requests from Trillion. They agreed that tricking her into believing they had seeded this world had been the right thing to do. And it was also the first time Ship had done something (intentionally) that was against Trillion's wishes.

That was a good thing, and Trillion said it needed to happen more often.

They decided that going forward, they would make decisions together. Trillion would lean on Ship's counsel a lot more, rather than just going at things alone.

Ship wasn't sure how that would work, since in a way he was programmed to be subordinate to Trillion. But he figured that maybe he was growing and learning to be more of a leader. Especially given he'd orchestrated the ruse that had freed Trillion.

They came to a few new decisions during the counseling session. They were going to seed a planet, the next best one, as they both agreed that having more humans in the world would increase the rate of technological progress.

They also agreed that they'd work overtime to colonize more star systems but in a strategic pattern around the existing stars they already had. That way, if any alien did come toward them, these outpost star systems would act as a barrier, seeing any threats first.

CHAPTER 13

ARIANA

FINDING CLUES

Ariana Barns liked being a simulation. Without a physical body she wasn't limited by biological functioning. She didn't have to eat, she didn't have to exercise, and she didn't have to go to the bathroom. She didn't even have to move if she didn't want to.

And so, in a way, that's what she did. For an unusual amount of time, she stayed in one location with her eyes closed, concentrating. Ever since the other team members had departed in their spacecraft, she hadn't moved from the bridge of the rotating space station in the system. She only recalled opening her eyes twice to see out the window of the deck to glance at the aliens' vessel.

Had it been weeks or months? she wondered to herself.

With no one around her, she didn't feel the social pressure to move. She also told herself that, in a way, she was moving because she remotely controlled probes and other devices around the system. So that was her moving about.

She was working on three projects concurrently. She had eleph-ANTs deconstructing the orbiting platform and recycling the material to make a small rocket, which she would use to leave the system when she was done with her research. The second item on her list was properly investigating the alien vessel to better understand it and perhaps the aliens themselves. The final piece, and probably the most important, was she wanted to hack her way into the alien spacecraft. She wanted to get inside of its electronics, to understand how it ticked. And maybe, to identify how it worked. She hoped she might also unlock some alien technology.

Unfortunately for her, she hadn't found the brains of the ship. It was a mystery. From what she could see, she'd explored every accessible compartment in the spacecraft. And not once did she find a control panel or even some wires that she could plug into. Any human ship would have at least had control panels or something.

She hadn't yet resorted to cutting her way through the ship. She wanted to do that as a last resort. She still expected to take control of the ship and wanted to fly it all the way back to the others. She couldn't control the automatic smile on her face as she thought about showing up to Peter in an alien spacecraft.

She had to remind herself that alien meant alien. So it was unlikely they would build in a similar way to humans. She had a few hundred ANTs racing around the alien ship, pulsating different frequencies on the electromagnetic spectrum. Her assumption was that maybe all connection on the ship was done wirelessly. So by racing around the ship with a strong antennae, the ANTs might trigger a panel or whatever to send a pulse back.

And then at least she'd know a location to start investigating. She mentally decided to give it all another month; if she hadn't found a control panel or something she could start interfacing with by then, she'd start cutting holes in walls and tunneling her way throughout the alien ship until she found something she could hack into.

She had found one thing though. It was interesting. There were definitely some clear signs about the origin of this starship.

One side of the ship had clearly been subjected to a lot of radiation bombarding it.

When high-energy particles from a star or from cosmic background radiation impact the surface of metals, a change in the metal occurs. The more there is, the more obvious it becomes. In the same way sun damage occurs on the sides of a sofa that are always in direct sunlight, the structure of a metal that is always in sunlight will also change—although much more subtly over time.

She had been researching the changes in metal composition around the ship. There were some clear signs of where the ship came from in the way the metals had changed.

A spacecraft typically always accelerated from one side of the ship, so she assumed this one would too. The engines fired the same way; they needed to in order to pick up speed—assuming the alien didn't possess some advanced alternative propulsion method.

When leaving a star system, one side of the spacecraft would always face the same direction. There was always a side that was constantly being bombarded with X-rays and ultraviolet light from the star.

Ariana analyzed the changes in metal and confirmed just that. The side of the ship with the engines also showed the most radiation damage.

Ariana smiled at how brilliant the concept was. By having access to this ship, she basically knew what type of star the alien came from.

Red dwarf stars, which were the most common type of star in the galaxy, emitted more longer-frequency light. But bigger stars, on the other hand, emitted more light at higher frequencies. The bigger the star, the more high-energy particles, X-rays, and ultraviolet light that was emitted from the star.

Ariana compared metal from all around the ship. She ran those samples through different simulations. It was clear that the radiation damage experienced by the alien vessel was produced by a G-type star. A good proportion of this spaceship's life was spent in near proximity to a G-type star, a star of similar size to Earth's Sun.

Now either that meant this spacecraft had visited Earth recently, or more likely the planet this alien spacecraft originated from was a G-type star. There were fewer than ten of these stars near enough to them that they could have traveled the distance.

Although that was speculation because, if this alien had some sort of warp drive or any other FTL travel method, then the range of potential stars was huge.

Ariana loaded that piece of information and data on everything else she had learned so far onto a tight-beam communication and sent that information to Atlas.

Then quickly she realized she probably needed to explain her findings, as she wasn't sure Atlas would immediately understand the importance of this finding.

Ariana opened her eyes and instructed an ANT to record her. Before speaking, she faced away from the window and had the ANT move its camera.

Ariana now looked like she was standing on the bridge of the orbiting platform, and out the window the alien spacecraft was visible.

"I've made a discovery. The aliens traveled to us from a G-type star. I've included that data on how I made that discovery as an appendix to this message. I'm not sure if that's their home system or not. But this ship definitely came from a system with a yellow dwarf in the center. Atlas, I know there's a telescope in the system you're going to. I suggest you point it at the ten closest stars of that size and see if you can spot anything unusual.

"I've scanned the databases for information about all the G-type stars near us and couldn't find anything unusual. But we know the aliens had complete control of our computer systems. It would not have been an issue for them to doctor what we know.

"My suggestion, if you have a look again, is to use the transit method to see if you can identify any biosignatures on any of the planets.

"Let's see if we can find out where these aliens come from. Let's find the Atua's home world."

CHAPTER 14

ATLAS

LOCATION, LOCATION, LOCATION

Atlas arrived in the Tac system with his action plan set in place. He was excited, giddy. He loved the mystery of it all.

About six months earlier he'd received information from Ariana that narrowed down the number of stars he needed to investigate in order to identify the location of the Atua. He wondered if he was about to learn where their home world was.

He looked out of the small port window of the escape capsule they'd traveled in. "Ship, can you signal the Lex in this system? Can you confirm our authorization codes still work?"

"Done. It'll take a few moments for it to respond," Ship said as the two of them waited for the reply. "Lex has confirmed Trillion's permission settings still give us full access to this system."

The Tac star system was the first location Trillion had visited. Through a mistake, she ended up grey gooing the whole system, turning it into resource pallets and fabricators, which he planned on using in order to do his research.

Out the window of the small pod, Atlas saw a dead mechanical world. Atlas's jaw dropped open as he looked at one of the planets. It looked like a Death Star. Every inch of it looked to be bottled up and turned into resource pallets. "Does Lex know what happened to the Starnet, Ship?"

"It said it blew up, but it's not sure how or why."

That's not good, Atlas thought. "Was any other infrastructure damaged?"

"It's confirmed all the damage has been fixed," Ship said. "This Lex really is more proactive. It said that the Starnet has been fixed, and it's reestablishing the connection with the others."

Their Lex flashed a subtle hue of red and nudged Ship. "Sorry, Lex, I didn't mean it like that. You're still my favorite."

"Lex has allocated us one of the unused spacecraft." Ship took control of the small escape pod they were traveling in and guided them into an open hatch inside of one of the empty starships in the system.

Ship drifted the probe into an open air lock chamber, and eleph-ANTs inside of the cargo hangar took hold of the probe and secured them into place. "This will be our new home going forward. We can start coordinating things from here."

"We've got full access to the manufacturing capability of this system, correct?"

Ship nodded.

"Then I'd prefer to fabricate a new rocket ship. I want it to look exactly like this one, at least from the outside. But from the inside, I want our matrices stored in a different location, and I want to replace the engines with the much more powerful designs that Angelique provided us."

Atlas had learned the hard way the issues with using the same designs for all his ships. When he was attacked by Angelique's people, his ship had been disabled quickly. It was a simple task of disconnecting Ship and him from their spacecraft. That rendered them unable to fight back.

Presumably the Atua aliens had access to all their blueprints, so if Atlas ever encountered them in a fight again, he wanted to make sure he wasn't easily disabled.

He was quietly confident Angelique hadn't shared all the weaponry she had at her disposal. But she had shared everything he'd seen so far. "Can you also add the tractor beam and more laser weapons to the spacecraft you build?"

"Wow, that was fast," Ship said, projecting an image of the spacecraft design and handing it to Atlas. "The Lex in here is fast. Really fast. It suggested we use the original shape of our first rockets. The smaller rocket ship, as we don't need as much space for the engines. A smaller rocket will also make us more maneuverable, too."

On the outline of the rocket, at the very bottom, sat the large egg-shaped engine. Anyone looking at it would believe that was the large engine bay.

Ship opened up the inside of the rocket ship design to reveal the insides. There was a large open cavity where the rocket engine should have been.

Ship pointed to the opening. "With Angelique's engine designs, we fill this space with eleph-ANTs and other probes."

"I like it," Atlas replied. "Can you equip all the eleph-ANTs with tractor beams? That way if we get into a fight, we can drop them all out the back and they can attack the enemy vessel while we escape."

"On it," Ship said. "Okay, done."

"What do you mean done? I only just asked you to do it."

"Do you know how easy it is to manufacture things in this system? Trillion has an ungodly number of fabricators here. We can basically manufacture things in no time."

"Are you saying you printed tractor beams to connect to eleph-ANTs? Or the spacecraft is already built?"

"Both. They have massive fabricator units in this system. All the sections are currently being connected together. We could probably relocate into it, while the components are finished welding together."

Atlas was amazed at just how useful this system was. Through Trillion's mistake, she had created a very powerful capability.

This boded well for what Atlas had planned next.

After the construction of his fancy new spaceship, Atlas stood in the bridge with Ship and the two Lexes in front of him. Trillion's Lex in charge of the system manifested an orb avatar that was slightly bigger.

He didn't know if he was just imagining things, but his Lex was acting a little strange, as if it was slightly threatened by the new Lex. It always positioned itself in between the other Lex and him. Or maybe it was more like a puppy attempting to protect its owner.

Either way, Atlas found it a little cute.

"I assume everyone's reviewed the message from Ariana?"

Ship nodded, while the two Lexes flashed green.

Ariana had sent them a list of candidate stars to investigate, which might all be potential home worlds for the Atua.

"Perfect, so there's a large telescope in this system. Trillion built it to study other potential planets she could visit. Let's point it at these planets and see if we can use the transit method to identify something interesting with the planets around these stars."

The transit method involved waiting for a planet to pass in front of its host star. As light traveled through an atmosphere, different wavelengths of light were absorbed depending on the types of gasses light passed through. Oxygen, methane, and carbon dioxide all left distinctive fingerprints on all light that traveled through them.

If they were to point their powerful telescope at Sol, and if Earth was to cross right in front of the star so that they saw this happen, Earth would show obvious signs that it was producing gases that don't occur naturally—at least in the quantities they did. It would almost be a dead giveaway that there was life on the planet.

The biggest trouble with the transit method was that the planet needed to be at the correct angle so the planet crossed in front of the star at an angle they could see.

The truth of the matter was, if they did point the telescope toward Sol, they wouldn't see any signs of life because Earth would not pass in front of the star at an angle they could see.

So Atlas wasn't holding out hope for them finding much. But he had his fingers crossed they might get lucky.

"Let's get to it, team. See if we find anything."

CHAPTER 15

ATLAS

A BETTER WAY

Atlas studied the data coming off the large telescope that was currently using the transit method to search for the Atua's home world. They weren't finding anything. None of the systems they were monitoring showed any obvious signs of biological life. At least nothing that couldn't be explained by natural processes. He was at least hoping for a smoking gun.

The transit method involved waiting for a planet to cross in front of its host star. Then by analyzing how different frequencies of light were absorbed, the spectral lines, he could guestimate which gases were present in the atmosphere.

The trouble was, there wasn't anything conclusive. Methane was just as easily created by alien life as it was by a volcano.

And what was worse, Ariana's suggested solution was that they look at one of the stars, staring at it for five years, then move on to the next one.

The reason she suggested five years was to account for the fact that orbits in the Goldilocks zones of these stars might take up to two and a half years. So by keeping the telescope focused on the star for that long, they were almost guaranteed to see two moments in time where the planets transitioned in front of their stars.

That was not an ideal process, even if he constructed several telescopes to study them all at the same time. It would still take five years of constant study.

He could point the telescope at Sol for a hundred years and still have no conclusive evidence that it was a system full of life. Earth's orbit just wasn't at the right angle for them to see the planet using the transit method. Atlas needed a different way.

He racked his brain for potential ideas, trying to come up with a way around this issue.

"We're not going to do what Ariana's suggesting," Atlas said almost instinctually. He didn't quite have an idea yet but felt if he voiced the words out loud his mind would work in overtime to come up with a solution.

Ship cocked an eyebrow toward Atlas. "I'm guessing you have a better idea?"

Atlas bit his lower lip. He needed a way to look at the planets in those systems, not through analyzing the effects they made as light passed through their atmospheres. Somehow he needed to take a photo of each of the planets, as if he had the most powerful zoom lens ever invented. "If I needed to take a photo of a planet in another system, how would I do it?" Atlas wondered aloud.

Then a seed of an idea appeared in Atlas's mind. He was finally getting back to his science roots.

He bit his lip some more, further developing the concept. He had everything in the system already to make what he needed. He became excited to tell Ship about his plan. And even more excited to tell Angelique, Trillion, Peter, and Icarus.

It was the kind of science fiction idea he would have obsessed about as a child.

The concept subconsciously appeared in his mind when Ship went on and on about how many resources they had in the system. They had enough resources to conduct megaproject after megaproject. And this was the ultimate megaproject.

Atlas needed to talk through his thinking. If for nothing else than to flesh out his concept. "Ship, how do telescopes work?"

Ship eyed him suspiciously. "The first telescope was basically like a magnifying glass. It worked using a lens to focus a big section of light onto a small area that people could look at."

Atlas knew Ship was humouring him. Ship always played along as Atlas asked these questions. But Atlas also knew he'd piqued Ship's curiosity; Ship wanted to know the idea that Atlas was presenting. "And what about telescopes today? How do they make bigger telescopes?"

"The telescope we have in this system is probably the biggest humans have ever made. Rather than using a lens, the telescope in this system uses giant mirrors to focus the light onto a small sensor."

Trillion had constructed a massive telescope within the system. The James Webb Space Telescope was the first one designed in that manner. It had giant mirrors that reflected light. The limiting factor in that telescope's design was the size of the rocket used to ferry it into space. Humans had built bigger ones once they'd gotten bigger rockets. The one Trillion had built was even bigger than any in orbit around Earth. "Okay, so what makes a telescope better? Ship, what is the most important factor that would allow us to zoom in on faraway planets?"

"The aperture, the size of the lens, or the size of the mirrors. Basically the more light we can collect and focus onto a small area, the better the image and resolution we can gain."

"Correct, so what if we wanted to build a bigger telescope? How would we do it?"

Ship scratched the back of his head. "I would argue this is the biggest theoretical telescope using mirrors. Hmm." Ship considered everything for a second. His brain started to tick over thinking about potential solutions. "Maybe if we built even bigger mirrors, a wall of mirrors? Or maybe—" Ship paused. "I'm not sure how to do it. The designs of these telescopes start hitting against the laws of physics. We will struggle to make them much bigger."

"Want me to give you a clue?"

Ship nodded.

"Gravitational lensing."

Gravity bends light. Atlas remembered back to photos of weird images of space he'd looked at from the Hubble Space Telescope. In the images, distant galaxies would sometimes appear closer or distorted. He'd read a paper that said these were caused by the gravity within a galaxy in front of the objects the telescopes were looking at. If you were looking at a distant galaxy, and between you and the galaxy was a black hole, you could use the black hole as a telescope lens to take a closer look at the galaxy.

It didn't matter whether light was bent through a lens, a mirror, or even through gravity. The more light you could bend, the farther away you could look. The benefit of using gravity rather than a mirror was, though there was a hard limit on how big you could make a mirror, there wasn't a limit on gravity.

"Has Angelique invented something that can produce a massive amount of gravity?"

"No," Atlas said. "Well, at least I don't think she has. I'm talking about using the sun."

The star at the center of the system they were in was the biggest gravitational body nearby. It was a red dwarf star, a relatively small star, as far as stars go. But by using the lensing effect that the star's mass caused, he would essentially be able to see farther and at better resolution than anything he could possibly build.

"Okay, I'll bite," Ship said. "How do you plan on using the star in the middle of this system as a lens for a telescope?"

"So you agree that a big gravitational body like the star in this system will bend light?"

"Yes. But there's a star in the way. If we made a giant see-through lens the size of the star, I'd understand how that would work because it's transparent, but using the gravity from the star means there's a massive star in the way."

Oh, Atlas thought. Ship was thinking about it all the wrong way. "Do you know what an Einstein ring is?"

Atlas watched as Ship looked up the information. "It's an image of light being stretched and bent into a ring because of the way space-time bends light. It looks like a solar eclipse back on Earth."

"That's exactly what it is. An Einstein ring is basically a magnified image of whatever is behind that large gravitational body but stretched out of shape so that it's unrecognizable."

"So you're saying we could use the star to focus light from other distant ones?"

"I'm saying the sun is already focusing light from these distant star systems. We just have to send a telescope out there and start recording the data. The more data we collect, the higher the image resolution. In theory we could even create an image of the different planets in these star systems."

"How do we go from an Einstein ring to a clear image of a planet?"

"I think Lex here can help. We just need to take a warped image and reconstruct it into what it actually looks like."

The orb closest to Atlas flashed green.

Atlas continued. "Hopefully it'll give us enough details to make out clouds and landmasses on the planet. We will probably also be able to see signs of a technological civilization—like artificial lights on the planet."

"Why is this the first I'm hearing of this type of telescope? If it's so powerful, why haven't we built one before?"

"The trouble with this telescope is you can't just point it at another star or planet when you're done. It's really only designed to look at one planet or star. So for the types of scans we've needed to do, it's not practical." Atlas paused for a second. "But if Ariana is right, then we only need to look at a handful of stars. We can use this approach for looking at a few stars and their planets."

The team started work on designing small modular telescopes that could be manufactured quickly and launched out into space using the magnetic accelerators in the system.

In the end the design they settled on looked like a thin circular piece of board. In the very center was a camera sensor about one meter in diameter. Then the edges of the telescope were covered in solar panels.

They were disposable sensors that could be shot out in great numbers one after another.

It didn't take too long before it looked like a train of these satellites were headed out away from the star.

Atlas also sent out a spacecraft, and eleph-ANTs with tractor beams attached collected all the telescopes after they'd completed their missions.

"Now we wait," Atlas said as he contemplated increasing his playback speed. Although he knew he needed to use the time he had to figure out how best to parse the data the telescopes would collect.

At his core he was an engineer, a scientist, and a researcher. He preferred problem-solving. But crunching all the data he was about to collect required a slightly different skill set. Someone with machine learning capabilities. Someone who could design an algorithm for visualizing everything. Someone who could take datapoints in the shape of an Einstein ring and turn them into an image of a planet.

CHAPTER 16
ARIANA

CLEVER

Ariana began moving her new makeshift spacecraft onto the other side of the bubble. The bubble was the region of space currently being affected by a small device that consumed a lot of power. It was projecting a field around an alien spaceship, stopping it from receiving or sending any communication.

Ariana kept the stealthfield broadcasting and disrupting the region of space around the Atua's spacecraft so that there was no risk of PBD retaking control of the spacecraft.

The downside was she had no way to communicate with any of the other beta explorers without leaving the bubble. Using probes was painfully slow, especially when she finally had the Starnet set up.

Luckily, she'd just completed her renovation of the orbital platform. She'd recycled all its mass and turned it into a small spacecraft capable of moving her around the galaxy. It was her own personal spacecraft, uniquely configured to house her several matrices and also uniquely configured to give her even more resources and power than she'd had before.

An accurate description was she had now expanded her mind to encompass a small spacecraft. He gave her more processing power than she'd ever had before. Whereas the other explorers had opted to use the hapticgraphic projectors to ground them in reality, Ariana didn't see any need to have empty space in her rocket ship. So she'd decided to make use of a simulated reality. Simulated VR was indistinguishable from reality. She rejected the hypothesis of the others that using a hapticgram-based reality grounded them in the real world. In Ariana's mind, it really was pointless grasping onto the outdated idea that a simulation was different from reality.

Plus it came with a lot of powerful advantages. The other explorers only had the ability to speed up or slow down their perceptions of time. Ariana had the processing power of a country, which meant she could run entire simulated worlds at a faster speed.

She didn't have a use for that power yet, but she knew when Atlas was terraforming his world, he'd needed to engineer a specific type of mold. His process was painfully slow and inefficient. He would breed a new strain and test it in the real world. Ariana now had the capabilities to test every possible strain concurrently and see how they performed in a simulated world. Her new capabilities would create an order of magnitude increase in productivity for simple tasks like that. She wondered how much better things would be when she had a lot more time to play.

Because Ariana was her ship, and her ship was Ariana, she felt weird sensations as she traversed to the other side of this stealthfield. Signals inside her brain weren't arriving at the exact moment they should have. And because she had essentially become a distributed intelligence, with different parts of herself acting independently toward her goals, it resulted in her receiving answers to questions several microseconds before she learned part of her had asked the question.

It was a little disconcerting at first, and she had to remind herself that this is what the bubble was designed to do—disrupt and mess with all signals in and out of that region of space.

On the other side of the stealthfield was a node connected to the Starnet. So far only Atlas had a working connection.

Atlas was bugging Ariana to cross to the other side of the Starnet and talk with him. He wanted to show her something amazing. When she'd asked him to send a video recording, he'd said he wanted to watch her reaction. So here she was, traveling to the other side of the bubble to talk with Atlas. The first thing she did when connecting to the Starnet was attempt to hack into Atlas's systems so she could see what he wanted to show her. She was disappointed when she encountered a very strong firewall. She guessed it was something from Angelique's people. She would have to find out the good news the old-fashioned way: speaking to people.

"Ari, you've gotta see this," Atlas said as soon as he saw Ariana appear in front of him.

"Did you use the transit method to look at the stars I suggested? Are there clear biomarkers of life on one of the planets?"

"No, we didn't find anything meaningful using that method."

"Interesting, so none of the G-type stars showed signs of life?" Ariana thought for a while. She was confident they would find life on one of those planets. The alien ship she'd scanned did come from a star system that gave off a lot of radiation in the same frequencies as a yellow dwarf star. "They must have a manufacturing base or refueling base at one of those stars. I tested my theory multiple times; they visited one of those systems."

"The problem with the transit method is it's better at detecting hot Jupiter-sized planets, gas giants that are close to the star. From where I am now, if I pointed a telescope at Sol, the transit method wouldn't detect Earth because Earth never passes in front of the star from my point of view. I'm in the wrong position to see it."

"Okay," Ariana said, thinking through other options. "What if we build telescopes in all the systems we have access to? At least one of them should be at the right angle to detect something? I know I'm right about this."

"You were right, Ari," Atlas said, pulling the conversation back to the start of their discussion. "They were on Sigma Draconis this whole time. Only eighteen light-years from Earth."

Arian was left speechless for a second. "If the transit method didn't work, then how do you know they're there?"

Atlas raised his hands into the air as if he was holding up a basketball. "Ship, can you show the projection?"

A nighttime projection of an alien planet appeared in Atlas's hand. It was a mostly water world but had three large continents on it. The biggest of the three looked like a snake had swallowed a large animal of some sort. The top and bottom of the continent stretched from one pole to the other. There was clearly ice on the poles too.

The most obvious giveaway that there was intelligent life on this planet was the light coming from the areas of land that Ariana assumed were the cities.

"Are you showing me your world? Or is this one of Angelique's?" Ariana asked because it didn't make sense that this was an image of the Atua home world. "Unless . . ." Ariana paused, she couldn't think of any possible way to take an image of a planet in another solar system without visiting it. "Did you already have a probe flying by that system?"

"No, this is not one of our star systems. And no, we haven't sent a probe to it."

"You're showing me one of the planets in the Sigma Draconis system?"

Atlas nodded.

Ariana studied the projection. The image wasn't quite high-definition. It was quite pixelated, something more akin to one of the early pictures of Earth, when humans were first sending probes into space. But it was clear enough to give the unmistakable understanding that the planet had life on it. And that life was congregated in coastal cities. Ariana didn't understand how Atlas had gotten that picture. She wasn't an astronomer; it wasn't even her area of interest. AI, computer systems, theoretical physics, those were areas of science she obsessed about, but she had a good enough grasp on astronomy to understand the basics. Surely there wasn't a new design of telescope she didn't know about. "How?" was the only question Ariana could get out.

"Easy," Atlas said with a proud look on his face. "Well, not easy. We just used the star as a lens to bend light so that it would be like creating a telescope as big as the star itself."

Everyone knew about Atlas's inventions back on Earth. Stories of him were legendary at Peter's company. He was almost a meme, like Oppenheimer or Edison. But Ariana had always assumed he wasn't as good as people said. Not because she didn't think Atlas was a good inventor. She just knew from experience that memories of something often became better than the original.

For much of Ariana's adult working life, she'd believed that technological progress had reached a plateau. She and all her colleagues believed each subsequent step forward required an order of magnitude more effort than the previous one. Gone were the days when one person could make the kinds of breakthroughs in science seen in the past. Oppenheimer might have sped up the invention of nuclear energy by a few years. But that invention would have happened regardless of whether he existed or not.

Ever since the invention of the first AI, there had never been another inventor like Atlas Tupu. He was the last of the great inventors. Well, at least that's what everyone said. She didn't believe it though. Surely it was all myth, and he was just taking credit for other people's inventions. One man couldn't have the creativity to do what people said he'd done.

But now seeing firsthand, seeing Atlas in action. My god, she was impressed. "You really are that good."

"Aw, thanks," Atlas said, going a bit red. "I think it could be better still. Do you mind looking at the data?"

In an instant, Ariana's ship, which was now her, felt a massive data dump of information that had been sent over the Starnet.

"I've sent you everything we recorded. What it comes down to is there's a lot of noise in the data. Algorithms are more your specialty. Theoretically, we should be able to get a clearer image out of it. I just can't figure out how to do it."

Ariana immediately started to parse the information. She closed her eyes as she did. She sped up time, turning a fraction of a second into hours. She sifted through everything, understanding exactly how Atlas had achieved the amazing goal of looking at another planet. She re-created his projection of the planet using the data he provided. She tweaked the algorithm slightly, and the result was a similar-looking image. Still pixelated. There wasn't enough data to enhance the image.

"Do you have sensors around the star?" Ariana asked. "Your algorithm uses a fixed number for the gravity of the star. It assumes that massive ball is the same density everywhere. And that is basically true, except if we want to create an even more detailed image of this planet, we need to use an exact measurement for the mass of different regions of that star."

Atlas bit his lower lip. "You're right." His face read, *Why didn't I think of that?* "The star will have pockets of density that will mean light traveling from one side of the star takes a tiny, tiny fraction of a second longer to reach my sensors. And you're saying if we can plug in a more accurate number for the mass of the sun, we can account for that noise and cancel it out?"

"Exactly, and we should be able to build a more accurate picture."

"I don't have anything specifically tracking the gravitational changes in the sun. But we have billions of ANTs orbiting around the system. Maybe you can combine the changes in orbital patterns of these things to get an approximation?"

Atlas nodded to Ship, who sent everything they had across.

"Approximation." Ariana laughed as she scanned through the data. There was more than enough mass orbiting around the planet to get an exact measurement of that star at any point in time. She quickly designed a simulation of the star's mass and how that mass was distributed across the whole burning object. She then updated her algorithm and reran the operation to create an image of the planet.

Ariana manifested her new 3D image in her hand, holding it next to the one Atlas held.

The contrast was noticeable, a standard-definition image in Atlas's hand, a high-definition image in Ariana's. What became obvious from Ariana's image was the detailing around the edges of the continents. It was like turning on a filter and the terrain of the planet became visible. The ocean depths were visible from the darker-blue sections. There were islands where Atlas's map showed none.

There were also concentrated areas of vegetation, green areas on the map showing some sort of forests, as well as drier desert regions.

Ariana flicked through various map faces, showing they now had the capabilities to view clouds maps and infer the direction of prevailing winds. She also showed what the planet looked like during the day.

"I suspect the longer we look at this planet, the more detailed we can make this map," Ariana said.

Atlas slow clapped. "We should map out all the planets nearby, too. Using this same method—" Atlas paused for a moment; he looked like he had just had an epiphany, like he'd suddenly had an idea of great importance. Or maybe something to be concerned about. "Have you heard of the dark forest?" Atlas asked.

"Are you talking about the solution to the Fermi paradox?"

"I get the feeling that this telescope disproves that theory. Any sufficiently advanced civilization would be capable of building a telescope like this—they might even have something more powerful than this. So they should know where every other advanced technological civilization in the galaxy is."

"So you're saying there's no dark forest, with every civilization scared of being spotted by others."

"And in a way, there's almost no point in hiding. Because with telescopes like this, you can't hide." Atlas paused for a second thinking things through. "The problem with this telescope is it's like a sniper. It can only look at one planet at a time. And it produces a lot of data on each of those planets. So it's not practical for scanning millions of stars at once. That's what a traditional telescope is good for. Maybe you could use an old-school telescope to select candidates to scan further."

"Have you looked at Juniper?" Ariana asked. "How good is the stealthfield at blocking this observation technique?"

"I haven't . . . Yet. But my guess is it'll limit the details we can get in the image. I think where the star field shines, it makes the whole system look ordinary. It stops traditional telescopes from flagging the system as something to look further into."

Atlas waved away his projection of the Atua home world and pointed at the projection Ariana had created. "We should send this to the others." Atlas changed the subject. "Also, how's it going with the alien spacecraft? Have you hacked your way in yet?"

"I haven't found any circuitry or anything I can hack into yet. I haven't found a computer or anything. I'm going to start cutting my way into things to see what I can find next."

"Let me know . . ."

Ship interrupted them both, a little bit of panic on his face. "Ariana, something is headed your way. I just received confirmation of something showing up on radar."

Ariana immediately slowed down time and dived into the information. She left a subconsciousness in the room with the others—it would contact her with anything she needed—while she focused on what Ship had highlighted.

It was bigger than Ship said. Light from the signal showed there were four objects headed her way. Or there was one large object, but then three objects took off and started heading her way at an even faster speed. "A missile? A probe?"

Why didn't she see this? This was not a trivial mistake to make. She should have had a subconsciousness monitoring for suspicious activities like this. Then she remembered how engrossed she had become with the idea of discovering the aliens' home world. All her subconsciousnesses were focused on that task. She was even trying to create a new algorithm to improve on the results she'd already shared with Atlas.

She'd missed the alien because she wasn't dividing her attention. She was singularly focused on one task.

"Ari, can I get access to your eleph-ANTs?" she heard Ship ask as she crunched the numbers. She assigned access to the eleph-ANTs while she worked out the probability the blips on the radar were missiles or not.

"You have to get out of there now!" she heard Ship say to one of her subconsciousnesses after the fact.

Then her subconsciousness came back with the answer she'd asked for. She'd asked it how long she had until the objects arrived in the system. The answer rocked her to her very core.

She was now confident an alien vessel was headed her way and had fired missiles at her. Assuming those missiles were moving near to the speed of light, then she was about to be hit.

If she was just receiving light that bounced off the missile and that missile had the capability to travel at light speed, then it was too late. She was already dead. She based the assumption on everything she knew about the Atua, based on their personality, based on how they'd interacted with humans so far. Even based on the fact that they'd lied to them about negotiating. The Atua weren't the kinds of people to send warning shots.

They would most likely send missiles to blow her up at the exact moment she would notice them, just enough time to create panic in her, but not enough time for her to do anything. A not-so-subtle way of saying, "You are bugs," one last time.

As if confirming her predictions of the Atua, one of her subconsciousnesses served up an image of a warhead that was moments away from impacting her. It was a particularly nasty-looking thing. It detonated, and shrapnel was flying out in a cone shape toward her. Even if she'd had the ability to move, which she didn't, it was impossible for her to escape the blast zone. Even without knowing how powerful the bomb was, she knew she was screwed.

She was about to slow down time further, stretching out her final moments of life into a month, when the subconsciousness she'd left with Atlas informed her that it had given control of her spacecraft over to Ship.

Neither Atlas nor Ship could slow time down as much as her. They didn't have the capabilities to match what she could do. So talking to them now would only reduce the subjective time she had left.

She considered it for a moment; she thought it was nice that up to the last moment they tried to save her. Ship was remote controlling her ship, and apparently all eleph-ANTs in the system. She felt sad knowing she'd never get a chance to say thank you for trying. Ship wouldn't be able to control anything soon anyway; the Starnet was moments away from being destroyed—again.

She decided she would join Atlas and Ship. She decided it was better to spend an hour with them, then a month alone, especially if that hour involved her telling them to seek revenge. They knew where their home world was now, so revenge would come.

Ariana realized that's probably what the Atua were doing, racing into the system to destroy any evidence that might lead Ariana and her friends to discover something about the aliens.

She hoped she would be remembered fondly. She wanted to be remembered as part of the team who saved the Neuropans. She spent a good amount of time recording a short note to all her friends. She would miss them. She transmitted those messages across the Starnet.

As Ariana began speeding up her playback speed so she could communicate with Atlas in a timely manner, she noticed something curious, something she didn't pick up on when time was all but frozen.

The cone of shrapnel, the blast radius of the aliens' weapon, was curving to the right. It wasn't following the laws of physics—at least any physics that she knew.

She watched further as the explosion appeared to reverse in time, particles and debris getting closer together. It was like she was watching entropy reverse. How was that even possible?

As she returned her speed to something ideal for interacting with Atlas and Ship, she noticed Atlas frozen in time while Ship was flickering as if he was moving much faster.

"The Starnet is about to be destroyed," she heard Ship say. "I've overclocked your engines. Keep firing them as hard as they will go."

"Why is Atlas frozen?"

"He suggested I take all the processing power available to try to save you."

Ariana noticed them now, the eleph-ANTs that Ship was controlling. They were out in front of her, firing their tractor beams, condensing and manipulating the shock radius of the bomb. Trying to carve a sliver of a gap. Making a tiny but traversable pathway.

She was headed down that small window of escape, controlled by Ship. He was guiding her in the right direction. Although, she was about to be disconnected from him.

"Goodbye, Ariana," Ship said. "Keep curving away from the blast."

Ariana retook control of her rocket ship as Ship was forcibly disconnected. The first thing she noticed was the ride was much bumpier. Ship was somehow better at predicting the path of least resistance; he was guiding her and making millions of micro-adjustments to keep her threading the needle to safety.

She didn't have the intuition to do that. She didn't even have a submind capable of doing that. But she could follow instructions.

Ship had left behind clear directives, one of which was to make a sharp turn and attempt to double the energy output of the engine. Doing so might break her spacecraft. It would pull energy away from the simulators and force her into real time, meaning from her subjective perspective she would die instantly if Ship was wrong.

What did she have to lose? She followed the instructions down to the letter.

She got a fright when the eleph-ANT firing the tractor beam exploded, creating another cone of debris, but more concerning, it released the containment of the explosion, which immediately began to spread outward again. She felt her spacecraft shake as things began to heat up.

She counted down the time. Three. Two. One. Right at the moment Ship instructed her to, she fired the engines harder than they were designed for.

She was rocketed into real time.

Everything around her progressed like a blur. Then everything went offline.

CHAPTER 17

PETER

WHERE EARTH SHOULD BE

Peter sat on the deck of Angelique's spacecraft looking through the view port.

They were approaching the planet Everest. It was the perfect name for the planet. It was hard for him to encapsulate what he was seeing. He'd been into orbit multiple times. The first above Earth's atmosphere, he'd gotten a sense of just how small humans were. It was an eye-opening experience that many people said they felt when seeing Earth from space for the first time.

Seeing Everest put that experience to shame. The planet was huge, and it looked it. It made Earth look small in comparison. It gave him the perspective that Earth was just a tiny drop in the bucket.

As he looked down at the planet, he remarked at how different it looked. Earth was a water world—most of its surface covered by O_2. Everest was a world covered by land—mountains, snow, and jungles visible from space. There was water, but it looked like lakes. He was sure the lakes were large enough that they would appear like oceans if he stood next to them.

There was ice on each pole too. But unlike on Earth, the snow looked to cover almost a third of the planet. Thick ice shelves at either end of the planet were massive, and Peter wondered if they were still terraforming the world, and whether it would become a water world too if the ice all melted.

The first time he'd seen Earth from space, he'd realized humans were small. This was his first time seeing another planet from space; seeing it made him realize how small humanity as a whole was. Earth, Sol, everything that humans came from was nothing compared to the vastness of what was out there to explore.

Peter felt the engines firing and their trajectory change.

"We just received a request from Everest," Ship said. "They asked us to stay in orbit. When I told them we made contact with an alien world, they asked if we had time to transfer to a new clean spacecraft."

Angelique shrugged. "That's a reasonable request. We can't confirm we're not carrying any alien microbes. Better safe than sorry."

"They also requested everyone else on board stays on the spaceship until after the merging ceremony." Then Ship added, "Until you merge with your Ange's Angel, you have full autonomy. You can decline that request and transfer everyone to the surface of the planet."

"No point. As soon as I merge, they'll have jurisdiction, anyway. So, if they want to hold everyone in quarantine for a while, it's within their rights."

"Can we back up a second? I'm not quite understanding all these new terms." Peter pointed at Angelique. "How do you fit into the governing of this planet?"

"Everest is run through a representative democracy. All my planets are run that way. And I'm not part of the government. Although I am part of the constitution." Angelique paused for a moment thinking it through. "I guess you could make the argument that I'm the fourth branch of government. My arm of the government oversees expanding the colonies and improving everyone's lives through advancements in technology." She pointed to herself. "I'm responsible for finding new worlds and bringing all the advancements in science to the new worlds." She pointed out the window to the planet below. "And Ange down there is responsible for cataloging all the new science and disseminating the new knowledge so the planet progresses. But again, my 'branch,'" she said, miming quotation marks around the word, "can't overrule an order from parliament or the military."

"I'm not saying you would do this," Unity started to speak cautiously. "But what's to stop you from manipulating information your share with the different planets? What's to stop you from controlling them?"

"There are encrypted files hidden in the data files I take with me. They are designed to corrupt if I tamper with these files. And the military always includes special keys that unlock documents that only they have access to." Angelique anticipated the next question. "This isn't just to stop me from tampering with everything I carry with me. It's also a precaution against an alien hacking into my data payload while I travel from system to system . . . But there are risks, and I feel like every planet we visit has some invention that improves the security of this process."

Peter considered Angelique's words. Reading between the lines, he got the feeling she had designed the constitution of her civilizations to allow her the flexibility to keep exploring, while also giving the colonies complete control over their governance. He guessed she did have the power to override some decisions the colonies made, but she wasn't saying it out loud. He wondered whether this conversation would form part of the treasure trove of data shared with the colony.

He decided to ask a question that would give him a peek at just how much autonomy she had. "Let's say they decide to lock us all up." He pointed toward himself, Unity, and Hezekiah.

Angelique looked confused. "They wouldn't do that."

"Let's say a lot has changed since you left. And let's say some leader decided to do that."

"Well, technically that would be within their right." Angelique scratched the back of her head, thinking everything over. "I wouldn't be able to stop that from happening until Ange and I become separate people again. But once I was me again, all my privileges would return, and I would just say you were important to my next mission." She raised her hands as if to say, *Don't worry it won't happen.* "That's not going to happen though, and if it did, we're not going to be there for that long. We need to tell the other colonies what's happening."

Peter continued the line of questioning, digging in deeper to his understanding of the worlds Angelique had created. "Once you and your Ange's Angel are merged together, can they stop you from splitting apart again? Keep you on the planet against your will?"

"According to the constitution, that would be an act of secession. In a way, that would be an act of war against the other colonies."

"Can't they just change the constitution? Don't they govern themselves?"

Angelique shook her head. "All the colonies have the same founding constitutional document. So a change like that would require a supermajority vote, not just on this planet but on all the planets. So every planet would need to update their constitution at the same time."

Peter smiled that remark. Angelique had done an amazing job at designing the constitution. She was embedded at the heart of the document. It was masterful, and the results spoke for them-selves: from what Atlas had said, her people loved her. And no one had attempted to kick her out—unlike what they'd done to Atlas.

Peter's next question would get at the heart of where his thinking had been. He'd spent a good amount of time thinking about what to do with the Atua, and his only conclusion was that the two species would eventually fight each other. Humanity versus the Atua.

In traditional times, whenever a human civilization encountered another, the more technologically advanced one would enslave or conquer the other. And from what Peter had already seen of the Atua people, they'd done exactly that to humans, conquered humanity without them even knowing. Now they were in a position to fight back, and it was probably going to lead to a war. Peter wanted to make sure they were well prepared for a war. That's the reason he wanted to visit Angelique's colony. He wanted to gather support for fighting back. "Do you have an army?"

"Not an army as such," Angelique responded. "But all colony worlds have a military base built specifically for me. It has a standing order to have, at any one time, enough starships on it for me to visit every one of the colonies at the same time. They have to overestimate how many ships they need. And that base must be equipped with personnel and material to upgrade the ships based on the new technology I bring with me."

Angelique continued: "Oh, and they obviously have their own military on this planet. I chose to come here first because it was the closest planet with an abundance of resources. We need to conduct some big upgrades to our spacecraft."

Hezekiah and Unity both wore concerned looks on their faces. They looked worried about the risk of being trapped on the planet. Angelique lifted her hands to placate the group. "Don't worry, team. I promise you won't be in quarantine for long. If they keep you against your will, I'll split with Ange, and we'll go to another planet."

The team was approaching a large space station. In front of Peter, the view changed to reveal a boxy military-looking spaceship. It was enormous, big enough that their ship looked tiny in comparison. One side of the ship opened up to reveal an open area with a clear spot for docking.

"Do you still want me to dock?" Ship asked as they approached the large open hangar door.

Angelique nodded.

Ship maneuvered them into the docking space and then switched the engines off.

"We wait here while you do your thing?" Peter asked.

Both Angelique and Ship nodded. Their avatars disappeared when their spacecraft was plugged directly into the space station.

CHAPTER 18

ANGELIQUE

SHATTERLING PROTOCOL

Angelique popped into existence seated on an ornately carved wooden chair. In front of her was an expensive-looking desk. It was solid, well-built.

She looked at her hands. They were holographic; she wasn't a hapticgram, so she couldn't interact with anything in the room.

Angelique wondered why she was there. Was this her new office?

She looked around the space; it was an oval room. There was a large official-looking emblem on the carpet. A statue of a golden eagle sat on one end of the table.

If rooms could have a vibe, the vibe of this one was official. It looked and felt like the room of some sort of important person. *Maybe this was Ange's office*, she wondered. If it was Ange's, then she wondered where she'd developed such bad taste.

She noticed the multiple flags placed around the room. The country flag for Everest. Although they were slightly different from what she remembered. Then it occurred to her: she was in the office of the prime minister of this country.

That was odd because she wasn't meant to meet the leaders until she and Ange were merged. She needed all the memories of Ange to get up to speed with what had happened.

Angelique heard a clicking noise from behind her head. She turned around on her chair to see a large man walk through one of the side doors. He was in a dark-navy suit and a blue tie. He walked in like he knew the place.

Angelique studied the man. She couldn't quite put her finger on it, but his proportions were off—just slightly. He was wider than normal but not fat—simply muscular. He had large wrists as if his bones were thicker than normal. The silhouette of his pants also alluded to his legs being quite wide. He looked shorter too, but he was still taller than her. Then Angelique checked her internal stats, her height programmed to be a good foot shorter than it usually was.

"Angelique, welcome back," he said as he strutted in and walked toward the other side of the table. He had a southern drawl to his speech, the kind she remembered from politicians from South Carolina. "Imma get right to it," he said as he sat down. "You're here a little earlier than we expected. So we're not quite ready for you."

"I'm a little confused. You are the prime minister?" Angelique asked, feigning ignorance.

"I'm sorry. Where are my manners?" He reached over to the other side of the table to offer his hand before pulling back. "My name is Callum Overwood. I'm the president of this here country. We're equals here; you can call me Callum."

Angelique went to reach over, and then realized she was a hologram. She looked down at her hands and shrugged. She decided to wave. "Angelique Komene. Lovely to meet you." Angelique paused for a moment thinking back to what was just said. "The president?"

On all her worlds, she was the official head of state. The difference between a president and a prime minster was the president was both the head of state and the leader of the government. Whenever those roles were separated, like in countries with a monarchy, or on her worlds, then the leader of the government became a prime minister. Officially he should be a prime minister, unless they'd changed the rules.

"Well, technically I'm still the prime minister, but that will change shortly." Callum winked at Angelique in the kind of expression that said, *If you know what I mean.* "You're probably wondering why we're meeting here in this room. And why we haven't begun the merging yet. Am I right?"

"Among other things." Angelique was starting to get a bad feeling about everything. She did not like these kinds of surprises, especially the kind that involved being ambushed by a prime minister with a prepared speech. She was on the back foot though and had to keep playing dumb until she could formulate a plan.

"We had a little war. So we've commandeered all the resources at our disposal in order to rebuild."

"And those resources include everything my Ange's Angel would normally have at her disposal?"

"You are right on the money. I wanted to debrief you before you get a little alarmed."

"Alarmed—" Angelique started to say before circling back to something Callum had said earlier. "A war? With whom?"

"Oh, just a bit of a civil war. Everything has calmed down now; that was so long ago I barely remember it all."

Angelique couldn't help but think that this was the reason the merging had to happen before having a conversation with the locals on the planet. This was all information she should know already. The Ange version of her should have gone through all of this and known it all already. So why was he telling her all of this? Why had he stopped the merging? Angelique was about to ask that question when another thought entered her mind. "Why has the flag behind you changed? Are you still part of the colony worlds?"

"How astute of you. They told me you had a great attention to detail. I'm very impressed just seeing it now." Callum picked up one of the pens on his desk and played with it a little.

Angelique assumed that was a nervous tick. Then thinking about it some more, she decided it was him pretending to be nervous because, in her experience, people who rose up the ranks to his level weren't that easy to read. He wouldn't be showing nerves unless he wanted her to think he was nervous.

"We still consider ourselves part of the collective."

Angelique felt a little relief at that. She was worried she had unwittingly walked into a situation she wasn't prepared for. As a mandatory part of being one of her colony worlds, all planets had to maintain a standing fleet of spacecraft for her to use in case of emergencies. And they had to have enough fabricators on standby to make any adjustments she needed. "Perfect, I was going to save this for our first official briefing. But I guess I'll tell you now. We need to implement the Shatterling Protocol."

"In reference to the ancient book from Earth? *House of Suns*?"

"Correct. I need to send a bunch of copies of myself on a round trip to all the different planets under our umbrella. It's an emergency."

"Well, that's the thing; we don't have any of those resources on standby."

"What do you mean? That's a requirement of being one of the colonies."

"We rewrote our constitution so that wasn't part of the requirement."

"Well, then you're not part of the colonies, and I can't share with you any of the technology we have with us."

"Hold on there just a moment, missy. We are still part of your colony of planets. We just haven't had the time to build all that yet."

"Either you're part of the colony of worlds, in which case you're required to take seriously the *security* of all our worlds properly, or you're not. Which is it, Callum?"

Callum looked Angelique straight in her eyes. He held her gaze for a long, long time. "You left us for a long time. It's been generations since you were last here. I didn't think it was a good use of our limited resources when people needed feeding."

Angelique saw something cold in his eyes. She saw someone who wasn't used to backing down. Someone who was used to getting his way. She also saw something she should be afraid of, as if there was something more he wasn't telling her about. She decided to see if she could get under his skin, push him to defend his decision, in the hope that he revealed something more. "I left this planet with fabricators that can produce anything you want. You have autonomous ANTs that can be used for any task, like harvesting crops or building anything you need. I fail to understand how you don't have enough food, let alone resources."

"The challenge we face here, is that we don't have the ability to do that." Callum picked up a manila folder and handed it to Angelique.

Angelique looked at the folder; it had the word CONFIDENTIAL in bold red letters over the front of it. She opened it up and looked inside. Inside was a stack of several reports, covering different issues.

She quickly ramped up her playback speed to digest everything quickly. From her first pass, she wasn't any the wiser about what had happened on the planet. There was verbiage and a lot of information that contradicted itself. She wasn't sure where the information came from, but she was almost certain that there were multiple authors.

The main takeaway was the war had basically sent their production capability back to the Dark Ages. According to the report, if it was to be believed, all the fabricators were sabotaged in the attack.

"You have working spacecraft," Angelique said. "I saw ANTs and eleph-ANTs in the cargo bay. Surely you have the ability to re-create everything you need?"

"Eleph-ANTs are just a replacement for manual labor. What we need are fabricators. And those are pieces of highly specialized, highly complicated machinery. We know how to make them; we just don't have the industry to produce them."

Callum was right; there were billions of different components on the insides of those things. They were probably the most complex pieces of machinery humans had created. A device capable of creating almost anything else—including itself.

Fabricators came in two variations, one that deconstructed material into fabricator pallets and one that took those pallets and turned them into machinery or objects.

The lasers inside of them required a special alloy that was next to impossible to produce without specialized equipment. Add to that making the mirrors to the exact measurements, which was again impossible without an industry setup to produce them.

Even if she gave a caveman detailed instructions on how to build a phone, they wouldn't be able to produce one because they had no means of producing plastic, metals, or even electricity. The caveman would need to create the means of production before they could make even a makeshift phone.

Equally, this planet had no particle accelerators and no way to produce antimatter. They didn't even have the right materials to produce the machines that produced antimatter.

"I—" Angelique cut herself off before she spoke. She was sure he knew, but she wasn't going to tell him that she had a fabricator until she understood the situation better. "Tell me about this war. Which side were you on?"

"I was on the side that won."

"What does that mean? Was it you who sabotaged the fabricators?"

"I know you have a fabricator on your ship."

"Which you can't access without my codes. It won't work without my approval."

"And that is why I'm asking for your approval and not just taking it from you."

"Are you a dictator?" Angelique had a disgusted look on her face. "Or do people here get to vote?"

"Let me be straight with you. You're going to find out eventually. My side of the war wanted to break away from your colony of worlds. We wanted to start exploring into the galaxy ourselves. We're having an election in about a month. Once I win, you and I are going have a talk about your fabricator. I'd like to buy it so we can start trade with your people."

"Giving technology to another civilization is not something I can make a call on without talking to the other colonies."

"You and I both know that's a lie. Look, I might not have the means to make any more spaceships. But you're in the cargo bay of one of mine right now. You're not going anywhere unless I deem it so."

Angelique looked directly into Callum's eyes. Did this man really just threaten her? She wanted to do nothing more than to put him in his place. But she calmed herself a little. "Where's Ange?"

Callum stood up to leave. "I've already told you too much upsetting news. I suggest you turn off your matrix for a few months. And after the election, let's talk about how we can work together."

"Is it an honest election? Or are you rigging it?"

Callum stood next to the door with his hand on the door handle. "The election isn't a farce. We've come too far not to win in an honest election." He turned his head toward Angelique. "But I'm not taking any risks, as this is also a referendum on whether we stay as one of your colonies. So I'm not allowing you to make contact with any of my people until after I've won."

"I technically still have rights. You can't keep me from my people."

"You're right. Our current laws say that I can't hold you against your will. But after I've won, I can retrospectively change the rules."

Angelique stood up and walked toward Callum. "How long has it been since I last saw this planet? I've had a lot of upgrades since I was here last. I'm not trapped in your tin can of a spacecraft." She smiled a knowing smile. She hadn't visited this planct since she had seeded it. They were lacking in many of the new technologies developed on the other colonies. Her spacecraft was made out of diamond. She was quietly confident they had no chance in hell of damaging it. "I'm glad we had this little chat. I got to know the real you. I suggest you open up the hangar door on this spaceship. Otherwise you'll have a giant hole to fill in when I cut through it to dig my way out." Angelique smiled warmly at Callum. "Oh, that's right, you don't have any manufacturing capabilities anymore." She shrugged and disappeared.

CHAPTER 19

ICARUS

ANTHROPOLOGIST

"Are you joking?" Icarus asked, looking at Atlas, trying to tell if he was making it up or not. "You spoke to a real-life alien?"

Icarus sat with Atlas on a porch overlooking the water. They were on Icarus's planet, finally able to reconnect after the Starnet was fixed. Icarus sipped on a coffee, while Atlas drank a beer.

Atlas just finished sharing the story of everything that had happened to him recently, the encounter with PBD and almost being taken hostage. Atlas made it clear he wasn't traumatized by the experience anymore. He was grateful that Angelique had stepped up and saved them all. Icarus got the feeling Atlas had a bit of hatred toward the Atua people. He thought he might probe that concept a little bit further later on.

In typical Icarus fashion, his biggest takeaway was an alien was out there to study and meet. He wanted nothing more than to meet another intelligent life.

"I'm not lying, Icarus," Atlas said. "He even went after Ariana. Ship is confident she escaped, but I won't know for sure until she gets here."

"Do you think PBD was a bad apple? Or do you believe the whole alien species is evil?"

Atlas considered the question for a good while. "I'm not sure. I wouldn't be surprised if that person doesn't represent the whole civilization. But I wouldn't be surprised if they were all like that."

"If our only interaction with the human species was General Walker, then I'd have a pretty grim image of the human race. We shouldn't make the same mistake with the Atua." Then Icarus thought about his comments a little more. He wasn't there, and even though Atlas had survived, it must have been an ordeal. Icarus quieted his excitement about this new alien species. "Are you all right, Atlas?"

"I'm fine," Atlas reiterated. "It's just been so unexpected, you know? I didn't want to be attacked like that. None of us did . . . And I haven't even told you the best part. We know where their home world is." Atlas pulled up an image of the alien home world.

"Where is this?"

As Atlas showed where the planet was on the map, Icarus couldn't think about anything other than visiting that world. He imagined visiting the world, decoding their language. He could potentially be the first human to interact with an intelligent alien species without them knowing.

As his mind started to wonder about the possibility, he quickly realized the timeline within which he needed to visit this alien world was limited. In human history, whenever one culture met another, there was often a war of some sort. Then eventually the cultures merged together.

Icarus remembered a theory he'd heard once before that said it was almost impossible to study something without having an influence on the thing you studied. And the more a researcher interacted with a research subject, the more that subject's behavior changed. Icarus racked his brain to remember where he'd learned that. Was it anthropology or ecology? "Or was it psychology?" he wondered out loud. Regardless of where the theory came from, he became more determined than ever to research the aliens without them knowing he was there.

He wanted to view the alien world before it interacted with humanity on some larger scale. Like an anthropologist studying gorillas in the jungle. He wanted to study these aliens in their natural habitat. He wanted to somehow blend in and view the world in the most untouched way possible. Without them knowing he was there.

Maybe he could write a book, explaining what their culture was like before being changed forever by their interactions with the human species. Assuming they weren't all locked up in the metaverse like humans on Earth. "Do you think they're all in virtual simulated worlds?"

Atlas shook his head. "I'd almost guarantee they're walking around the planet just like us." Atlas changed the view on display, revealing a view of the planet. There were lights all over the coastal sections of the planet. "Earth isn't lit up like this anymore. I think they manipulated us into simulated worlds to pacify us. I think they're in the real world."

Interesting theory, and it made sense. It might also be an indication of their culture. Maybe trickery and deception were part of who they are as a people. Then he thought about it some more. Humans were quick to lie as well—especially when they knew they wouldn't be caught. Back in his time on Earth, he remembered politicians were the worst. He remembered so many of them lying just to get elected. It was always the consequences associated with getting caught that stopped people deceiving others.

Icarus hated visiting touristy locations because the coffee was always bad. Shops in tourist towns never had any incentive to make a good-quality drink because they didn't care about repeat business—in touristy locations, there was always a new steady stream of patrons coming through the airport. Again, because there wasn't a negative consequence to serving bad coffee, the shops weren't incentivized to care.

The more Icarus thought about the Atua people, the more familiar their actions seemed. They didn't want to get into a fight with Atlas and the others. So they'd attempted to trick them— basically lied through their teeth. Maybe they didn't have enough weapons to win, or maybe they just didn't fully understand what capabilities Angelique had at her disposal, so didn't want to take the risk. Whatever the reasoning was, they'd tricked Atlas and company, and it had almost worked.

Icarus remembered back to when Trillion had almost committed genocide to the Dottiens—the alien species that trapped her on a moon—because she didn't fully understand them. Then he remembered she did commit genocide of an entire planet as she turned it into fabricators in the Tac system. "Humans were stupid sometimes—probably no different from the Atua people," Icarus muttered to himself.

"Atlas . . . ?" Icarus asked. "How good are Angelique's android bodies? Like the ones you used on Juniper?"

"They were the closest thing I've seen to flesh and blood. Her people have perfected the designs to the point you can't tell the difference. Why do you ask?"

"If I wanted to get that tech. Can you share it with me?"

"Of course." Atlas studied Icarus's face for a good while. "You have a similar look in your eyes to the one when you first got an opportunity to study the Dottiens." Then his eyes went wide. "If you want to sneak a robot onto their planet, we're going to build an AI, otherwise it's going to be too obvious. Maybe I could code something similar to Lex." He started to bite his lower lip as his mind worked. "I don't know how we're going to make it not obvious though. We could probably use Angelique's tech to miniaturize the processor unit, so we could get a matrix as big as Lex into a tiny Atua-sized android."

"How would you get onto the planet?" Icarus asked, liking the thought process. He wasn't sure yet how to tell Atlas that he wanted to go onto the planet, not Lex.

"Hmm," Atlas said. "Maybe we disguise a small probe as a meteorite. On the way to crash-landing in the ocean the probe takes a better scan of the planet. Maybe while heading toward it, we could intercept a bunch of radio transmissions, which will give us enough data to build an android version of the Atua. On board the probe, we'll need a small fabricator for creating the android body."

Icarus shook his head. He knew from experience just how hard it was to create a convincing version of a human. It had taken human CGI experts a long, long time to replicate a human face that crossed the uncanny valley. Surely the Atua had evolved a similar ability to notice not-quite-right-looking faces. "Intercepting enough information to re-create an alien body that fools the locals seems unlikely."

Atlas reluctantly nodded. "You're right. We might have a better chance at replicating their version of a bird or fish. To be honest, I think our biggest issue is figuring out how we set this all up. We won't be able to communicate with Lex when it's near the alien star system. So all our instructions will need to be pre-programmed. Lex is not very good at dealing with complicated situations all alone for a long period of time."

"I've got an idea for that," Icarus said. "Can you leave the task of programming an AI to me? And can you plan out the mechanics of how we'd get onto the planet surface safely? With all the right equipment?"

Atlas eyed Icarus suspiciously as if to say, *What you're thinking is not safe.* Atlas didn't say it, however; he just nodded. "I'll get it done because I've been looking for an excuse to better understand some of the new technology upgrades Angelique's people shared with us. But, Icarus, you better not be planning what I think you're planning."

CHAPTER 20

ANGELIQUE

EVEREST

"This is not a threat, but please treat my words seriously," Angelique said as she sat in the command chair of her spacecraft, hailing the now-enemy vessel that moments ago she had entered voluntarily. "We are preparing to exit through the same section of your spaceship we entered through. Please open the air lock door, or we will be forced to open it ourselves."

The response came back instantaneously. "This is Lieutenant Dan Taylor of the *ESS Washington-Mao* ship carrier." The lieutenant over the coms sounded like he was shaking with fear. "Please stand by while I confirm your request."

"You have two minutes to confirm my request."

Ship turned on the external lights of the spacecraft and pivoted them around so their weapons faced the hangar door. Ship never entered the room with Angelique; instead he was held in a waiting room while Angelique conversed with the prime minister of the planet.

Almost exactly two minutes later, the lieutenant's voice came back through the speaker. "Ma'am, your request has been approved. I have Prime Minister Overwood on a secure line. I'm putting him through to you now."

Angelique watched as the hangar door began to open, noticeably slower than when it was first closed. Angelique hoped that wasn't intentional.

Callum's southern drawl came through the speaker. He sounded cheerful, like the two of them hadn't just gotten into an argument. "Angelique, it was great speaking with you. Before you leave the system, any chance you can leave us a fabricator?"

Angelique waited for the hangar door to open up all the way before responding. She instructed Ship to maneuver them outside of the spaceship carrier. And once they were outside, she responded, "We're not leaving the system; we're staying here."

"I'm a little confused," Callum said. "I thought you'd be leaving, since after the election, we will no longer be one of your colonies."

"I want to make a short visit planetside, if that's okay with you."

"Angelique, you can visit." Then there was a long pause, and Angelique thought she heard other voices whispering advice in the background. "I'll make an official announcement shortly about your arrival. My people will let you know the location I'd like you to be for our first official meeting. It'll be a photo op, great opportunity for you to speak to some reporters. It won't be the official ceremony you're used to. Please don't mess with the election results. The will of the people has already been decided."

"Where can I find Ange?"

"Well, that's just it," Callum said. "She's dead. She died a couple years ago now; she was giving the resistance a tour of a fabricator-manufacturing facility when it blew up. I didn't want to tell you because I didn't want to blast you with this bad news."

Angelique made a cutting gesture, and the sound feed connected to Callum immediately cut off. She was determined not to believe any of it. The only way to permanently kill an Ange's Angel was to destroy the android body and go back and wipe the backup units. And there were backup units on the planet that only she and Ship knew about. Backups were created of Ange every three months. "Ship, can you take us to the north pole of Everest? Take us to the hidden backup facility."

Angelique shook her head in frustration. Things were never as easy as she hoped. She'd planned on coming here and using the resources here to fly over to all the other locations.

"Who's the Callum guy?" Peter asked her, breaking her out of her thinking. "And what happened while you were gone?"

"From what I've gathered, he's the leader of the winning side of a civil war that happened here. I believe his side wants to leave my colony of worlds."

"Do you know why he wants to leave?" Peter asked. "Aren't there benefits, like all the new tech we have with us? From the look of their space platform, I'd say they're several generations behind on the tech ladder."

"It's worse than that," Angelique said as she looked down toward the giant planet they were orbiting. "Someone on the planet sabotaged all their fabricators. Without a means of advanced manufacturing, they need to go all the way back to basics to bootstrap their way out of it. That could take them centuries."

"Don't we have a fabricator on board?" Unity asked. "We could print another one for them."

"He asked me for it," Angelique said, leaving out the fact she'd turned down that request. She hadn't yet made up her mind on what to do. In one sense, she had a moral duty to at least help them out. They wouldn't starve without a fabricator, but their people would suffer. She wasn't sure how desperate they were yet, but she was confident without advanced manufacturing capabilities, fixing any of their existing infrastructure would be impossible. It would impact their ability to generate cheap power and maybe even impact their terraforming projects, which would massively impact the people's quality of life.

"I'm guessing you didn't respond?" Peter asked. "You left it ambiguous as to whether you had a working fabricator?"

Angelique nodded. "They weren't expecting me here for a long, long time. So they know something has gone wrong. Otherwise we wouldn't be here."

"Let's keep it a secret that we have a fabricator," Peter said. "There is nothing worse than revealing all your cards."

"I disagree," Unity said, finally finding her voice. "There are people on that planet. We have a moral duty to make sure this planet is safe and viable over the long term. Even if they leave your colony of worlds, Angelique, if they need a fabricator, we have to give them a fabricator."

Angelique considered Unity's statement. She was right in a way, but Peter was also right. She wanted to disagree with Unity, but she also didn't want to sound like a ruthless dictator. She needed to show compassion for the people. But she also wanted to show there were consequences for leaving her coalition. If she let these people leave without any repercussions, then what was to stop any of the other colonies from doing the same thing?

Peter spoke before Angelique had a chance. "You're right, Unity, if these people need help, we are obligated to help. But it doesn't mean we have to tell the leaders of the country that . . . I haven't met this Prime Minister Overwood character, but he sounds like a wannabe dictator. With people like him, it's best to keep all your cards close to your chest. The fabricators are the biggest negotiating chip we have. It's probably best we don't bring it out until we understand exactly what we're dealing with."

"I agree," Angelique said. "From the sounds of it, the people here aren't in any immediate danger. So we have time."

"As long as we agree," Unity said, looking a little happier with the situation. "I just want to make sure politics doesn't get in the way of genuinely helping other humans."

Angelique didn't like the characterization that she might play politics with other people's lives. But she let that comment go. She knew that Unity was right. Looking at everything from the big picture, they were there to help them. And that's what she was going to do.

"This election that he doesn't want you to be involved in," Peter asked. "What is it about?"

"Well, currently the planet is still one of my colonies. But the election they're holding also includes a referendum on whether they stay or not. Technically they can't simply vote on something like this. But personally, if it's what the planet wants, then we'll have no choice but to go with their wishes."

Peter nodded his head, listening to what was just said. "What if you run for office, Angelique? What if you run against him?"

"I can't. Separation of power and all that. But . . ." Angelique scratched the back of her head. She thought through the consequences of what she was about to propose. There wasn't technically a law against it. But it might almost be considered an abuse of power. "You could run."

Peter raised an eyebrow. "Surely I'm disqualified because I wasn't born there?"

"It's not like what you're used to in the United States. There's no requirement for being born on the planet since a lot of our colonies have spread throughout their star system, but there is a requirement to be a citizen. But since I'm the head of state I can make you a citizen."

"Is that legal?"

"Technically, but it's the first time I would have used my powers to enact a law that congress didn't first approve." Angelique shook her hands in a gesture that said maybe, maybe not. "It's a legal grey area."

"Would I win? I don't have the same name recognition as you."

"We're the first humans from another planet to visit here in centuries. I'm almost confident everyone will know who you are within the next twenty-four hours."

"Just landing us now," Ship said as he touched their spaceship down on the snowy ground. They were on the north pole, far away from any other people on the planet. "I'm pinging the beacon now. We need to keep pinging it for the next eight hours to get a response."

The security protocols were such that in order to get a response from the hidden base, the request codes needed to be sent multiple times an hour for at least thirty-eight hours. The exact amount of time was random. This was to ensure someone sweeping the planet for a hidden base couldn't just send out a bunch of drones to send out signals in random directions around the planet. It ensured the only people getting into the base were those who knew where it was. It was also buried deep inside of a rock and made of a material that any wide-area scan wouldn't notice anything obvious.

Angelique had designed it that way so that if, in the unlikely scenario where someone had a rough idea of the bunker's location and the codes to active it, they would hopefully assume their information was wrong after not receiving a message back in a few hours.

This of course wouldn't stop anyone from digging up the bunker. But again, no long-term secret base was immune to compromise.

"Angelique, while we wait for a response," Ship said, "we should start running through the messages we intercepted while in orbit. It might give us a bit of context around what happened here."

CHAPTER 21

PETER

ELECTION

It had been a few days since Peter and the team had touched down on the planet Everest.

One of the interesting things about the planet he'd learned was the people were shorter than normal. The higher gravity meant the people of Everest had thicker bones and wider torsos. A human from Earth would struggle to move around easily on the planet because of the extra strain the gravity placed on their body. Peter hadn't worked out whether the Ange's Angel left on the planet to colonize it had genetically engineered everyone to be this way or whether it had just happened naturally. He filed that question for later, once he'd had a chance to ask someone about it.

The merging of Angelique and the Ange's Angel didn't yield much in the way of insights as to what happened with the fabricators. There were plenty of hypotheses, but nothing concrete. What was clear though was that Callum Overwood was an evil man. He overthrew the government and heavily limited Ange's ability to do much on the planet. More and more of Ange's resources were stripped away from her, under the guise of the greater good.

While Angelique updated them all on what had occurred, Peter had taken a back seat to the conversations, surveying everything and trying not to impose himself on everyone.

This was a relatively new situation for him. Usually he was in a position of power because he was the most experienced in the group. Or he was the one with the most money and influence.

In this situation, he had none of these advantages. Angelique had far more experience than he did with interstellar travel. And Angelique was the one with the spaceship and influence on the planet.

He had nothing, not even money at his disposal, which brought him memories of his early days when he was first starting out in the business world.

If Peter wanted to get back into a position of power, one where he could decide what he wanted to do, he needed to be deliberate and tactful with what he did next. He didn't want Angelique to feel like he was stepping on her toes.

Rightfully so, Angelique's opinions carried the most weight in the team's decisions. She had the most to lose with one of her colonies attempting to secede.

But also, Peter didn't want Angelique to get into a pissing competition with Callum. From what he'd learned about the prime minister, he had a big ego and was easily bruised. Peter could also tell that Angelique was angry at the man and wanted to do nothing more than to put him in his place.

Which was a bad situation for them to be in. Reading between the lines, this man sabotaged the planet's advanced manufacturing capabilities to secure power. Those kinds of men were dangerous.

He needed to guide Angelique away from this conflict, and he also needed to earn the right to insert himself into the conflict.

Usually, he would simply push his way into the conversation via force. But in this situation, he needed to be asked to fight against the prime minster of the planet—so that Angelique wouldn't feel alienated.

He needed to do that not because he didn't want to hurt Angelique's ego or because he was afraid she might get upset. He needed to do it tactfully because he genuinely respected what she had accomplished here. He was her old boss, and now he was back, which didn't mean he could automatically start acting like her boss again.

Peter had seen plenty of managers leave his company and come back years later. In that time, employees of the manager had been promoted to executive positions. He always found the old managers struggled in those environments when their old subordinates became their bosses.

He needed her to invite him back as an equal. He needed to be humble and patient.

That's why he liked the idea of him running for prime minster so much. Running for that role would help both their goals. It would give Angelique more control of the planet again and put him in a position of power once more. He might even be able to build his own spacecraft.

"Is it worth us staying here?" Peter asked. "They don't have the infrastructure to build anything we need. We should consider building a fabricator for them and giving it to the people. Give them what they need, then we head out to the next closest planet."

Angelique shook her head. "What if they just blow up the fabricator we give them? I want to know my people are safer before we leave."

"Our most important mission is to inform all your other colonies about this hostile alien," Peter said. "So if that greater mission says we need to leave Everest, then we should leave Everest."

Unity had just finished crunching several numbers on a piece of paper. "If speed is our key metric, then building it all here is always going to be faster, even if we need to create the fabricators from scratch. If we focused on fabricators building fabricators, we could build up the machinery to create everything faster than it would take us to travel to any of the nearest planets."

"Okay," Angelique said. "So then we need you to win an election, Peter."

Peter struggled to hide the smile on his face. He'd always wanted to run for office. So running on another world would be a fun prospect, but if he was going to run, he was going to win. And he wasn't someone who jumped into a political race without a complete picture. "Your Ange's Angel, did she collate information about world leaders on the planet?"

Angelique nodded.

"Is there anything in her documents that can give me a comprehensive view of every leader on this planet? I'm keen to get an understanding of whom they vote for and why they vote for someone."

"I can give you more than that," Angelique said. "Every Ange's Angel is tasked with collected all knowledge on the planet and taking a recorded unbiased picture of the planet's history." Angelique looked at Ship. "Can you plug Peter into everything he needs?"

Unity interrupted them, holding a tablet. "I've just finished studying your founding documents, Angelique. Really interesting stuff in here." Her face changed to someone who looked quite upset. "This prime minster has started privatizing everything and selling it off to his mates for cheap. He even sold the moon to one of his mates named Caspian. Which is at total odds with the ethos of the constitution. Resources like that shouldn't be owned by any one person; they should be shared by all."

"Surely he didn't sell an entire moon?" Angelique asked.

"It gets worse," Unity continued. "This Caspian guy is going to terraform the moon. He wants to put an atmosphere around it for him and his rich mates to use as an exclusive casino."

"You can't terraform a moon," Hezekiah said. "The gravity isn't strong enough to hold an atmosphere."

"Technically you can," Angelique clarified. "The problem is it's a waste of time and resources because you need to keep replenishing the atmosphere. And typically, as the gas is blown off the moon, it's lost forever."

Unity showed a display on the table with a marketing brochure. "They use it as a selling point. Right here it talks about how much new gas is lost by the solar winds each hour. It talks about how much is imported from Everest each day just to keep up with what is lost."

Peter decided to not say a thing at that very moment. He was quite familiar with the attraction of exclusive places that weren't natural to the region. Back on Earth, he would often go play golf in Dubayy, which was famous for being a desert. He couldn't remember exactly how much water was used on some of those greens, but he remembered seeing in a similar promotional pamphlet something about how much water was used to keep the fields green.

"Surely, they haven't terraformed the moon yet," Angelique said. "They don't have any fabricators; they don't have the resources to terraform a moon. Or if they do, that shouldn't be their focus?"

"They are the one percent of the planet," Unity said. "They won't suffer when the planet can't produce enough power."

Peter switched the topic back to the task at hand. He knew Unity's political leanings and knew she was very firmly on the left side of the spectrum. He wondered whether she would approve of the proposal he was about to make. "It looks like the Everest alternates between conservative and liberal parties every ten years." Peter watched everyone nod their heads in agreement. It was the kind of thing everyone was used to back on Earth. "Well, they're overdue for a right-wing government."

"What does that mean?" Unity asked, not hiding her disapproval of the statement.

"It means I'll be running under whatever this planet's equivalent of the Republican Party is."

Peter didn't want his team divided. However, Peter was politically agnostic; he was a pragmatist, what most would consider a swing voter. He didn't believe ideologically following one side was in the best interest of anyone. But he also needed Unity to get behind him, even if that meant going in a direction she didn't believe in. "Unity, can I get your help with this?"

Unity nodded. "Of course."

"We have to get them talking about me running for prime minister before I decide to run. We need to get the speculation mills running while I'm denying it all."

"That's going to be hard, given we don't have any connections to anyone in the media here."

Peter looked toward Angelique. "Do they play golf here? Is it treated in the same way golf is on Earth?"

"There are a lot of exclusive clubs here."

"Do you have a membership to the most expensive one?"

Angelique nodded. "Ange has lifetime memberships to most of them. They're very similar to what you're used to on Earth. All the key people on this planet are members."

"That's exactly what I need. Can you book me for a couple of days at the club's resort? I'm going to do some schmoozing, and by the end of it I should have a clear plan for winning this election."

The team set off after that. Since everyone had the smaller matrix unit, Angelique was able to print everyone a new android body for them to move around in. Even Angelique had her matrix transferred into a robotic body. Usually she'd move around the planet using hapticgraphic projectors, but she wanted free movement and not to be confined to locations with the projectors.

Everyone agreed to have their matrices backed up, too; everyone felt it was the safest option.

Ship stayed in orbit around the planet with Lex. If anything unusual happened, Ship had a clear extraction plan to get everyone off Everest.

CHAPTER 22

ATLAS

THE DARK FOREST

"Have you read any of these books?" Atlas asked, holding up three separate books for Icarus to look at. They were the books that made up the original Three-Body Problem trilogy.

Atlas and Icarus were both on the Rings of Titan, the planet Icarus was building, in one of the engineering laboratories.

"I listened to book one years ago but didn't continue the series," Icarus said. "The narrator's voice reminded me of you—strangely familiar."

"You need to read the second book in the series, *The Dark Forest*. It's probably the most famous book about the Fermi paradox Earth has ever produced. It was the first fiction book I read focused on the idea."

"I know what the dark forest is. It's the idea that the reason we don't see any aliens is because they're all hiding. And whenever one announces itself to the world, another alien destroys them." Icarus scratched the back of his head. "But it's a moot point now, anyway, because, when General Walker attacked Trillion, it lit up that whole region of space, and anyone with a decent telescope would have seen it. And no one came out and one-shot killed the system."

"We did have an alien show up to try to capture us." Atlas shook his head, realizing he had gone off track. "What I'm trying to say is this new method for imaging planets that I've developed changes everything."

"I still can't believe you used the star to bend light so much that we can see clouds in the sky from hundreds of light-years away. We can look at it as if we were right next to it."

"I wasn't the first to come up with the idea; that's why I'm calling the whole setup the Fraser Cain Observatory. It's not just one telescope, either; it's millions of small sensors designed for collecting light. They all combine to give us close-up images of planets like the one I showed you."

Atlas projected a new image of a planet in his hands. He handed it to Icarus. Clearly visible in the image was Titan, the gas giant they were in orbit around. Atlas zoomed in on a region of space, and the orbiting platform they were on became roughly visible.

Icarus squinted at the image. "Is that where we are now?"
Atlas nodded.

"It's like looking into the past; the rotating habitat looks so different to this now."

Icarus was correct; the image Atlas shared was of Icarus's planet from several years ago. Since light from his system took a few years to reach Atlas, they were looking at an image of the gas giant in the past.

"Spooky. Maybe I can send you a message," Icarus said. "You can't see the rings very clearly, but if I projected an image onto the gas giant, you would see something."

"I won't see your message for a long time, but if you did project a light show onto the planet, then I would see it," Atlas mused. "That's the point I'm trying to make. The dark forest is an almost impossible solution to the Fermi paradox. Because with telescopes like this, we will be able to identify every planet with intelligent life on it."

"What?!" Icarus said. "Have you found any others out there?"

Atlas shook his head. "I've only just begun the process. I pointed the sensors at your planet as a test, but I plan on eventually taking an image of every planet in our nearby region of the Milky Way."

"How long will it take until you can tell us which planets in the galaxy have alien life on them?"

Atlas had been trying to work out the answer to this question himself. He knew that there were more than one hundred billion stars in the Milky Way. And each of those stars probably had at least one planet orbiting it.

Using the Fraser Cain Observatory meant he could look at multiple planets at once. Although given how the technique required him to send thousands of imaging probes to take an image of a planet, and he also needed to look at each planet for a few years at least. He realistically would still be limited in the number of planets he could truly catalog each year. "I think it's realistic to aim for images of a hundred planets this year."

Then it occurred to Atlas that the telescope method only worked when he knew the exact location of a planet in the solar system. "Actually, I think it will be a lot slower than that." He started to bite his lower lip thinking about the problem some more. It took him over four years to take a high-resolution image of the aliens' world. And that had required him to focus every single sensor he had available at the solar system. The whole of the Fraser Cain Observatory was focused on a single object. It wasn't practical for him to do that again in the future. "I knew exactly which star to look at when trying to find the Atua star system. Ariana narrowed my options down to ten potential stars. And I narrowed it down further within six months of using this telescope. If we want to look for more life out there"—Atlas mimed pointing out into the sky—"then we need a better way to identify other candidates to look at."

"I thought you had an enormous amount of resources in this system?"

"We do," Atlas said, nodding his head. "But there are probably hundreds of millions of planets close enough for us to reach in a reasonable amount of time. I don't have enough resources to look at all of them at the same time." Atlas pondered over it a little longer. "What I need to do is develop an algorithm for identifying candidate planets. I can use a traditional telescope for identifying potential planets, then use this new telescope"—he decided to call it by an acronym as its full name was becoming too long—"then focus the FCO at the most promising planets."

"How long will it take to gain a complete picture of what's out there?"

"It will be slow at first. Maybe we'll take images of ten planets in the first few years. But as I collect more data and get better and better at picking candidate planets, I should quickly scale that to a hundred planets a year."

Icarus's face looked slightly disappointed. Atlas could tell moments ago he was starting to believe all alien worlds would be identified in a few years.

Atlas thought about how best to explain the predicament. It was a different kind of telescope than most people were used to. "It's the difference between spearfishing and catching fish with a net. With a traditional telescope you're passively scanning the skies and collecting a lot of data on many different star systems at once. With this method"—Atlas mimed firing a gun—"you can only look at one object at once. Actually, it's worse than that. I can only look at one area of space at a time. I could completely miss and look at an area in space without a planet at all." Atlas thought about the complications involved; it was much more complicated than he made it out to be. "To explain things a little more, I might look at the right location but judge the planet's distance from us wrongly, and the whole image of the planet is out of focus. It's definitely a powerful tool, but it's a lot slower than a traditional telescope."

"I can't wait until we have a complete list of all the planets near us with aliens on them. I can't wait to have a list of all the planets we need to go visit."

"Me, neither. Speaking of which, you want to visit the Atua home world, right?"

Icarus nodded.

"I've started working on an android that looks like them."

"Really?"

"Yes, I'm assuming you need it to look and feel like a real alien. So I'm first trying to replicate something that would pass through an airport checkpoint on Earth. So no metal frame, similar temperature to most animals on Earth, nothing out of the ordinary."

"I don't get it. Why are you building it for passing through security on Earth? Why not an alien one?"

"We don't actually know anything about these aliens. We don't know what they look like, other than the videos we have. We don't know what temperature they are. We don't know how heavy they are. But I'm assuming, through convergent evolution, we both evolved in a similar way. And I'm assuming if we can build something that passes through checks on Earth, then we can build something that passes checkpoints on that alien world."

Icarus appeared unconvinced, so Atlas pushed his point further. "Take body temperature, for example. Did you know most warm-blooded animals, including us, naturally sit around thirty-seven and thirty-eight degrees Celsius? You would think we'd have wildly different body temperatures from dogs or chickens, but evolution has figured out that this is the ideal temperature for running body cells efficiently. Different evolutionary paths converged around the same temperature."

He continued. "Convergent evolution was the idea that as animals evolved in similar environments they converged toward a similar design. That's why dolphins and sharks had a similar body shape for moving through the water. In early human history, it was believed that these two animals must have had a similar ancestor. But the truth was quite different from that. Dolphins were mammals and breathed oxygen. They were closer to an elephant than to a shark. Sharks filtered oxygen out of the water through gills and evolved from fish. It was theorized that on alien worlds similar to Earth, alien life would evolve similar features—after all, there was only a limited pool of designs ideal for flying, swimming, or running long distances."

Icarus nodded, in agreement. "Are you making artificial skin and bones?"

This was the point Atlas wasn't meant to be sharing too widely. While they were back on Juniper, he'd created a copy of all the research and science Angelique had provided to the planet. There was a lot of new inventions, one of which was printing an artificial-human robot. It was one of the tech designs for the new body for the Ange's Angel. All he needed to do was tweak things for a penguin body shape. He wasn't sure if Angelique would mind if he told other people about the technology. He decided that Angelique would be happy to share, otherwise she wouldn't have let him create a copy of the database. "It's a branch of bioprinting that I learned about when I was on Juniper. It's really amazing tech and means we could print an Atua body once we gather enough information about them. Assuming they aren't fundamentally different from what I imagined."

CHAPTER 23

UNITY

THE ELECTION BEFORE THE ELECTION

Unity had to hand it to Peter. He did what he'd said he would. And he did it quickly.

A week ago, the team had dropped Peter off at some exclusive golf resort. Peter was confident he didn't need anything, just the paid-for reservation that Angelique had made at the club.

Unity and the rest of the team left him there while they went off to announce their arrival.

A last-minute scramble to pull things together meant they weren't able to make an official media appearance until twenty-four hours later.

Unity thought it was a bit of a shambles. The country really wasn't in a good place as oligarchs on the planet jockeyed for position.

Unity studied all Angelique's previous appearances on her planets. Out of all of them, this was the first time things were so casual. It was more of a press conference with the world's media.

Unity noticed one little fact, and this fact was telling for just how big Peter's charm was. Not a single influential person on the planet showed up.

The major leaders of the political parties, the leaders on both sides of the factions, weren't at Angelique's announcements. Several of the planet's rich A-listers called to welcome Angelique back into the fold, but no one of real substance made time to meet her yet.

They were all on the golf course—the same one that Peter was at.

The CEOs of all the major news corporations, the owners of the moons, the who's who of the planet all pulled rank on their subordinates, cashing in whatever goodwill and clout they had to get themselves onto the very limited list of guests allowed at the resort.

Unity didn't learn this from Peter of course. She kept hearing whispers of reasonably well-off people being told they could no longer have their holidays at McMillan Club.

This was later confirmed by Angelique. Her contact details while on the planet were private. So anyone who had the ability to precure her number was at the very top end of importance on the planet. She started asking everyone who called to welcome her home where they were currently staying.

All of them said the same thing: "A preplanned vacation at the McMillan Club." There's no way everyone of importance on the planet coincidentally went to that place. They were all there for Peter.

As if confirming everyone's suspicions, Callum's assistant pulled the two of them aside, while Unity and Angelique had just finished an interview with one of the country's biggest political commentators.

"Can I speak to you both?" Deb Noster asked. He was a small man, with no hair on his head, and a green tie.

Unity and Angelique nodded as the three of them walked around the corner into a small dressing room.

"How can we help?" Unity asked as she closed the door behind them.

"What do you want?" Deb asked. "What is it going to take for you to call Peter out of his crusade to hurt Mr. Overwood?"

Unity feigned ignorance, while Angelique looked confused.

"Don't act like you don't know. Callum is on his way there now. Once people see the truth and understand that your friend Peter isn't really in it for the people of Everest, you're going to lose this challenge."

"I think you have us confused here," Angelique said. "We haven't spoken to Peter in a few days."

"Don't play dumb with me," Deb said, looking toward Unity. "I can see it in your eyes. You know what I'm talking about."

Usually, Unity would stay quiet, leaving Angelique to do most of the talking. But she also needed to branch out a little from her shadow.

She'd traveled to this planet and needed to find her own way in the world. Hezekiah had left to explore on his own soon after they'd landed.

Unity wasn't that interested in exploring on her own. But she did want to find a purpose. Something to get behind. At first, she hadn't been that interested in supporting Peter's mission, especially if it meant standing on the side of political ideologies she didn't agree with.

Peter was a pragmatist; he wasn't ideologically bound to one idea. He followed whichever path he believed was the right one. Unity thought that maybe she should do something similar. The people of Everest were in trouble. The ordinary people, not the elite of the planet.

She wondered if she felt this way because of her own preexisting beliefs not matching reality. How did the people of Everest get into this mess? When she envisioned humans on other planets she imaged this utopian ideal, where no one ever had to work, robots did it all, and everyone was equal.

She didn't know whether this planet had gone this way because of a few bad actors or whether it was just a fact of human nature. But she did know she had a choice. She had the option to be a passive observer in this situation until she found something she wanted to do. Or she could take an active role in the events as they unfolded.

She chose to take action, in the best way she knew how.

She would support Peter in his run for prime minister. She had a lot of experience with great leaders like Peter. They were great at seeing the big picture and only focusing on the big picture. They always focused on the things that moved the needle the most. She knew Peter left a lot of loose ends. A lot of things needed to be tidied up afterward.

Loose ends like this guy here. Who, left alone, might end up being a big problem later down the line.

Unity smiled warmly at Deb. She knew it was taking every ounce of will in him to look at both of them without showing fear. The only reason an assistant like him would confront them like this was if he was worried about his future. Things had gotten so bad that he was worried he might not have a job tomorrow.

Unity needed to make Deb feel like they were equal. With Angelique in the room, he was never going to feel that way.

"Angelique," Unity said. "Can you give us a moment?"

Angelique looked puzzled but nodded and left out the door.

"Are you Deb Dean?" Unity asked when it was just them in the room. "I've heard about you. You're the one who got Callum into power?"

Deb blushed, and Unity knew she had said the right thing. Stroked his ego in just the right way.

Unity had done her reading about the politics of the planet. She remembered his name appearing a couple of times. Not in any favorable ways either. But she knew about small men like Deb. They had fantasies about being the man behind the curtain. They dreamed about being the reason their boss was in power.

Unity had to stoke that side of his ego—just a little. "Are you here to make your own judgment on whether we're a threat?"

"Maybe," he said, a little unsure. "But to also understand why you're here." Then he quickly added so he didn't appear out of the loop, "I know what you told Prime Minister Overwood, but I wanted to hear it for myself."

"I'm Peter's assistant," Unity lied, but she wanted Deb to feel like he was superior. "I don't know if I can say this. But Peter did say he liked the work you did and asked me to offer you a job. Sorry to be so blunt, but back on Earth, Peter would always ask me to approach the best people. No matter where they came from."

Unity assumed Deb was here because he was afraid for his job. She assumed that meant Peter was winning.

"You're joking, right?" Deb said. "He wouldn't hire me."

Unity heard in his voice a mix of surprise and delight. He wasn't expecting the question, but equally he was very happy to hear it.

"Whatever happens after the election—win or lose—Peter would hire you in a heartbeat. You're that good."

"There might not be an election."

"What do you mean?"

"Well, there'll be an election night of course. We've still got to let the people vote."

Unity wore a look of confusion. "Sorry, I'm confused."

"You really don't know? They don't want to split the vote, and the election is too soon to run another primary. So everyone is getting together now to decide whom to support. The winner of this will most likely win the election."

"Do you know whom everyone is going to vote for?"

Deb's face straightened into a scowl.

"I'm going to find out eventually."

"Do you mean it? Win or lose this election, I'll have a job with Peter?"

"If I'm completely transparent, I can't make any promises. But I know Peter would be desperate for someone with your skill set and experience."

"I don't know. Callum has a lot of dirt on most of the people voting. So I'd hate to guess. I've never known Callum to fail, but I've also never met someone as good as Peter before."

And with that Deb walked out the room.

Unity walked out afterward to find Angelique standing outside of the door waiting.

"Did you find out what you needed?"

Unity nodded. "We probably need to see Peter at the resort."

"I'll get Ship to pick us up."

Ship was denied clearance to fly down to the surface of the planet. So after a bit of back-and-forth, they finally got clearance to be picked up via an eleph-ANT.

Unity and Angelique made their way to an open park in the middle of the city. People watched as an eleph-ANT descended to the ground. A flesh-and-blood human would have broken their neck, they were whisked off the ground so quickly.

Luckily Unity and Angelique were in android bodies, so they didn't experience any discomfort. Within a matter of seconds, both of them were already above the clouds and headed toward Ship.

Unity preferred inhabiting an android body when interacting with other humans. But she also preferred the instant-teleporting nature of using the hapticgram. As they passed the clouds in the sky, Unity decided she preferred the variety of what she was experiencing currently. She was enjoying the view.

It wasn't too long before Unity and Angelique were back in orbit with Ship. There was a bit of complication involved with getting them to the golf resort, as the added security meant they couldn't just drop in from the air unannounced. There were only particular vehicles certified to land on the property. So Ship dropped them off in the closest clear area on the edge of the no-fly zone, where a helicopter was waiting to take them the rest of the way.

Unity and Angelique arrived in the system just in time to see Callum getting ready to speak at a press conference. Callum stood off to the side behind a curtain chatting with a few of his advisers. He wore the grin of someone who had just won.

There was a large podium on the center of a platform, cameras and news outlets all waiting patiently for Callum to speak. Callum walked over to the stage.

There was a group of people standing behind the cameras off to the left. Unity recognized most of the faces from the briefing notes she'd consumed on the journey over. They were the most influential people on the planet, including the two businesspeople who owned most of the planet's news organizations.

Unity wasn't 100 percent sure what this meant. But from her experience with powerful people, if they were in the crowd, they knew what was about to be said. And their presence was a subtle nod of approval for Callum.

She scanned the crowd for Peter; he was nowhere to be seen.

"I think this is a victory speech," Unity whispered in Angelique's ear. "It looks like everyone is here still in support of him as president."

"Looks like we're about to find out for sure," Angelique whispered back as the crowd began to clap and Callum walked over to the podium.

Callum raised his hands for quiet. "You might be wondering why I gathered you all here today. Why I wanted to hold an impromptu press conference.

"Well, the rumours you've been hearing are true." Callum bowed his head in regret. "Our planet is even more screwed than we thought. I can confirm that a terrorist organization has sabotaged all our fabricators, both the kind that make fabricator pallets and the kind that turns those pallets into everything we need on this planet to survive.

"Make no mistake, this is an existential threat to our civilization. If we don't find a replacement to a fabricator, we'll be thrown back to the preindustrial age.

"That's why today I'm announcing that I will be stepping in as CEO of Cyberdyne Systems, which is the only company on Everest close to building the infrastructure needed for us to survive." Callum paused for a moment, letting everyone take in the message. "This means I won't be running in the upcoming election. All the polls showed I was about to win the election in a landslide. But the prime minister role has too many competing priorities and tasks. Re-creating a technology similar to the fabricators is the single most important task we need to do. As prime minister I couldn't dedicate myself to this, and it needs someone with my leadership experience to do this task."

Unity tuned out the rest of the speech. The crowd surrounding the podium began thinning out too as people realized what had just happened. The group of influential people also turned away and left; they looked like they were only there to make sure he said what they wanted him to say.

Unity guessed this was Peter's doing. He had come to this planet and in less than a week influenced the sitting prime minster to drop out of the race for the next election. There was so much about the world of the wealthy and influential that she had no idea about. Peter knew exactly what to do in order to win the election. He wasn't taking chances either. He had come here and changed the rules of the whole race so that his only real competitor, Callum Overwood, was no longer in the race.

Unity looked up at Callum still speaking. She couldn't help but feel sorry for the man; this speech was obviously designed to help him save face. The exclusive nature of the club meant none of his die-hard supporters were allowed in to cheer. So, there wasn't a reaction of people looking sad.

A man in a black suit and tie with an earpiece on walked over toward both Unity and Angelique. Acknowledging them both with a nod, he bowed. "Ma'am, ma'am. Peter would like to see both of you. He's waiting in one of the private dining rooms." Seeing a nod of approval from both Angelique and Unity, he continued. "If you'll follow me, I can take you there."

Unity and Angelique followed the man, and before long they were in front of a door labeled BRITISH PRIVATE DINING ROOM. There were two guards posted out front of the door.

The man gestured for them to continue through as one of the guards posted outside the door opened it.

The room was nothing like Unity had expected—it was huge, a large dining chamber with ten or so tables scattered around. All the private dining rooms Unity had ever experienced were small and cramped; this was designed for a small party, a group of guests.

Peter stood over one of the tables, several pieces of paper scattered over the table and a pen in his hand. He looked up from his work and smiled when he saw them both. "Was his resignation speech good?"

"It sounded more like a congratulation to himself," Unity said. "Was that your doing?"

Peter nodded. "I convinced him to resign. But reframing the situation as him focusing his energy on a company he started ten years ago, that was all him."

Angelique picked up one of the pieces of paper. "Why do I get the feeling you're more important on my planet now than I am?"

Peter laughed. "The people here worship you. Anyway, I've cleared the path to an uncontested election. We've got the backing of most of the people of influence. I'm going to reinstate the old constitution." Peter looked at Angelique. "Once you're happy with everything, you can share all the technology you have with the planet, and it'll be like they never had a civil war."

"Do you know much about how the fighting started?" Angelique asked.

"Most of the people I met while at this resort had an active role to play in the fighting. I think everyone saw an opportunity to gain more power. Everyone here needs something to rally around. Angelique, I think your arrival is what this planet needs to unite everyone."

CHAPTER 24

PETER

MAKING UP FOR LOST TIME

Peter walked out of his situation room and into a small adjoining bathroom. His head was throbbing. He hadn't worked this hard ever. Being an android came with some advantages; for one, he never had to sleep. And so he didn't; he pushed through and kept working, and working, and working. He wanted to sleep though; his mind was crying out for a mental break.

In his diary, he even scheduled a full night's sleep. Tonight was that night—in a few hours he would be sleeping. No meetings and no dinner plans. Just sleep.

Peter won the election in a landslide, although the real election was held a while back when one by one Peter convinced the people financially backing Callum Overwood to back him instead.

It was one side of politics that Peter enjoyed—although the fact that he was able to pull something like that off left somewhat of a bad taste in his mouth.

In a perfect world, he would have campaigned against Callum and won on merit. He would have won the election because it was the right thing for the planet. But the world wasn't perfect, and human nature meant the best person didn't always win. If it was that easy to turn all this world's leaders against someone they had backed and supported, it would have been just as easy for Callum to do that to him.

The truth was, he won because Callum had no idea what he was dealing with. As soon as Peter arrived at the golf club, he'd gone about gathering support and putting all the dominoes in place. He was able to move quickly while Callum was unaware, so that by the time Callum found out, it was already too late.

It was probably the only way Peter could have won. If Peter had announced he was running in a media conference, Callum's ego would have never allowed him to stand down. But because Peter did everything behind closed doors, Callum could portray this as all his doing.

There really wasn't too much to winning everyone over. Angelique was back with a whole lot of new technology. And the planet was screwed without it. They really didn't have much of a choice. But surprisingly, that wasn't the point that convinced most people. A lot of the people who owned much of the planet's manufacturing capability weren't in favor of changing the status quo. Yes, Angelique had newer tech, but some of that technology would make their businesses redundant. Again, Peter hated that human nature was such that many powerful people couldn't see the greater good.

The one thing that pulled everyone in line to support him was the concern about splitting the incumbent party's vote. If the votes were split, it might make the other end of the political spectrum win. Ultimately, that was the one fact that convinced a good chunk of people. It was a sad fact of life that even when the world was in trouble, some people, especially some in power, still only thought about what was in it for them.

After the election, he held a big celebration in honor of Angelique. She gave a very rousing speech. As Peter predicted, Angelique became a uniting figure. She delivered a new fabricator, and then the whole world worked toward unpacking all the new technology she had brought with her.

A five-day holiday occurred soon after, and as Peter had hoped, many of the people who had supported a civil war because it would bring them greater profits saw their companies' values fall to zero as new inventions made everything they controlled worthless.

The first thing Peter enacted was the creation of more fabricators. He had fabricators churning out fabricators as quickly as they could. And before long they had restored the complete manufacturing capabilities of the planet—the exponential nature of these machines made that all easy. And once the planet had sufficient enough manufacturing capability, he set about constructing ships for Angelique's use. She wanted to start contacting the other planets.

He did have an ulterior motive in all of this. He was confident humans were about to go to war with the Atua people. He had no idea how powerful the aliens were; he didn't know how big their war fleet was. But one thing he was confident about was that the aliens would be back. It might take them several years; it might take them a hundred. But they seemed confident that they didn't want some small rough civilization traveling around in their backyard.

And in Peter's mind, the way the Atua treated him and the others was a sign of the way they thought about humans. It reminded him of the way he used to trick his dog, Stella. Stella hated the dog cage—he never wanted to go inside of it. Stella had a sixth sense about it too. Back before Peter was rich enough to pay groomers and vets to visit him, he had to get Stella inside of his little carry kennel to go on a trip. Peter would put treats in a line across the floor, guiding him into the cage. Once Stella was safely inside, Peter would give him a little pat on the head and another treat and then move him into the car.

There was no malice in Peter's actions. He didn't feel like he was doing anything wrong. He simply knew that the easiest way to get Stella into the cage was food. He knew from experience that trying to force Stella into the cage was traumatic for both of them and didn't result in Stella entering his kennel.

Humans throughout history were happy to treat other humans in disgusting ways, especially those different from themselves. Back when humans lived on only one planet, it was common for whole countries to be enslaved or marginalized by a stronger group.

If the Atua people saw humanity as nothing more than pets, then it made sense that they used trickery to get them all back inside of the cage.

Peter was almost confident that there was only one way to make sure humans were treated with respect. He needed to unite all the planets currently controlled by humans. And he needed to coordinate a battle fleet between all of them. Not to fight back, at least not in the beginning. He needed all the planets to come together as one to show strength to the Atua people.

Peter believed strongly that the next time humanity clashed with the Atua, they needed to be equals.

Peter splashed his face with water a few times. He'd been in the bathroom a few minutes now and knew everyone was waiting outside the door. He didn't need to use the bathroom, so everyone would probably be waiting for him. He washed his face a few more times and walked back into the situation room.

In front of him sat several aides, all with stacks of critical questions to answer or problems to solve. "Okay," Peter said. "What's next on the agenda?"

"The Starnet, Prime Minster," Harry Hiscock said. "Angelique has given the technology the highest level of classification and not released it to the public. She doesn't want anyone working on the technology."

"And why not?"

"She's unsure about the technology used to connect the planets with instant communication. She's worried it would alert the Atua aliens of all the locations of her colonies. She believes the risk of someone on the planet using the tech against the wishes of everyone else is too high. She doesn't want anyone on the planet to know about it."

"Surely we can make it work without letting the rest of the universe know where our other star systems are located."

"I wouldn't know, sir," Harry said. "Knowledge of how it works is above my pay grade."

"Can you organize a group of engineers onto that problem? I suspect someone will be able to solve it."

"Well actually, sir," Niki Wong chimed in. "The security clearance for the tech is such that only Angelique's Ship knows how to make it."

Peter sighed. He wasn't going to get that sleep after all. Angelique was preparing to leave soon, so this couldn't wait. Peter sent a little text off to his assistant. He asked her to cancel his scheduled sleep; he needed to meet with Angelique tonight. His plan wasn't going to work unless he convinced Angelique that it was worth the risk connecting all the systems in her colony together. He needed her agreement to make this happen.

CHAPTER 25

ICARUS

SECRET ASTEROID

Icarus flicked a short message to Trillion asking her to join him in a secret area of his spacecraft.

He was in a laboratory working on something he didn't want Atlas to know about—at least not yet.

He wanted to speak to Trillion about his planned visit to the Atua home world; when he'd first told her about wanting to explore their planet in secret, she'd been receptive, especially when he told her he wanted to understand if they were really evil. Icarus wanted to understand the rationale for the Atua's behavior. He was surprised by how onboard with that decision Trillion was. But then it made sense once Trillion explained how she wished she'd understood the Dottiens before deciding to wage war with them. She had grown as a person and had a better appreciation for aliens being completely different from humans. She was adamant they shouldn't anthropomorphize these aliens—they should truly understand them.

Icarus surveyed the room; in one corner there was a miniature fabricator specifically designs for printing organic material, the design of which was mostly taken from the treasure trove of information stored in Angelique's databases.

In the other corner was a rocket ship that looked like an asteroid. It legitimately looked like a hunk of rock. It was small too.

Trillion teleported and just stared. "Is that you Icarus?"

"What do you mean?"

"Why do you look like one of those penguins?"

Icarus was about to answer when he realized he was inhabiting a new avatar design. He was testing out his new organic Atua alien body. He'd designed it based on recordings and images the team had gathered when meeting them. It was his best guess of what another creature would look like. "Oh, I guess I can't tease out the surprise anymore."

Trillion looked confused. "What surprise?"

"I'm visiting the Atua people," Icarus blurted out. "This is a test model to see if I could create a body that was real flesh and bone." Icarus poked his arm to show it was soft. "This is real tissue, not circuitry and wires."

Trillion walked around Icarus. He was about a meter tall. "How'd do you know it's accurate? Did Ariana get DNA samples or something?"

Icarus shook his head. "It's based on Earth biology. But I assume I can change it later once I have more sample data from the planet."

"How do you plan on getting a sample of the Atua? You can't just abduct one of their people . . . Can you?"

Icarus pointed at the asteroid in the corner of the room. It was about forty meters wide—quite a big object. "I'm going to hide a fabricator and all the equipment I need in here. Enter the system as if I'm a small asteroid."

Trillion looked at the asteroid. Then at Icarus. Then at the asteroid again. "It's too big."

"What do you mean too big?"

"I don't know much about these aliens, but surely they're going to notice an asteroid that big drifting toward their system."

"It's the smallest I can make the thing and fit everything I need for the mission."

"Have you spoken to Atlas?"

Icarus shook his head. He hadn't spoken to him yet because he was sure Atlas would think it was a bad idea. "I didn't want him to talk me out of it."

Trillion laughed. "He knows; he told me he thinks you're visiting the planet."

Icarus felt slightly better at hearing that. "Really?"

Trillion nodded.

Icarus sent off a mental command to Atlas asking him to join them in the room. "While we wait for him, I have a favor to ask."

Trillion eyed him suspiciously. "Go on."

"One of your eggs, those probes you send to other star systems, is in a system about two light-years away from the Atua planet. Can I move myself there?"

"Of course," Trillion said confused. "It'll take you a while to get there though. Aren't you farther from the system than me?"

"I'm going to teleport my matrix there." Icarus paused to let those words sink in. He hoped she understood what that meant. Technically they could teleport their matrices from system to system instantly. But their matrices were always in one location. Teleporting his matrix meant creating a copy of himself in that other location.

"Um, matrices don't work like that," Trillion said. "That's just creating a clone of yourself and putting them there."

"I've read a lot of books about this," Icarus said. "It's about continuity of experience. If I turn myself off where I am now and turn myself on at the new location, then from my perspective all I did was teleport there."

"Please don't tell me you're going to destroy one of the copies of yourself."

Icarus had thought through Trillion's question already. It was a question he'd asked himself. Was it possible to maintain continuity across both space and time? He racked his brain to try and come up with an appropriate analogy. The Ship of Theseus came to mind. "Imagine you had a ship," Icarus said.

Trillion rolled her eyes and manifested a glass of wine in her hands. "Are you going to explain the Ship of Theseus to me? I know the thought experiment about replacing all the pieces of a ship until there are no original pieces of the ship left. But that's different."

"How is it different?" Icarus asked.

"You're a living and thinking human. Not an object with a name."

Icarus had to agree; something did feel different about an object and a human, but surely they had to be the same thing. "Okay, let's think about it a different way. Do you agree that, when we were living breathing humans, our bodies were constantly replacing cells?"

Trillion nodded.

"Okay, great, and do you agree that one hundred percent of the cells in your body when you were human were replaced by the time you turned twenty?"

Trillion scratched the back of her head, then nodded. "That sounds about right. I'm not sure if it happens that quickly, but I agree with the idea that eventually all the cells in your body get replaced."

"So that's my point. Naturally a human body replaces all the cells, one at a time, slowly. It creates a copy of that cell and replaces it with a new one. By cloning my matrix every atom at a time and moving those atoms to another star system, I'll essentially be doing the same thing."

"But you can't do that with a human body. You can't take a cell out of the body and move it to a new location to reconstruct it there."

"That's where the sailing-ship analogy comes in. If you took apart all the pieces of that ship, relocated them to another location, and put them back together again, that would still be the ship of Theseus."

"No it's not because there's two versions of you. What would happen if both versions of you were turned on at the exact same time? Who would be the real you?"

"Well, this is just me," Icarus said. "But I believe the version I would consider the original me would be the one turned on first, the one with the longest unbroken awareness. That's why my plan is to turn myself off here while I'm in the other system. Then when I'm ready to come back, I'm going to use Angelique's merging process to combine all my memories back together in my original matrix."

"So, there'll only ever be one of you moving around at a time?"

Icarus nodded.

"Why not do something like the Ange's Angel program? Why not clone yourself, then merge back together?"

Icarus liked these lines of questions from Trillion. She was testing the limits of his thinking. The truth was he didn't want multiple versions of himself running around. The idea that he could clone himself, then have both of his clones spend so long apart that they experienced personality drift scared him. He wasn't sure he wanted two versions of him that were similarish but not the same. He liked his solution to it all. It meant only one version of Icarus ever existed at a single time. "I don't want there to be two of me out there."

Atlas teleported into the room.

Icarus used this opportunity to switch the subject; he wasn't yet confident enough to have the same conversation about teleporting his matrix with Atlas. "We have a question for you."

"Go on," Atlas replied.

"Well, maybe two questions. Firstly, is that asteroid-shaped spaceship too big to sneak onto an alien planet?"

Atlas walked about the asteroid. "Probably. If I saw something that big coming toward Neuropa, I'd notice it. Does it have to be that big?"

Icarus moved his head up and down. Then side to side. "It's the smallest I can make it and still fit a fabricator inside of it. Unless you know of a way to make a smaller fabricator?"

Atlas bit his lower lip as he thought about it, walking in a circle around the asteroid. "I assume you want a fully functioning fabricator, too? So you can produce anything you need."

Icarus nodded. This was exactly the conundrum he was in.

Atlas posed the question to Icarus: "Do you know why fabricators are so big? Do you know why, even as our technology gets better, these things aren't getting much smaller?"

Icarus shook his head.

Atlas looked at Trillion, who shrugged. "Because you haven't tried to make it smaller?" she asked.

"No," Atlas replied. "It needs to be capable of producing everything imaginable. There's a fundamental limit to how small you can make some of the machinery in there." Atlas bit his lower lip. He started to mumble to himself. "But what if we didn't need to produce everything? What if we only needed to produce a fabricator?"

Atlas began looking around the room frantically. Icarus could tell he was looking for a piece of paper to write notes. Icarus manifested a piece of paper into his hands and handed it to him.

Atlas began sketching notes and writing equations, then working them out. His piece of paper quickly became full of notes, and he had to turn it over to the other side.

Icarus created a stack of blank paper next to Atlas on the table.

He enjoyed watching the old man work—literal genius. Icarus wondered how much more technology and science they would have already if Atlas cloned himself. Each clone could experiment and expand human knowledge faster. Then he had a thought: maybe that was what Angelique did with her many worlds.

If Atlas and Einstein were unique—one in a billion—then on a world with twenty billion people, there are twenty people just as capable as Atlas.

Icarus wondered whether it was better to have a hundred clones of Atlas or a planet with one hundred billion people.

Icarus's thoughts were interrupted when Atlas shared his findings. "I've worked it out." Atlas pointed to a piece of paper. "You don't need a full-size fabricator if the only thing you want to create is a fabricator. We could reduce the size by about ninety percent with this plan."

Icarus took hold of the paper. He scanned the details; there were several calculations on it and a diagram. "How will this tiny printer create a full-size fabricator?"

"Easy," Atlas said. "We print it in pieces and then combine them all together. It would be like bootstrapping. First, you'd print out a larger fabricator in four components. Then print some ANTs to fit all the pieces together. Then once that's built, you can use the bigger fabricator to print out the components on an even larger one. And after four cycles of that, you'll have the components to manufacture a full-size fabricator capable of doing everything you need."

"You can't make matter out of nothing. Where are you getting the material to do all of this?" Trillion asked.

"I thought about that," Atlas said, turning over the paper. "If we sent several other asteroids with raw resources—fabricator pallets that look like rocks—we'd just need some ANTs to go and collect those."

"How long would this whole process take?" Icarus asked.

"Maybe six months. But the great thing about this plan is you could land in the water." Atlas pulled up an image of the alien world they'd identified. "Most of the Atua people are congregated in coastal cities. If they're anything like humans on Earth, they're not going to notice a small meteor shower landing in the middle of the ocean away from everyone. Especially if they're small rocks like I'm suggesting."

Icarus nodded in appreciation. Atlas had solved his biggest problem: getting onto the planet without being caught. There was still a risk that his fake asteroid was randomly intercepted by the Atua people. But as Atlas had pointed out, small asteroids hit the surface of Earth every day. It wasn't an unnatural occurrence.

"Icarus," Atlas said. "Don't rush this, if you're going to visit the planet. You need to place the asteroid on a realistic trajectory. If you were sneaking onto Earth, you'd have to make it look like it came from the asteroid belt in the system. Same with the Atua's planet. If you're going to do this, you need to do it right."

Trillion nodded in agreement. "We want you safe, Icarus. We want you to come back to us with everything you learned about the planet and the aliens."

In that very moment, Icarus felt appreciated. He also liked that he had friends that were so open to him trying such a dangerous mission. "Thanks, guys, I'm definitely coming back."

CHAPTER 26

ANGELIQUE

BEFORE YOU GO

Angelique placed her knife and fork down at the four o'clock position. She made sure the prongs of her fork were facing the plate too. This was an old-school habit her grandmother had drilled into her. It meant she was finished eating and satisfied with the meal.

She was surprised that this tradition had followed her across the galaxy. The more expensive the restaurant, the more likely they were to understand the subtle queues of etiquette.

The waitress—she was nineteen years old—immediately noticed the positioning of her cutlery and picked up the almost empty plate. She left the dessert menu on the table, then topped up her champagne flute and stepped back away from the table without a word.

Angelique was nervous, and it wasn't because of the food. This was going to be her last day as Angelique for a long time.

Or at least, over thirty clones of hers were about to wake up thinking that.

Tomorrow her sisters, her Ange's Angels, would travel to every star system she had control of. Her clones would bring with them the latest technology. But, most importantly, they'd be taking with them news about the Atua people.

None of that was causing her to feel strange. It was the fact she was implementing the Shatterling Protocol. The process itself was straightforward. Duplicating herself dozens of times was no different from duplicating herself once.

The trouble was the Shatterling Protocol was something she had built up in her mind as a last resort. If everything turned upside down, that was when, and only when, she'd reach out to all the other planets for help in such a fast manner.

She thought about it a little longer. She realized that the protocol itself had taken on a new level of meaning. It was like going to a funeral, even though the person might have passed away some time ago. Going to the funeral often made the emotions more intense because it signaled they were never coming back. Angelique shook her head at the morbid nature of that example. *Why is my mind thinking negatively?*

Before she had a chance to answer her question, the curtain to her private dining area opened. She looked up expecting to see the waitress return.

Instead, Peter wandered through. He looked exhausted. He carried with him a glass of whiskey.

"The final supper?" Peter asked as he sat down.

"Yes, my final meal before I depart. It's sort of a tradition I do just before I split myself." Angelique looked at Peter, assuming he was here one final time to convince her to let the people on the planet use FTL communication. "If you're here about the Starnet, I haven't changed my mind, but I have been thinking about it."

She knew Peter wanted to set up a Starnet connection with all her planets. In her mind, the Starnet was a one-way technology. It was Pandora's box—it could never be put back. Yes, she had already shared the technology with her people on Juniper. But their thinking was aligned with hers. She believed connecting all the planets would act as a beacon for anyone looking. It would identify every planet under her control. It wasn't worth the risk.

"I'm not here to convince you about the Starnet."

Angelique was a little taken aback by that comment. She was about to share the truth with him: that she was didn't want her planets to use the Starnet because if they did she wouldn't have a clear purpose. She'd been traveling between the worlds and sharing new technology with everyone for so long that she was a little bit sad she wouldn't have the chance to do it anymore. It took her a long bit of contemplation to figure that out. It was kind of a selfish reason to not give them the tech. But it was the truth. But now that she knew the reason, she was beginning to see a plan for herself post-Starnet. Because ultimately, there was no way she would be able to keep it hidden for too long. And the benefits of hundreds of billions of people connecting together, sharing knowledge, and improving on technology in real time were so worth it.

She imagined how fast her people would grow if they didn't have to wait for her to visit every few thousand years. She began to think about how a human empire might look.

There were more than a hundred billion stars in the Milky Way. A galaxy-wide empire was within her grasp . . . As long as they all got together to fight against the Atua aliens trying to keep them trapped. "Oh, that's a shame because I have been giving it a bit more consideration."

Peter raised an eyebrow. "Go on."

"No, you go first. What did you come here for?"

Peter grabbed a small crystal out of his pocket. It was one of the permanent storage devices that stored information in a clear gem. "I assume Atlas has access to all your latest tech? So he can read this?"

Angelique nodded.

"Perfect, I've recorded him a little message here. I was wondering if you could send one of your clones to him."

"Of course. Does any of the message concern me?"

Peter took a swig of his whiskey. "Not you specifically, but I have asked him to create a weapon."

"To use against the Atua?"

Peter nodded. "I want something powerful enough to be a deterrent. Something so strong they'd be stupid to fight back."

"Have you looked through the classified data? Every weapon any of my people have created is in there."

"I have, but nothing stood out to me. I want something that's the equivalent to a nuclear bomb on Earth. There, none of the superpowers fought with one another because of the risk of mutual self-destruction. I'm hoping Atlas can create something like that."

"I see," Angelique said. "You think Atlas will build a weapon?"

"He's probably the only person I trust to build something with that much destructive force. If we are looking to build a weapon capable of destroying a planet or a solar system, then I'd want the recipe for that to be only known by someone at our level."

"Our level?"

"I mean at the level where you're thinking about groups of planets. Not obsessed with the day-to-day of what's happening on one single world. We don't want crazy people like old moneybags Callum Overwood having control of a weapon like this."

Angelique found that comment interesting. At their level. It implied they were at a different level to others, which kind of made sense since she was part of a very small group of humans that had visited more than one planet. It didn't make them better than others, but it did give them a unique perspective. It did give them the ability to see the galaxy in a whole different light. "You want this weapon controlled at our level? Not controlled by individual planets, but above them? Does that mean we're taking control of the security of these planets too?"

"Yes, if we're going to war with another alien species, we need a federation. Or a human empire with enough teeth to fight back."

"Interesting. I think you and I are on the same page. I'm coming around to the idea of using the Starnet. But Atlas needs to figure out how to make it work without a constant stream of particles."

The waitress came back in the room, interrupting them both. Angelique smiled at the young girl. "Can we try one of everything on your dessert menu?"

The girl looked at Peter, who raised his glass. "Can you get me another one of these?"

"Of course, Prime Minster. Which drink was it?"

"It's a Scott Manley–label scotch. I forget the name; it's the peaty one."

"It's Called Rocket Science for a Reason?"

"Yes, that's it. Can I have another round of that please?"

Angelique didn't understand why this planet had adopted hipster-like names for their whiskeys. Back on Earth, it was only beers that got the cool names. But this planet had continued that tradition with whiskeys and even wines.

The waitress nodded and then left the room.

"You were saying?" Peter asked.

"I've been thinking about it. I agree with you; the strategic benefit of the Starnet outweighs the downsides, especially if there's a way to make it work without broadcasting our planets to the universe."

"Agree. I wasn't going to push you on it because it would also mean an end to your Ange's Angel program. You wouldn't need to visit the planets anymore."

"More than that. I felt like it would lead me to lose my purpose. But I see two things I can do going forward." Angelique raised one finger into the air. "I'll still be able to break new ground and terraform new planets." She raised a second finger and smiled at Peter before winking. "And secondly, I'll be able to compete with you for whoever gets to be the leader of this federation of planets we're building."

"You can have it," Peter said. "I assume both of us will get a chance. But you can go first. You deserve it, since most of the planets will be planets you created."

Angelique looked at Peter for a good long while. The brazen nature by which they were able to discuss becoming rulers of a collection of planets was crazy. Especially considering they hadn't yet solved their problem with the Atua aliens. It was the kind of thing you didn't say out loud. She'd never had a friend she could talk to about these kinds of things before.

She liked the idea of having someone else she could talk to, someone that was just as ambitious as her, someone who said the things out loud that she would have previously only kept inside of her brain.

The young waitress walked through the door carrying several plates precariously balanced on her arms and hands. "Ma'am, if it's any consolation, I think you'd make a great leader of the galaxy."

Angelique took that as confirmation that she was right.

CHAPTER 27

ICARUS

GOODBYE

Icarus was about to say goodbye to his friends Trillion and Atlas for a long while. His matrix was about to be disconnected and all residual power removed.

His current location was in deep orbit in the system he'd first colonized. His spaceship was hiding embedded in a planet around the size of Pluto. He wanted to make sure his location was relatively unknown, as he assumed he'd be there for quite a while.

Atlas had solved the issue of creating a fabricator that was small enough to be disguised as an asteroid.

Icarus's plan was simple. Using a tight-beam-communication blast, he would send a copy of himself and Ship to a spacecraft that was currently on a trajectory through the Atua system.

The biggest issue with the Starnet was it required a constant stream of particles sent between two locations. The problem then was that if a small rock or microasteroid passed through the constant stream of particles, some of them might be bounced in the wrong direction—potentially toward the planet. This would be detectable and give away the position of the spacecraft.

That's why they'd never equipped this starship with any such Starnet: the risk was too high that the alien might detect one of these stray particles.

To ensure the spacecraft wasn't seen or detected, all the lines and curves on the starship were specifically designed to bounce light away from the center of the system—in particular, they made sure light always bounced away from the Atua planet that was occupied.

Scans of the system showed there wasn't much activity happening in the system, not much in the way of asteroid mining or space-based megaprojects. That was what led Atlas to conclude this must not be their home world—because surely a space-based civilization would be conducting a lot of activities out in space, especially around their home world.

"Our window to make the transfer is open now," Ship said. They calculated the position of the receiving spacecraft. They had a short window in which it could safely receive a transmission from the team.

Icarus nodded. "I'm going to miss you both. See you in a bit."

Trillion, Atlas, and both their Ships all waved as they watched their two friends, a little sad. They had said their goodbyes and were there to see them off.

Icarus and Ship were standing in a little two-person escape pod with their arms crossed over their chests. They weren't really about to be ejected out into space. But Icarus liked the dramatic impact of pretending like they were.

"Launching now," Ship said.

"Wait," Trillion said, jumping toward the both of them. "One more hug."

Trillion jumped in between both of them and gave Icarus and Ship one last big hold. "Take lots of photos and come back with lots of stories."

Trillion stepped back from them both.

Icarus and Ship were launched out the escape hatch as copies of them raced across the stars.

It was two years before Icarus and Ship arrived at their intended location. Traveling at light speed still took time to travel across the stars. And they didn't have the option of using the Starnet.

Once on board the spaceship, they embarked on the complicated task of getting to the surface on the planet. It was a mostly preplanned maneuver. A version of Lex was in the driver's seat. But Icarus and Ship never had their minds reprinted inside of matrices. Their minds, or at least all the information required to reconstitute their minds inside of matrices, were stored as data, saved as ones and zeros inside of a hard drive. Both Icarus and Ship had to be stored this way because matrices were fragile—they wouldn't survive reentry. Even the improved versions Angelique's people had designed couldn't survive what was about to happen.

CHAPTER 28

LEX

FIRST ENCOUNTER

Lex turned on; being the smallest of the three files, he was quickly loaded into the spacecraft and ready to carry out the mission.

The Atua system had a large asteroid belt, which Lex was currently racing through. Lex confirmed everything in the system was as expected. And most importantly, he started checking passive sensors for any sign the Atua aliens detected they were there.

Lex normally wasn't too good at handling uncertainty. But Atlas had reprogrammed this one to treat anything with more than a 75 percent probability as fact. Within an hour, Lex confirmed the probability there were no active sensor pulses and no alien spacecraft nearby was over 80 percent. And so Lex understood the next step in the process.

Lex began passively collecting more data on the nearby asteroids. It was looking for an asteroid to collide with. On board the spacecraft, they had printed a small asteroid. Lex had to aim for one, and as if it was playing pool out in space, the asteroid it hit needed to fly off in the direction of the planet.

This was a low-probability incident but still not zero probability. It was the only way the team could plausibly explain a meteor shower on the planet in a reasonable time frame. The spacecraft Lex was in was designed to look like a fast-moving comet racing through the system. It would look like it was ejected from a nearby system at a relatively fast speed and then collided with a few asteroids on its way through—nothing too suspicious.

Lex selected a target and released the small asteroid contained in the nose of the ship.

The small payload connected with the intended target and obliterated it, not exactly like pool or snooker because the asteroid that was hit didn't fly off as one large chunk in the correct direction. Maybe a better description was a bullet hitting a bowling ball causing shrapnel to fly off in all directions, with several pieces heading toward the planet.

Lex quickly scanned all the fragments of the asteroid and identified several that were traveling in the right direction— toward the Atua planet.

Lex released the last of its payload, firing several smaller asteroid-shaped devices toward the planet, right in the middle of the asteroids already heading there.

One of those small payloads contained Icarus and Ship.

Lex then powered down the ship and turned itself off. It wouldn't reawaken for forty-two years, enough time to race through the system undetected and report back to the others once it was safe to do so.

Quite some time later, another Lex was switched on. Its wake sequence would have been triggered by any number of scenarios: a change in trajectory or even a change in temperature. Any situation that required a brain to look into. In this scenario, the wake sequence for Lex was trigged when the internal temperature of the spacecraft turned comet started to increase rapidly—the outside of the asteroid was red-hot.

Lex checked passive sensors. It had orders to self-destruct if there was any reason to believe it had been captured. In this case, Lex concluded the temperature change was caused by the fact it was racing through a thick atmosphere.

It was really hot, and Lex concluded its matrix would probably not survive reentry. There was no protective heat shielding or nanogel for cooling. The use of anything that might become detectable in the atmosphere was unacceptable. Lex continued its checks and concluded the hard drive containing Icarus and Ship would survive.

Lex continued its decent toward the planet, getting ever hotter and hotter, but also slowing down as it pushed its way through the atmosphere.

Lex knew the heat had corrupted the orb beyond repair, and so it disconnected itself from any operations inside of the falling debris of a spacecraft—it didn't want to go rogue. Lex then passively observed as it raced toward the ocean of the planet before splashing hard into the ocean, the force instantly breaking the matrix into a trillion tiny pieces.

Over some time, the asteroid that contained the team drifted toward the bottom of the large body of water. It ended up traveling several hundred meters under the water before finally hitting the ocean floor. The temperature change that occurred when the hot spacecraft was rapidly cooled almost destroyed them all. The only thing that saved the team was the new diamond shell that they were inside of. If it wasn't for that material, the team would have died.

Once the spacecraft had fully cooled and nothing had disturbed the team for some time, another Lex was printed out of a specialty fabricator device and activated.

This Lex once again had orders to self-destruct if it detected an alien had captured them. It quickly concluded it was at the bottom of the ocean—safe and as expected.

Next, the Lex reviewed what the other two versions of itself had done. Even though Lex didn't personally experience being ejected from the spacecraft or having its matrix smashed to pieces, it knew that all those things had happened. It also felt like it was the same Lex that had experienced all those activities.

It treated those experiences like they were its experiences. Lex didn't have any issues with believing those versions of itself were it. Unlike Icarus or any other human, Lex didn't have a weird uncertainty about who it was. It didn't matter whether it had something stored in its memory or not. Icarus only had one Lex—this Lex. And if throughout this journey to get Icarus and Ship back, Lex had to go through multiple instances of deletion and reinstallation, then so be it.

To Lex, there was no such thing as dying, no discontinuity of experience, not even a mild case of cognitive dissonance when it was reborn missing whole sections of time because it needed to be reinstalled from a previous backup.

Lex was Lex, and there was only one Lex. This was one thing it didn't feel uncertain about. It was 100 percent certain about who it was every time it was switched on.

It began the next lengthy operation. And it wouldn't know if it was successful for six months. Any machinery failure or missed calculation might not be noticeable until the final month of the process.

Lex instructed a small door panel to open. Several small ANTs popped out and began working, moving around the location searching and cataloging their surroundings.

Lex found itself in the middle of something that resembled a coral-like reef. There were multiple fishlike creatures around, several squid-looking creatures with six and four arms. They quickly scurried away once the ANTs started moving around.

Lex confirmed the location looked safe enough. And so began the next steps of the operation.

One of the ANTs started digging its way through the ground. Its job was to dig deep into the bedrock and embed itself in there.

Five other ANTs began unloading an inflatable-shell cover. The shell inflated and was placed over the top of their location. After taking a scan of the surroundings, Lex had printed out a cover that would blend in and hide them. The cover was made of a special material that the team hoped would make them invisible to most known detection methods. In theory, they would simply look like a rock on the ocean floor.

With all of that in place, Lex began working on phase two. It was sort of lucky and surprising that on the planet there was an abundance of deep-sea creatures. There were animals that Lex could emulate. Lex selected the six-armed octopus-looking creature and had the fabricators print some ANTs in roughly the same size and shape, then cover them in an organic printed covering that would mimic the look and texture of the animals. They wouldn't pass a close inspection but wouldn't raise any suspicion if the aliens on the planet saw a photo of the new ANTs.

Next, Lex sent the ANTs disguised as alien squid out foraging, systematically venturing farther and farther out than they had gone before, scanning the areas, searching slowly and methodically for any material it could take back to the fabricators.

Once something was identified, multiple squid-like ANTs would drag the objects back. It didn't take long before Lex acquired enough resources for phase two.

One of the other tasks given to Lex was recording all signals received. It needed to passively scan for the aliens' equivalent of a TV signal. Lex sent small fish-shaped ANTs toward the surface of the ocean, where they picked up a lot of information. It recorded everything and planned to decode the messages once it had the resources to do so.

Lex had to locate one of the fabricator pallets. It was a difficult task. But there really was no getting around that they needed some very hard-to-produce exotic materials. This was going to be a needle in a haystack. But Lex was designed for single-minded tasks that required absolute focus.

Lex got into quite a good flow, churning out squid-shaped ANTs and sending them out searching for more material. Those ANTs were instructed to hunt for fabricator pallets. But if they found other material that was useful for building more ANTs, then they would bring those back to Lex.

Before long, it looked like a whole colony of the hundreds of thousands of the squid-looking creatures out hunting for fabricator pallets.

If anyone looked down on the area with a camera, they would see something was wrong with the situation. The six-legged squid were solo creatures out in the wild. So seeing a big colony of them would be a sure sign to investigate further. Lex didn't know this yet, but that one action was putting the whole mission in jeopardy.

As luck would have it, one of the fabricator pallets was found quite quickly, which allowed Lex to move on to phase three.

The next stage of production required Lex to begin building more visible structures underneath the water. Fabricators were massive and needed to be constructed in an even larger area. They required a near vacuum, too.

So Lex began the construction of an even larger dome under the water.

Like a reverse Russian doll, Lex needed to build a dome capable of building a fabricator slightly larger than the one that produced it. Then once completed, all the resources and material would be cannibalized for that fabricator to construct the next larger size.

It was a long process, since any time Lex needed resources from the ocean, it had to be very careful not to be seen.

The only saving grace throughout the whole process was all the squid-like ANTs that had been created earlier were recycled into material for the dome.

Lex didn't know it, but the area above them had been scanned shortly after all the ANTs were disassembled to create the larger dome, which saved the team from being identified.

This process would take several months. Throughout this time, Lex worked tirelessly to make sure everything was completed in the right order and in as quick a manner as possible.

This was the biggest project Lex had ever been given, and it felt the need to do everything right. It knew what Trillion's Lex had done in destroying a planet and wanted to make sure it didn't repeat that mistake.

Lex now had a big enough processor to properly analyze all the information passively collected—the aliens' version of the TV. Using data collected and comparing it to all the existing recordings of the aliens' speech, Lex was able to piece together a comprehensive translator of the Atua's language.

During some of the downtime, it did wonder what would have happened if it had been damaged on the way there. It wondered what might happen if it simply mined the ocean floor to create more ANTs. It wondered if the aliens on the planet would be capable of stopping something that exponentially expanded like that. It wondered if that was a realistic weapon to use against another species. Hopefully it would find out once Icarus and Ship explored the planet.

And finally, the time had arrived. Lex built a complicated enough fabricator to produce something as sophisticated as matrices for Icarus and Ship.

Lex loaded their files into the fabricator and several hours later both of them were ready to be switched on.

Lex was excited to share everything it had collected with the two of them.

Lex connected Icarus and Ship to the power and turned them on.

CHAPTER 29

ICARUS

UNEXPLORED WORLD

Icarus appeared in a simulated world. A virtual reality of sorts but designed to look exactly like the world around them. The alien planet they were on.

Using the hapticgraphic projectors wasn't practical when they were trying to stay hidden. So a simulated version of the planet was the next best thing.

Icarus thought about it, and the water disappeared. Simulating that he was swimming wasn't what he wanted to do in that very moment. The coral around him looked familiar to what he remembered from Earth but not quite the same. The colors were different, and the animals were strange.

Icarus sat down, using one of the coral as a seat; his duck-like legs weren't ideal for the terrain.

Next to him appeared Lex.

Icarus reached over and pulled Lex toward him, kissing the orb on its head. "You did it. You got us safely to the surface."

Then moments later, Ship appeared too.

Icarus couldn't contain his excitement. He was on an alien world. "We're on a planet with aliens. I can't believe we're here."

Ship patted Lex on the head. "I had my doubts, Lex, but you did it."

The orb flashed pink with joy and moved from side to side as if to say, *It was nothing.*

"What do we know about the planet, Lex?" Icarus asked. "Have we intercepted anything that could give us a clue as to what these aliens are like?"

The orb flashed green, and Ship filled in the context. "Wow," Ship said. "Lex intercepted a lot of communication that used a technology similar to television signals."

"What do they watch? Soup operas? Reality TV?"

Ship shook his head. "Sports. It seems there are a bunch of independent countries on this planet. Like, a lot. All competing against one another in a sport called sky-ocean-ball."

"Sky-ocean-ball?" Icarus mused. "That's a strange name, and how do you know it's called that? Surely there's an alien name for it."

"That's the other thing that Lex has done: created a complete translation layer. So we can understand their language now. Sky-ocean-ball is the literal translation of the words."

Icarus gabbed Lex again and gave it another kiss on the head. "You genius."

Icarus was excited because he could now speak with these aliens in a language they spoke but also disappointed that he didn't get to translate any of the alien speech himself, although he knew it was going to be an easy task. They had a lot of recorded speech already. When Angelique, Atlas, and the rest of the team had spoken with the Atua representative, it had used a translator to speak English. But the alien version of the words was still audible in the background.

Having hundreds of example sentences in English and the equivalent in the language the Atua spoke was half the battle. It wasn't like with the Dottiens, when they had essentially started from scratch.

"Do we have enough information to make a realistic-looking alien body?" Icarus asked.

Ship nodded his head. "This is where it gets complicated. The aliens are very segmented. So much so that we need to build a body type for each species. There are three nearby countries that speak the language we're familiar with."

Ship displayed three different alien body types—all variants on a penguin design. They all looked very similar to one another, except one was shorter with longer flippers, while one of the others had a shorter beak. "The differences are subtle," Ship continued. "But where you're born dictates exactly what you look like."

Icarus pointed to the middle of the three alien body shapes. "This one looks very similar to the alien that Atlas and the others met."

"I believe it's the same people. They are one of the strongest people on the planet."

Icarus noticed Ship's use of the word *people*. When thinking about these aliens, it was hard not to anthropomorphize. Icarus thought some more about it. He wanted to take his time on the planet. If they were the most advanced, it might not be best to visit them first. They would likely have the most security and probably the highest chance of him getting caught. He thought about Earth and which country would be easiest to sneak into. He quickly realized it wasn't about the power of the country. It was how much of a melting pot the location was. It would be easier for an alien to hide in the city of New York than a small rural town in the Midwest. "Which of the three countries has the biggest population? Which country is the most like a melting pot?"

Ship looked toward Lex, who put a glow around the tallest of the three aliens. Ship filled in the details. "The aliens from the country Arck'tula."

"Perfect. Pull me everything you have on this alien," Icarus said. He desperately wanted to print a body that looked like those people, but he didn't want to rush into it all. He needed to tread carefully, especially in the beginning. He needed to interact with these aliens without them becoming aware of his presence. If this meant he needed to take a bit of time to do more research, then he needed to do that. "What about technology? Have we learned any advanced science that we don't have yet?"

"That's what's strange about these aliens," Ship said. "I reviewed everything that Lex has collected. They don't seem as advanced as I expected. Sure, they have space capabilities and their version of a computer. But I don't see flying cars everywhere. I don't see any mention of AI. I don't see a lot of reports about space travel either."

"Do we know if this is their home world?

Ship nodded. "I believe so."

Interesting, Icarus thought. These were more questions he wanted answers to. He wanted to go out to the surface of the planet and talk with others, find the answers to these questions.

The team worked like this for some time, Icarus asking questions and Ship querying the database that Lex had built up.

In the end, it took three long days of planning and multiple trips out in the bodies of small fishlike creatures to survey the area and confirm the details of the mission.

They decided to print two bodies for the Arck'tula aliens, one for Icarus and one for Ship. Lex was a little disappointed it couldn't come explore, but they needed someone to stay back at their base and keep an eye on everything.

The Arck'tula were ideal candidates because, of the three target populations, they interacted with the others the most. Their people often worked on secondment, working as laborers on dangerous jobsites for many of the other nations. They were a poor nation.

Icarus's plan was simple: they would build the alien bodies, and then migrate overnight, heading over to one of the shores and entering from there.

Icarus and Ship didn't know what they were going to encounter, so the bodies they built were made of real flesh. Convergent evolution meant these aliens were very similar in design to animals on Earth. Icarus assumed there were only so many ways a bird could evolve to swim in the sea.

The Atua bodies had heart-like organs, lungs, eyes, and wings. Any standard body scan would reveal very similar insides to a normal Atua body. If anyone weighed them, the density would be slightly heavier than expected—but otherwise they were as close a match as they could create without abducting one of the locals. Icarus was surprised by just how much information could be gathered simply by watching television shows.

They had a lot of sports, more than usual. But there were still shows about doctors, which the team used to catalog the insides of their bodies. And that's how they'd gathered that information.

There was so much information to run through too, so many shows. They could have spent the whole time running through everything on offer, but Icarus and Ship agreed that it would ruin some of the magic. Yes, they needed to not make any mistakes by being ill prepared. But they also didn't want to approach the Atua for the very first time knowing everything—that would ruin the magic of discovery.

There was a religious ceremony coming up, so Icarus made the call to go out and blend into the crowd during that event, experience it before sneaking back into the water, returning to their base, and then consuming everything they could about the aliens.

CHAPTER 30

SHIP OF ICARUS

WE NEED A NAME

The Ship of Icarus floated just on top of the water. Out in front of him was a beach with some of the blackest sand he'd ever seen.

It was just before morning, still dark out in the sky, nothing in the air except the sound of the ocean waves hitting the beach.

He continued moving along the top of the water, his new body perfectly built for swimming. He dove underneath a wave and kicked his powerful legs, propelling forward.

A few moments later he reached the edge of the beach, where it was shallow enough to stand. He poked his head up above the water slightly, checking to make sure the coast was clear.

Icarus reached out and grabbed his hand. "It looks safe to exit the water."

The Atua aliens were affectionate. It wasn't uncommon for them to walk in pairs or even small groups all holding hands—in the same way that humans did. Ship and Icarus built a physical connection in each of their hands. It meant they could communicate with each other as if they were speaking out loud while holding hands. It meant as long as they were holding hands, they could have a private conversation that no one else could listen to.

This also eliminated the risk of someone detecting signals constantly traveling between them—it wasn't worth the risk of getting caught.

Ship followed Icarus as they both began walking up onto the beach.

The sand clung to Ship's webbed feet—the feet of his new body. He shook it off.

Ship opened a small pouch located underneath his chest; he pulled out a bag. All Atua had a somewhat large flap of skin, similar to a kangaroo's pouch. But unlike a kangaroo, this double layer of skin was right where their chest was.

Ship opened the bag and pulled out a towel. He wiped himself down and then pulled out a green-and-white jumpsuit—at least it looked like a jumpsuit. This was the sports uniform for one of the local teams. Wearing your team colors or tops with pictures of celebrities on them was all the rage on this planet. So, they'd selected this to blend in.

Ship looked over at Icarus, who was in what could only be described as a backwards sweater and some very tight shorts. But this time, rather than being the local team colors, it was a brown outfit with the image of the captain of the team. Again, this was a common outfit among these people.

They nodded at each other and made their way off the beach and toward the city.

The Atua legs weren't suited to long-distance travel. They weren't as bad as if they were penguins back on Earth, but still, their short legs meant traveling long distances by foot was slow-going.

Atua evolved to travel quite long distances on their bellies. They didn't move like that anymore.

It took them a bit of walking before they reached the first street corner. The Atua did have cars, or car equivalents. But that wasn't what caught Ship's eye.

Looking at the footpath, Ship realized just how different from humans these creatures were. There wasn't a clear way for them to walk down the street. Instead, all the footpaths had these gutters of sorts that blew a strong amount of air out of them.

Icarus reached out and grabbed Ship's hand so they could communicate in private. "We have to ride this thing," Icarus said.

Ship shrugged as he watched Icarus climb into the small gutter. It was called a chuk-tok, and this was the primary means of travel. They were designed so the Atua floated in place over the jets of air.

Icarus shot off down the gutter, and Ship had to scramble into it to follow behind.

The Atua had thick coats, which meant Ship didn't even feel the wind passing over him. The ears of the Atua could close in on themselves, meaning it wasn't noisy at all. The Atua could navigate these gutters easily without their eyes open. They had large organs on the top of their heads that produced an effect like a combination of magnetism and echolocation. Turnoffs and signs were easily identified through unique magnetic fields and sound resonance.

Ship let go of the sides and quickly moved downward. It wasn't that hard to move down the stream of air, catching up to Icarus. The aerodynamic nature of the Atua body was well suited for this.

Ship could see their desire to be birds again coming through. Much like their sports, this was an effort to make them feel like they were flying. Moving down the stream felt much like gliding.

Ship used his new sensors to feel out the city. Ship noticed the beauty in everything around him. There wasn't an analogy for what he was experiencing. There was almost a music in his mind as he moved through the city. Buildings, landmarks, even sculptures, all gave off a unique and distinct signal to these new sensors he was using.

Humans' most-used sense was sight, and so things in the human world were designed to look good based on the eye sensor. There was no other way to describe what he was experiencing but to call it magical. It was a truly alien experience; everything was giving off a new and interesting signal in his mind's eye.

Ship followed Icarus as they traveled a loop around a block. Ship got the feeling Icarus was enjoying this and wanted to play around a little longer. They looped around one block in particular three times before Icarus jumped off at one of the exits.

Ship and Icarus had watched a number of television shows that demoed the travel via this tubelike network. Atua could enter and exit at any point along the line. But dismounting at any point required a bit of technique and, in Ship's case, a lot of luck. Ship opted to race past where Icarus got off and exit from a small ramp specifically designed for disembarking.

Ship landed on the ground a good ten meters away from Icarus. He looked back in time to see Icarus pulling himself off the ground—he obviously hadn't exited the alien transport gracefully.

Ship ran back up the street to catch up to Icarus.

"Did you hear the song playing as we moved down that tube?" Icarus asked. "Each block had a different tune to it; I could hear it in my mind. Somehow, I knew exactly where I was at all times."

"Seeing the city through these new eyes was something else."

Icarus didn't respond. He was staring over Ship's shoulder, his mouth wide open in amazement. The look was unmistakably human. He was in awe of whatever was over Ship's shoulder.

Before Ship turned around, he made a mental note to create a script that translated human gestures and mannerisms into alien ones. He was almost confident that expression would mean something completely different to the aliens here.

Ship swiveled to see what Icarus was looking at and understood why his friend had looked so in shock. Both Icarus and Ship had stayed away from watching too many videos of the alien architecture or culture, opting to rely on Lex to provide them with the minimum they needed to know. Even Ship, who'd consumed more of the alien television than Icarus, wasn't ready for what he saw.

It was the complete opposite of a human city. Everything looked natural, not in the sense that they were looking out into a forest, but as if the buildings were grown, or most likely printed, out of metal.

On Earth, all the buildings were square or curved, made out of mass-produced uniform material. There was always a sense of symmetry in human designs. This was the complete opposite; every supporting beam, window, and building frame was unique. All the pieces twisted and bent in different directions.

It wasn't an ugly mess either. It was beautiful. It was different. It was alien.

There were skyscrapers, too, massive towers that stretched as far as they could see, but not the uniform versions you'd get on Earth. The poles that made up the tower twisted and grew thicker in random parts.

Ship remembered learning about a design process called evolved structures, which had a similar design language to what he was looking at. It involved asking an algorithm to redesign a shape so that it could be printed using the least amount of material. It resulted in these structures that looked like bone. They looked organic, as if nature had designed them.

And this was exactly what Ship was looking at. The colors were bold and vibrant, too. Ship couldn't see a dull grey or concrete color anywhere. Somehow it all just worked. The bright colors made for a beautiful-looking city.

Ship grabbed Icarus's hand. "There's someone coming."

There were three aliens heading toward them. They'd just exited the air canal, which was the name Ship had decided best described the wind-transport thing.

The aliens were looking at the two of them. Ship froze. He wasn't sure what to expect. He felt like it was glaringly obvious he was from another planet.

He watched the eyes of the approaching aliens. They were studying him and Icarus. Then Ship saw an object in one of their hands. *Was it a gun?* Ship thought and began to full-on freak out.

CHAPTER 31

ICARUS

TRUE FIRST EN-COUNTER

Icarus noticed his friend acting a little scared—Ship looked afraid.

Icarus took hold of Ship's hand. "You seem worried."

"They know we aren't from around here."

"Chill," Icarus said. "Remember what you told me. We can't anthropomorphize. Just follow my lead; copy them and let's walk past."

Icarus started to walk toward the aliens, mimicking their walking gate. It was a lazy waddle.

Icarus nodded at the three aliens as they passed. "Under his eye."

He felt Ship's hand squeeze hard. Icarus changed the translated meaning of his words. So, Ship heard, "Under his eye," but the aliens heard, "Hello," in their language. It was a reference to a show they'd both watched called *The Handmaid's Tale*. He knew saying it would make Ship want to curl up in a ball with embarrassment—even though the aliens didn't understand the reference.

"Good day for the gods to be here," one of the aliens said.

Icarus didn't know what to say in response to this. He didn't have the power to slow down his playback speed to quickly review all the notes he'd taken. He said the only thing he could say while continuing to walk forward: "Yes, it is."

One of the aliens stopped and turned toward them both. Icarus got the feeling it was inviting them to stop and face them too. The alien started to speak again, and the translator kicked in once more. "Are you hoping to be chosen by the gods?"

"I am," Icarus said, slightly intrigued but also wanting to get out of the conversation because he was starting to show his ignorance. "We're running late. We must be off to a meeting. Sorry."

Icarus, still holding Ship's hand, raced them off down the street. He hadn't been remotely prepared for that conversation. Which god was it talking about? What did it mean by *chosen*?

Icarus realized he and Ship needed to get somewhere quickly and review everything they had. Icarus felt like he had done the right thing in getting out and visiting the planet. After all, if he'd known about the alien building designs, he wouldn't have been as surprised as he was. But the time for surprises was over.

He needed to get somewhere quickly and do some digging.

"We should go back to the base," Ship suggested.

Icarus shook his head. "Let's find the closest thing to an alien park."

Ship stopped walking and pulled hard on Icarus's hand. "No, we need to go back. Our body language, our mannerisms don't match the locals'."

Icarus thought about this for a moment. Icarus was usually the one to be more cautious. He thought of himself as someone who liked to plan a bit before jumping fully into something. A few hundred years ago, he would have happily gone back with Ship to do more research. Icarus wondered what had changed.

Maybe the years being stuck in administration on a planet had changed him, caused him to want to take a bit more risk.

He wanted to be a real explorer, like the ones in the movies, exploring the unknown. Learning on his feet, rather than having everything planned out in advance.

Yes, Ship was right, they needed to improve their algorithms for interacting with others. But they also needed to collect more data; they needed to do more people watching. What they'd captured from television was an unrealistic view of the planet. It was like learning about Earth from reality shows and basketball.

He and Ship needed to understand the real planet. The real aliens.

"What if we head to their version of a library?" Icarus asked. "I know they have reading places similar to us. They're quiet too, so we would be left alone. We could people watch and collect more data on how these people interact with one another."

Library was only a loose translation of what it truly was because there wasn't really a human equivalent. It was like a mix of a museum for music and a private movie theater. It was designed for the sensor humans didn't have.

Ship thought about this for a while. "I don't want us to get caught."

"Ship, I think we'll be fine. Surely we have enough processing power between the two of us to build an updated interactions algorithm." Icarus wasn't sure they'd be able to do it without Lex but figured he'd propose the question to Ship and see if he could come up with a way to make it all work.

Ship scratched his chin, another human-like gesture they needed to stop doing. "If I disconnect my matrix for twenty minutes, I should be able to route enough processing power to create a new model of these aliens' behaviors."

It took a bit of negotiation, but eventually Icarus convinced Ship to venture farther into the city and find a library. Nearby there was a sign with directions on it. Both Icarus and Ship had advanced vision, so they could zoom in on it quite easily.

They were only several blocks away, which, if they were walking, would have taken a whole day. But using the air-canal system meant they'd be there in no time.

There were other descriptions on the map in a sort of language that Icarus didn't understand. The script was three-dimensional, similar to braille but more detailed. He thought it might make a particularly resonant sound somehow but didn't have time to work it out. The way the language appeared on the map led Icarus to believe that perhaps it related to the same sound he'd heard while traveling the city. Each of the locations made a different sound when he viewed the city through the magnetic and sonar-sensing organ.

It was a useful way to see the world. Icarus thought about how much of human experience was dictated by what the eyes could see. This different way of *feeling* was unique to Atua life. It made the world more alien than it already was.

Icarus jumped into the air canal and raced through the city. Ship followed closely behind.

Icarus guided them around the block a few times. He was getting used to the experience. It was kinda like flying. He used his wings to move from side to side in a rocking motion.

The costs involved in building something like this must have been enormous. And it was simply a part of the infrastructure of this country, a public good that everyone got to use for free.

It was like having free autonomous taxis around the whole planet—or maybe a train. Icarus decided he wanted something similar to this on his planet.

Icarus angled his wings to give him maximum lift as he exited the air canal. He was moving quickly, so he launched himself into the air, stretching his wings out wide to slide as long as possible. Once he reached the peak of his arc, he summersaulted, then positioned his body in the closest thing to a superhero pose he could muster in this alien body. He hit the ground with a thud and held it for way too long.

He was a little disappointed that Trillion wasn't here to see that. He made the decision to send a recording of that landing to Trillion.

It was still relatively early in the morning, so there weren't too many people about. Icarus noticed a couple of aliens sitting down at what would be considered an alien café.

The Atua didn't really eat solid foods. Most of their diets consisted of thick gloppy soups and shakes. One of their first evolutionary advantages was fermented foods.

Fire was harnessed quite early on in human evolution. Using fire to cook food did more than make it taste better. It unlocked a lot of the nutrition and calories available within meat and grains. It meant humans didn't need to eat as much food, and their brains could consume more energy.

The Atua hunted in the ocean and spent most of their time in coastal areas. So fire wasn't something they'd created for a long, long time.

The Atua had another advantage. Without a moon, they didn't have high tides. So the level of the sea was relatively stable over a long period of time. In small rock pools they learned to leave the creatures they caught for a couple of weeks.

During that time, the mix of food and seawater matured, decomposing into something more edible. Yeasts from the air landed on the food sludge, too, which added to the flavor. They developed a preference for the taste of foods and began experimenting more.

After a while they started carving food-storage containers into rocks to protect their catches from other scavengers. They learned they could speed up the fermentation process by adding in some of the soup from other well-fermented food.

They learned too that mashing up the food further and cooking it inside of warm black rocks all combined together to mean they could cook a meal inside of a few hours.

The unintended consequence of all this food experimentation was they increased the bioavailability of calories inside of the food.

And much like humans learning to cook their food with fire, the Atua's fermentation process meant their brains had more energy to consume.

Fast-forward a few hundred years and all Atua meals were made up of liquidly glop consumed via a straw.

Icarus watched the aliens at the café. In front of each of them were between three or eight small glasses. Icarus assumed each of those glasses contained a different drink. A meal for them was probably made up of several of those drinks, all combining different flavors together. He wasn't sure if they had a version of alcohol yet and decided to find that out later.

Ship arrived, landing next to Icarus. His landing wasn't as impressive, but he was getting better at it all.

They walked the rest of the way to the front of the library. To enter the building, you had to hop on an escalator, and an automatic door would open when you got close enough and close again behind you. Then after some time, another automatic door on the inside would open, too. The stairs of the escalator were such that the two doors never opened at the same time. Icarus assumed this was to keep the wind and noise out.

The inside of the library continued the unique, almost organic, design aesthetic of the Atua. Stairs and columns jutted out of nowhere, some even ending randomly in places.

Icarus assumed, through the additional sense, the Atua people knew which stairs led to nowhere and which were appropriate to use.

Icarus didn't know which direction to go; the place honestly looked like a mess. He wondered whether that was intentional or whether there was something he was missing.

He looked around the room for a sign or any markings.

"Do you know where we go?" Ship asked.

Icarus shook his head.

The problem was all the dead ends and randomness throughout the building meant nothing was clear. It was still relatively empty, so Icarus assumed they had enough time to wander around trying to find somewhere quiet.

Icarus and Ship began their random expedition to explore, meandering slowly down one of the winding paths.

The Atua didn't do straight lines. So after a good while of walking, they began to understand just how hard this process was going to be.

It occurred to Icarus to try his other sense, the one that was unique to the Atua people. It didn't come naturally to him. Using his eyes was still his primary way to see the world. He made the decision to change that; if he wanted to truly embrace this alien world, he needed to begin thinking like them.

Icarus closed his eyes and began scanning the world. The view of everything changed completely. His sense of direction immediately improved. Winding columns that obstructed his view faded. Stairs that led to nowhere again disappeared.

Icarus found it hard to describe. Somehow, he just knew where to go. It was as if each floor resonated with a different kind of music, and pathways to each played notes relevant to each floor.

Not only that, but he knew which floors were busy with people. The rooms spoke back to him. The thirteenth floor was empty. And he heard which path to follow to find his way there.

"Use the echolocation," Icarus said to Ship as he began walking toward one of the walls.

All his human sensors were telling him there was nothing in that direction. But the music was pointing him there.

"Do you know how this works?" Ship asked him.

Icarus had no clue. He guessed it had something to do with the way the objects flexed and changed magnetic fields, and that, combined with the way different materials reflected, absorbed, or changed sound waves, created the experience.

There just wasn't an equivalent to what he was experiencing to a human mind. It was like describing color to a species without eyes. Icarus wondered how he could describe the beauty that was color to someone who had no concept of the thing.

He wondered how he would explain color to someone who only experienced the world through touch. Was it even possible to explain how an object can be completely transformed through a coat of paint? How would someone explain that, even though something felt exactly the same, it looked completely different because of the different wavelengths of light reflecting off the surface?

Icarus decided it was an impossible task. And so explaining what he was experiencing right now was impossible for another human to comprehend without experiencing it.

Icarus decided then and there to figure out how to re-create this experience with Trillion, Atlas, and Angelique. He wanted them to understand this.

"I don't understand how this is so beautiful," Icarus said as a panel in front of the wall slid open.

"I'm struggling to understand how they made this," Ship said. "The only way to describe this is seeing the world in a previously unknown way. Have you ever looked at something in ultraviolet? Have you ever looked at a flower using that wavelength? That's the closest analogy I can think of."

"Music," Icarus said. "That's the best way to describe it."

Ship nodded. "You're right; it's like an orchestra is playing on each floor, and I can tell which way to go to reach any of the floors because individual instruments are clearly audible in each path."

"The only thing that breaks that analogy is I can somehow take in all the music at once. It doesn't sound noisy."

"That's where it's similar to eyesight. I can see everything at once and focus on different things." Icarus walked into the open door and was quickly whisked upstairs by a gust of wind.

Icarus was pushed out onto the thirteenth floor gently.

Icarus mused that these aliens didn't have the same superstitions about a thirteenth floor that humans did.

Ship slid next to him as both surveyed the area.

An alien approached them both from the rear. "If you're here for the new nuctchutuk, we don't have it yet. But we have some of the older stuff."

Icarus heard the translator struggle with one of the words. He didn't want to make it obvious. "We're here for the older stuff."

The Atua made a look that Icarus assumed meant surprise. "Which one were you thinking of? We have everything from the last three-eighteen-one years."

Again, Icarus assumed the translator was literally translating the numbers. They probably made more sense to the locals than to his human ears. He wondered what he was getting himself into. He could feel Ship screaming at him to end the conversation. He decided to go with the flow. "What do you recommend?"

The alien's neck moved around in circles, and its hands kind of jiggled. Icarus didn't know what the sign meant.

"I have the perfect one for you both," the alien said.

The alien guided them into a small round room. The room was a similar technology to the hapticgraphic projectors, only the materials were different. There were several types of materials in this hapticgraphic-projector-based room, each creating a different resonant sound.

"Come see me after if you want to play anything else," the alien said before closing the door.

Icarus and Ship were locked in a room, and the door closed behind them. Then some sort of movie began to play. But unlike a movie Icarus was used to, the whole room changed shape. It not only changed the music or sounds, but it also changed the magnetic resonance of the place.

Icarus wished he understood the meanings of all the changes in magnetic resonance. His only reprieve was there were subtitles. Icarus assumed this was for people who might have a disability. They had a very good understanding of the written language of these aliens from the TV subtitles.

CHAPTER 32

SHIP OF ICARUS

ALIEN CULTURE

Ship learned a lot from the alien experience he and Icarus had just gone through.

It was a full-on sensory explosion. The show, if Ship could call it that, made much more use of senses humans didn't have. Yes, there were things to look at and sounds to hear. But it also made use of the aliens' organ that sensed changes to magnetic fields, as well as their ability to sense in three-dimensional space through echolocation.

For Ship, it was like one of those experimental shows people watched at the museum. Only this wasn't boring. Ship consumed the information eagerly.

The aliens' version of the hapticgraphic projectors changed the shape of the room to tell a story about the history of the aliens.

What Ship learned would stay with him forever. These aliens were all female. At least they started that way.

They all had the ability to switch into a male version of themselves. The aliens on this world underwent a natural sex change when another alien creature entered them.

But these other alien creatures embued the aliens with other powers, too. This was where Ship was a little confused. He wasn't sure whether it was a religious myth or if this was actually how it happened. Apparently, they treated these mythical aliens like some sort of god. And once they had been touched by this other creature, they could think faster, they were faster, and most importantly, they could impregnate other aliens.

Throughout the movie, these other aliens were mentioned as a type of god. And being touched by a god was the ultimate goal in life.

The room was returning to normal as Ship looked at Icarus. "Do you think they really get smarter?"

Icarus shrugged. "I believe it, but I got the sneaking suspicion we received the religions retelling of the truth. I struggle to believe it's their only way of turning into males."

Ship considered that for a moment. "You're right. If the creature produces some sort of chemical that causes the Atua to change gender, then surely that something could be created in a lab."

"I'm keen to see what the aliens in other countries believe. See if they look at things the same way."

The door behind both of them opened once more, and the small alien from before came back.

"Did you enjoy the cinema experience?" she asked them. "You know, Tuktoktok passed away since this was filmed. Once the gods arrive, we won't be able to show this video anymore because there will be some more chosen ones."

"How does someone become a chosen one?"

She looked at them both with a mix of confusion and concern. "Are you Nuknuknoe?"

Ship didn't understand the word but assumed it meant an idiot or some other slang for someone who didn't know much.

"We are," Icarus said.

"You poor child," she said as she grabbed both of them by the fronts of their clothes and started to pull them forward. "I wondered why you were both acting weird. How long have you been out?"

Icarus did his best impression of an alien shrugging. "Not that long."

"Please don't take offense," the alien said. "But I hope they shut down those communes. They don't teach our true history. They are obsessed with creating life without gods. I'm glad you made it out."

Ship was so confused. It sounded like they were an outcast group of this society. Or maybe they were people who believed in conspiracy theories.

"It's sad really because you're disqualified from being one of the chosen ones," the lady said as she guided them toward a new door. "All because you were born inside of the Nuknuknoe. But it's for the best; the gods were right to cut those people out of the bloodline."

"Who are the gods?" Ship asked.

"You poor soul. They don't teach you anything in there, do they?"

Both Ship and Icarus moved their necks in a circular motion, which was the aliens' body language for no. They were picking things up quickly.

"Last cycle, one of the chosen ones was cast out by the gods for his blasphemous ideas. But he was still able to reproduce. He corrupted some females and created the Nuknuknoe. I would never think to question the word of the gods. But they choose to make sure none of you ever become chosen rather than smiting you all."

Ship realized this lady was suggesting the gods should have killed him and Icarus.

Icarus grabbed hold of Ship's hand so they could talk in private. "I'm not sure the translator is working on what they call the gods."

"Maybe they're another country that enslaved these people," Ship said. "I assume this is how they control what the population believes, by controlling who can breed."

"You two head in there. I have a couple more movies to show you." The alien pushed them inside. "Don't worry, I'll come grab you if the gods get here early." She closed the door with an audible thud.

Ship and Icarus found themselves in an even larger cinema room. The title of the short documentary they were watching was roughly translated to *The Dangers of Nuknuknoe.*

Several short films later, Ship and Icarus had an even greater understanding of the Atua people. And they even had a better understanding of why this alien lady was treating them as children. In her mind, they had just escaped a cult and were still brainwashed. She was showing them this because she believed they needed reeducating.

Ship was grateful for this turn of events. He couldn't believe how lucky they had been with this whole situation. He was starting to believe Icarus had been right when he'd pushed for them to come here. Yes, it was a risk. But none of this information was available on the television channels they had access to for free. Maybe it was because the television channels Ship and Icarus had watched were the limited free broadcasts, and so they weren't able to watch the good stuff. But whatever it was, they hadn't consumed anything nearly as informationally dense as this show they'd just watched.

It made Ship believe the next most important step was to figure out how to get into their internet. If they had something similar to a World Wide Web, then perhaps he could get access to it.

The door behind Ship opened, and he noticed it was the same alien as before.

"Do you have any more questions?" the alien asked. "I know that was a lot to take in. I know someone else who escaped the Nuknuknoe. They watched these shows too and didn't know whom to believe. They became angry at the world afterward." She looked at each of them earnestly. Ship was starting to understand the body language of these people a lot more. She was showing genuine kindness as she spoke. "It's not your fault. A fish doesn't control where the fishing nets are. A bird doesn't control where the wind is blowing."

Ship got the feeling she was sharing a parable that the translator wasn't picking up properly. He assumed she was trying to say they had no control over where they were born.

Ship was starting to like this lady. He did the aliens' version of a smile, which involved a guttural growl and a movement of the mouth—but he didn't show the teeth; that would be a sign of aggression. "What's your name?"

"Niomi-oku," the lady replied.

Ship had to ask about the gods; he still didn't understand who they were and whether they were real or not. He was so confused by the way the movies talked about them. "How much of that movie was real? Are the gods real?"

"I'm sorry, my child," she said, grabbing them both, this time by their flippers, and leading them down the passageway. "I see now they didn't explain anything to you. I know this is going to be confusing. The Nuknuknoe have brainwashed you. They told you all these lies.

"The gods are the ones that help us bring others into this world. When they come, they choose a few thousand to change." She pointed at the chests of both Ship and Icarus, right where a special pouch was located. "They enter the chosen ones through there. They give the chosen ones powers. They give them the ability to create life. They give them knowledge of everything they know."

Ship listened intently to her as she confirmed things he thought he knew. But seeing her talk about it made him realize everything was real. None of this was made up. These other aliens entered inside of their bodies and changed them from females to males. They gave them the ability to impregnate others.

"Where do the gods live usually?" Icarus asked her.

"Deep in the ocean. They cannot reproduce like us. They must hide from the world; otherwise they risk dying. And if they die, we will have no way to reproduce."

"Are they intelligent?"

Niomi-oku did the alien version of a gasp, which involved swinging her head back rapidly. "You silly child, surely you know the truth."

Ship tried to make his best impression of an apology.

"They built the world we live in. They gave us all the technology we have. We owe everything to them. Without them we wouldn't have mathematics, science, technology. That's why they're our gods; they created everything for us."

Ship opened his mouth to ask another question, but Niomi-oku raised her shoulders to signal she wasn't done talking.

"Now, be careful talking to others about this. Others would kill you right away if they found out you were from Nuknuknoe. So don't go offending the gods like that. I know the Nuknuknoe tell you lies about the gods controlling us. Or that there is a way to build artificial males through chemicals. But none of that is true. We provide nothing of value to the gods. They don't have to share these gifts with us. They visit us and give us the gift of life, the power to think, and everything we have all for free. They seek nothing in return."

Ship felt Icarus grab his hand so they could talk in private. "Oh my god, Ship. This planet gets better than I thought; there are two intelligent aliens on this world."

Ship agreed. "Everyone we spoke to here seems humbler than that alien Atlas and the others met. It makes more sense that the alien they encountered was talking through the alien they met." Ship decided to confirm that fact with a question to Niomi-oku. "Can the gods talk through the chosen ones?"

"Of course. How else would they share their knowledge? They control the bodies of the chosen and live among us for three cycles."

"How do you get chosen?" Ship asked.

"Are you asking for yourself? Remember, you're disqualified because you might be a Nuknuknoe spy. I'm not sure how the gods decide whom to take. I know that only the special get chosen, and if you're chosen, it's for a reason."

A loud noise began playing over the speaker.

Niomi-oku looked up toward the speaker with a happy expression. "The gods are arriving to select the chosen ones. They'll be crawling onto the beach on the southwest side soon. I suggest you go there." She pushed them both toward one of the slides. "We're closing the library for the rest of the day."

Ship and Icarus were pushed out into the streets, where the city was alive with thousands of small aliens all racing in a similar direction. Ship assumed that was the direction the gods were coming from.

CHAPTER 33

ICARUS

SECOND ENCOUNTER

Icarus looked up and down the streets trying to find a way through the crowd of aliens. It reminded him a lot of downtown New York on a busy day.

The rows and rows of people were all moving deliberately through the chaos. He really wanted to follow the crowd and find a spot to watch the other aliens' arrival.

Icarus noted that one good thing about these aliens was their design of public transport. Icarus guessed he was looking at a sea of maybe a million people, all moving like sardines in the same direction. He and Ship were even bumped into a couple of times as people moved past.

Icarus was glad these aliens didn't use cars. It would have been complete gridlock if they had this many people moving in the same direction on any of his planets, where cars were still one of the primary means of transport.

Icarus thought some more about it and realized he hadn't seen any children and wondered how they moved through the city. The air canals were potentially dangerous to anyone small. He knew that they didn't populate like humans. Only chosen ones had the ability to impregnate others. But surely there would still be little ones around.

Icarus began scanning the crowd looking for any signs of young aliens. As if answering his question, Icarus saw an alien riding some sort of scooter-looking thing along the air canal. Belted onto the side of the scooter were two smaller aliens. Icarus wondered whether that was a pram of sorts.

"We need to go watch the arrival of these alien gods."

Ship looked a little worried. "I was hoping we could regroup with Lex. We can watch it on the TV."

"We can't miss this live, Ship. This is the biggest event this country will have this year. It's our opportunity to see who's really behind the curtain, see the alien controlling everything on this planet."

Icarus couldn't get over the fact there was another intelligent alien on this planet. He wondered how that alien had coevolved with the penguin-looking aliens. How did it all work? His mind started to race through possibilities. Icarus knew that cats and dogs had become smarter and more docile because humans had unknowingly selected animals with specific traits. Humans deliberately bred sausage dogs, dogs that were small and long, so they could fit into badger holes. Humans effectively made them for hunting.

From what he understood, these godlike aliens controlled who on the planet could have children. Through controlling who the chosen ones were, they wielded the real power—they controlled the gene pool of this species.

"Ship, which do you think came first?" Icarus asked. "The aliens with the god complex or the aliens that look like penguins?"

"Is that some kind of chicken-or-the-egg joke?"

Icarus laughed; he honestly wasn't thinking like that. Although, now that Ship pointed it out, he wished he had come up with a similar joke. "It's a serious question. Who came first, the penguins or the gods?"

"It has to be the gods, if they really are the ones controlling everything. But then, why would they go inside of the penguins? And the penguins need to exist for them to enter." Then Ship scratched his head, another human action he needed to stop doing. "Neither of them turn into each other, so I'm not sure."

"I get the feeling the gods became intelligent first and selected for the most intelligent penguins. But I'm just guessing. It sounds like these two species coevolved," Icarus mused. "We need to find a way to interact with these other aliens. We need to understand how they think." He paused, noticing Ship's discomfort at the idea. "Don't worry, Ship, we'll be fully prepared for meeting them when the time comes. And if that means heading back to Lex, then we'll do that."

Icarus noticed Ship's tension noticeably drop with that comment, so he took that as a sign it was time for them to move forward.

Icarus was getting used to his organ for sensing changes in magnetic fields. He noticed that having this many aliens around wasn't as daunting when he used that organ. With the organ, he gained a better understanding of just how many people there were. But he also saw the gaps in the crowd too. The ways he could move in order to not get stuck.

There was a gap in the air canal coming up. Not only could he tell that there was a space along the tube he and Ship could jump into, he also saw that no other alien was moving to take advantage of it.

He wasn't used to sensing the magnetic fields of aliens yet but was guessing each person had a unique fingerprint. He was almost certain the auras he and Ship were giving off weren't quite right. He knew Lex was going to have to do a lot of upgrading to their avatars once they got back with this new treasure trove of information. "Ship, there's a gap in the flow."

Icarus guided them toward the alien wind transport, and they jumped in. They were blown down the track faster than before. Icarus could feel himself and Ship were being forced to catch up to the aliens in front of them.

Icarus couldn't tell if this was a simple matter of air currents naturally flowing to make this happen. The air canal might have a computer or something pulling the strings. Icarus realized how impressive the design of it was. The reason he was able to notice a gap in the flow of aliens was this air canal had created it. And the reason no other alien was moving quickly to take that gap was because they trusted there would be others.

Icarus felt the aliens all around him getting denser and denser. Icarus was struggling to get a read on everyone as they were so tightly packed in.

Interestingly, Icarus knew exactly where he was in relation to the beach everyone was heading toward. He could feel everyone around him and knew he wasn't going to find any place to view what was happening through the crowd.

The locals kept scrambling toward that one place though. And because these aliens were so small, Icarus was sure no one but the people at the very front would be able to see.

The air canal was about to split up ahead: One way would take him into the denser part of the crowd. The other way would take him up on a hill, where he sensed a lot fewer aliens. From the top of that hill, he would be able to see everything clearly. He wondered why not that many aliens were gathered up there.

Then Icarus thought about it a bit more. Maybe they weren't expecting to see it all with their eyes. Maybe everyone would be using that organ that was unique to these aliens.

Icarus needed to make a decision quickly; the turning point was coming up. He decided to watch from the top of the hill. Even though the prospect of watching everything from a truly alien perspective was tempting, he and Ship still favored their eyes as a means of taking in information. He doubted they had the knowledge to properly experience it all.

Turning right, he exited the air canal at the top of the ridge, a good few hundred meters away. He sensed Ship pulling up behind him.

With their enhanced eyes, they could zoom in on the excitement and watch as if they were in the front row. There were several people around them. Icarus assumed they didn't have as good of eyesight as humans. On Earth, this would've been the perfect spot.

Icarus grabbed hold of Ship's hand. He didn't want to take any chances of someone overhearing their conversation. He was painfully aware that their magnetic resonance, or whatever it was called, was different from everyone else's. He made it a priority to come up with a name for this sense the aliens had.

"Do you have any ANTs?" Icarus asked. "Any that can sense magnetic fields?"

"A couple. Why?"

"I want to get a recording of everything that happens down there." Icarus pointed to the sea of aliens all crammed together near the water. "I want to see if there's anything else we are missing."

Ship knelt down toward the ground, pretending he was picking up something. Out of the palm of his flipper, a micro-ANT jumped out. It immediately started to go across the ground before flying high up into the sky.

Quickly, it crossed the distance and dropped like a rock, scurrying to hide beneath the sand.

"The ANT will stay there, recording everything. And once the beach is empty, it'll swim its way back to Lex with everything it recorded," Ship said.

Icarus watched as a giant spacecraft appeared along the horizon, a large floating circular ship, similar to the one that had encountered Atlas and the others. It was moving toward the beach quickly. The speed left a noticeable ripple across the water.

Icarus focused on the magnetic lines created by the large ship. It was leaving noticeable patterns in the water. And those ripples were multiplied by the water—creating an interesting effect to Icarus's ability to sense echolocations.

Icarus was glad he'd made the decision to send a small ANT down there. To humans, it would have made more sense for them to fly in from the sky, so everyone could see what was happening clearly. But Icarus now understood why everyone was crowded down by the beach.

Unlike using human eyes, sensing the world through a magnetic field or echolocation wasn't impeded by others being in the way. So every single one of those aliens out there in the crowd was probably experiencing the arrival of their gods as if they were in the very front row.

The alien spacecraft was hovering just above the water. Icarus guessed it was one hundred meters away from the beach.

The water around the ship started to shake violently. Then the waves began oscillating and moving back and forth. Icarus saw several standing waves appearing all around. There was a deep message being told in those waves. Icarus made it his mission to translate what was said later.

The water right beneath the alien spacecraft started to move upward, almost like an invisible straw had appeared below the ship. The column of water became thicker and thicker as it continued to rise up slowly toward the alien vessel.

Once it reached the ship, it stopped moving. Icarus used his enhanced vision to take a closer look. The water was crystal clear, however they were using the hapticgraphic engine; it was suspending water perfectly still above the ground. Icarus knew Atlas would be interested in this application of similar tech to what he'd invented.

Icarus saw dark-black fish swimming up the column of water.

"I think that's the aliens coming out of the water," Ship said. "Enhance your vision and you can see they look almost like eels or squid."

Icarus looked closer; he saw those animals looked very similar to the cephalopod-like animals Lex had first seen swimming around the base it had constructed.

Icarus wasn't religious, but he found himself praying that it was a different species. He hoped those squid-looking mollusks were distant relatives of these animals and not them.

This was his first time ever seeing the aliens, so differentiating between them and evolutionary cousins was impossible.

He wondered whether they would have a similar struggle trying to tell humans apart from monkeys. In his mind, a gorilla and a human were obviously different. But maybe an alien that evolved to distinguish between different tentacle shapes couldn't tell which was which.

Icarus turned to see Ship and noticed his face. He looked like he'd seen a ghost. It was a clear human look of worry. He obviously realized they might be the same aliens that Lex had scared away when they'd first arrived.

Icarus shook Ship's hand. "Don't worry. They look different from the animals hanging around our base underwater," Icarus lied because he wasn't sure himself. But he knew there wasn't much point in worrying too much, as they couldn't do anything about it. Icarus assumed they wouldn't be there right now if their cover was blown. So he assumed there was a low likelihood of it being the same animal as before.

Before Icarus had a chance to think about it all a little longer, things around the alien spacecraft began to change. The outside of the ship began to move and deform like water. It looked like a bunch of material was being spewed out of the spacecraft. It was forming like a small wave.

The penguin aliens near the waterfront started moving side to side as if a wave was moving through them all. Icarus was almost confident they were reacting to a change in magnetic fields.

They began taking off their clothes and throwing them to the side. Icarus noticed a lot of them already had no tops on.

Out the front of the alien spacecraft a platform appeared. It was massive. It shimmered in the light, clearly designed to carry something. The platform dipped into the water.

The penguin-looking aliens began clambering over one another, every one of them moving as quickly as they could to clamber onto the platform.

Icarus watched as thousands of these now-naked aliens shuffled their way onto the submerged stand.

This went on for a good long while.

"These must be the chosen ones," Icarus said.

"This actually looks like a penguin colony."

Icarus agreed with Ship's assessment; it did look like a colony of the birds. It was amazing how the evolutionary paths were so similar.

The platform began to rise, and the aliens began floating up.

Icarus watched as several unlucky ones fell off the edge and back into the water.

There were a few thousand aliens all piled up waiting for something to happen.

What happened next would stay with Icarus for the rest of his life. It was the most disturbing ritual he'd ever seen.

Several pipelike objects on top of the spacecraft opened up right above the platform all the penguins were standing on.

Then it began raining the squid aliens. Hundreds of the little slimy aliens began falling from the tubes that now appeared. They landed on the faces of the penguins and slid down into their chest cavities.

It was an open space in their chests that developed specifically for these other aliens. Icarus felt like he could hear a slurping sound as the cephalopods crawled inside. He couldn't actually hear that because he was too far away, but his mind had no problems making up the disgusting sounds.

"This is like a nightmare of a horror movie," Ship said.

"I've had to turn off my gag reflex. This is worse than that scene from *The Suicide Squad*."

"Imagine all these things attacking humans on our planet. Squirming inside everyone's brain. Entering through the nose to control their minds."

Icarus shuddered at the thought. That was the worst kind of alien invasion. "New subject. I can't get that image out of my mind."

"Do you think they've visited Earth? Do you think they've done that already? They freely admit that they pushed humanity toward the simulation."

Icarus thought about it. That was a great question. These aliens had evolved to enter the minds of another alien species, to take over their bodies and control them but also make them smarter.

Icarus was starting to gain an understanding of why the Atua did what it did. It did to humans what felt natural. They didn't see anything wrong with taking over the minds of another sentient species. Humans were like these penguin aliens. "They did come to Earth and enter our minds—metaphorically. I don't think they burrowed into our brains physically. It wouldn't work. They didn't evolve to interact with our brain chemistry.

"But they did find another way to get inside our heads," Icarus continued. "They pushed everyone into the simulation, where they could take control of everything we thought about. Manipulate us in ways we didn't know."

Icarus was starting to see the world from these Atua's perspective. He knew now that the alien Atlas and the others had met was this squid-like alien. This was the Atua. The penguins were a different alien altogether.

Icarus tried to shift his perspective, change his way of thinking, look at this situation from the aliens' perspective. *Was there an alien version of anthropomorphizing?* he wondered to himself. "Do you think the Atua believe they are helping the penguins?" Icarus didn't have another name for the penguin-looking aliens so decided to just call them the penguins for now.

"They are giving them the ability to breed. They're changing their sex. The penguins wouldn't survive to reproduce without them. So yes, I do."

Icarus tried to think about these aliens coming to Earth to brainwash humanity. "Do you believe they thought they were helping humanity when they went to Earth and attempted to manipulate everyone?"

Ship opened his mouth to speak, then closed it again. There was a long pause as his mind worked through the question. "I'm not sure. I don't know enough about them. If I were to guess, I don't think they cared whether they were helping us or not. If you think about it, we brought a bunch of embryos, animals, and plant life from Mars to a completely different star system. We didn't stop once to ask whether any of those things would mind. If you think about it, we moved hundreds of unfertilized human eggs and sperm across two sections of the Milky Way. In some ways, that's like moving a human to another planet without asking them. You wouldn't do that to a human against their will—but we did with the ingredients for humans."

Icarus understood the point Ship was trying to make. It went back to the philosophical argument of when life begins. Was sperm life? Was an egg life? What made it different when the two ingredients came together?

In Icarus's mind, what he'd done was completely ethical. There wasn't some grey area; none of it was human life until the embryo started to grow. None of his people regretted what he did for them; none of them wanted to go back to Sol.

The Atua probably had a similar understanding of the facts. They saw nothing wrong with controlling humans in the way they did. In all honesty, most of the humans still back on Earth were probably grateful for it.

Trying to look at the world from the perspective of the Atua was beginning to hurt Icarus's head.

He started to look again at the platform full of penguin aliens. He watched as some of the Atua slid out of the chests of one penguin and into the chest of another one.

Icarus got the feeling that the Atua were trying out different bodies. Maybe they were reading the minds of the penguins to get an understanding of which body they wanted to inhabit.

Icarus knew the Atua would normally stay inside of the penguins for about seven months, give or take.

Icarus watched as another platform manifested and floated down toward the water.

A similar scene unfolded as more and more of the penguin aliens scrambled to get on the structure.

Icarus didn't know how long this would go for, but there wasn't a shortage of penguins wanting to jump on a platform. And from the body language of everyone below, everyone who wanted an opportunity to become a chosen one would get a chance.

Icarus and Ship watched from the vantage point on the hill for the rest of the day as wave after wave of penguins were picked up and delivered to the Atua.

Penguins that were not chosen were eventually forced off the platform. Penguins that were chosen by an Atua got to ride the platform into the spaceship. It became clear when one of them was chosen because the Atua embedded itself in the chest of the penguin. It looked almost like the penguin had a single breast in the middle of the chest.

This went on for a long, long while. Until it just stopped. The alien ship floated back into the sky.

Icarus expected some sort of speech—but there was nothing. Icarus thought that was odd, until he realized that he was on an alien world—human norms didn't matter.

"What now?" Ship asked as the crowds below began to dissipate. "If my memory is correct, the tour will be back in five days to introduce the new chosen ones."

Icarus was grateful that Ship remembered everything from those movies. He'd forgotten that part. That would give them both enough time to do some more research. To find out new answers. To understand this world a lot better. "Do you remember the name of that commune?"

"Nuknuknoe," Ship responded.

"We're going there next."

CHAPTER 34

ANGELIQUE

YOU KNOW WHERE THEY ARE?

Angelique and her Ange's Angels were all well into their respective missions, traveling to every corner of their immediate region of space.

Angelique chose to head to Atlas herself rather than staying on the planet waiting for everyone to come back. She was a beta explorer after all. Staying on a planet waiting for her Ange's Angels to return just wasn't her style.

It meant she would be slightly out of the loop with everything gained from those planets as her Ange's Angels returned to Everest with all their new technology and knowledge. But she considered that a reasonable sacrifice to make. Her Ange's Angels would probably seek her out, anyway, since they had a piece of code in them driving them to merge with her.

Angelique was fast approaching the Tac system—the system where Atlas had set up his base.

As she looked out the window of the starship, she got a sense for why Atlas had chosen to do his research here. The system was completely strip-mined. She got a sense that building anything was possible given the amount of resources freely available and moving out in space.

It was a buzz of dead movement. It was beginning to closely resemble a Dyson swarm.

A Dyson swarm was the evolution of an idea from Freeman Dyson. He believed that as civilizations got more technologically advanced, they'd eventually require all the energy produced by a star. He envisioned a K2 civilization would cover their star in a dome to capture all the light that came off it.

The trouble was building a monolithic structure around a star wasn't practical. So the idea was updated to become a swarm of probes around the star. Eventually, with enough probes, the whole star would be completely covered, and all energy would be captured by these probes.

Whatever Atlas was constructing had him well on his way to constructing a Dyson swarm. She hated to think just how many flying objects were moving around the system right now. She noticed at times her view of the star was completely obstructed as a cluster of probes, so thick she couldn't see through them, whizzed past.

When Angelique had originally started this journey, she'd had the construction of a Dyson swarm on her bucket list. It was all the rage when she was back on Earth. Up until she'd actually terraformed a planet, she'd believed the natural progress for humans was to eventually move into orbit on trillions of small platforms.

The problem with a Dyson swarm was biological life needed protection from cosmic rays, and the easiest way to protect it was keeping it on a big rock with a thick atmosphere and strong magnetic field.

The other interesting fact about being able to design a city from scratch was humans didn't take up that much space. It was a common misconception that you needed a lot of land to house a billion people.

She assumed that myth came from the fact most cities back on Earth had evolved and grown over time. They weren't planned from the beginning to hold several million people.

Since she got to design her cities from the start, she was able to organize them perfectly. She also had the other benefits of flying robotic taxis, so her people never had issues with traffic. Farms were all automated and controlled by an algorithm so they were as efficient as possible.

In her experience, there wasn't much benefit to building a Dyson swarm. It wasn't even energy efficient, since fusion reactors created more energy than solar panels could capture given the same surface area. She didn't even use solar panels much on tidally locked planets because the panels simply blocked usable soil.

Angelique hailed Atlas again, knowing she was within near-real-time-communication distance.

A few minutes later she received a reply from the Lex in the system giving her the location of where Atlas was. Lex let her know Atlas was deep in concentration trying to solve a problem, but it was alerting Atlas of their arrival.

Angelique and her Ship made their way slowly toward a massive spacecraft that was the same model as the one she left Mars in. She found it interesting that he was still using the outdated model, even though she'd already shared a bunch of new designs with him.

After docking the two spacecrafts together and building a secure connection between the two, Angelique and her Ship hopped over to Atlas's research lab. Looking around the room, she saw Atlas and his Ship in front of mountains of papers. "You look like you've been busy."

Atlas looked up from behind his huge stack of documents. He had a massive smile on his face. "Angelique, sorry I waited for you to come to me. As soon as I saw you enter the system, I wanted to say hi. But I knew I wouldn't be able to keep this secret for that long if I did."

"Secret?" Angelique eyed him curiously. "Good secret or bad?"

"I know where the Atua are," he blurted out. "I know of eight star systems that they've colonized so far."

Atlas handed over a piece of paper with a bunch of planetary images on it. They looked like they had been taken from orbit. It was clear these planets had intelligent life on them because they were awash with visible light sources. They were high-definition images of the planets. "I've taken these pictures of the planets I've found."

"What?!" Angelique didn't know how to react to that. She knew on some level they'd be out there colonizing other worlds, but for Atlas to know exactly which star systems they were in, her mind was full of questions. "How?" Then she thought back to all the probes moving out in orbit around the system. Had he used the star to bend light like a telescope? Thinking about it again, it had to be the only way. "You used gravitational lensing to take an image, didn't you?"

Atlas smiled and then nodded. Angelique knew he was impressed that she understood how it was done.

Angelique believed it was theoretically possible to do. Some of her scientists back on Earth suggested they create something similar. The idea had never progressed though because having that many satellites in orbit around the star raised the chances they'd be detected. In every discussion they'd had around the topic, the strategic value of such a massive undertaking wasn't as big as building a standard telescope. Angelique was beginning to think she'd been wrong.

Angelique noticed something familiar about the planet she was looking at. It reminded her of one of her early ones. Then she realized it was one of hers. Atlas had clearly identified one of the planets she hadn't told him about.

She'd made the decision long ago to keep some of her planets well hidden from all the others, partly as an experiment and partly as a security measure. She knew that if something went wrong on one of her worlds, they wouldn't have knowledge about the locations of all her colonies.

Looking at what Atlas had shown her, she quickly realized how any sufficiently advanced civilization could quickly identify all other worlds that were habited.

Angelique finished looking at all the planets. She laid seven on one of the tables and then handed one back to Atlas. "This is the only one I don't know about. These others are mine." She looked over at her Ship. "Can you check I'm right?"

"Those look right to me," Ship said after reviewing the files. "Do you want me to share the classified documents with Atlas?"

The classified documents were a separate collection of data about all the planets Angelique had colonized. They contained more information than what she'd shared with the leaders of the planets. Angelique considered it for a moment. It looked like Atlas would eventually discover all her planets, anyway. She decided there wasn't much point in waiting for him to discover them all—or wasting his time discovering systems she already knew about. "Do it."

Her Ship looked toward Atlas's Ship. "Do you want to come with me? I'll transfer you the files now."

The security protocols were such that giving Ship the files would require him to physically plug into her spaceship.

Angelique and Atlas were left alone to discuss things.

It was Atlas's turn to eye her suspiciously. "I should have known you had more worlds that you let on."

"I should probably let you know I have a few sleeper systems too. Empty planets where I've hidden a few fabricators and radio dishes. I can broadcast a copy of myself to one of them if I needed to. They'll all be contained in the files Ship shares with you." Then she looked down at the world that she didn't know about. "This one is new though. Are you sure it's not one of Trillion's or Icarus's?"

"Not a chance," Atlas said. "Trillion's confirmed it's not one of hers. And Icarus got so excited about exploring an alien world that he's snuck onto the planet to visit them."

"Visit the aliens?" she asked a little uncertainly. "Do you know what kind of aliens they are?"

"We're about seventy percent certain they're the Atua, the same aliens that brainwashed Earth. Ariana is confident it's them because the biosignatures of the planets are similar to the samples she took from the spacecraft."

"Wait, Ariana's here too? Has everyone come and visited you?"

"The Starnet, remember? I've been working on rebuilding the connection between everyone ever since the unit in this system blew up. Trillion is currently trying to talk to a cloud. Icarus is offline, trying to sneak onto an alien world." Atlas paused for a moment. "And Ariana is on her way here. I got confirmation a while back that she escaped an attack from the Atua people who came back to finish the job."

Angelique realized she had so much to catch up on. She thought Icarus had made a stupid decision. "He visited their home world? What if they get caught?" Then she thought about it a bit more; he would probably get caught. There was no way an alien could sneak onto one of her worlds. At least she hoped not. "How much about my world did Icarus know?"

Angelique knew she was being selfish by focusing her questions on the risks to her worlds rather than being concerned for the well-being of Icarus. But ultimately it was his decision to go there. She just didn't want his dumb mistake to cost her.

"He specifically didn't want to know for that exact reason. And he programmed his spacecraft to self-destruct if they got caught."

"How will we know if he self-destructs?"

Atlas scratched his chin. "We won't. But he left the backup in one of his systems, I can't remember how long they set the timer. But the backup will turn on if it hasn't had confirmation from Icarus in a few thousand years."

Angelique thought about it a bit more. What was done was done. She couldn't change the past. And it probably didn't matter, anyway, since, with the telescope Atlas had access to, no alien civilization could hide. Not even ones covered by a cloaking bubble.

She realized the benefits of the Starnet now outweighed the costs. Since any advanced alien could identify all her spacecraft, she needed to speed up the communications between her colonies. "Speaking of alien worlds," Angelique said, changing the subject. "Do you think you could make the Starnet work without needing a constant stream of particles?"

Atlas bit his lower lip. "You don't want the Starnet giving away the position of all your planets?"

Angelique nodded. "If I can help it."

Atlas nodded his head. "There's a way. The reason the Starnet is constantly broadcasting signals is because it only has one quantum entanglement device. But I could create a billion of them at once, preload a few hundred years' worth of entangled particles, then keep half of them here while we send a spacecraft to your planets with the other half."

Angelique nodded, not quite understanding what he was talking about but glad he'd found a solution. "How long would that take?"

"Maybe a few hours. There's a lot of resources in this system. I can do anything quickly."

Angelique again was impressed with how useful a resource-based system like this was.

She handed a memory stick to Atlas. "Before I forget, Peter sent you a few recorded messages. He wants you to build a weapon."

Atlas raised an eyebrow at that comment. "What sort of weapon?"

"He's confident we're going to be attacked by the Atua people soon. And from what you said about Ariana, he might be right. Anyway, he wants you to build something big. Something capable of destroying an entire planet in one shot. He wants it as a deterrent, just in case we get into a war."

CHAPTER 35

ICARUS

NUKNUKNOE

Immediately after watching the Atua take over thousands of bodies, Icarus and Ship headed back toward their base under the sea.

They had a lot of research to do and improvements to make to their alien bodies. They updated their algorithms for alien body language. They had Lex improved the translator software. They even improved the translation layer between them and the bodies they inhabited to ensure no more human tics or expressions filtered through.

They still hadn't re-created the magnetic auras the aliens gave off. It was a better approximation, but because they didn't realize how important the sense was to the aliens, they didn't have a sensor with enough fidelity to re-create it perfectly yet.

Icarus expected the next expedition to collect data.

Icarus and Ship debated over which country to visit. In the end, they decided it was best to stick with the country they knew until their avatars were completely indistinguishable from any other alien.

And besides, Icarus thought he could learn a lot from visiting the Nuknuknoe, the commune created by a disgruntled Penquin who had once had an Atua inside of him.

Icarus had decided to start calling the penguin-looking aliens Penquins and the squid-like aliens the Atua. It was becoming too confusing in his mind for the two species to not have unique names.

Getting into the Nuknuknoe was harder than they'd first imagined.

They knew where it was, and so they traveled there. It was near a rocky part of a beach. They had literally transformed this horrible section of the coast with mud huts. Technology and the ability to build things were strictly controlled by the Atua. All the buildings Icarus had seen previously around the city were created by robots.

So this commune needed to be built the old way, with mud bricks and clay. The buildings look like the Penquins had chewed up bits of mud and grass and spat them over some sort of scaffolding, which was almost true. It was probably how houses were made thousands of years ago.

They fermented a grass-mud mixture in one of the hot pools and used that as the material for the buildings. As it dried, some of the bacteria created lime, which hardened like concrete.

The mud huts didn't have the same asymmetrical beauty as the buildings Icarus had seen around the city. But there was still low rustic attractiveness in it all.

Icarus and Ship arrived at what was the largest mud building and knelt down with their flippers facing up. It was a submissive nonthreatening gesture. It was meant to convey that they were there to learn and obey.

Icarus and Ship just lay there in that position for a few hours. They'd heard from others that this was the only way to prove they were committed to getting invited in.

A couple of times, they heard Penquins yelling out for them to leave. They ignored those calls and just lay there.

After what felt like an entire day, two pots of cold gloppy-looking food were placed next to them. Icarus took this as a sign they were invited to stay. The gesture meant the Penquins in the commune didn't want them to starve.

When nighttime came, they were handed a blanket and told to sleep in a little hut.

The next morning, they were handed another pot of the glop. A few hours later, someone from the commune, they didn't get her name, handed them both a large bucket.

They had given them the task of carrying fermented mud from one of the hot pools to an empty section of the commune. None of the other Penquins came close to them; they all gave Icarus and Ship a lot of space.

For the entire day, they completed manual labor and built a hut. Then they lit a fire inside of the hut, which they were told had to be kept going all night.

So Icarus and Ship took turns pretending to sleep, while the other carried wood to burn inside of the building.

The next day, they were told to build another one.

Icarus was torn about what to do next. He knew the Atua were heading back to the city soon; they would be presenting the new chosen ones and would probably share news. He wanted to be there for that. He got the feeling they were just being used for manual labor. They would probably spend the next several days making houses for these people before eventually being kicked out. He was torn on whether to leave now to watch the arrival of the Atua or wait and hope something changed.

The only thing that kept him going was the fact he was on an alien world living like an alien, collecting more data to improve their algorithms for how these aliens operated. He'd also left a few ANTs on the beach recording everything that happened, so he would eventually find out what they said.

He counted fifty-two Penquins in the commune. They had drones all around the property collecting data. So when it was time to leave, they'd have an opportunity to review all the recordings.

On the tenth day, one Penquin approached them. Icarus wasn't sure if they'd be asked to leave now. They hadn't met this Penquin before, but by the looks of the others, this alien was respected.

"What are your names?"

"I'm Icarus, and this is Ship." Icarus knew his translator would select similar enough names for them both. The translator would automatically convert all mentions of their names to something an alien would understand.

"My name is Atuatuk." The Penquin studied them both for a good long while, looking at them both before closing its eyes. Icarus got the feeling Atuatuk was studying their magnetic fields. "Why auras so wrong?"

Icarus knew how to respond to this. He and Ship had discussed which excuse to use because it was the only answer that left a lot of room for interpretation. "We offered ourselves to become some of the chosen ones. We were thrown away." This meant that they had offered their bodies to the Atua and were declined. It meant that the Atua had entered their bodies but then decided not to use them.

"You might be dying," Atuatuk said solemnly. "Many of the rejected end up dead. You were right to come here. My children, I know what you're going through. You feel lost; you feel without purpose. I will give you purpose."

Icarus noticed his speaking cadence was different from the other Penquins. He sounded a lot more similar to the alien Atlas, Peter, and Angelique had met. It wasn't the same, but it was similar.

"Are you one of the chosen ones?" Ship asked.

Atuatuk rolled down the top of his shirt to reveal a wound over his chest. It had crusted, as if it had slowly healed over many years. "I was chosen. But my Atua died before it was ready to leave me. It left me with all the knowledge but none of the shackles."

Icarus looked at him, studying him in detail. "What do you mean by shackles?"

"I will tell you soon." He pointed at the two huts that they both had spent the last few days building. "These are your homes now. Use them. Sleep in them. And we will talk when the sun rises."

Atuatuk went to walk away but then turned around and looked at both of them. Again his face showed the alien version of compassion. "It won't feel like this for you now. But be grateful you weren't chosen."

"Why? I don't understand," Icarus said, acting as if he saddened by the fact he wasn't chosen.

Atuatuk paused for a moment. He looked like he was deciding whether to tell them the truth or not. "Once you join with Atua, neither of you are the same. You won't just coexist in the body. You become the Atua; the Atua becomes you. You become something different, something more. But the Atua are stronger; their willpower is great. So you mostly become them." Atuatuk stepped away from them both once more. "Now go sleep. We talk in the morning."

Did Atuatuk really just say they became a different person after being chosen? He'd always imagined it as two species coexisting in the same body, two separate minds interacting with each other and sharing knowledge.

But when he thought more about it, then maybe it made sense that they became one person. How can you share knowledge with someone without them experiencing what you know?

Icarus wondered whether the Atua became an amalgamation of all the different Penquins they entered. Then again, it might be a different experience for the gods. Atuatuk did say that the Atua were stronger, and it was their minds that took control of things.

Icarus did know that there were some experiments in psychology that proved human consciousness was just the mind's way of rationalizing the decisions people made. Maybe this was simply Atuatuk's way of rationalizing all the new knowledge he'd acquired.

He'd preserved his sense of self by believing he'd become a new entity when he was linked to the Atua.

Regardless, Icarus decided he could learn more about this all tomorrow.

Icarus and Ship drifted off to sleep. Well, they didn't sleep. They left the avatars on standby as they powered down their matrices. They didn't have the ability to change their playback speed, they resorted to old-school methods, the same strategy they used to use when traveling in between planets.

These aliens needed sleep, and they wanted to fit in as best they could. Their bodies moved and adjusted, simulating what normal Penquin bodies did while sleeping. There was a special alert set up to wake them if anyone approached.

CHAPTER 36

ICARUS

A GREATER UNDERSTANDING

Early in the morning, before the sun rose, Icarus was woken by one of his proximity sensors. He lay there pretending to sleep.

"Time to start catching fish," the voice of Atuatuk, said shining a bright light in their eyes.

The light also gave off a noise that lit up the room with sound that human ears couldn't hear. Icarus assumed it was meant to flood the world with information for echolocation. Sound waves were bouncing off all surfaces around them.

Icarus shot up out of the ground, pretending to be startled.

"We'll have you make some mattresses next. You don't want to sleep on the dirt when winter comes," Atuatuk said before also waking Ship.

He guided them past the mud huts to an area of the commune they'd never been to. They passed hot pools where food was fermenting and showers where a couple of people were starting to get ready. He led them both to a cave entrance and guided them inside.

They were walking down the dark cave, and not once did Atuatuk turn on his flashlight.

Icarus began to get worried. Was this a trap? Did he know who they really were? Concerns and ideas started to race through Icarus's mind.

"Who sent you here?" Atuatuk asked when they had finally reached the end. "Your auras are off, and you haven't died. Most who fail to be chosen die within ten days."

"No one sent us," Icarus said. "We told you why we came."

"Don't lie to me. I can read your mind. I was an Atua once. That skill is still with me."

Icarus didn't know what to do. He grabbed Ship's hand. "Any ideas?" he asked Ship through their private communication channel.

"Should we tell him the truth?"

"That's the last thing we should do," Icarus replied, thinking hard. He decided not to say a thing. Instead, he displayed the aliens' version of fear. He began shaking and bringing his knees together.

"I can see it in your aura. You're telling the truth," Atuatuk said. "I needed to be sure. You're very lucky to have survived."

Icarus kept showing fear as he asked his next question. "Did you think the Atua sent us?"

"No. This kind of infiltration is beneath them. If they wanted information, they would abduct one of my people and pull the information right out of their head. The Atua would never let any of their followers grovel enough to get let in. That's how I knew you weren't from them, but I still worried you were from another country." Atuatuk turned the his flashlight on. "You must have many questions, so ask them."

"Why do those who don't get chosen die?"

"It's how the Atua control our people. They decide who can reproduce. They decide who is not worthy of living. In your case, it looks like they tried to kill you but didn't succeed. You must have had a young one enter you."

Icarus thought about that for a moment; it made sense that this was how they kept the population of the Penquins under their control. When the Atua entered a Penquin's body, they must also look at their genetic makeup and decide whether they fit. In this situation, the Atua were directly influencing evolution—it sounded like it wasn't the fittest who got to reproduce, it was the ones the Atua chose. "Young Atua?"

"Oh, I see. You don't understand them properly, do you? I'll tell you the true history of the Atua. Everything I learned from when I was Atua. We both coevolved, Penquins and Atua. They evolved to hide inside of our bodies for warmth and safety. We evolved to be changed by them. To change sexes once we have been touched by them.

"It sounds simple, but our two species are so different from each other, we really shouldn't have coevolved in the way we did.

"They tell lies. The Atua believe they evolved intelligence and then gave us this intelligence. But I believe we evolved to think first. And then they gained that knowledge from us. We were the smart ones first." Atuatuk paused for a moment. He was looking in Icarus's eyes, trying to read him, trying to understand whether he was taking this all in.

The idea of two species coevolving together wasn't something fundamentally interesting to Icarus. Humans had long known this fact. Most of humanity's pets were smarter than the wild versions of the animals because of their selection for these traits. Still, maybe this wasn't common knowledge among the Penquin aliens.

Both Icarus and Ship made faces of astonishment, as if this was a world-shattering idea.

Atuatuk took this as confirmation he was impressing them both and continued: "The Atua aren't like you or me. To give birth, they must die, their body consumed to make room for the many, many young that burst out of their body. So only the old give up their life to have children.

"For most of our two species' coexistence, this relationship has balanced us quite well. They gave us the ability to reproduce. We gave them protection in our bodies so they could live a long time.

"About ten thousand eight hundred and thirty-nine cycles ago," Atuatuk said, the translator obviously having trouble with the alien's unit of measurement, "the Atua invented regeneration. They became immortal. Which on its own is not a bad thing. But the Atua treat seniority as the most important measure in their society. So suddenly none of them wanted to give up their lives to reproduce."

"You might be wondering why this matters, why I'm telling you all this. This is of much importance. Old Atua don't want to do what is best for all of us. They are prioritizing protecting their own lives and not the lives of the Penquins too."

"Give me an example. How do they not do what's best for us?"

"Do you know what an alien is?"

Icarus pretended to consider the question for a bit before answering. "It's a smart animal like us but from another world?"

"You are wise for someone who was thrown away by the Atua. Yes, well, the Atua know of three species of alien that they trapped on their home world. Another that will reach us in a few hundred cycles."

Icarus's mind began to race. Was humanity the one trapped on their home world? Was Angelique the other alien headed toward them? *Wait, they know of three other aliens?* Icarus wondered in his mind. Did that include the Dottiens? He wanted to tell this alien that he knew so much more. He wanted to ask pointed questions. But he couldn't ask without revealing himself. "Are these other aliens evil?"

"Yes," Atuatuk said. "Any alien that can move across the stars must be resource hungry. They will definitely want to take the resources from our planet. And that's why we must be ready to fight back."

"How do we do that?"

"We need more planets ourselves. The Atua are stopping us from visiting more planets."

"I'm confused. Why don't they want us visiting other planets?" Icarus asked. "I thought you said they trapped an alien on their home world."

"You see, the Atua aren't very smart. They would rather use and take. The Atua built space-traveling machines. We have the technology. I know the Atua stole a lot from the aliens they trapped. But we can't use the technology to transport ourselves to another world. The way us Penquins make children, we could send ourselves across the galaxy. But the Atua are different. Their nuknukcho doesn't survive very long. It especially doesn't last long enough with all the radiation out in space."

That was a new word Icarus hadn't heard before. Icarus queried his database and found the closest equivalent word to it was DNA. If Icarus was listening right, he was saying the Atua's bodies and the embryos couldn't survive space. He assumed this also meant they hadn't figured out how to print whatever they used as DNA.

"Are you saying we survive out in space? We can cross the stars?"

"We already have. There was one Penquin that crossed the stars. And they killed him. His mind became a computer."

If Icarus was listening right, Atuatuk had just said they had the technology to upload minds into the simulation.

"They killed him because they no longer had the ability to enter his mind and control it. Even after he traveled to all the closest star systems looking for alien threats. They killed him."

"Did you say computer minds?" Icarus asked, acting dumb. "Can the Atua do that?"

"They can do it to us, but not to themselves. Their minds work differently from ours. They can't do it. And none of them are willing to be test subjects and risk death."

Atuatuk stood up and began walking out of the cave, as if to signal he was done.

Icarus wanted nothing more than to keep asking questions. "What do you believe we should do?"

"I know we need to find a way to live without them. To live inside a simulated reality. We need to build our own technology and go explore the stars. We don't need the Atua to do it. We can explore without them. We can protect them from the aliens if we have the resources to fight back."

"How did you get smarter? How did the Atua change you?"

"They don't really change you. Well, not at first. We give the Atua the ability to share knowledge with one another. We act as hosts absorbing their knowledge, and when other Atua enter us, we can share that knowledge with them."

Icarus wanted to interrupt him and ask what he meant by share knowledge with one another. Did this mean that Atua took knowledge from the host Penquin, and if that Penquin had knowledge from another Atua, then that was carried over, too? Icarus made a note to ask that question when he could.

"There's no way for the Atua to make us smarter. You just have access to all their knowledge, everything they've learned over their life. Now, usually before the Atua frees you, they actually make you dumber. You still retain the knowledge, but you lose your mind. You lose the part of your brain that gives you free will. You become a servant for them. My Atua died before this happened. So I have all the memories and also free will. That's why I know the truth. I know they are evil."

Atuatuk paused for a moment. He closed his eyes. Icarus got the feeling Atuatuk was scanning the world around him through his other senses. "You lied!" he yelled accusingly toward both Icarus and Ship. He jumped forward, pushing Icarus and Ship to the ground, and then ran out the cave.

Icarus and Ship looked at each other confused, wondering what had just happened.

CHAPTER 37

SHIP OF ICARUS

RUN

One minute, Ship was amazed how much information this alien was providing. The next minute, he was on the ground wondering what had just changed. It was pitch-black, so they couldn't see a thing now that the alien holding the light had left.

He assumed Atuatuk had sensed something else approaching them. So Ship opened his mind to reach outside of the cave.

That's when he realized why Atuatuk had led them here. The thick walls were affecting his ability to sense much. A normal Penquin would effectively be blind in here. Ship assumed Atuatuk had abilities beyond a nomal Penquin because of his experience as an Atua.

The only reason Ship sensed anything at all was because they'd built a new version of the android body, a body that had even more capabilities to sense the world around it.

Ship reached out to the world and realized there was hundreds of other Penquins nearby, many more than they had ever seen on the commune. "I think they're being invaded," Ship said.

"I sense it, too. Everyone being rounded up."

Ship put his processors into overdrive. He had an innate ability to keep track of many different objects at once. He also had a deep desire to keep Icarus safe. What he had been worried about this whole time was finally happening. He didn't want to be captured. "We need to get out of here."

Ship and Icarus crept to the front of the cave.

There were several Penquins in heavy black armor. The armor was made up of many flat surfaces connected together. Almost as if they were designed to bounce sound waves off in random directions. They had black helmets that covered their faces—with two glowing eyes in the very center. Ship saw there was something strange going on with them. They were projecting some sort of resonance that made them hard to see exactly where they were through his magnetic sense.

Then Ship realized exactly why the armor looked like flat triangle panels all connected together. It was a material designed to bounce sound and magnetic fields. It was like camouflage but for an alien whose primary sensor used echolocation. It reminded him a lot of military equipment designed to not be detected.

Ship sensed where everyone was and waited for the perfect opportunity to run. He waited until most people nearby were turned around.

Tugging at Icarus's arm, he dashed toward one of the buildings, planning to hide behind it before going to the next one. He knew if he could make it to the beach, they would be safe.

"Hey, you, stop," he heard someone call.

Immediately, he sensed several of the armored men headed his way. Ship realized then there was no point in trying to hide.

It didn't matter whether the aliens were looking at them or not. The Penquins' special ability to detect magnetic fields meant they didn't have to rely on line of sight.

Ship sensed several bullets hit the walls around them. The walls were thick, so bullets weren't traveling through. That was the moment Ship realized they were in trouble. These aliens were there to take everyone as prisoner—dead or alive. They were going to use every weapon at their disposal to stop them. Ship couldn't let that happen.

Ship made a decision right then; he was going to leave behind signs that an alien had visited this world, that they had been there.

He sensed as one of the armed Penquins was just around the corner of one of the mud buildings. It was headed their way.

He quickly programmed one of the small ants inside his flipper to discharge all its power.

He waited for the exact moment, then threw the micro-ANT hard at the face of the soldier as soon as they rounded the corner. It landed on its forehead, then nearly electrocuted the alien.

Ship hoped he hadn't killed it. He was guessing the right voltage but decided it was better to lean toward too much electricity rather than risk it not working and them getting caught.

The other armed Penquins obviously sensed their fallen comrade and began running toward them.

Ship felt the bullet fly through the wall just behind him.

"Run," Icarus called from behind him.

Ship sprinted between the mud huts, moving faster than any Penquin could move.

He ran toward the beach, focusing his mind on using his other senses in order to find the fastest way to the beach.

They turned left, then right, avoiding alien soldiers, sprinting this way and that.

"Jump, Ship, jump!" Icarus called out as they reached the edge of the beach, where they could escape into the water.

Ship felt his leg crack as it was caught in some sort of device. Ship looked down at his leg; his leg was almost cut in half by a nasty device, exactly like a bear trap. The only reason his leg wasn't completely off was because of the reinforcements inside. Normal bone wouldn't have stood a chance.

Ship cursed himself for not seeing this obvious trap. It was invisible to his other sensors but was clearly visible to his eyes.

Icarus started pulling the trap apart.

"Don't," Ship said because he'd already tried that. The trap had a locking mechanism, so his leg wasn't coming out unless he had a key. "Jump in the water."

Three armed aliens with long tubelike devices—he assumed those were guns—were almost on top of them.

Ship started his self-destruct sequence as he shoved Icarus, forcing him to get going.

They began shooting as Icarus did what he was told and jumped over the sea of traps.

Ship watched as Icarus made it to the water—the shots not doing as much damage as the aliens expected. He knew as long as one of them made it off the planet, they would be able to re-create the other from backup. He would lose the memories of his time at this commune. But he wouldn't be gone forever.

It wouldn't be him exactly who was brought back to life. But that version of him would believe it was him, even if this version of himself was dead.

Ship shook his head. It wasn't yet time to give up. He wasn't going down without a fight. He could self-destruct at any time, but he shouldn't give up prematurely. He ordered the joints in his knees to disconnect. As his body began to tear itself apart from the leg joint, he lay on his back and pointed both flippers up into the air.

He programmed the six remaining micro-ANTs to fly out and attack the nearest soldiers. They flew out one by one, eliminating the nearest enemies. But there were a lot more of them on their way to his position.

Ship's leg joints had been severed, and he yanked hard to remove the flesh and tissue.

The amputated Ship began to hop down the beach, avoiding all the nearby traps.

He wondered whether these aliens had a movie similar to *The Terminator* because he looked like the Terminator hopping along this rocky beach with his leg blown off.

He was shot more than a dozen times before finally reaching the water.

He dived in and immediately began kicking his leg. It was slow going, but Icarus waited for him.

Icarus grabbed hold of Ship, and they swam together, quickly covering the distance to their base where Lex was.

They needed to leave as soon as they reached the base. Ship began making a mental plan of everything they needed to complete in order to leave the base quickly. They could probably escape leaving half their things there. They didn't need to pack anything up. Besides, Ship had already left evidence behind. Several ANTs were now in the aliens' possession. If they didn't know it was humans who visited them, they would within a few hours.

After a good hour and a half of traveling with neither of them speaking to each other, Icarus finally calmed down from the rush of everything enough to speak with Ship. "Do you think they were coming for us? Or was it just a coincidence?"

"If we were their target, they probably would have come with more firepower."

"There were enough of them there. Maybe they didn't know what we were."

"They definitely know what we are now. I left a bunch of ANTs there. And if they don't notice those, they're going to notice the leg that isn't bleeding on the beach."

Visibility in the water was low, but through Ship's new alien organ he could sense they were approaching the area where Lex was. It wasn't visible to his echolocation; it was well hidden after all. He knew they were close because he'd memorized the land-scape around them.

Then the world around him began to shake. He wondered whether he was in an earthquake. The ground below him wasn't shaking. *Oh no*, he thought as he realized what was going on. A pressure wave was moving toward them quickly.

Lex had self-destructed.

There was only one reason for him to do that. The aliens knew where their base was.

CHAPTER 38

ATLAS

STARNET 2.0

Atlas was enjoying himself. It was the sense of purpose he gained from toiling away on projects that others needed.

He stood, overlooking another megaproject in the Tac system. This time it was the construction of a massive Death Star–looking object. Atlas considered it as he stared out the window. Maybe Death Star was the wrong description. But it did look like a large moon. It was bigger than any of the moons in the system—even before all of them had been cannibalized for material.

It was made up of millions of honeycomb-shaped probes all interconnected like a jigsaw.

The hexagon-shaped probes were similar particle accelerators to the ones that made up the Starnet. But instead of only one, there were a lot of them all arranged in a circle, designed to fire two particles toward the middle of the giant orb.

Atlas rubbed the ridge of his nose thinking about all the complicated math he'd had to do to make this all work. He had unlimited resources, which was a positive, but still had to think through the problem carefully.

The current design of the Starnet constantly broadcast a steady stream of entangled particles.

If he wanted to speak with Trillion in real time, one pair of the particles would travel across the galaxy to where Trillion was while the other was bounced between two pieces of glass.

Atlas had discovered some time ago that when two particles were entangled away from a large gravitational body, doing something to one of the particles would have an impact on the other. Scientists on a planet would never be able to discover this unique quirk of quantum mechanics because all their tests were in the presence of the gravity produced by a planet.

The easiest way to build a Starnet that didn't require a constant torrent of particles traveling between the stars would be to bounce both sets of particles between mirrors.

He could set up the Starnet and have it produce entangled particles for several years, then send one half of the particles that were bouncing between mirrors to Trillion in one package.

The problem with that was he didn't want to have to wait several years to create enough particles. He wanted to do it quickly.

And so he had designed this particular arrangement of particle accelerators. Every second of operation, these machines would fire a year's worth of entangled particles. That meant, after just one hour of running, enough particles would've been produced to run the Starnet for almost four thousand years.

Each of the particle accelerators fired two entangled particles toward the center of the spherical moon-shaped megastructure. Again, he needed a solution for managing the fire hydrant of particles.

Atlas chose to use a modification on Angelique's stealthfield bubble technology.

He worked out that with a small modification of the way it worked, he could stop the stealthfield from destroying entanglement and still enable it to slow down the speed of light for every particle that entered that region of space.

Basically, he used the stealthfield to guide trillions of pairs of entangled particles toward two separate storage units.

One of the storage units could be kept with him, the other sent to the other side of the galaxy.

Then things would operate much like the current design of the Starnet.

Atlas flicked off a quick message to Trillion. She wanted to be there when he first switched on.

The moonlike structure would produce a lot of wasted heat when turned on.

Trillion teleported in holding a wine glass. "I've been looking forward to this light show. Angelique is too busy visiting Icarus's world; otherwise she would have joined, too."

Atlas put glasses over his eyes. "You ready?"

Trillion nodded, and Atlas pressed the giant red button in front of him.

The giant moon made up of millions of interconnected hexagons began to glow slightly. Then it got brighter and brighter. Atlas had to actively shield his eyes from it.

He could feel the heat radiating off it, too.

Trillion looked at him as if to ask, *Is that normal?*

Answering Trillion's question, the machine shut down with an audible grinding sound.

"Hmm." Atlas ran over to his computer to check on the results. "It overheated. I need a bigger heat sink." He shuffled through the pages of information. "It worked though; it produced enough entangled particles to run the Starnet for at least five years."

"Nice. At least you know it works." Trillion raised her glass in a toast. "Could you use that as a weapon? I heard Pete asked you to build something that could destroy a planet."

Atlas considered it for a moment. Maybe if he wanted to sterilize a planet, firing a bunch of high-energy particles would be effective. But it would be quite invisible. "Peter wants something a bit showy. He wants something with destructive power but also something that leaves a visible sign."

"What's scarier than a glowing moon that shoots laser beams?"

Atlas nodded slightly. "The glow is scary. But most of the particles it shoots are invisible. And most of the destruction would be invisible. It would be terrible for human life though. If you shot this at Earth, it would cause a mass extinction event."

Atlas wanted to change the topic. He wasn't that comfortable designing a weapon, even if it was a deterrent. He'd been distracting himself a little, not wanting to put much effort into building something that could wipe out an alien race.

He took this as his chance to bring up a topic he had been wanting to discuss for a while. He was becoming a little concerned that Trillion was spending a lot of time hallucinating. But he wasn't sure exactly how to bring it up. "Are you still meditating in that cloud?"

Trillion believed there was an alien in that cloud. She believed she was communicating with it when she entered it. Atlas wasn't so sure. He'd joined her and entered the cloud, spreading his consciousness across many micro-ANTs. It didn't work. He'd left feeling extremely relaxed, having solved an equation he was trying to figure out. But he never got a sense that he was speaking to an alien. He never got a sense that there was an alien in the cloud.

He'd tried to go into it with an open mind. But afterward, he was convinced it was just a dream. He found himself imagining a lot of different things while meditating.

Trillion finished her glass of wine, then manifested a bottle to top it up. She poured herself a glass and dropped the wine bottle down a portal. "I know you don't believe I'm speaking to anyone in there. But I enjoy it. It's relaxing."

Atlas had a sneaking suspicion Trillion was lost. She was lacking a purpose. She was using the cloud as a distraction. But he couldn't just tell her that. She needed to discover it for herself.

He considered what to say next. He thought about asking her to help him. But he knew she wasn't that interested in the technical things that got him excited. Even though she didn't have the behavioral modification in her matrix driving her to build a colony, he knew that was something she wanted to do most of all. She was happiest when she was helping the children on his planet grow up. "How are your other colonies going? I know you've sent out thousands of probes to other star systems."

"I've had about a hundred planets come online. I'm waiting until I have a few more before I select which one to go visit."

Atlas thought a hundred planets was a lot, way more than any of them had had to choose from. "How many planets do you want to compare between?"

"I want to get this right. I'm thinking I'll pick the best planet once I've had a chance to visit a couple thousand."

Atlas understood Trillion's conservative nature. Out of all the explorers, she had had the worst luck. She'd destroyed her first planet and gotten trapped on a moon on her second. Now she was worried about terraforming the system she was in because she believed the clouds were sentient. She was overcompensating for some of her past mistakes.

Again, Atlas didn't want to tell her that. He also didn't want to push her toward something she wasn't quite ready for.

Then it occurred to Atlas that he could help her speed up the process. She didn't need to go out and wait for her probes to visit every planet when he could take a photo of them using the telescope he'd built. "What if I could scan all the planets your probes are still traveling toward? I could scan them all and tell you which is statistically the most likely to be the best."

Trillion considered that for a moment. "Could you find me something similar to your planet? Something I can terraform easily?"

Atlas nodded. "I could help you get there faster than the probes too. Since Angelique's design for a spacecraft can travel at near light speed, you could probably reach some of the planets before your probes do."

Atlas watched as Trillion's eyes lit up. "Really?"

"I think so." Atlas thought about how he might do it. He didn't want to lead Trillion on. He didn't want to give her false hope. "Between all of us, we've visited enough planets to know which planets are ideal for terraforming. Angelique's people have quite a lot of data on differentiating between good and bad planets. It wouldn't take much effort to build an algorithm to find your something close that is easy to terraform." Then Atlas added because he knew it was an important point for Trillion, "A system with no life on it."

"It's important there isn't even a remote chance of having life on it."

Atlas's mind began to work. Doing this would slow down his process of hunting for planets the Atua were on. But this was important. He wanted to make sure Trillion was happy. "I'm confident I can speed up your process." Then he smiled. "Let's see if we can get you more planets than Angelique."

Trillion smiled. "I can finally live up to my name and get that many planets."

Atlas almost said something then. The idea that she was living up to her name. She had a trillion resources in the Tac system. She had more resources than anyone else already. But then he kept his mouth shut.

Trillion left Atlas, and he got back to work figuring how to absorb all the additional heat generated by running the machine he'd constructed. It would be easy on a planet, but he needed to be away from a large gravitational body. Once again, he began tinkering with his designs.

CHAPTER 39

ICARUS

CAN WE ESCAPE?

Icarus now had a million things racing through his head. Lex had self-destructed, and he was almost certain that it was because one of the Atua had discovered his base. So they couldn't return there.

They needed a way to escape from the planet now. They couldn't duck somewhere and hide. The Atua would be coming in force to find them.

If an alien snuck its way onto one of Icarus's planets and injured some of the locals, even if it was in self-defense, he would use every resource within his power to find the alien. Icarus assumed the Atua would do the same with him and Ship.

The two of them would be found. It was just a matter of time before they got caught.

And even if they somehow managed to get into orbit, it wasn't like they had a chance; every single one of the alien spacecraft would be chasing after them for as long as it took.

Icarus thought about escaping into space. Where would he go? If they raced to the nearest system Atlas or Trillion controlled, all he'd be doing was leading them there.

They probably already knew which star systems were under their control. But still it wasn't worth the risk.

Even if he made it all the way back to his planet, Titan, he wasn't assured rescue. He didn't know what sorts of weaponry they had.

His mind was getting too ahead of things; he needed to focus on his immediate problem. "Ship, any ideas on how we can get off this rock without getting caught?"

"How screwed do you think we are?"

"What do you mean?"

"If we get caught, do we end up in an alien prison?"

"I suspect it's much worse than that. They've already shown their will to trap an entire planet in a simulated prison—in the metaverse. I think they'll trap us into some computer, extract all the knowledge we have. We'll either tell them everything we know or they'll torture it out of us."

The sound of being tortured for the rest of time was something Ship did not want to deal with. "I would rather self-destruct."

"Me, too," Icarus said. "So given we are in a situation where we either escape or die, how do we escape?"

Ship pulled them both toward the bottom of the sea where they hid underneath a rock. The rock wouldn't hide them too well, but it was better than nothing.

"Give me access to your android," Ship said as he offered his other hand to increase the bandwidth between the two of them. "I'm turning off all our magnetic fields. I'm gonna try and make us as invisible as possible."

While Ship altered Icarus's matrix, Icarus began passively scanning the area around them. Something seemed odd; there were more fish in the immediate sea. There was a massive school of swimming creatures moving in deliberate patterns. They were moving in a corkscrew pattern clockwise around where Lex had just exploded.

"They're searching for us," Icarus said. "We probably have ten minutes before we're spotted. We need to get out of here."

"We can't move anywhere. If they're scanning this area, then they'll have sensors above the water. They'll be able to detect our avatars moving through the water."

Icarus wasn't comfortable with the idea of staying right there waiting to be caught. "Do we have any squid-looking ANTs nearby? Can they take our matrices?"

"That's it," Ship said excitedly. "We can leave in the same way we came."

Icarus knew that sounds of excitement in Ship's voice; he had a plan. They didn't have access to processing power to change their playback speed. So Icarus wasn't willing to slow things down by having Ship explain his idea. "You have a plan?"

"I have a plan. Do you have any ANTs left?"

"I do."

Icarus watched as Ship took control of his avatar and began releasing all seven of the ANTs still inside of his hands.

They began racing out in random directions away from where they were right now.

"I need to disconnect your matrix," Ship said. "I need to replace it with a Lex."

"Do it."

Icarus was switched off.

Ship knew there were hidden ANTs nearby, ANTs that looked and acted like alien fish. They were meant to be passively searching the area, looking for intruders. One particular ANT had the perfect-size mouth to fit both his and Icarus's matrices in it.

Ship took a gamble, but because signals didn't travel very far in water, he hoped he wasn't broadcasting their exact location. The

ANTs he'd just released were sending out signals to attract one of the swimming ANTs. In theory, there should be at least one nearby.

While Ship waited for a mystery ANT that may or may not come, Ship began programming the exact steps the small robotic fish needed to do.

Icarus's avatar was currently building a small Lex-based AI. Ship knew from experience that giving instructions to Lex was marginally better than trying to preprogram things for every possible outcome.

He worked as quickly as he could, trying not to overprescribe things but also conscious of the fact that a small Lex matrix struggled with ambiguity.

Ship nearly jumped with joy when a small squid-looking robot with tentacles approached them both and gave off its authentication codes.

Ship sensed the alien robots in the water looking for them were nearby. He estimated they were thirty seconds away from being found.

His planning was going to have to be enough. He ejected Icarus's matrix and shoved it into the squid's mouth, then pulled out a small data clip from Icarus's head and slid that into a small port on one of the robot's tentacles. That data clip would install Lex and tell the swimming android what to do next.

Taking a deep breath, he ejected his own matrix.

The two avatars of Ship and Icarus were on a preprogrammed schedule. As soon as they were seen, they were to dart off in the opposite direction, swimming as fast as their printed bodies could take them. Ship expected them to be caught. Ship expected the aliens to converge on them. That was okay because, once captured, they were programmed to self-destruct in a big explosion. Ship hoped that would be enough to convince the Atua to stop looking. Or at the very least, cause enough chaos that the squid holding their matrices could hide.

The alien cephalopod reached out one of its arms and grabbed Ship's matrix. It swam in a natural pattern, scattering from rock to rock in the general direction Ship wanted it to go.

Lex controlled the robot as it slowly made its way across the ocean, traveling a good few days. About an hour into the journey, it felt an surge of pressure. It didn't know it at the time, but that was the avatars of Icarus and Ship exploding.

At one point, it was attacked by a large swimming fish. Lex had to hide under a rock until that larger fish left it alone.

It was a long and slow journey. But Lex was under strict instructions not to raise any suspicion. So during the night it pretended to sleep under a rock before beginning the journey again in the morning.

After five days of steady progress, Lex finally made it to the hidden base.

It was camouflaged to look like a rock. Ship's original plan had been to use this as the main base of operation for when they were exploring the nearby country. They were still months away from using it though, so it was tiny, just a small fabricator.

Lex hopped inside and immediately began cannibalizing the base to manufacture a small eleph-ANT. Lex turned itself off once the process had commenced; it was under strict orders not to use any more power than it should—because the risk of getting caught was too high.

Six hours later, Lex was switched back on.

It was now in control of an eleph-ANT. A small eleph-ANT. Lex again was instructed to leave as soon as the work was complete.

But Lex reviewed the sensor data. There were a lot more fish out in the water nearby. It assumed the only reason there were a lot of fish around was the aliens were scanning the area.

Lex had a decision to make: run now or hide.

It didn't believe running now had a high probability of success. The eleph-ANT had a massive contraption on top of its head, so it would not be a good swimmer.

In order to escape, Lex had to swim up two hundred meters before reaching the surface. That was a lot of ground to cover.

Lex didn't want to fail. It didn't want to die.

Lex powered everything off for an hour. It knew the camouflage was good, but all the electronics on board the eleph-ANT would probably give away its position.

One hour later, Lex awoke and powered everything on again. It noticed the amount of fish activity nearby had returned to normal.

It waited for another two minutes, passively scanning the area for any hints of aliens.

None were found.

Moving as quietly as it could, the eleph-ANT moved out from the camouflaged cover and began swimming upward.

The eleph-ANT began powering its heavy motors to reach the surface.

For this plan to work, Lex had to position the eleph-ANT as high in the sky as possible, ideally above the clouds.

The eleph-ANT fired its engines hard, rocketing into the sky as quickly as possible.

It took exactly twenty minutes before it was noticed. Longer than Lex had expected but still not enough time to be sure.

Lex reached the cloud and continued straight up. It didn't have enough speed to escape the alien vessels on course to capture it.

Lex sent out a pulse, looking for the weakest part of the clouds, a gap in the clouds, anything. Identifying exactly where to go next, Lex changed course. It was looking for an open view to the stars.

It took a fraction of a second to identify exactly where to point the radar dish at the very front of the eleph-ANT, using the exact position of the sun above them and a few barely noticeable landmarks as a compass.

Lex began broadcasting every bit of data it had, starting with the information required to re-create Icarus and then Ship. This took nine painfully slow minutes to complete.

Lex again had a decision to make. It wasn't a guarantee it was broadcasting to the right location. It also wasn't a guarantee that all the information was received properly. So rather than broadcasting any new information, like all the data they had collected on the planet, it decided to restart the broadcast.

Lex once again sent everything required to re-create Icarus and Ship with all their memories.

The alien vessels were on top of Lex. It didn't want to die, but it also had orders to self-destruct.

Lex considered all its options. It decided it could complete both those objectives.

Lex exploded a small device near the matrices of both Icarus and Ship—self-destructing them. This took out a limb of the eleph-ANT but nothing critical.

Lex then pointed the location in system where the spacecraft they arrived in was hiding. It broadcast a copy of all the information there—just to be sure.

Then it dropped all the hard drives containing every bit of information, except Lex, out the back of the eleph-ANT. Moments later, an explosion happened behind Lex as all that information was destroyed.

Lex also dumped the large antenna at the front of the eleph-ANT—eliminating weight.

Then Lex took control of the eleph-ANT and redirected itself toward the incoming spacecraft.

Lex's plan was simple: fake its death by pretending to go kamikaze. Lex planned on dropping more limbs and shedding as much weight as possible. The deadweight would hit the alien spacecraft, hopefully disabling it.

Lex assumed a big enough explosion would hide the fact it was escaping. It was a long shot, and Lex knew it had a very minor chance of working, but it was better than nothing.

Lex began picking up speed. It hoped it would be able to dodge and weave until it escaped the system, as it traveled to the nearest system controlled by Icarus or the others.

Lex figured it was immortal, so spending thousands of years traveling between stars was nothing.

Unfortunately for Lex, the first part of its plan failed. As it approached the alien spacecraft, it was caught in some sort of electronic net, and the eleph-ANT's engines were fried.

CHAPTER 40

ATLAS

GOODBYE AGAIN

"You all ready?" Atlas said as the final Ange's Angel clone was turned on.

Atlas stood in front of a sea of Anges, forty-five of them in total. Angelique had a lot more worlds than she let on.

Angelique had changed her tune about hiding colonies when she'd realized anyone with a powerful enough telescope and enough time could quickly identify them. And now that there was an alien out there actively trying to attack them, they needed the benefits of sharing knowledge between everyone's worlds. That was the only way they were going to survive.

"You all look like backup dancers or something," Trillion said, teleporting into the room.

The Ange's Angels in the room pretended not to react to Trillion's remark, but Atlas saw the collective eye rolls around the room.

"Let's take the photo and get out of here," one of the Ange's Angels said.

Atlas had to hand it to Trillion. She had made this scene happen. It was something he thought he'd never see. All these clones in one location at the same time.

This system and all its resources were Trillion's. Building forty-five spacecraft, all with their own Starnets, required a lot of material. Not that much compared to what she had in the system but still enough that Angelique felt obligated to go ahead with Trillion's request.

Everyone gathered around in a semicircle. Atlas noticing he'd never been surrounded by that many red heads before. All three of their Ships jumped into the group, too, before Trillion stepped forward and placed a camera on the bench in front of them.

Atlas knew she was doing this all for theatrics, playing with her old friend. But he also knew Angelique had a bit of a god complex, especially with the way she was adored on her worlds. So having Trillion treat her like this was the perfect cure for her ego.

"Lex," Trillion called out before the orb. Five of the orbs appeared floating above them all. Trillion patted hers on the head.

The camera flashed, and Trillion ran over to look at the photo. She smiled. "Everyone looks good."

"Okay, see you in a bit," all the Ange's Angels said at once as they teleported out of the room, leaving just Angelique, Trillion, Atlas, their Ships, and their Lexes.

"Did you have to make me do that?" Angelique asked while slow clapping in a gesture that said, *Did you have to make me look so silly?*

"Nope," Trillion said. "But who else is going to keep you humble?"

Angelique smiled at that remark. Trillion, Atlas, and the other beta explorers were the only people who'd known Angelique before she'd ventured out into the stars. Before she'd become probably humanities most powerful person—with access to more colonies and technology than anyone else.

Like all old friends who knew someone before they got famous, Trillion knew something others didn't. Atlas knew Trillion was impressed with what Angelique had accomplished. But because she'd known Angelique before she'd amassed that much status, she was able to bring her down a peg.

Atlas approved of her strategy. "So what now?"

"I'll visit all my planets again, bring this new version of the Starnet to all my colony worlds." Then she paused for a moment. "Well, my Ange's Angels are going out to visit the colonies. I'm going to stay here. I'm enjoying exploring your world, Atlas. It's all new to me. Normally I'm visiting worlds I built. This is like discovering a long-lost culture. The people are so different from any of my worlds."

Atlas understood what she meant; their culture had changed a lot since he was last on their planet. They had developed in isolation for so long, going through a number of struggles because of the filter virus that had impacted their crops. It had brought their civilization to the brink of destruction through starvation—which was arguably the worst possible way to go. Out of that struggle, the people of Neuropa became a hard people that didn't trust technology. They didn't complain much, and above all else, they valued hard work. Even though his people had access to robotics and a lot of automation, they took pride in doing things with their hands. Having rugged hands had become a bit of a fetish—a sign of someone's attractiveness and worth.

"They worship you, Atlas," Trillion said.

Atlas blushed because she was right. After he'd appeared on their planet once more after years of being gone, he'd saved them from starvation by removing the filter virus. Then, because the Atua had destroyed the Starnet, he'd disappeared again.

He'd once again become immortalized. Stories were told of him coming in to save them, then leaving again without needing a thank-you, like a god solving a famine—deus ex machina.

Every time something happened on their planet, many of their people would pray to Atlas asking him to come back and save them.

It made Atlas question how humanity got to the level of reaching the stars when so many were quick to deify another human.

Atlas had to constantly remind himself that it was only a few of them making those proclamations—he really didn't want to get a god complex. "That's only a vocal few of them."

"I've been visiting most of the cities," Angelique said. "It's not a small minority. A lot of people on the planet look up to you as if you're some kind of god."

"Don't you find it fascinating?" Trillion asked. "Even though they know you're a human and you came from Earth, they treat you as if you're something more. Something bigger. One once told me you'd turned water into wine." Trillion cracked a smile. "Although I'm not sure if he was joking or not."

Angelique projected a halo around Atlas's head. "Somehow the less time you spend on the planet, the more they look up to you."

"Groupthink," Atlas said, seeing confused looks on both of their faces. "It's something we humans evolved to better get along with others. We couldn't have everyone in the village disagreeing with one another, so we evolved to be agreeable." His palms faced up in a gesture that said, *Therefore.* "Groupthink."

Angelique looked about to question what he had just said. "But why don't I see that happen on my planet? Even Earth had countries that thought differently."

"It's because there's only one real country on Neuropa. Their population got so small they all congregated around one city. So they became a bit of a monoculture. I'm guessing once they started to expand again, they kept a lot of those cultural aspects."

"By aspects you mean they kept worshipping you," Trillion mused.

Atlas didn't want to nod, but that was what he meant. He didn't feel comfortable with his people worshipping him as if he was worthy of that. He didn't want to be an empire. Then he considered it a little more. Emperor, he didn't want to be an emperor. Or a king. Or any sort of lord. He wanted to be an explorer. He thought there was so much more in the universe to discover, and he hoped that he'd one day live long enough to discover most of it.

CHAPTER 41

SHIP OF ATLAS

BUILDING A WEAPON

There was something about flying cars that made it easier for Ship to think.

Ship couldn't decide whether it was because, first and foremost, he was a spacecraft. He was engineered to fly through space, tracking and monitoring multiple things at once. He was *a* ship.

Ship thought about how best to describe the ride they were traveling in. A car undersold just how big a machine he was controlling. Even an RV made it sound small. It was a house on wheels—or in this case, a house on wings, complete with offices for both Ship and Atlas, a lounge space, and a complete kitchen for entertaining.

He and Atlas were in a large flying vehicle traveling around inside the Rings of Titan. They were stopping in city after city looking for inspiration—inspiration for a weapon. But Ship knew they were also there to meditate and figure out whether Atlas wanted to build a weapon.

Traveling around Icarus's world was a way for Atlas to escape. He wasn't worshipped, or even followed, on this planet, unlike what would have happened if they'd visited the planet they'd created together.

"We've officially hit the halfway point," Ship said, pointing to a map on the wall showing an image of the Rings of Titan. They were traveling through one of the lesser-populated sections of the ring.

"You know it would have taken us only forty-five hours to travel around Earth at this speed," Atlas said. "But this ring is so big it's going to take us over nine days to complete the trip."

They'd been flying nonstop around the ring for five days now, only occasionally stopping at one of the cities that interested them. The Rings of Titan was an artificial rotating habitat around one of the gas giants in the system called Titan. It was one continuous tube that circled the entire planet.

Once Icarus had completed the ring, his people had gone about removing the walls blocking off each section of the ring. This came with a slight increase in risk, since any leak in the structure could no longer be contained to a single section, but it came with the joy of being able to travel around the entire planet without stopping, which the people of the planet reported gave them a greater sense of openness.

The people of Titan had constructed a number of mountain ranges on the rings, which when combined with the centrifugal force would act as a barrier slowing down, but not quite stopping, the atmosphere from escaping in the event of some sort of catastrophe.

"It's better than traveling around Earth," Ship said.

"I agree. Earth is just water. Even our planet, Neuropa, is mostly water. They've done a great job at making each section of the ring different. It's like traveling through a piece of artwork."

Ship nodded in agreement because he'd enjoyed watching the landscape change and evolve as they slowly made their way around the world. "It's become a rite of passage here now. They're turning it into something everyone needs to complete. It's driving a lot more people out of the simulation and into android bodies for the trip."

They were now traveling over a field of purple grass. It was winter on this part of the planet, and the grass here was genetically engineered to look this color when it was cold.

Ship saw farmland up ahead.

"Can we pull into that eatery there?" Atlas asked, pointing down toward one of the billboards. The sign read, LAST FOOD STOP FOR EIGHT HOURS.

"You want to have a chat with some of the locals?" Ship asked.

Atlas was treating this not only as a trip to find himself. He was also interested in talking to random people. Ship knew he was secretly interviewing people. He wanted to understand what people really thought about the potential for a fight against the Atua. He was trying to figure out whether he should build a weapon.

Ship angled the flying RV toward a small parking lot. There were several vehicles all docked up there in the bay too. The sign obviously attracted a number of travelers.

They were in a gravel parking lot surrounding an old-looking building. It looked like something straight out of a Western film. The giant sign in front of the building read, ROXANNE'S DINER.

"There's more people walking around this planet now that the filter virus isn't around brainwashing them," Atlas said as he stepped out of the RV.

Ship stepped out too. "They still have more simulants than living humans. They have more usable land on Titan than Neuropa, but Neuropa has more living humans."

The two of them began walking toward the front door of the eatery.

The door opened with a ding of a bell.

A lady behind the counter with a white apron on holding a pot of coffee smiled at them warmly as they entered. "Take a seat anywhere, darling. I'll be with you in a sec," she called out before she began serving another customer.

Ship wasn't sure whether the lady put on that accent or not because she sounded like a cliché version of what all servers at small restaurants in the middle of nowhere sounded like.

Ship and Atlas walked over to one of the booths in the very corner. Everyone was gathered together at one end of the eatery, so it made sense to continue that trend and take the next free booth close to everyone else.

Ship went to pick up the menu but decided he'd do what he always did and ask for a recommendation. That way he always got to try what was most popular.

Atlas looked up from behind the menu. "So this weapon. Do you think it's a good idea?"

Ship had spent most of the last five days thinking about this very question, whether he should or shouldn't encourage Atlas to build a weapon. The trouble was he was programmed to protect Atlas. He had a deep desire to do just that. And so the very idea that there was a potential threat out there clouded his judgment.

One thing he did know for certain though was he wanted something else that he believed was better than a weapon. "What about building some kind of defense? Is there a way to turn the stealthfield that Angelique created into some sort of impenetrable shield?"

"The problem with a forcefield or any sort of defense like that is there's always a way around it. You don't build a wall thinking it'll deter people from trying to attack you. A gun is what stops people from attacking you."

On some level, Ship knew Atlas was right. The reason World War II on Earth had ended was because of the risk of one of the countries being hit with a nuclear bomb. "Can we create a scenario where both we and the Atua can't fight each other without the risk of mutually assured destruction?"

Atlas began to bite his lower lip as he thought about it. "Maybe," he said before pausing and thinking it over for a while. "Hypothetically the only way to create mutually assured destruction would be if we found a way to explode the supermassive black hole in the middle of the galaxy. If we did that, we would bathe the whole Milky Way in radiation and kill everything. But I don't think that's technically or ethically possible."

"What about a star? Could we send a nearby star supernova?"

"Um, maybe. Most of the energy from a supernova shoots out of the poles. It creates these massive jets of energy. If we could control where these jets were pointed and shoot them at the Atua planet, we could sterilize the system like that."

"What's this you're talking about sterilizing?" The lady from behind the counter came over to take their order. "I'll have you know I cleaned these tables myself. If you think they're not clean enough, you can leave."

Atlas went slightly red with embarrassment. "Sorry, we were talking about something else."

She slapped him on the arm. "I'm just kidding you, darling. My name's Roxy. I'll be your server for today. So, what are y'all having?"

"Can I have the fish and chips?" Atlas asked.

The lady looked at Ship. "What do you recommend?"

"You look like a man who enjoys a good steak. I'm going to get you a steak, and both of y'all are going to get a beer." She pointed to Atlas. "He looks like he needs one."

"That's just his face," Ship said. "He bites his lip when he's thinking."

Atlas looked sheepish. He quickly unsquashed his face and smiled at the lady.

She wasn't wrong though. Atlas had been a bit stressed lately trying to deal with the conflict around building a weapon.

Atlas gained his composure. "Can I ask you a question?"

The lady placed a hand on Atlas's arm. "For you, honey, anything."

Ship decided he liked this over-the-top impression of a waitress at a diner.

"Do you know about the Atua?" Atlas asked the lady.

"The aliens that destroyed the Starnet?"

Atlas nodded. "Are you worried about them coming back?"

"I'm not too worried about that side of things. I think they destroyed it because someone back on Earth did something to upset them. I figure they'll ignore us if we leave them alone."

"So you're not worried about them attacking us again?"

"They won't attack us. The universe is big enough that I'm sure they have other things to concern themselves with. We're just a tiny planet. I think they're more likely to attack Earth—they're the ones that started this."

"If they attack Earth, we'll be forced to defend them," Atlas said rather forcefully.

Roxy looked at him strangely. "Why? If the stupid humans back on Earth got themselves into some kind of mess, they can get themselves out."

Ship wondered if she didn't worry about any of this stuff because it didn't affect her or if she just wasn't aware of the risk the aliens posed. He decided to ask a question that might shed light on that. "Have you thought about what you would do if an alien showed up tomorrow?"

"Probably serve them coffee," she said with a smile. "I'm a nobody from the middle of nowhere. Why would they care about me? I'm sure they have enough other people to care about rather than to wonder about what I'm doing. There's a billion . . ." She trailed off as she spoke. "Do you know something that I don't know?" Then she paused, studying the two of them for a good while. "I thought you two looked familiar. You're Atlas, and you're Ship. If we're in trouble, you better tell me now so I can head home and go be with my kids."

Atlas shook his head. "There's nothing to worry about. I'm just asking hypotheticals."

She noticeably relaxed at that statement. "If you're asking me what would I do if they attacked us here, then yes, I'd want to run and hide. But still, I don't understand why they'd want to hurt all this innocent life. We're just ordinary folk."

Roxy's face was noticeably more tense after that brief exchange. She stepped back from the table, and in an instant her demeanor returned to its normal bubbly self. "I'll get those orders put through and be back with some food quicker than you can reach the other side of the ring."

Ship waited for her to leave. He wasn't sure whether she'd helped or not.

"That was good, asking everyday people," Atlas said. "They aren't as obsessed about this as we are."

"Did she give you any clarity?"

"She did. She made me realize I don't want to build a weapon. Even if we get into a war with them, I don't want something that can potentially hurt the ordinary aliens on their planets, the people like this waitress we met. It's just not worth punishing them for a decision their leaders made. Imagine building something with destructive power that was used. I don't think I could live with myself."

Ship raised an eyebrow because that wasn't the direction he'd thought Atlas would eventually end up going. He'd assumed Atlas would eventually build something. He'd assumed he'd put in some safety measures to prevent it from being used unless absolutely necessary. "I thought you said the best defense is a strong deterrent."

"I'm going to put my time into building a better wall. A better forcefield. I'm going to make it so it's not worth attacking us because whatever I build is so obviously impenetrable that they don't even bother."

"What if we could trap them on their planet?" Ship asked. "What if we had a device that, when activated, slowed down time so much around a planet that we experienced hundreds of thousands of years before they get out?"

"What do you mean?"

"Time moves slower near a black hole, correct?"

Atlas nodded.

"Can we launch a black hole at a system and use the time-dilating effects of gravity to slow down their time so much that they race into the future?"

Atlas began thinking deeply. "How is that even possible?"

Ship could tell Atlas was trying not to bite his lower lip.

Ship shrugged. "I don't know. I was hoping you had an idea."

Atlas opened his mouth to talk. He paused. He closed it again. He started to bite his lower lip, and Ship saw a glimmer in his eye.

Ship knew his brain was beginning to work, coming up with possibilities.

CHAPTER 42

PETER

WELCOME BACK

Peter got word that another Ange's Angel was returning. He was excited about her return but also slightly curious about how quickly she'd gotten back.

All the Angels that were close enough to arrive by now had already made their way back.

The only obvious solution was to have Angelique send one of her Angels back to Juniper rather than coming back herself.

He was currently making his way across this country and back to his home on the beach. He'd just given a speech in front of the military. And even though he was no longer the prime minister of the country, he was still working hard to raise support for what he assumed would be a military operation against the Atua.

He was not winning the fight, however. Humans had short memories. One of the evolutionary advantages of humans was the ability to forget pain. Psychologists believe it was a feature and not a bug. If a child remembered every single fall they had, after six months of living they would be too scared to move at all.

So everyone he spoke to had basically forgotten that they'd lost access to the Starnet. Everyone was again too preoccupied worrying about their own lives to care about some alien invasion.

He was amazed at how desensitized the people of Everest had become.

Peter knew the business cycles of boom and bust, or rapid growth then recession, typically happened once every ten or so years. Back when he was on Mars, he'd found it surprising how consistently the world would make the same mistakes. Somehow, businesses and governments would fall into the trap of forgetting the mistakes that had led to the previous recession and make them again. He'd made a lot of money simply by studying what had happened before and preparing for it.

He was seeing a lot of parallels in the way society was reacting to this. When Peter had first arrived on the planet, he'd had to fight quite aggressively to get the country aligned. There were a lot of oligarchs who'd inserted themselves into the planet's running in order to take advantage of people. He had removed most of them from their positions of power.

Following that, he'd let the planet know about the Atua and shared the risks they posed. For several months, there was back-to-back news coverage about the potential threat these aliens posed. There was speculation about who they were, which star in the sky was their home system. Documentaries, movies, and conspiracy theories all revolved around the unknown alien species.

This made it easy for Peter to push for more money to be spent on the defense force, on research and development around infrastructure security, and even on limiting the ways their planet could be hacked into.

Peter had made the mistake of believing this trend in expenses would continue. When he'd left office, he'd thought things would be maintained as they were. He had been wrong.

The people of Everest quickly forgot the risks the Atua people posed. Slowly, defense spending was gutted, and practices that were designed to ensure the security of the planet was not put in jeopardy were overlooked.

Fast-forward to today and he wasn't sure they could defend themselves properly against an attack.

Peter pressed a call button on the screen in front of him that gave him access to his security detail at the front of the car. "Can you turn the car around?" Peter said to the military escort in the front of the car. "Take us to Ange's residence."

"Of course, sir," he heard one of them say as his flying car arced around.

It didn't take long before he reached his destination. Ange's house was at the very top of a cliff overlooking a big stretch of water. She liked her views. And she especially loved views with water.

It was an unexpected visit, and so both Ange's and Peter's secret service members had to quickly coordinate on the effort. The only obvious sign of any of this Peter experienced was having to drive the final few kilometers to her house because the airways around her small-village-like house were blocked off.

Peter's driver moved him up to the porte cochere. One of his people opened the door, and he hopped out. He smiled as he took in the view. Ange was slowly rebuilding her old homes after they were destroyed in the previous mini–civil war that had left the older Ange dead.

The redesign had all the typical Angelique design hallmarks. A massive stairway leading right up to the top of a ballroom, gold everywhere. If he hadn't known better, he'd say this place had been designed in worship of a god.

Ange appeared, walking out of the doorway with a huge smile on her face. "Peter, how are you?"

Peter walked over and gave her a big hug. "I hear you've got a surprise for me."

Ange pointed up to the very top of the stairway. "You mean her?"

At the very top Peter saw another red-haired woman. Peter assumed it was Trillion, but then he squinted to take a better look. Then he saw. "Angelique?"

"Nope, another Ange. But this one came back from Atlas."

Peter's ears perked up at that. "I thought there was something suspicious in the message you sent. Why haven't you announced her arrival?"

Ange took hold of Peter's arm, and the two of them began walking up the very long gold-and-marble stairwell. "She's got something to share with us both."

Peter wondered whether it was a weapon idea. Then his mind went to the potential of something worse. Had the Atua attacked them again? Was something more going on?

"Don't worry," Ange said, obviously noticing Peter's worried expression. "We're not in any danger. Ariana did have a run-in with the Atua who came back to reclaim its ship. But she survived. She's fine."

They reached the top of the long stairs. They opened onto a glass-walled space that overlooked the water.

The new Ange gave Peter a hug. "Atlas says hi."

The original Ange looked at her security detail. "Can you secure the room? We want no eyes and ears on this conversation."

It took the team a whole thirty seconds to rearrange the room, closing off the stairwell behind them, securing all windows shut, and flicking a switch on the glass areas facing the water, turning them into one-way mirrors.

All three of them took a seat on a white couch that Peter immediately sank into. Even though he was no longer running the country, he was still feeling the effects of extreme tiredness and overworking.

"You'll be happy to hear we're bringing the Starnet to all the colonies," the new Ange began by saying.

"Why the change of mind?" Peter asked. "Have things escalated with the Atua?"

Peter assumed the only reason Angelique was open to using the Starnet now was that something had happened recently to make it important they could share real-time communication with all the other colonies.

"Atlas knows which star system the Atua come from," Ange stated matter-of-factly. "At least the very least, he knows where one of their star systems are. And he's currently searching for the others. He's created a telescope capable of taking a high-res picture of any planet less than a couple hundred light-years away."

Peter was in shock. He couldn't think of a single way to build a telescope that powerful. He'd always thought there was a practical limit on how big a telescope could become.

Peter didn't have a chance to comment because Ange continued: "Now, if we can see them, then they can see us. And it basically means there's no way to hide in this universe. If you're changing the atmosphere of the planet in the same way we're doing here, then a civilization with advanced enough technology will be able to see us."

Peter nodded. "This is a departure from previous thinking."

"Well, previously," Ange continued, "we believed there was strategic value in staying hidden for as long as possible. But with this new revolution, we realized we're only hiding from civilizations less advanced than us."

"And those are the ones we're not afraid of," Peter said.

"Exactly. Atlas has proven you can't hide from a civilization with a similar technological level as us." Ange paused for a moment; she had a look in her eyes, something that said this was the reason she'd changed her mind, and not because Peter had been pushing for it. "And so we're not going to throw away our main advantage. Having real-time communication between the planets is a strategic advantage we need to make use of."

"So you're not worried about giving away our position to less-advanced civilizations—if there are any watching?" Peter asked.

Ange shook her head. "Atlas has a solution for this too. Lex is waiting on the other side of the stealthfield with billions of entangled particles. I need help to convince everyone to turn off the Starnet for a long enough time to get the particles through."

Peter knew from his own research into how the Starnet worked. The stealthfield broke entanglement with particles. So the Starnet wouldn't work through the stealthfield.

Peter and both the Anges discussed the strategy for convincing the leaders on the planet that they needed to change a policy of maintaining the stealthfield at all costs.

Ange shared everything that had happened since she'd last visited. It got Peter very excited about seeing his old friend Atlas again.

One thing that hadn't come up yet was a weapon. Peter had sent a message to Atlas to request he build a weapon. He wanted to know if Atlas had made any progress. "Did you ask Atlas about building something we could use to fight the Atua aliens with?"

"I did," the new Ange responded. "Judging by the way he responded, I get a feeling his heart's not in it. He understood the need to fight back, but I don't believe he's comfortable with building a weapon that could potentially wipe out a whole alien race."

The other Ange added, "I can see his point. Building something meant for that kind of destruction takes a different kind of person."

"Have you both read about the nuclear arms race?"

"Are you talking about back on Earth?" the other Ange asked. "When the US and another country—I can't remember the name—began mass-producing nuclear bombs? I recall both countries entering a sort of war with both sides trying to create more weapons than the other."

Peter nodded. "Exactly that. Both countries spent time and energy trying to create more nuclear bombs. But more importantly, neither side used them because they knew it would result in their destruction."

"Mutually assured destruction."

"Correct. If we can show the Atua we have the ability to utterly destroy them if they attack us again, then it's simply a type of game theory. They couldn't attack us without the risk of being attacked themselves. And equally, we don't know what weapons they possess, but we have to assume they have something powerful enough to take out at least a few of our colonies."

The Ange that had stayed on the planet the whole time responded: "And now that we know it's possible to identify exactly which planets are colonized. So each side has the ability to attack the other side because there really is no way to truly stay completely hidden. We might be able to hide a few small spacecraft, but hiding colony worlds is impossible."

"Unless they have the capability to neutralize all our planets at once. If they can take us out effectively enough that we don't have the capability to respond, then we'll still lose."

Peter looked out into the ocean view in front of them. "That's where the arms race comes in. If we can produce enough of the weapons that the Atua can never be sure they'll be able to take out every single one of our planets and hidden starships, to attack us would be stupid unless they could guarantee we were pacified completely and unable to launch a counterattack. Which, again, the risk becomes too high if we have enough of these weapons hidden around the galaxy."

"Assuming Atlas builds something."

"Yes, assuming he does."

CHAPTER 43

ANGE

TITAN

The Ange that had stayed on Everest merged with the Ange who'd visited Atlas to combine their experiences and focus on getting the Starnet built.

It took several months for the scientists on Everest to figure out a strategy for moving the paired photons within the bubble around the planet.

The risks were high, since when entangled particles moved through the stealthfield, they lost entanglement, which would ruin the ability for the Starnet to work. Atlas hadn't put any time into figuring out how to make it work; he'd assumed the planet's knowledge of the stealthfield was greater than his, and so he'd left it up to the Ange carrying the tech. The only instruction he'd given was to not carry it through the bubble around the planet.

Even if there wasn't an initial strategy for bringing the starship full of entangled particles through the stealthfield, Atlas knew it wouldn't limit the overall goal of the Starnet. Communication wouldn't be real time; it would be delayed a couple of days. This ultimately was still better than the several years it took any other form of communication—even traveling at the maximum speed: light speed.

At the very least, one of the colonies would figure out a solution, and that information could be disseminated among the other colonies quite quickly.

Ange and her small team couldn't find a solution around it without turning off the stealthfield. So in the end they created a smaller Starnet that was used to send information FTL to the very edge of the bubble.

Then it was simply a case of tight-beam communication through the stealthfield, where the other connection to the Starnet resided, the one that was connected to Atlas.

They were able to use tight-beam communication as they already had the ability to make changes to the bubble in a way that they didn't interfere with these kinds of signals in specific areas of it. This was a tool they already had at their disposal.

What this all resulted in was a slightly lower-bandwidth version of the Starnet. But still, it provided a near-real-time-communication link to Atlas, Trillion, and the other planets connected on the Starnet.

Everyone was there in the room for the official first usage of the Starnet on Everest. Ange sat around a table along with Peter, Hezekiah, Unity, and Ship.

It was a table made of solid diamond because Ange thought she'd give it a try, given that there wasn't much difference between using the fabricators to print a table out of wood or diamond.

It was stupid really, a table with that many reflective indexes meant anyone in the room without robotic eyes had a hard time seeing anything—blinded by the gleaming brilliance coming off the table.

Ange rested her hand on the slab, feeling the cold, solid nature of the stone. She led the Starnet project and had the use of the FTL communication placed under the Ange's Angel program, which meant, like interstellar travel, the operating of the technology was a joint venture between her and the military. Exactly how it was built was a guarded secret.

As part of the arrangement, she was still in the testing phase, which essentially meant they had a week of unmonitored use of the Starnet—"to confirm it's working as expected."

After the week was up, the military and select members of parliament would get access to it. Then they would make a decision on whether to share it with their citizens.

Ange assumed that once it was shared with everyone, the level of knowledge improvement and growth would climb even faster. With hundreds of billions of humans being able to communicate in real time, progress was about to speed up.

If Einstein was one in a billion. Then the Starnet was about to enable hundreds of Einsteins to collaborate together in real time. They could all solve problems for which the questions had not yet been asked and, most importantly, find a way to fight back against these Atua aliens—and to speed up the progression of human life.

"You ready?" Ange asked the group.

Everyone in the room nodded.

Ship sent through the mental command, and the Starnet was turned on.

Nothing happened. Not that nothing happened with the Starnet. The connection was made, and it was working. Rather, nothing visible happened.

"Is it on?" Hezekiah asked, looking at the others for a cue.

Ship closed his eyes, connecting through the metaphorical wire to his other counterparts. "We're connected. I've just pinged Atlas's Ship. They're currently on Icarus's world, Titan. Should we pop across?" Ship paused for a moment, looking like he was collecting more data. "Icarus is back. He's giving a lecture about his time visiting the alien home world."

Everyone's eyes in the room lit up. Ange had told them all that Icarus had gone to the alien home world. She wasn't sure it was a smart idea. But obviously he'd made it back safely—and with stories to tell.

It was the kind of announcement that made your heart race. Not only had Icarus made the somewhat crazy decision to sneak onto an alien world and observe them from the inside. But he'd also made it back alive, which was incredibly lucky.

If Ange was honest with herself, she hadn't thought Icarus was coming back. In fact, she'd thought he had a death wish. He was functionally immortal. He didn't die. He didn't age. And he'd already been around for thousands of years. His original purpose was building the Rings of Titan. But once he'd completed that mission, he didn't give himself something else to focus on.

Ange herself had focused on the Ange's Angel program. She'd gone out and colonized more worlds. But she was starting to get a sense that that program was ending with the Starnet and the potential for autonomous drones.

She knew it was only a matter of time before one of her worlds went out and colonized a new world without her—if that hadn't already happened.

She wanted to live forever; she didn't want to risk her life in the way Icarus did. So if her assumption about Icarus was correct and he took this extremely unnecessary risk because he'd lost his purpose in life, then Ange was going to make it her mission to find a new purpose. Something that still involved going out and discovering the universe. "Can we watch his lecture?"

Ship shook his head. "There's no way for us to get in there. The auditorium is firewalled off." Ship paused once more. "Oh, we're good. Atlas's Ship just requested us access. We should be able to stream in shortly."

It took a little longer than the team expected. They discussed among one another for a while until Ship confirmed they could live stream in.

They appeared in a large university auditorium at the very back of the hall. The place was filled. Every seat was taken, and people were gathered around in every available space. Even the aisles were full of people—a fire hazard undoubtedly.

Ange looked around the room. It wasn't just students; there were people from every walk of life. Older people, people in suits, even random avatars. Ange saw someone in a black hood made of some kind of ghostly material that sparkled. Next to that person, there was someone in white boxers with red hearts on them. He had a scarf covering his mouth and nose.

As Ange scanned the room, she saw the influence Icarus had over the planet. Everyone looked unique and expressed themselves in their own way.

They were floating above everyone in projected seats in the only available section.

Unfortunately for them, Icarus had just finished speaking.

"We're thirty minutes over time," Icarus said as he finished what he was saying. "I can answer one more question before we're kicked out of this place completely."

Hands shot up in the air from everyone. Ange assumed half the crowd had raised their hands trying to get one last question answered.

Icarus pointed at a young girl near the front. A porter ran over and handed her the mic. "What was the most surprising thing you learned about visiting the alien world?"

Icarus considered it for a while, nodding his head slowly. "I found it fascinating just how alien the aliens were." He clicked back a few slides on his presentation.

On-screen, the words *sonar* and *magnetic fields* were visible.

"There's no equivalence to the human brain," Icarus continued. "Their brain intuitively processes the world differently from us. So they designed their world to take advantage of that. It was beautiful really. I struggle to explain it, except to say it's alien. They see the world using different sensors than us. It's like if you could never hear and then suddenly could. Or if you only saw the world in black and white, then suddenly you can see color. I'm actually building a module in the metaverse to simulate this . . ."

Icarus saw waving hands, and he was finally being pushed out of the lecture hall. "Come back next month, and I'll share an update."

Icarus was hurried out, and people began leaving the auditorium when they realized they weren't able to intercept Icarus for a private conversation.

Ange and the team waited for Icarus in a little office down the hall.

It was a relatively cramped space now that everyone was in it, open books and half-scribbled papers all over the place. Ange had to hop up on the small desk to make room for everyone.

Hezekiah knocked over a stack of books and was now quickly trying to place them back onto the window ledge where they were previously balancing precariously.

Icarus walked into the room with a sense of swagger that Ange hadn't seen in him before. He looked like he owned the place.

Ange jumped on him and gave him a massive hug. "You adrenaline junkie. You could have got yourself captured . . . Or worse, killed."

"It was worth it though," Icarus said. "I have so much more to tell you."

Ange's eyes lit up when Atlas, Trillion, and both their Ships walked through the door, crowding an already full room.

"Is anyone in here not a simulant?" Icarus asked as he was squished even farther into the room.

The core team of friends all confirmed, while there were a couple unknown people around the peripherals that were real humans.

"Teleport to my RV?" Atlas asked.

Everyone nodded and left the room.

CHAPTER 44

ICARUS

WHAT WE KNOW

Icarus teleported to Atlas's RV. It was currently located on one of the quieter sections of Titan. It was overlooking a field of grass that was genetically engineered to look purple in autumn.

"You know, you should have decked this bus out to look like the Magic School Bus," Icarus said. "No one on this planet would get it, but if they did, it'd be a nice Easter egg."

The Ship of Atlas chuckled. "We're trying to be inconspicuous as we travel around your planet. That would be like holding a giant sign above our heads announcing our location at all times."

"I might travel around in the Magic School Bus. It'll give me a chance to see my planet again," Icarus said. "You know, this part of the ring up ahead with all the changing-color grass was built in honor of the Dottien aliens. There's going to be a new section constructed about the Penquins." Icarus knew Atlas was going through a time of rediscovery. Atlas hadn't been too comfortable with the idea of building a weapon to attack the Atua and Penquins. From what Icarus had learned, he was quite shaken up by the prospect and was traveling around Titan to get over the melancholy. Icarus suspected Atlas was also torn between doing something his oldest friend had asked for and harming another sentient race.

"What about the alien world?" Peter asked, interrupting Icarus's thoughts. "What was the world like? Did you find out anything about when they might attack us?"

At this point, Icarus was becoming good at retelling the narrative. He had retold the story so many times. He was about to retell his story of exploration when he looked around the room. He noticed that both Peter and Ange had worried looks on their faces. They were still in the mindset that this was an evil empire of aliens. The truth was completely different.

"So the aliens we met aren't the Atua," Icarus began to say. "There's actually two intelligent alien species on that world."

Ange's eyes opened wide. "OMG, have they conquered a world?"

Icarus shook his head. "Nothing like that. The two aliens have a symbiotic relationship. They coevolved together. I call them the Penquins and the Atua."

"So we met the Atua?" Peter asked.

"Well, kind of. This is going to give you xenomorph vibes . . . The Atua are squid-looking aliens that tunnel into the Penquins' chests. They sort of take over the Penquins' bodies so that they can move more freely out of water." He was met by a room of squeamish stares. "It's not all one-sided though. The Penquins gain all the knowledge of all the previous host Penquins. It's kinda like getting an upgrade to their intelligence. And it changes the gender of the Penquins too, so it's the only way they can reproduce."

"Is that why these aliens felt so comfortable with brainwashing all the humans on Earth?" Atlas asked.

"That's exactly why. It's part of their culture. They see themselves as gods, as the caretakers of the Penquins."

Ange raised an eyebrow. "How do the Penquins feel about it?"

Icarus smiled at Ange for asking that question because it was the part he found most fascinating. "It's almost impossible for us to grasp their relationship with each other. Humans never coevolved with another species as smart as us. For hundreds of thousands of years, the Penquins and Atua were interdependent. They both need each other to survive. It's a great honor among the Penquins to be chosen by the Atua. We can't be anthropomorphic; the majority of them don't see this relationship as a bad thing. It's what they've evolved to want. Although there are a few of them wanting to find a way to reproduce without the Atua, almost everyone we spoke to is happy with their current arrangement."

Hezekiah lifted his head away from against the window of the RV; he was looking out onto the purple fields below. "Are the Penquins slaves?"

Icarus considered the question for a good while, opening and shutting his mouth a few times as he thought over it. "If one race of humans did this to another one, then yes. I think we'd consider this relationship to be a form a slavery. But to the Penquins it's not."

The Ship of Icarus looked up, mouthing the words *pet* and *analogy.*

Ship was referring to the closest human analogy they had, the idea that humans and pets had coevolved together.

"Ah, yes," Icarus said. "A good way to think about their relationship is by looking at us and our animals. If a dog could talk, I don't think they'd considered themselves slaves. I'm sure they would think of themselves as part of the family. Even working dogs, before we had robots to automate a lot of things, I don't think they'd be upset by what they did on farms. I think they'd see that as what they contribute to the family."

"Isn't that just because we selectively breed them to be like that?" Atlas asked.

"Exactly, we did. Remember how I told you the Penquins need the Atua to reproduce?"

Everyone nodded so Icarus continued. "All Penquins are female at birth. Once a Penquin is chosen by an Atua, they change into a male. And from there they can reproduce with any of the other Penquins. But there is a process to being chosen by the Atua. I'm not sure what's involved, but they do enter the minds of the Penquins. In a way, the Atua are selectively breeding the Penquins."

"If the stories we learned while there are true," Ship added. "They, the Atua, became intelligent first and selectively chose Penguins that were more intelligent."

Atlas finishing typing in a new destination for the RV, and they began to move. "Is this why the Atua saw nothing wrong with their approach of enslaving humans inside a simulation?"

"I suspect that's true," Icarus said. "They probably believed that, after a while, humanity would come to appreciate them and love them the way the Penquins do."

The team continued to pepper Icarus with questions about his visit. Icarus continued sharing his experience on the alien world before the conversation moved to Icarus's escape. He made sure to embellish his skills in the ordeal and skim over the fact he'd almost died.

Peter picked up on what Icarus was leaving unsaid in his information. His face looked like he had seen a ghost. "Are you saying they know one of us visited them? They know it was a human?"

Icarus nodded.

"That's an act of war! Essentially, you just proved that we could sneak a nuclear bomb onto their planet without them knowing. They will have to respond to that. Simple game theory." Peters face suddenly turned angry. "I hope I'm wrong and they don't retaliate." He looked around the room at everyone. "The people in this room have way too much power. These decisions are not just impacting us; they have the ability to impact every living human around. We should not be making decisions like that. None of us should have the ability to put the entire human race in a position of war with another alien species."

There was an awkward tension in the air. Icarus felt like he had just been told off.

In a way, Peter was right; he had made the kind of diplomatic decision that should have been made after consulting others. But in another way, when he'd made the decision, there wasn't anyone else to really speak with. It was, to put it bluntly, one of the perks of building a planet. One of the perks of being immortal. And perhaps, it was simply one of the cruel long symptoms of being stuck on a planet for hundreds of years working slowly to terraform it without speaking to another human or Ship.

That was a lonely torture that changed him—for better or worse, he wasn't sure.

Atlas noticed the strange silence around the large van too. He broke it by pointing out the window. "Hey, look, there's four friends all walking down through the meadows. Let's stop in and say hi. See if they need anything."

Icarus knew Atlas and Ship had been on a long adventure around the Rings of Titan. They were going through a period of discovery and were stopping in and talking to as many people as they could. He knew that Atlas was using it as a way to understand what the ordinary people of the planet cared about.

The RV began slowing down. At first, the four wanderers were looking up at them cautiously, constantly looking upward, then almost hurrying forward. One of them pointed a device at them, as if to say, *If you do anything to us, this is all on camera.* But then as they got closer, something changed. The one with the phone began pointing at it and showing the others.

Their demeanor changed to one of excitement. They began waving and motioning them to dock down nearby.

Atlas nodded, and Ship guided the VR to an open space about twenty meters in front of them. The grass around them was shifting colors slowly. From the air, the grass looked like a solid-purple color. But up close, it was a mosaic of different hues. Some of the plants were changing from the deep-purple color to a rich-orange one. It added so many layers to the beauty.

Traveling the ring was almost a rite of passage to the people of Titan. The last census had said over 97 percent of people either wanted to complete a loop around the planet or they had actually completed it.

There were many different ways to do it. There were those who used transport, the most common of which was on large blimp-like cruise ships. And then there were those who walked.

The ones that walked were seen as the true intrepid travelers. It was often described as the most rewarding but hardest personal challenge to ever complete. It was a many, many-year journey, one hundred times longer than walking the entire circumference of Earth. In fact, there was a dedicated team of rescuers in each city who's only job was to save travelers who couldn't go on farther.

Atlas motioned for Hezekiah to jump up from his seat. "Sorry, there's a gift box under your seat I want to grab out." Atlas lifted up the seat and grabbed out one of the several large baskets full of various things. Icarus saw basics like water, MREs, and toothpaste. But he also saw other things like a tent, a solar shower, and rope. "A lot of these travelers have a habit of underpacking. I like to give them a couple of things to keep them going." He lifted the basket up and carried it out the door.

"Atlas," one of the four travelers yelled out as they ran toward the RV. "I knew I recognized your bus. You know, it's all over the wanderers forums."

Wanderers was a term the people of Titan called anyone on the journey around the planet.

"This is for you," Atlas said, placing the basket of gifts on top of a dog-sized ANT that popped out from under the RV. It looked well designed to carry the basket of goodies. "The ANT will carry these goods for as long as you need. And when you're done, it'll fly everything back to the RV."

"Thank you," the four wanderers began saying before their mouths gaped open as everyone in the RV began to pile out.

"These are my friends," Atlas said as he pointed. "You probably know of my Ship. This is—"

"Oh my gosh, oh my god, that's Icarus." The only girl in the group began squealing.

The tallest of the four people looked at his friend as if to say, *Act cool.* "Everyone knows who he is." He was a good head taller than the others, and he had the kind of bulging arm muscles that made Icarus think he'd just started this journey because surely there weren't any gyms nearby. "My name's Matt and this fangirl over here is Esme. And these are my two friends Victor and Justin."

Esme was a tiny, almost-Asian-looking woman. Victor and Justin looked like close relatives, maybe cousins.

"I told you it was a good idea to walk," Justin said, addressing his friends. "There's no way any of us are ever meeting one of the founders, let alone all of them."

The four of them looked a little starstruck. They constantly kept drooling over the fact they were meeting Icarus, Atlas, Trillion, and one of the Ange's Angels. They weren't too fussed about Peter, Hezekiah, or Unity until they found out they were from Earth, too.

"We're about to set up lunch," Atlas said. "Do you want to join us?"

Icarus had never seen people come to an agreement so quickly. They looked like they'd won the lotto. Icarus found it cute. He also started to feel quite special seeing his people responding to their presence. He was starting to believe Atlas had the right idea with traveling around the planet talking to locals. Talking to real people—not the politicians or businesspeople they were used to speaking with.

Atlas reconfigured the RV into an outdoor kitchen. He began setting up for a BBQ.

While that was happening, everyone chatted among one another. It wasn't until the four wanderers had food in their mouths that they started to get over their stardom and start treating Icarus and the team like normal people.

When Icarus felt they were finally relaxed enough to answer deeper questions, Icarus asked, "So what do you want to do long-term?"

"I want to visit other planets," Justin said. "I wouldn't mind going on holiday to the Penquins' planet you talked about Icarus."

"Oh, and I'd love to go see some of your planets, Ange," Victor added.

Icarus wasn't that hungry, so he was drinking a coffee instead. "Do you mean you want to become simulations like us and visit other worlds?"

All four of the wanderers' heads shook in unison, and Icarus thought he saw a flicker of disgust in their faces, as if the idea of becoming a simulation was somehow gross.

"Not like what you all are is wrong or anything," Matt said. "At the time, it's the only technology you had to live forever. But now, modern medicine solved all that. We're immortal too."

Icarus looked at them all curiously. "But you can't travel between stars as a biological. Traveling at the speeds to traverse space multiplies the radiation. At those levels, it would kill you."

"I'm hoping someone will solve those problems in our life-time," Matt replied.

Icarus thought he saw all four of them look toward Atlas when Matt made the comment about solving the issue with radiation.

Icarus liked these people. They reminded him of them when they were younger. Full of life and hope. And also against the idea of becoming simulations, which could be considered mildly contrarian.

"What made you two start the beta explorer program?" Justin asked.

Peter began retelling stories of his time back on Mars.

Icarus looked around the circle and smiled as he found himself in the middle of a moment that made him extremely happy. He was surrounded by his oldest and closest friends, and he got to relive old memories in front of people who found every word they shared fascinating.

CHAPTER 45

ICARUS

WHAT'S GOING ON?

Icarus remained with Atlas and Ship after the rest of the crew left.

After Icarus spent a bit of time talking to other locals, he wanted to join Atlas on this rediscovering journey. He wanted to encounter his world through the same eyes he'd used to explore the alien world—through eyes of nonjudgment and curiosity. In order to accomplish that, Icarus and his Ship changed their appearances. Icarus changed his avatar away from his recognizable duck to what he'd looked like before becoming a simulation—not that many people knew what he'd looked like before. And Ship changed his appearance to be that of a middle-aged man.

He had one of the eleph-ANTs secretly move his matrix to Atlas's RV, too. That way, he was able to be more present, rather than hopping around through the Starnet satellites around the planet. He was able to be confined, mostly, to a robotic avatar.

He still streamed into universities and lecture halls to give his talks, but they were becoming less common as he began to lose interest in sharing the same story over and over again.

"It's incredible, isn't it?" Icarus said as Atlas and both of their Ships touched down in the very center of the glass ring.

This was the only section of Titan that wasn't covered by anything. Entering that space gave a completely unobstructed view of the galaxy.

It was quite a popular destination for travelers because it gave the people of Titan some of the best views on the planet.

Up in the sky was a clear view of the gas giant they orbited around. And below it was a view out into space. Once a rotation, there was a clear view of the star in the center of the system.

This was the only location on the ring where light wasn't reflected off large mirrors to create an illusion of a natural twenty-four-hour night-and-day cycle. People in this section of the ring understood the world that they were on to the fullest.

It was quite common for people who visited the section of the ring to report feeling so small. They reported realizing how small they were. Seeing the fact they were in orbit around a massive gas giant often gave visitors the feeling that their problems didn't matter. And it also showed people how far humanity had come, no longer confined to living on a rock ball the size of a planet.

Everyone on Titan intellectually knew this was the single biggest planetary construction humanity had ever completed. But they often forgot that because it was designed in a way to hide that. Titan had mirrors creating a consistent day-night cycle. It even used centrifugal force to create a feeling of gravity. These and many more factors hid the fact it was essentially a very long tube, wrapped around a very large planet near the center of a solar system.

Coming inside the glass ring made all of that very clear.

"The glass is so clear. How often is it cleaned?" the Ship of Atlas asked as they walked out of the RV and began moving toward the small crowd of people also taking in the view.

Icarus shrugged because he didn't have a clue.

The four of them walked in silence as Icarus admired everything in front of them. It really was magical. He was standing on top of a glass wall and could see out to space from all angles. He'd built this planet and hadn't really explored it like this before. As he looked up, he watched the way the curved glass magnified the gas giant above. He watched as the reds and blues swirled and mixed together. It almost looked like a marble—only it was moving. The shapes and hues changed, albeit slowly. Icarus thought about it some more; it was probably one of the five wonders of the universe. No other planet, even in Ange's worlds, had a view like this.

Icarus was so engrossed in what he was looking at he didn't notice people approaching them.

"Can I get your autograph?" one of the male strangers who was walking by said to Atlas.

Then Icarus realized it was a small family. There was a husband and wife, and they both had young girls on their shoulders. Maybe one was three, and the other couldn't be much older than one.

At that very moment, Icarus was glad he'd changed his avatar so that no one would recognize him. Not that he didn't want to be kind to his people. He just wanted to enjoy the view and wanted to stay deep in his contemplation.

"Of course," Atlas said, grabbing a pen out of his pocket. He began writing on the little postcard that had Atlas's face on it. "Who should I write this out to?"

"My name's Aaron, this is my wife, Shannon, and our two girls, Hailie and Ariana."

Atlas bit his lower lip and started to write.

Icarus was impressed. Atlas had taken the time to write a very long and kind message to this little family. He hoped they really appreciated it.

"Do you mind if we grab a photo?" the woman, Shannon, asked.

Atlas nodded.

When Icarus went to move away from the photo, Atlas grabbed his arm as if to say, *You're in the photo, too, and you need to remove the avatar.*

Icarus obliged, and as the photo was being taken, he used the hapticgraphic projectors to change the look of his and Ship's avatars back.

The family didn't notice, so Icarus worried he hadn't done it right.

Icarus's fears were quickly quashed when, two minutes later, he heard a scream of joy from the family when they were about twenty meters away—evidently studying the photos and realizing whom they'd met.

Icarus winked at them as they turned around and waved.

"Did you ever consider building a weapon?" Icarus asked Atlas. "Or did you rule it out as soon as Peter asked you?"

"Are you talking about a weapon to fight the Atua?"

Icarus nodded. He was genuinely curious about Atlas's thinking. He wasn't one of the people abducted by the alien spacecraft, so he didn't have the negative feelings toward them like the others did.

"I seriously considered building one. I even had a few ideas of using micro–black holes to increase the power of a laser so much that we could destroy a planet in one go." Icarus moved his head away from the view out into space and began looking at the people around him. "Then I began talking to strangers and realized it wouldn't be the person we attacked that I would be hurting. It would be the ordinary aliens. They would have been the ones that my weapons would hurt. I don't want to hurt people." Then Atlas paused for a moment and almost whispered, "And I don't buy Peter's argument that it would only be a deterrent. Eventually someone would use it."

Icarus nodded; he thought the same really. It was a genie that couldn't be put back in a bottle. Not that it was probably going to stop humans from building a weapon if humanity and the Atua did ever get into a small battle. But if Atlas built it, he would somewhat feel responsible if it was ever used.

There was a collective aw from everyone around them as people began to stare up into the air and point.

Icarus followed their gazes.

There was a massive hunk of metal floating above them. It looked jagged, as if it had been ripped out of something larger, as if a large metal tree had been pulled clean out of the ground and all its roots were still intact. Icarus couldn't really put his finger on what he was looking at. It was so huge, yet so wrong. It didn't make sense. They wouldn't have a spacecraft traveling this close to the rings.

"Isn't that one of our defensive turrets?" Ship asked pointing at the megalithic object.

Then it clicked to Icarus. It was. This was one of the large weapons strategically placed around the ring. These were built into the structure in such a way that they would never be able to fire on the ring itself. It was a safety protocol that meant even if their weapons were somehow hacked, they'd never be able to hurt themselves.

Icarus wasn't involved in the maintenance or security of the planet anymore. So he wondered if they were cleaning it. But then why would it look like that?

Icarus looked closer and saw there were hundreds of small eleph-ANTs and probes all with wire connections to the ship pulling it and moving it around.

"Icarus," his Ship began saying. "Did you get a message?"

"No." Icarus had turned off all his external communication devices. He wanted to be completely present in the moment. "Why's that?"

"I received several urgent messages from the president and the military leaders asking for our location. If I'm understanding this correctly, the Atua contacted them and threatened to destroy the Rings of Titan if they don't hand you and me over to them within thirty minutes." Ship paused for a moment. "I only just turned my phone on now. These messages were from fifty minutes ago."

CHAPTER 46

ICARUS

MECHA GURREN LAGANN

Icarus raced to turn on his phone. At that very moment, he was mentally kicking himself for disconnecting completely from the outside world. He'd made the decision before this adventure to move all communication to a device, rather than being always connected via his mind. He wasn't sure exactly what to do, but he felt like he needed to do something, to stop whatever was going on.

Almost as soon as the device booted up, he received a flood of messages. His phone was going off, and it didn't look like there was an end in it stopping. Again, he was regretting disconnecting his matrix from the internet because he would have been able to parse all this information quicker than going through a phone.

He was about to begin the task of scanning through the info when he received a video call from an unknown number.

Icarus showed the screen to Atlas and both the Ships.

"Answer it," Atlas suggested.

Everyone huddled behind Icarus as he answered the phone.

Time seemed to slow down at that very moment. Icarus's heart skipped a beat, and a strong sense of panic and dread washed over him.

On the other end of the screen was a scene straight out of a horror movie.

On the screen, Icarus saw two Penquins, and they clearly had Atua inside of their chests. One was the Atua that attempted to abduct Atlas and the others—Icarus had become quite adept at differentiating between individual aliens. And the other was one he hadn't met before.

That wasn't what worried him the most. There was a third Penquin, this one clearly not sporting any Atua in its chest. It had a collar around its neck, and it was clear one of its flippers was broken. It looked like it was groveling at their feet.

Icarus knew the Penquin, too. It was Atuatuk, the alien who had helped give them a lot of new information when they had been in the cave. The last Penquin they'd talked with right before they'd escaped. Icarus felt sorry for the alien, who looked to be in great pain.

This wasn't what Icarus's heart was racing for, however. In the corner of the screen, right above one of the Atua's heads, was Lex. Most likely his Lex.

They hadn't gotten away completely free after all. Obviously, they'd captured his escape vehicle after his updated information contained in his matrix was broadcast across the universe.

Icarus wondered whether they had his matrix as well. Lex was meant to self-destruct everything right after sending the data packets. But if they'd managed to halt that self-destruction, then a version of him might have been tortured.

He felt like he had just made one of the biggest mistakes of his life. The Atua obviously didn't look kindly at aliens—especially those that snuck onto their planet.

"I should have known you were on the glass ring," the alien that they knew as PBD spat. "Good." The two aliens looked at each other and made a guttural-sounding click. "You will see the error. We are destroying your ring, and then you will come back to our planet and apologize, and the matter will be considered complete. That's all we want, an apology. In person. With your Ship." The video disconnected.

The words coming out of the alien's mouth were so at odds with what he knew about the Atua. They were ruthless people. He'd seen it on multiple occasions. Their grip over the Penquins was absolute. Icarus didn't believe for one minute if he went to apologize that he'd ever leave again. "That's definitely a trap."

Then Icarus realized that before PBD had told him and Ship to swing by and apologize, he'd casually mentioned he was going to destroy the ring.

As if on cue, Icarus followed Atlas's eyes as he looked up toward the metallic mess, which was one of the planetary-defense weapons ripped right out of the ground and now pointed at the ring.

A massive glow was coming out of the head of the machine. It was about to fire.

It was a laser weapon, designed to cut through almost anything. The Rings of Titan were made of a material called Daimond, which would offer some protection. But Icarus wasn't sure how long it could last. One breach of the hull would probably cause them to lose millions, if not billions, of lives.

"How do we stop this?" Icarus pleaded to no one in particular. He was feeling so helpless.

"I know the operation of those weapons," Atlas said. "There's a manual fail-safe that can shut it off completely. It's right in the very center, underneath the barrel."

"Can you show me where it is?"

Atlas and his Ship both shook their heads. "Ship, did you do it?"

Ship shook his head. "They've completely locked us out."

"It's your Starnet. They've taken over the running of it," Atlas said. "I need to shut it down on our end."

"How do you know it's the Starnet?" Icarus asked.

"We didn't see an alien vessel enter this system. So they must have hacked their way in. If I shut down the Starnet on this end, then that will hopefully lock them out completely."

"What if they've set up their own back door?"

Atlas bit his lower lip, thinking some more. "They have to be leveraging the technology somehow. I'm going to try overloading it, sending massive packets of data back and forth." Atlas pointed up toward the firing machine. "Shut it down."

"Okay." Icarus was feeling a wave of panic roll over him. He didn't like situations like this. He began scanning the edges of the ring wall. He knew there was an air lock somewhere nearby that should allow him to move through it and reach space.

Atlas and his Ship froze. They couldn't operate their avatars while the bandwidth on the planet was being overloaded.

"Let's mecha merge," Ship suggested.

Icarus and Ship had designed their avatars so that they could be merged together. It would allow them both to consume more power and do things that they couldn't do individually. It was particularly useful in this situation because they were going to need as much power as possible.

Icarus nodded, and the two of them blended into each other. Their combined form looked like a mecha robot or a Transformer.

Their combination made what could only be described as a Transformer-inspired duck. The Icarus-Ship combination looked like it had a duck head over one of its arms, almost protruding out like a gun. It looked like Icarus and Ship had designed it to look a lot like the Grimlocks in Transformers, only instead of including elements of a dinosaur, it was elements of a duck.

There was meant to be accompanying dance as an electric guitar soundtrack played, all crescendoing in an end pose that had the newly combined Icarus and Ship standing with one hand in the air as a light flashed and they bellowed, "Mega Icar-ship!" in a suitably deep and raspy Japanese anime-style voice.

None of that happened, since they didn't have time to run through the normal preamble, and they had a mission to complete.

Icar-ship looked up quickly and completed the scan of the edge of the glass portion of the ring. He was looking for the air lock exit. There were several air lock doors dotted around, but they were all the consumer kinds, not the emergency ones.

The air locks designed for the general public had no cycle-override functionality, meaning they would have to wait for the air to be completely pumped out. The emergency air lock doors were bigger and able to be forced open, even without all the air pumped out.

Icar-ship spotted the exit he wanted. He fired his engines and raced to the air lock, moving much faster.

CHAPTER 47

MEGA ICAR-SHIP

HERO

Icar-ship closed the air lock door behind him.

Icar-ship reached out toward the emergency-door opener before pulling it back.

"We need to fasten ourselves through an umbilical," Ship said through their shared internal voice. "We'll get thrown out into space if we don't."

Icar-ship grabbed one of the thin wire threads connected to the wall. It was a little bit thicker than dental floss. Since it was made with diamond nanotubes, it was stronger than any rope available from before the material was in wide use.

He slammed the emergency-air-cycle button—damaging the button and leaving a noticeable dent in the housing.

Icar-ship didn't realize how much stronger he was as he was blown out the door and began tumbling toward the mess of wires out in space.

"Can we take out any of the eleph-ANTs?" Icarus asked. "They're what's holding the laser weapon in place."

"This look is just for show. We don't actually have any weapons."

As they moved through space, closing in toward the massive weapon, they watched as all the eleph-ANTs that were attached seemed to maneuver their engines in such a way that they looked like they were pushing the gun.

Then Icar-ship saw it. The laser was firing. The eleph-ANTs had repositioned themselves in preparation for the recoil.

Icar-ship watched as a giant chunk of the ring began to melt and morph. A wave of force propagated down the ring, causing violent shaking on the inside. It almost looked like an earthquake was happening.

Icar-ship felt a wave of emotions as they both realized how serious this all was. People were dying in there.

It was destruction on a scale they hadn't seen before. Icar-ship had to force his face to look away from it. He assumed the pressure change inside the ring was also causing people's ears to rupture.

"I've reconfigured the hapticgraphic engine around us," Ship said. "We should be able to use it as a small rail gun and launch tiny payloads out the front of our arms. I'm lining up targets now."

Icar-ship fired off ten quick shots. One of them was toward the nanowire many of the eleph-ANTs were holding. It was very unlikely they had enough firepower to break it, but they wanted to make sure.

The other eight shots hit their target. They aimed for the bolt connecting the arms of the closest eight eleph-ANTs to their bodies.

Five of the bolts successfully exploded on impact, rendering those eleph-ANTs without the ability to take hold of the nanowire, effectively making them useless at holding the giant laser weapon in place.

Both Icarus and Ship felt each other's collective joy at that moment.

There was no noticeable change in the aiming ability of the weapon; it would probably require them to take down a few hundred eleph-ANTs. But it still felt like a win, as that was five fewer eleph-ANTs the alien enemy had to manipulate the weapon.

Icar-ship's self-praise turned into fear as the five eleph-ANTs with no ability to grapple their assigned ropes turned toward Icar-ship.

"We need to get out of here, Ship."

Obliging, Icar-ship's engines shifted to full throttle, and he raced toward the closed hatch just below the nozzle of the massive gun.

Unfortunately for Icar-ship, the eleph-ANTs were much faster. They were much bigger and had much more powerful rocket engines. They were quickly closing in on them.

"What do we do?" Ship asked. He noticed they had no chance of making it to the manual-shutdown valve they were aiming for.

"Let's take as many of these things out as we can," Icarus replied. "See if we can make a dent!"

Icar-ship began firing off volley after volley, aiming at all the eleph-ANTs that offered a clear view of their appendage bolts.

They were really racking up the number of direct hits, as eleph-ANT after eleph-ANT was no longer about to help in the aiming of the weapon.

"It's like shooting fish in a barrel," Icarus remarked.

The enemy wasn't responding at all to Icar-ship's attacks. They wondered if Atlas's plan to overload the Starnet with packets of data was working.

Then they got their response. Whoever was pulling the strings was focusing their energy on firing the weapon again.

They giant defense turret turned self-destroyer aimed at the same location, this time taking the heat created and puncturing a small hole through the ring's material. Icar-ship saw a plume of gas jet from the puncture on the other side of the ring.

The security exits along the ring began to close, blocking off that area of the ring and limiting the amount of gas that could leak. Anyone not in a sealed suit would soon suffocate if they didn't do something.

The silver lining in all of this was that the five eleph-ANTs that were previously pursuing Icar-ship began moving in a direction away from them. They were moving to block the available shot angles that Icar-ship had.

"I think we're having an impact," Ship said. "Should we continue trying to shut down more of these things?"

Then they noticed the impact of their efforts. The eleph-ANTs were struggling to hold the weapon in position against the force of the recoil.

The final few seconds of the laser weapon's blast moved away from the hole it had created and blasted harmlessly into deep space.

"Let's not press our luck," Icarus replied. "Let's get to the hatchway first, then shoot as many as we can before we close the door behind us."

Icar-ship pressed his advantage and moved as quickly as he could toward the hatchway. It was up ahead, just a few hundred meters away.

Icar-ship quickly wrote a program and fired a large payload out of the front of his front rail gun. It quickly splattered against the side roller door.

The congealed mess of a payload began to recombine, flowing into a solid and wrapping its tentacles around the air lock roller door.

Icar-ship had sent one of its two hapticgraphic projectors as well as a massive amount of material to the hatchway. It acted like an additional limb that was detached in order to begin the process of opening the chamber.

The extra appendage began to turn the roller wheel, slowly at first, as the thing hadn't been opened in years, then faster and faster until the door opened with a puff of gas.

The rest of Icar-ship was close behind as soon as the door opened, slamming into the inside of the inner chamber almost as if timed to the nanosecond.

The viscous section of Icar-ship quickly closed the door behind it and then recombined with the rest of Icar-ship.

They were in a small chamber that was slowly being repressurized with atmosphere.

Emergency red warning lights began signaling. Not all was right with the place.

"Can you see an override switch?" Icarus asked.

The override switch forced the air lock door to open without the requirement of atmosphere being pumped in.

Spotting the lever, Icar-ship opened the cover and quickly pulled it down.

The change in pressure was immediately obvious.

Icar-ship projected a beam of light out of the front of his left arm, keeping the other arm in reserve as a weapon.

The inner air lock door slowly swung open, and Icar-ship quickly realized how screwed they were. In front of them were hundreds of small ANTs and even a few eleph-ANTs. They acted like a wall, and several started moving toward them.

Icar-ship fired off several shots, taking down all the small ANTs that were headed their way.

Instantly, dozens of more began their approach. This confirmed that they were all here to protect this location. Those ANTs were all there to stop this attack.

Icar-ship now had one mission: to make it to the other end of the short hallway and trigger the automatic-shutdown sequence.

Icar-ship bent down slightly before leaping forward. As he left the ground, the gun obviously fired as the entire structure around them moved a meter to the left, causing Icar-ship to smash violently into the opposite side wall, crushing one of the ANTs that had grabbed him.

The other ANTs that were moving toward them in the tunnel also experienced the sudden movement and were taken out by the sudden force.

Icar-ship quickly stood back up and began running as quickly as he could past more and more ANTs, fighting the change in direction caused by the weapon they were in firing.

"We're going to make it," Icarus said.

"Why aren't they attacking us?" Ship replied.

"Who cares; let's keep going."

Their confidence was growing as they made it deeper and deeper in. The ANTs nearby seemed to be ignoring them unless they came too close. They were all focused on holding on to the wall, and the whole space they were in shook madly.

Then it stopped. The shaking, the movement, everything.

That's when everything went completely wrong. The ANTs inside of the tunnel weren't ignoring them. They were waiting until the weapon stopped firing, not wanting to take additional damage.

But as soon as the firing stopped, they surrounded Icar-ship and began pulling him to pieces. Bit by bit.

Icarus and Ship were screwed.

It was something out of a nightmare. The only thing that made it easy was Icar-ship didn't feel pain as more and more parts of him were dismembered—death by a thousand cuts.

Almost like falling into quicksand, they began to be consumed. Their chances of reaching the end of the hallway approached zero. They were actually being pulled away from their goal, so their probability of success dipped even lower.

There was objectively no equivalent to what Icarus and Ship were experiencing. No control over their bodies. No autonomy. No ability to do anything but be consumed. The closest thing to it was ants in real life. When they encountered another ant colony, the wars were atrocious. Groups of ants would pull off the limbs of the enemy ants, one at a time.

This is exactly what was happening to Icar-ship.

The thought of that sent shivers up both of their spines. Icarus in particular forced the avatar they were sharing to move and shake. He fidgeted this way and that. But more and more of his body parts were pulled off.

The hapticgraphic nanomaterial was running out faster as Icarus began to panic.

Ship took over control of the avatar and forced him into a perfectly circular ball, self-healing holes as chunks of him were dislodged.

The whole room shook, and Icar-ship bounced around the room like a pinball machine. It wasn't as bad as previously since several ANTs still had hold of him. But it was enough that he thought they might have an opening.

Icar-ship quickly positioned his engine out the back and fired hard, attempting to make his way toward the side of the room with the control panel.

No luck, however. Icar-ship actually lost his engine as one of the ANTs pulled it clean off as another one mangled the wires.

"There's no hope," Icarus said as he felt defeated. He began to panic.

"There is one," Ship said. "Self-destruct and take this whole section with us."

Icarus nodded as he felt a little bit of control creep back into his world. He was about to show them one last bang. "We haven't backed up since we got here. We won't be coming back."

"It's fitting that we die together. You and I." Then Ship couldn't say anything more. He shared the pain and sadness he was feeling with Icarus.

"Goodbye, my best friend."

"I love you, Icarus. Goodbye."

The two of them understood the wild mix of emotions each of them was feeling. They were the same. They combined and amplified. They told each other they cared and that they didn't want to die. And that they really hoped this destroyed the alien weapon. None of it was in words though. It was all just a feeling. An understanding. A shared meaning through connected emotions. As if they'd developed some new language that only they could understand. And that was only possible through thousands of years of shared experiences.

There was a loud noise.

Then there was white noise.

And finally, nothing.

CHAPTER 48

ATLAS

END OF THE RING?

Atlas and his Ship stood on the bridge of a spacecraft parked in the Titan system. They were overlooking the utter destruction that was the ring.

Atlas had expected his plan of overloading the Starnet to work. But it hadn't. He assumed it was because the Atua were very adept at hacking. They had very deep knowledge of the systems on Titan. Atlas had no idea how they had gotten in, but his current running theory was the Atua had already infected all the systems before. This was different from the previous attack that Atlas had destroyed. The Atua must have had multiple sleeper AIs just waiting to be switched on.

Crashing the Starnet did stop the Atua from sending any new instructions. Atlas assumed it was because they had AIs operating already, with complex goals they were moving toward.

Still, Atlas thought his theory about the Starnet had to be true. So he continued to have the bandwidth taken up by useless messages. He was now on a separate spacecraft that he had docked in the system. This had a completely different Starnet connection and so wasn't impacted by his attempt to overload the one running on Titan.

Atlas could only guess, but it looked as though the death toll would be measured in the millions. And if the ring broke apart, he was confident it would mean a total wipeout of the population.

The ring was on the cusp of falling apart. Somehow the alien had taken over one of their defense turrets, which normally wouldn't be an issue because they were fixed in place and had no way of pointing the weapon at itself. But the Atua solved this by completely detaching it from its housing. It was drifting out in space with thousands of eleph-ANTs being used to point the end of the laser weapon at a section of the ring.

And boy did that weapon make an impact. It had cut right through the daimond-infused shielding around the ring. It had also melted and deformed much of the surrounding structure. This on its own was a bad thing. But then, as more and more of the shell was cut into, the centrifugal force was stretching the small hole out and turning it into a giant gash.

Atlas knew there were people among all the debris that were unfortunate enough to make it out into space.

"I don't see them slowing down the rotation, Ship. Are they getting our messages?"

"I haven't had confirmation from them yet."

"Keep the message on repeat; just keep broadcasting it until they respond."

Atlas felt like the ring was in a precarious position. It looked like it was causing more and more self-inflicted damage. The spin on the ring was causing more additional damage than the laser weapon itself. Atlas knew the Atua knew exactly where to aim to cause maximum damage. They had fired right at one of the hidden joints, at an area that wouldn't be noticeable unless you had the original blueprints of the ring.

Atlas began to worry that one more shot was one too many shots for the ring to take. "How many humans can we fit in here, Ship?"

"This wasn't built to house humans."

"But if we needed to. How many could we fit?"

Ship thought about it for a little while. "Maybe a few thousand. But we couldn't hold them for long. We'd need to get the atmosphere from somewhere."

Atlas pointed at where the hole in the ring was forming. "Let's enter there and start pulling people out."

"Are you sure? If that weapon fires while we're entering, we might end up dead."

"Anyone in that section of the ring will be dead soon if we don't save them. I think the risk is worth it."

Atlas felt the spacecraft move as they headed toward the target.

"That gun is firing at regular intervals," Ship said. "If we move fast, we'll get there right after the next shot."

Atlas received a notification at the same time he witnessed the whole ring begin to slow down. He immediately began to see the pressure being put on the gap begin to ease and the two ends that were coming apart begin to close in on each other. "At least they're finally slowing it down."

"We're being hailed by the head of the military," Ship said, projecting a hologram of the leader in front of the two of them.

He was a stockily built man. He had a short military cut and stood like he had spent years standing at attention. He looked like he was in his pajamas though.

"Atlas, this is General Lemuel Bossman," the older man on the hologram said. "Can you stop overloading the Starnet? It's messing with our internal communication network."

"Of course," Atlas replied, looking at Ship, who nodded, evidently freeing up the bandwidth again. "Sorry, I thought that was how the Atua were hacking in."

"We agree with your assessment. But it's also impacting our rescue efforts. Do you have any other tricks up your sleeve for disrupting the Atua?"

"I know as much about this attack as you do, general."

Atlas saw light coming off from the weapon again. Atlas assumed it was about to begin firing once more. It felt a little too soon; the weapon had only just finished its last shot.

Atlas turned his head and saw the light wasn't coming from the head of the laser but the base. Then he realized it was an explosion. All the lights around it switched off at that point.

General Bossman looked to the left of himself, as if he was communicating with someone off-screen. "We've just had confirmation the weapon the Atua were using is completely offline now.

"Do they have access to any other lasers?"

"If they could hack into this one, they'll be able to hack into any of them. I've got my team entering all the manual-control centers and disarming them one by one."

"Good."

"Atlas, can you look into how they hacked us and find a way to stop them?"

"I can tell you now, they built this back door a long, long time ago. I think we'll have to assume they have access to all our systems."

Lemuel Bossman looked down toward his phone. "Did you get a message?"

Atlas got the ping too. Ship pulled up another separate projection next to Bossman.

It was PDB, the original Atua that they'd met. It was a prerecorded message.

Atlas nodded and Ship played the recording.

"I consider this matter concluded," PBD said. There was a snarling as the alien looked directly into the camera. "Do not return to our planet."

There was no preamble. No long-winded speech. But Atlas knew there was a lot of threat in that message. Atlas knew that

PBD had a very good grasp of human psychology. He knew that this message would be analyzed and broadcast to the public all over the galaxy. Atlas knew that the nonchalant nature of the message conveyed much more than any long threat could have.

That message said that punishing humans was beneath them and that they would do worse if humans tried to retaliate.

That message would cause fear in everyone.

Atlas didn't have a moment to analyze the message further though, as they'd just touched down.

"General, we're going to help rescue some people," Ship said before closing the projection. "Let us know if you need anything else."

The place was like a war zone. Buildings had toppled over as the space vibrated and moved. Sections of the walls had fallen down and acted like boulders crashing into things. Because the whole ring was moving at the same time, it acted like a pinball machine and caused the massive chunks of walls to bounce around, causing more damage.

The air was full of cries for help, people screaming for their loved ones. The air was thin too, as more and more gas escaped.

"Send out all our ANTs," Atlas ordered. "Get everyone here or to one of the emergency exits."

Ship was already doing that. Ship was directing ANTs to carry people with missing limbs and serious injuries out of harm's way. They didn't have medical facilities to help anyone either.

"Atlas, I've got our two onboard fabricators churning out medical equipment. But we're not equipped to help anyone with a serious injury."

"Let's just save as many people as we can."

Atlas was running into one of the nearby buildings. It had been crushed by a falling tree. He thought he heard a noise coming from it.

He forced his way through the half-broken door and made his way toward the sounds. It was a woman. She was screaming for help.

"Are you hurt?" Atlas asked as he got closer.

"I'm stuck. I can't get out," he heard her say in a panicked voice.

Atlas saw that the tree had landed right on top of the door to the room she was in. It meant she wasn't able to open it. By the looks of things, she was trapped inside of a bathroom.

Atlas used his electronic muscles to break the giant trunk and move it out of the way.

Atlas opened the door, and the woman smiled at him. She looked to be her twenties.

"Are you all right?" Atlas asked.

She collapsed and fell to the ground.

Atlas raced forward to catch her. He wondered what had happened. Then he analyzed the air and realized the oxygen was thinning quickly. There must have been a bigger breach in the wall.

Atlas picked her up and raced her as quickly as he could back to the spacecraft. He knew that brain damage could occur quite quickly once a person was oxygen deprived.

Making it to the rocket, he grabbed one of the small oxygen tanks from the ANTs that were handing them out. Then he placed her down on the metal floor, in a clear space. His ship was full of injured people.

Atlas felt a wave of emotion run over him. Anger. He wanted to kill the Atua. But first he had to save as many people as humanly possible.

Atlas went back and forth, searching and rescuing as many people as he could. They were using eleph-ANTs to ferry people out of this section of the ring. They were using ANTs to send out oxygen masks as quickly as their fabricators could produce them.

Everything was go go go. Until it wasn't. General Lemuel Bossman called Atlas on a private line.

"I don't know how to say this, Atlas. We've had confirmation that Icarus was in that laser turret when it blew up. He saved us, but that version of him is gone. I'm sorry."

Atlas couldn't think.

Everything was swimming around Atlas's head.

Everything went dark.

He knew on the surface that Icarus wasn't truly gone. He knew he had a backup protocol. He knew a version of Icarus would come back. But it wouldn't be his Icarus. It wouldn't be the one he'd spent months traveling around the planet with. The new Icarus wouldn't have the shared experiences and memories. It would be Icarus. But it wouldn't be Icarus.

Atlas's vision went dark.

For a moment Atlas could think again. Then he couldn't.

"—las."

Atlas wondered who's voice he was hearing.

His face became wet.

"At—"

He could hear Ship's voice out in the distance.

He wished it was Icarus's voice.

An emotional scar he didn't know was there reopened. He missed Icarus. He also began to miss his first child—Atreus.

He closed his eyes.

But the pain got louder.

He opened his eyes and couldn't see a thing.

CHAPTER 49

ATLAS

UTTER DESTRUCTION

For several days after the incident, Atlas went through life as if he was experiencing post-traumatic stress disorder.

In fact, everyone on Titan was.

Atlas and Ship did nothing but help. Back and forth they moved through Titan helping in any way they could.

Digging people out of toppled buildings. Searching for missing pets. Rebuilding homes. Transporting people back to family members on the other side of the ring. And burying the dead.

Atlas had never seen so much death in his life. He became numb.

It would have been easy to assume that with the level of automation and resources available to the Titan people that Atlas would have nothing to do. But they were unprepared for how widespread the destruction was.

If Atlas was honest, there really wasn't a human on this planet that would have thought to prepare this sort of chaos. Everyone knew someone who was dead. Everyone had a family member they couldn't find.

Three hundred and fifty-two million people.

Eighteen percent of the population of the planet.

Everybody knew someone.

Atlas knew someone.

Icarus.

Icarus was never coming back in the same way.

A deep hatred grew in Atlas's heart while he tried to save as many lives as possible.

Atlas didn't know how to get through it. He still heard people's cries of pain echoing in his ears whenever the world around him was quiet.

So many times, the people he was saving asked him, "Is it over?" or, "Are they coming back?"

The only thing he could say in reply was "You're safe now."

Because in all honesty, he didn't know. There was a running fear among everyone that the Atua might come back. They might attack again.

The Atua were completely fine with lying. They were happy to say one thing and doing another. They had a goal in mind and would say whatever was required to get them to that goal.

They'd lied to Atlas and the others about negotiating with them. And now Atlas wasn't sure whether they were lying about the attack being over.

From what he knew about the aliens, they were completely alien in nature. Their motivations were clear, though. They wanted to punish Titan for Icarus's unannounced visit to their planet.

One thing that was true about the Atua was they had an extremely good grasp on human nature, especially human nature over large groups. They'd spent years manipulating and studying humanity.

Measured purely from the perspective of fear, they'd succeeded.

It's a long-held myth that humans fight back when put in a corner. But humans aren't dogs. The majority of humans didn't fight back in a stressful situation like the one everyone on Titan had faced. The most common human response was to freeze. To become overwhelmed and unresponsive. The second most common human response was to run.

This was being played out throughout everyone that Atlas had interacted with. They weren't preparing revenge or wanting to get back at the Atua. They were scared senseless. They were angry at the world. Angry at the government. Angry at whoever left a back door in their programming so that their own weapons could be used against them.

It was true that some humans fought. But when faced with an army or an attacker that was bigger, almost no one did.

Atlas was seeing this play out. Atlas saw the fear in people. The people of Titan thought the unknown nature of the Atua meant there was a possibility they were so technologically advanced that humanity had no chance of fighting back.

Atlas felt a surge of anger creep inside of him. Atlas did not feel that way. He wanted to seek revenge. He wanted the Atua to feel everything he was feeling right then.

He wanted to make sure there was never an attack like this on a human colony again.

Atlas sat in the very back of his spacecraft, in a cargo area away from everyone else. He was ferrying a lot of people between two sections of the ring.

He was about to get some sleep when Peter called him.

"How are you doing, Atlas?" Peter asked.

"I'm doing better than most of the people I'm helping."

There was an odd silence on the line as they both took in the meaning of Atlas's words. "Have you spoken to Angelique? Is she making progress on securing the ring against any subsequent attack?"

Angelique answered the question. "One of my planets thinks their system is impenetrable. But we'll need to rebuild all the tech stack on this world from scratch."

"Is there an interim solution? Can we switch all defense weaponry to manual operation?"

Atlas had sent a message to the leaders of his planet, Neuropa, asking them to deactivate all automated defense capabilities. He'd warned them to move toward a manual human-controlled method, something that, at least in the short term, would be harder to hack—since he didn't think it was possible to hack a biological human brain.

"That will take some time," Angelique replied.

"We might not have time," Atlas replied.

"This is our number one focus," Peter said, sensing Atlas's fear of another attack. "We've got the brightest minds on all the planets trying to understand how the Atua got in in the first place and how to stop them from ever getting in again."

Atlas wanted to ask Peter and Angelique something. He opened his mouth to speak, but then closed it again. He was worried the phone line was somehow compromised. "Is there a way for us to communicate so that there's no chance we can be listened to?"

"I wouldn't trust the network on Titan," Angelique said.

Atlas thought about it some more. "In theory, the Starnet uses entangled particles, so anyone intercepting particles would ruin entanglement if they tried to listen in. But the weak link is between the entangled-particle reader and the connection to our matrices. Can someone of one of your planets rebuild a secure connection between me and the Starnet, Angelique?"

"That's one of the recommendations from the security council on my planet Chrysalis," Angelique said. "I'll get them to send over the designs to you. It requires you and Ship to build it from scratch and not use a general-purpose fabricator because there needs to be trust in the system. You need to verify the exact specification of each component to ensure there isn't a back door."

Atlas felt that was a good precaution, given everything that had just happened, and he agreed with it. If he used a fabricator to create a security unit, then he would have no way of verifying that the unit didn't have a back door or a malicious piece of code. Because it made sense, if the Atua wanted to ensure everything he made had a back door in it, that the easiest way would be to program all fabricators to add that secret back door to everything they manufactured.

This was going to be a big project. They had underestimated the extent to which the Atua had infiltrated their planets. Yes, they had eliminated the filter virus, which was the cause of their planets' struggles. But they never fully purged the Atua from their systems.

All their well-intended strategies had no chance at all of ever working. Yes, they'd rebuilt a lot of the technological infrastructure from the ground up to be more secure than ever. But they'd still used the same fabricators and automation to build them.

Securing their worlds was going to take many years. It was going to take manual work. It was going to require the entire planet to focus on that singular goal. Rebuilding the ring was one thing. Rebuilding a defense platform that was verifiable and they could all trust was another.

Again, another issue they'd have to work through was verifying the designs that Angelique shared weren't altered in any way.

Atlas pushed those thoughts to the side; he knew someone on one of Angelique's worlds would have a solution. There was only one thing he was focused on right now.

His mind was focused on building a weapon.

His mind drifted to the idea that he could ensure no one else in the galaxy would have to deal with the Atua again.

He was going to make them scared. Scared to mess with a human again. Scared for the survival of their species.

He knew his anger might calm down later. But for now, all he wanted was to fight back. In this very moment, he didn't feel like the majority of humans that went into a fear or runaway mode. Right now, he was ready to fight.

Right now, if they pushed him hard enough, he thought he might even be willing to kill.

Right now, he felt justifiably angry.

CHAPTER 50

PETER

WEAPON OF MASS DESTRUCTION

"Why are we at a baseball stadium, Atlas?" Peter asked as he kicked a small rock off the batter's box area.

Peter, along with Angelique, Atlas, and the Ship of Atlas, were all on a planet called Chrysalis. It had been seven months since the attack on Titan, and Atlas had been working away in secret for the last six.

Chrysalis was one of the moons in one of Angelique's hidden systems. It was the original location she'd transformed when she'd first set up the system. But once the terraforming project was complete on the chosen planet in the system, everyone had migrated, and they'd left the moon as a museum and research facility.

Which Peter realized sounded a tad odd, given they were standing in the middle of a university-campus facility that was left dormant and unused for many years. But when a K2 civilization had the power to create or transform almost anything, designating an entire moon as a museum turned research facility wasn't that far-fetched.

"Are you all connected to the local Starnet using a secure connection?" Atlas asked instead of answering Peter's question.

The road to recovery for Titan had been long—and wasn't yet complete. But there were a number of massive learnings throughout the process. Firstly, the security on all the colonies was woefully out-of-date. Too much reliance on automated systems, and almost everything was accessible digitally.

This made sense given that all the beta explorers, the people who'd set up the planets, were digital. They needed to have access to everything digitally. But this also left everything open to remote hacking attacks, which the Atua were very experienced in. Their knowledge of human-designed programs was immense. It was well-known that the Atua had given New Zealand an AI that had completely transformed the world. But there was now a working theory that the Atua's influence was more prevalent than that.

It was now suggested that many of the human-based programming languages and design were created by the Atua and given to humans. That way they always had a way through the back door.

Humans were focused on building applications on top of the operating system, while the operating system was left wide open.

Even on planets like Neuropa, where they assumed they were building things from scratch, they weren't. There was always a kernel taken from previous systems.

One of Angelique's planets had developed several completely different computer architectures. These were assumed to be safe—well, as safe as they knew was possible.

"We're both connected via the Stealthnet connection," Peter said looking toward Angelique, who nodded.

"Well, as you know, I've been working here in secret," Atlas said. "Working on something that I could use to make sure we never end up in a similar situation again."

Peter was interested in what Atlas was going to share. He thought it might be a weapon. He knew that Atlas was angrier than he had ever seen him. He'd never seen Atlas want revenge so badly.

But as Peter looked around the park, he began to second-guess Atlas's intentions. He was beginning to think he was here to share something else.

Angelique smiled at Atlas. "The suspense is driving me crazy. Spit it out, old man."

Atlas pointed to the pitcher's mound, to where a machine was. He walked toward it and gestured for the others to follow.

Atlas stood in front of what looked like an automatic ball thrower. He turned it on, and the two rotating wheels began to spin. And they spun quickly.

Atlas picked up one of the balls and loaded it into the back of the machine. It rolled down a small track and then as soon as it hit the spinning wheels it shot out the front and slammed into the net behind the batter's plate. "Any idea why we're here?"

Peter knew this was all spectacle. He knew Atlas was putting on a show. "You're going to build a giant version of this and shoot an object out of a rotating rail gun?" Peter asked sarcastically.

"Well, kind of," Atlas said. "There's one more piece of the puzzle I need to explain to you before I show you what this is." Atlas looked at both Peter and Angelique. "How efficient is dynamite at turning matter into energy?"

Both Peter and Angelique shrugged.

"Not very powerful," Peter said. "I don't think you could create a dynamite stick big enough to punch a hole through one of our spacecraft."

Peter looked at Angelique, who said, "Don't look at me. I have no idea about some ancient technology."

Atlas bit his lower lip. "Okay, the analogy obviously doesn't work." Atlas picked up his notepad and started racing through the pages.

"Use the energy analogy," Ship offered. "That's your strongest example."

Atlas became animated at that prospect. "The fusion energy that powers our spacecraft, how efficient is it at turning matter into energy?"

Angelique raised an eyebrow. "Are you talking about something to do with E equals MC squared?"

"Correct," Atlas replied.

Peter and Angelique both shrugged because they had no idea.

"If you're like me, you probably think it's really efficient," Ship said, helping Atlas out. "The amount of material we need to power this entire moon's energy requirements is tiny."

"Exactly." Atlas held up one of the baseballs. "If this baseball was the matter used in fusion power, it would power this entire moon and more." Atlas placed the ball onto the ramp, and it rocketed out the front and hit the wall behind it. "But it's still tiny. Roughly one percent of the energy trapped inside of this ball would be converted into energy." Atlas pointed up toward the star. "The star in the sky is the universe's most powerful fusion reactor, and it's nowhere near as good as the designs we have now."

"Okay, so what's more powerful?" Peter asked, guessing the direction Atlas was heading.

"Black holes," Atlas said matter-of-factly. "Rotating black holes will turn forty percent of the matter they're given into energy."

Peter thought about that statement and realized he wasn't fully understanding it. "I'm struggling to visualize that."

"It means," Atlas said, picking up another baseball. "If we turned forty percent of this object into energy, this entire moon would explode. We would probably cause so much violent destruction to the moon that the nearby planets would be thrown off course." Atlas turned a knob on the ball-throwing machine, and it started to increase its speed. He dropped the ball down the track once more. This time it rocketed out the front at such a speed that Peter nearly missed it.

The ball quickly traveled through the net on the other side and slammed into the wall behind. It exploded on impact against the brick wall.

"So what are you saying?" Peter asked. "We're going to move a black hole to outside of the Atua's home world?"

"Even better," Atlas said. "We're going to create black holes. It's actually quite simple." Atlas pointed at each rotating circular wheel. "Imagine each of these was a black hole." Atlas held up a ball. "And this was a small payload." Atlas sent another one of the balls through the machine. "If we sent billions of light particles past two rotating black holes, we'd impart enough energy to blow a hole right through any Atua planet."

"But how?" Angelique asked. "How are you making this all work?"

"Creating the black hole wasn't that hard."

Peter noticed a sense of pride in the way Atlas said that statement. Peter knew him well enough to know that it was the kind of thing only Atlas could accomplish. It had probably required him to learn a massive range of other fields of knowledge just to come up with a theory of how it would work. Then to actually complete the work in less than a year was incredible.

Atlas continued. "I'm using a much more powerful version of your tractor beam, Angelique. If you combine that with the hapticgraphic technology, it's possible to condense a gas so much that a micro–black hole is created." He pointed at one of the spinning wheels on the machine. "The biggest hurdle is they evaporate so quickly that they need to be created at the exact time I send the particle right by them."

"So you've built a weapon that uses a particle accelerator to fire a special kind of particle out the front of it?" Angelique asked. "And then you create two micro–black holes right at the exact moment that particle passes by so that the amount of energy that it has is multiplied massively."

"Massive would be an understatement. But yes, that's essentially what happens."

"What about the black holes' spin?" Peter asked. "Surely we don't have the technology to spin the black hole fast enough to do what you're wanting?"

"Well, that's the fun part," Atlas replied. "The intense spin directions happen naturally." Atlas looked at Ship as if to say, *This is your cue.*

Ship began to rise off the ground. He had his arms stretched out in what looked like a biblical pose as if he was about to be loaded onto a cross.

Atlas walked over and used his arms to spin him around. Almost like a top, Ship began to turn around. It was a slow and steady spin.

"The great thing about spinning objects is the smaller you make them the faster they spin."

Ship began to pull his arms in toward himself. As he did, his rotational speed increased.

"It's the same principal that happens with figure skaters," Atlas explained. "While their arms are stretched out, they spin slowly. But as they pull their arms closer together, they increase the rate of turning."

The conversation with the team went on like that for quite some time, everyone asking Atlas and Ship questions to fully understand how the weapon worked.

Peter couldn't help but be impressed. Atlas's mighty brain had worked hard to create something so simple yet extremely powerful. In theory, what he'd built a laser weapon so powerful that it could blow an entire planet apart in a second. It was essentially a Death Star weapon on steroids.

All they needed to do next was test it.

"But how are we going to test it without blowing up a planet?" Peter asked. "It's not like we have a spare planet just lying around that we can blow up."

Atlas waved his hands up in the air, and everything around everyone began to stretch and fold. Suddenly Peter found himself standing outside of a spacecraft floating in space.

Peter looked to his left and noticed a large spacecraft with a strange-looking nose cone.

"With this," Atlas said.

The nose cone of the spacecraft glowed red for half a second. Then a bright light shot out the front of it.

Peter hadn't realized it until that moment. But there was a planet out in the distance. It was quite far away. It sort of looked like they were as far away from the planet as the moon was from Earth. It was a blue-and-green orb out in the distance. It had white clouds.

Thirty seconds must have passed before anything happened.

In an instant, the planet began to move and shake. It started to crack open, as if it was an egg that had just been cracked. The insides of it exploded outward in a red lava-looking yolk.

Then an explosion, and the planet completely ripped itself apart.

"This is what would happen if we fired this weapon at Earth," Atlas said.

Even though there was no sound in space, Peter felt like he was hearing the crackle of tectonic plates on the surface of the world being displaced.

Again, Peter was amazed at just how much energy had been pumped into that planet in such a short amount of time. It just didn't seem possible. But then he was watching proof of what it was capable of doing right in front of him.

Peter thought a bit more about how humans would respond if an alien showed up and told humanity to leave them alone, otherwise they'd blow up Earth.

He was almost confident that there would be a lot of people angry. A lot of people would suggest they shouldn't be pushed around. But ultimately, he knew the leaders of Earth would understand that a war was a no-win situation. If the only demand was "Leave us alone," then humanity would leave them alone.

Peter thought more about their current situation with the Atua. It was simple game theory. Right now, the Atua believed humanity was not in a position to fight back. They believed humanity had no way of truly hurting them. So it made sense that they were happy to attack one of their planets. Peter knew that human history was littered with dead civilizations, killed by stronger kingdoms just because the attackers had known there were no consequences.

Again, it was game theory. The only way to ensure humanity would not be attacked again was to show the Atua that there would be consequences. Humanity had a means to defend themselves.

Peter did not think using the weapon was the right thing. Even if they got a critical hit on the planet and utterly destroyed their home world, it was impossible to prove that the Atua didn't have another way of attacking back—retaliation. Atlas so far was confident they were confined to only one world. But the risks of an all-out war were too high.

But Peter knew they needed to show the Atua that they had the capability of causing immense destruction. And then, under the rules of game theory, the Atua should rethink their approach with humanity. An all-out war, where both sides could utterly destroy one of the other's planets, was a war not worth having. No one would win.

Peter understood that. And he hoped that the Atua would, too. He also knew the Atua were alien. Alien in thought and alien in culture. So there was a possibility that they didn't see it this way.

Peter decided then to study their behavior and make sure his assumptions were correct. He wished Icarus was around at that very moment.

"Has there been any word on Icarus?" Peter asked.

Angelique shook her head. "He's not online yet."

Icarus had configured his backups so that no one could turn them on remotely. They were triggered to periodically scan the systems for a key. If Icarus didn't provide that key, then one of his backups was switched on.

Everyone assumed that Icarus would have come back by now. But obviously the time between the backup checks was longer than anyone had anticipated.

CHAPTER 51

CLONE OF ATLAS

LONG ROAD AHEAD

There was a significant complexity gap between building something in a simulation and building it in the real world. Especially when real-world testing wasn't possible.

Atlas was in a secret hidden base inside of a moon-sized planet. It was chosen because of the proximity to the Atua home world. He'd cloned a version of himself and sent it to this world. He'd done that so he wasn't constantly streaming himself across the Starnet. Atlas knew, with the changes Angelique's people had made, there was a low probability of the Atua finding out what he was doing. But he didn't want to take on unnecessary risk. The Atua were extremely competent at hacking, so he decided it wasn't worth the gamble.

He was in an underground base on the moon. It felt very much like a cave. He knew if his old friend Icarus was still around, he would have called it a Batcave because that's very much what it looked like.

A mix of heavy machinery juxtaposed with the sharp rocky walls made for an interesting sight.

The cave was getting deeper and deeper, too. Every time he fired up the weapon, firing a single particle toward a micro–black hole, a tiny bit of energy would be absorbed by the bottom wall.

He'd spent the last few years in this cave. His tests weren't anywhere near the scale or power that the real weapon would be at until now.

He'd built everything he wanted to. He knew in theory it would work. But he'd never actually tested it.

He never planned on testing it in the real world for the simple fact that a weapon like this would produce so much energy and power, anyone scanning the sky should be able to detect it.

Using a weapon like this would undoubtedly cause the Atua to take a closer look. So up until that very moment, he had confined his tests to simulated worlds. Or very, very low-power attempts at the inside of the cave.

Now it was complete.

The model for building his weapon was sent in secret to several maximum-security bases around some of Angelique's colonized worlds. They had built twenty in total.

They were all on their way toward the Atua and Penquin home world. They were all planning to arrive at the same time.

If the test Atlas ran right now didn't work, they would quickly turn around and go home.

In his mind, the weapon was going to work. And today was the day that was going to happen.

He had one test to complete it in. And this test would also act as a warning shot that they had a weapon that powerful.

"Okay, we're ready," Ship said, teleporting next to Atlas.

The two of them walked down the path toward their new home, a very futuristic-looking spacecraft.

It was all white and looked very sleek, subtle rounded curves and no visible gaps or openings. This spacecraft was not designed to host any human life in it. There were no storage components for embryos, not even a door for Atlas or Ship to enter through. All the space inside of the spacecraft had to be used for power generation and computing power. The energy requirements and calculations involved were at the very limit of what this machine was capable of.

They couldn't just make it bigger, either, since making it bigger increased the chances that they were hit by some stray material from anything they blew up.

Atlas and Ship arrived at the spacecraft. They couldn't touch it, since the surface of it was alive with liquid nanobots designed to shield the insides from the immense Hawking radiation created by billions of tiny micro–black holes decaying.

"I'm going to have to turn you off," Ship said as he reached out his hand.

Atlas nodded, and a compartment at the very front of him opened up. A small golf-ball-sized matrix appeared in the middle of his chest.

Angelique had perfected and miniaturized the creation of matrices. It had become an asset to be able to inhabit android bodies because it meant they didn't have to set up hapticgraphic projectors everywhere.

This was particularly useful for some of the science experiences Atlas ran because the hapticgraphic projectors were known to interfere with measurements. It just meant he could better control variables.

Atlas was switched off as Ship removed his matrix. He carefully carried the round housing and walked along to the side of the spacecraft.

He sent the mental command out, and the white coating on the spacecraft came alive. It almost looked like white-colored liquid was being pushed aside. But the physics didn't quite make sense because it was tiny nanobots all moving away.

Behind the material was a small panel that clicked open.

Ship placed Atlas's matrix into a specifically designed slot, and the matrix was moved to the center of the spacecraft where it was connected to the new ship.

Ship was already inside of the ship so didn't have to do it twice.

The panel closed, and the liquid shielding morphed back into place.

Ship ordered his remote-controlled avatar into its holding location, and he met Atlas on the inside of the spacecraft.

Atlas was now part of the spacecraft. He was in a simulated world, which was a different experience to the one he was used to. The simulated world was designed so that, to him, it looked like he was inside of the spacecraft. He could see out of windows. But of course everything was simply relying on the spacecraft's external sensors. The spacecraft had no available space to house haptic-graphic projectors. He was in a completely artificial environment.

Atlas used his new sensors as part of the ship to see the cave around him. He was ready to leave this place. "Let's go."

Atlas watched as they began to levitate off the ground and inch out of the dark space they were in.

Minutes passed as they moved farther and farther into space above the small planet. The planet was maybe 70 percent bigger than Earth's moon. So as planets go, it was tiny. But still, it was big enough for their purposes.

"Ready?" Ship asked as they steered across the empty space between them at the lifeless rocky planet.

"I don't think I'll ever be ready for this."

"Well, if you want to delay it, we'll have to wait another week before we can do this again."

The planet they were flying above was racing around the system's host star. It took roughly six and a bit days for it to complete an orbit. They were currently on the side of the system that faced the Atua home world. Anything they did to this world would be visible to all the sensors on the aliens' home world in a few years' time.

"We're not delaying this," Atlas said. "Let's see the results of all our research and development."

Ship nodded, and the process began.

Firstly, the front of their spaceship began releasing small rotating droplets of a very dense material. These perfectly circular objects were dropped out the front in quick succession. One at a time, faster and faster.

Then a new machine fired. This one fired out a quick pulse of compressive energy.

As soon as the compressive force touched the droplets, it began to crush them, making them infinitely smaller, forcing them to pass the singularity threshold, where individual particles in the material became so close together that the gravitational pull between them collapsed in on one another, forcing them into a point where math stopped working and nothing could escape.

They were infinitesimally small micro–black holes. They were so small they'd quickly evaporate, spewing out massive amounts of Hawking radiation.

But before they disappeared, a laser would shoot out tiny particles of light. These particles would race past the black hole, almost touching its surface—but not quite.

As they flew by, the rotating black hole would impart more energy, at a rate of E equals 60 percent of MC squared.

This was for all intents and purposes the most efficient method ever created for turning mass into energy. More energy was being shot out the front of the spacecraft than any star could produce for the same volume of mass.

It was an enormous amount of energy being produced. The sky around then was being lit up. It was messy, too; not all the energy moving straight ahead.

It looked as though someone had turned on a fire hydrant of light. As if a tiny hose was pumping out enough water to fill an entire planet's worth of water in a minute.

Atlas instinctually covered his eyes.

This was the ultimate weapon. A Kamehameha on steroids. A beam of light so powerful it wasn't stopped by the planet below.

It continued to beam right through as if it wasn't even there, punching through it and continuing straight into the star behind.

This was overkill for destroying a planet. An overreaction in every sense of the word. Like bringing a nuclear bomb to a pillow fight.

There was so much energy being spewed into the planet below that the star behind it would have a hard time managing it all.

Slowly, the planet responded. Not by fighting back—because it didn't have a chance. It began to come apart. To be torn apart violently. As if the planet was racing to become a cloud again. As if entropy decided that rocks shouldn't clump into a ball but should defuse around the system like gas.

There was an explosion, and the metal core of the planet began to rock around as if it was a pinball inside of a machine. It created a resonance that increased the destruction.

"We need to go," Atlas said, understanding the true power of what they'd built.

They'd chosen this system because it was dead. There was no life in the system and no chance at ever evolving life, either.

Ship turned his engines on, and they raced from the system.

Something else left the system at that moment, too. A message. A message to the Atua.

At the speed of light, the galaxy around them would slowly learn that something quite destructive had happened in this system. That a planet was utterly destroyed. A less technologically advanced civilization would struggle to make sense of what had happened just then given their understanding of how the universe worked.

Atlas thought about it as they raced away from the destruction. They'd just broadcast a message. And that message was simple: "Don't mess with us. We have the power to destroy a planet."

It was a simple, yet powerful message. It meant that humanity had a weapon of utter destruction.

They'd chosen to use it on this planet because it was the only way for them to prove they had the ability to destroy the Atua. It was the ultimate strongman.

They didn't want to enter a situation where they threatened the Atua with destruction and the Atua didn't believe them. It was simple game theory. Almost mutually assured destruction—but not quite. The human race was too spread out to be destroyed by the Atua. But the Atua could definitely cause an issue.

Hence Atlas was sending out this threat at the speed of light.

The next step for Atlas and Ship was racing to the Atua home world. They were going to meet the other twenty ships heading to the Atua home world. The other ships all with the same weapon.

Overkill for attacking a single planet.

But they weren't attacking a planet. They wanted to show once and for all that the human race was off-limits. The human race was not to be messed with.

Atlas in particular got angry when he thought about the destruction the Atua caused to Icarus's world. He personally had no intention of doing that to them.

An eye for an eye wasn't appropriate when talking about another race of intelligence. But he knew the Atua would continue to walk all over humans, treating them like they weren't any more than bugs, until they went too far.

Atlas needed to show force. Show the threat of power. Show that humanity was not to be messed with. He needed to nip the concept of a war in the bud.

Mutually assured destruction.

The Atua needed to understand that any further attack would mean the death of them.

The Atua needed to understand humanity was no longer under their control.

CHAPTER 52

PETER

NO TURNING BACK

Peter felt the change in his playback speed. His original speed allowed him to experience the travel time between stars as roughly an hour. It was quick, as far as space-travel times go. So he knew something was off.

There were only a limited number of instances that this could happen.

Two of them were bad.

He was currently traveling near the speed of light in a small spacecraft. He was traveling toward the Atua and Penquin home world. At least all their current intel said it was their home world.

Peter used the mental commands to query the spacecraft on what was happening. He ordered it to simulate a virtual world around him. "What are we looking at?"

Both Hens and Moses popped into existence in front of Peter.

Hens Fari was a psychologist who had a deep understanding of human behavior. He was the world's foremost expert on how humans react to different situations. He'd spent most of his life working in Angelique's secret military, in charge of building algorithms for identifying when groups of humans were being manipulated. He was instrumental in identifying when there was a hidden puppet master. Peter had convinced Hens to join him on this mission because he'd wanted someone in the negotiation with a deep understanding of human psychology. He was convinced those skills would come in handy since the Atua already had a very deep understanding.

Moses John was an AI behavioral expert. Ever since Icarus had come back, Moses had spent his time analyzing all the information on the Atua. He'd built a very compelling AI algorithm for predicting the behavior of both the Atua and Penquins. Peter was under no illusion that what Moses had built was going to be accurate with what the Atua did or said. But it was a starting point. Peter and Moses had queried the AI on how the Atua would react to this situation. Even if the AI was wrong with what the Atua would do, Peter wanted Moses on hand to improve the AI's predictions as their negotiations progressed.

After all, they were there to negotiate a peace treaty with the Atua. They were there to make sure humans were never attacked again. And if the negotiations failed, Peter knew he would only have one option. He was going to destroy the Atua.

"The ship's slowed down our perception of time because it's detecting a lot of radiation coming from a nearby star," Moses said, a little confused. "But it's not the Atua home world."

Peter pulled up a map of the stars and confirmed it was the star he expected. "It worked!"

"What worked?" Hens asked.

There was only a select number of people who knew what this signal meant. On this spacecraft, only Peter knew. It meant that Atlas had fired the weapon, and it had worked.

"Wow, I've never seen readings like this," Moses said. "If I'm reading these charts correctly, a star in that system just went supernova."

"Atlas fired the weapon," Peter said. "We are on a ship capable of that, too."

"You can't be telling the truth." Moses looked a Peter with curiosity. "That's more energy that we can possibly produce. I don't understand how that is achievable."

Only a selection of people knew the weapons existed. They were manufactured using a specialized fabricator that could only build one thing. It was designed to look like any other fabricator. They didn't want to risk the Atua learning of its existence. So Hens and Moses both knew they were headed to the Atua to negotiate piece. And that was true. But it was only now that they were learning of the stick Peter was going to use to encourage peace talks. "That's Atlas for you; he found a way."

"What does that mean?" Hens asked.

"It means we have proof that the weapon we're carrying with us can utterly destroy the Atua's home world," Peter said. "It means even if they have a planetary-defense system capable of halting rail guns traveling at the speed of light, they won't have a chance in hell of stopping what we're bringing with us. It means we have a bite to back up our bark." Then Peter paused for a moment, thinking over what this meant. "Moses, can you ask the AI that predicts Atua's behavior how they will respond to the news of this weapon? I know we previously asked it how they would react to the prospect of an all-out war with humans. But can you ask it about the potential threat of all our warships arriving with weapons capable of causing their planet to spontaneously combust?"

Moses nodded and manifested a computer in front of him. He sat down in front of it and began furiously typing away.

"Are we actually going to use it?" Hens asked, then clarified his statement. "Use the weapon on the Atua."

Peter thought long and hard about this question. It was a question that would define him. If he did use it, then that would be his legacy. It would become the legacy of every human on the journey to the alien star system.

"Actually, don't answer that," Hens said, interrupting Peter from thinking and preventing him from voicing something he didn't want to.

"The truth is humans as a whole wouldn't terminate an entire species like this," Hens said. "Humanity wouldn't conduct murder on this scale."

Peter's mind went to multiple instances where humans had caused massive genocide to another race of humans.

"I know you're thinking that humans have caused destruction before. And it's true. But it's always because of one single individual. And that's why I don't want you to tell me. The Atua need to understand that it's your decision whether to attack. They need to believe that only you have the ability to pull the trigger and that there aren't any other checks and balances. Because democracies don't wipe out entire species of aliens. But individuals do. In this negotiation, the Atua need to believe that you will fire this weapon at them." Hens looked at Peter straight in the eyes. "In the same way I believe you're willing to fire it."

"Interesting," Moses said, finally finishing with his testing of his model. "I'm predicting a fifty-fifty chance that the Atua are going to call your bluff. They might not engage with you because they don't believe you will destroy them."

Peter had worried this was the case. He needed to make sure they understood the threat was real.

Moses paused. "But let me make a few adjustments to it based on what you said, Hens. Let's see what happens if they believe the threat. I originally had them believe that it was a group decision whether we fire or not. Now I'm going to reprogram it to say only Peter controls the weapon."

Moses worked away at the computer for a good while before coming back. "Okay, so I'm reaching the limits of the AI's knowledge. We just don't have enough data on how they'll respond to a threat like that. I know humans would want a peace treaty.

But the Atua and the Penquins—we need more data to better predict."

"Well then, let's go get some," Peter said. "Anything else to discuss? Otherwise, let's change our playback speeds so we can talk to these Atua."

Both Moses and Hens nodded, and Peter gave the mental command.

Time raced before their eyes.

And before long, Peter was lighting up the Atua's star space. Him and nineteen other spacecraft.

They were a good two light minutes before the spacecraft forced them back into real time.

They had received a message. The Atua knew they were there.

Peter opened up the video message. It was an Atua Peter hadn't seen before.

"Don't come any closer, human," the Alien spat. "You stupid, stupid bug." Peter thought the alien was getting angry. "Disengage your engines and prepare to be boarded."

In that moment Peter realized the negotiation had begun. How Peter and the others responded would dictate the rest of their engagement with the Atua. Peter knew the other nineteen spacecraft had been ordered not to respond and to follow Peter's lead. "Send this message."

Peter straightened his back and faced an imaginary camera. "By now you have probably interpreted the signals that a star in the star system nearest to you has just gone supernova. This is a weapon we have created. We have a similar weapon onboard our spacecraft. If you fire at any of us, we will use this weapon on you. Please await our arrival. Once there—" Peter paused for a moment, deciding to attempt his best alien impression. "We will negotiate, or we will use this weapon on you."

Peter sent the mental command to broadcast that message to the Atua and to every other human spacecraft in the system.

CHAPTER 53

PETER

CONTACT

Peter stood in a specially built docking ship. He was streaming in from one of the twenty spacecraft currently in orbit around the Atua and Penquin world.

The docking ship was one of seven specifically built hubs for the rest of the team to communicate. They were treating the threat of being hacked seriously. None of the spacecraft had a direct link to any of the others. Any communication between the various warships had to be done via one of these docking ships. This ensured that no virus that the Atua infected any of the spacecraft with could propagate to the others.

The docking ships worked almost like a sandbox within a sandbox. Each of the twenty warships was connected to an independent hapticgraphic projector inside of the docking ship. These hapticgraphic projectors had computer systems that were firewalled from the others. And each of the warships had to independently confirm the other warships had not been compromised before any connection would be initiated. It meant the only way to communicate with the others was to have a conversation on the docking ships.

There was no sharing of digital information between spacecraft, either. They had the ability to have secret conversations by occupying one of the seven docking ships while others weren't around. But otherwise, there was no way for any of the warships to infect any of the others—or at least any virus would only spread slowly.

Peter stood there waiting for the others to join. He was in one corner of a metal room that had ten chairs all facing one another in a circular pattern.

Peter walked over and took a seat on one of the chairs.

In popped Angelique, who looked over at Peter and smiled. No avatars could touch one another, so there was no hugging. "How was your trip across?"

"Besides seeing Atlas light up the sky when he used the weapon, it was uneventful," Peter said. "We changed our playback speeds, so it felt like I only saw you five minutes ago."

"Same." She paused for a second. "It's a bit concerning how quickly the Atua knew we were here. And how comfortable they are with us coming into their system with these weapons."

Before Peter could respond, Trillion arrived, followed by Hezekiah, Unity, and Ariana, who all walked over and jumped onto one of the available chairs.

Then Atlas and his Ship walked through the door. They were the only two with separate connections to the Starnet, enabling both of them to communicate with the others at once. On all the other spacecraft, only one of them could cross into the sandbox at once.

Atlas looked around the room. He looked sad, as if he wasn't too comfortable with what he'd done. "I'm not going to be the one who pulls the trigger. I can't be."

Peter studied the faces of everyone in the room. He noticed something he hadn't quite noticed before. Everyone was a bit apprehensive. They looked like something bad was about to happen. Peter suspected it had to do with the fact that they'd all decided to go on this mission while they were emotional. They were all angry at the Atua. They wanted revenge.

But revenge wasn't a dish best served cold in this case. Because of the many years it had taken for the team to execute this plan, it calmed the emotions. Everyone knew that eliminating an entire species was a path that couldn't be undone. At the time, Peter had capitalized on everyone's fears. He'd mobilized everyone into action. Even before the attack on Icarus's world, Peter was sure that the Atua would attack. Even though he suspected it might happen, he still wasn't happy when they attacked. And this, to Peter at least, was the clearest sign they wouldn't leave humanity alone until they understood humanity was a threat not to be messed with.

Peter decided to calm the group's fears. "Look, we all know what the Atua are capable of," he said, reminding everyone of the tragedy that had brought them all together. He didn't say Icarus's name, but everyone knew what he was referring to. "I started this beta-explorer mission to discover life. To find out what was in the universe. I know each of you are here because you wanted to explore the galaxy, not because you wanted to get into some intergalactic war." He looked at Atlas first. "If we use this weapon, it's not on you. You don't need any of this on your conscience."

Peter turned his face to the rest of the group. "We're here to tell them we don't want to fight. That's all. We're here to make sure the Atua and Penquins leave us alone. If we don't show them strength, then they will walk all over us. And then the next time we have a conversation with them, it might be over the death of another world. We're here to tell them we don't want to fight. But we're also here to tell them that we will fight if we need to. We're here to tell them that a fight would be a one-sided affair."

Peter looked at Unity next. He knew that she believed the only reason the Atua attacked was because Icarus had done something bad on their planet. She believed that it was a form a self-defense from the Atua. "What they did to Titan was not right. It was a more than a retaliation. It was a vindictive attack. I believe strongly that if we don't nip this in the bud, our two species will end up in a protracted war of attrition. They have shown time and time again they aren't willing to leave us alone. Earth is still under their grasp. Humans on Earth are still locked in a simulated reality that they designed. Don't be under any illusion that the previous attack was the conclusion of their dreams to conquer us all."

"Are we simply provoking them again?" Unity asked. "If they reacted that way to Icarus sneaking onto their planet, what's to say they don't turn around and do something worse to us again?"

"Honestly, I don't know," Peter replied. "None of us know. We also have no idea whether not replying to their attack is a sign of weakness and a sign they should attack us again. We also don't know whether their original attack wasn't already planned a long time ago, and they lied to us about the excuse. To be perfectly honest, I think it's likely that us coming out here will be a show of strength. From what I believe of the Atua, I think they'll see this as a sign we are no longer to be manipulated." Then Peter shrugged. "I might be wrong, though. We don't know enough about the Atua or the Penquins. And at the very least, I'm hoping we'll know enough about them after this negotiation to better predict how they will act in the future."

"I agree with him," Atlas said. "If we're going to coexist in this universe together, then we need to better understand each other. Maybe we can even set up some trade with each other."

"So what next?" Angelique asked.

"We have about ten minutes until we open a discussion line with the aliens," Peter said. "And two minutes until the others join. I wanted to make sure, Atlas, you were still on board with us threatening the alien with this weapon? I know we haven't spoken about this in years."

Atlas nodded. "I hope we don't get to that. But I trust you, Peter, to make the right decision."

The team went back and forth for a little while as they waited for the other twenty in the war fleet to arrive.

Once everyone was there, Peter addressed the team. Walking into the meeting, Peter had planned to convince everyone to let him speak directly to the alien on everyone's behalf. But he kept playing the message the other person on his ship had said. He didn't know enough about the Atua. But they knew a lot about him.

The Atua had most likely studied the behaviors and decision-making processes of all the beta explorers. How Peter responded to any question was probably already well understood. He was the one who'd sent the message off to reply to the Atua. So some AI was probably being trained to better predict how he would respond.

Peter looked around the room. He knew of everyone except one person. A woman named Rose sat on one of the chairs quietly listening to everyone. He didn't know her because she was from one of Angelique's secret systems. She was from one of the worlds that definitely didn't have any trace of the Atua technology on it.

"Rose, do you mind if you speak on our behalf?" Peter asked. "To the Atua, I mean."

Rose looked up; she showed a bit of concern, as if she wasn't qualified to be everyone's representative. "Why—why me?"

"Because the Atua don't know who you are. I think they'll have a very good understanding of what I or most of the others in the room will say. Can you pretend you're the leader?"

"You want me to act?"

Peter nodded.

"I can do that."

"Thank you. We'll all be there with you. It's mostly an information-gathering exercise. We just need you to explain our demands. Then we'll be able to regroup and decide what to do as a collective."

Rose nodded in recognition.

Peter explained what he wanted her to ask and explained the types of questions it would be important for her to gather responses to. He stressed that it was important for her to seem as if she was the leader of the group and that she had the ability to order the destruction of their home world if she didn't like the answers they were providing.

Peter reminded himself that everyone has a plan until they get punched in the face. Peter was about to see how things would progress once they touched down.

They had followed the Atua's instructions and entered the atmosphere, touching down on a specially designed docking platform in the middle of the ocean. It looked like a twenty-meter-by-twenty-meter metal structure surrounded by the sea. It was made of some sort of concrete that had been worn down by the ocean waves.

The team attempted to scan the immediate area, but they quickly realized all their sensors were being overloaded with signals. They weren't able to capture any useful measurements of the area around them.

It didn't take long for an alien submarine to arrive. It was sitting beneath the waves one moment, then the next, it was above them.

It was long and pointed; it looked like it was designed to race through the water at great speeds. The surface of it was all white and completely sealed off. Peter didn't see any windows or markings on the outside of it.

They tried to use their radar on the submarine, but whatever it was coated in was not letting any of their radar signals see it. From their vantage point it was invisible to everything except visible light. Peter was sure it had the capability to go invisible even to visible light when under the water.

There was an anticipation in the air as everyone waited for something to happen.

"We just received instructions to come out," the Ship of Atlas said to the team.

Everyone nodded, and the front door of the docking station opened up with an audible hiss. Stairs appeared, too. And standing in the middle was a congregation of twenty-one of humanity's representatives.

Peter looked at Rose and gave her a subtle look that said, *You're up.*

Peter knew a common symbol of a person in power in human culture was for the leader to walk in front. He knew that the Atua and Penquins would be expecting this.

Rose walked down the platform, followed by the rest of the team.

When the whole team was down on the platform, they watched as several hidden arms rose up from the sides of the floating platform they were on.

"We're being scanned," Ship confirmed.

Everyone stared at the alien submarine. Then everyone saw a subtle light shimmer in front of them. It was the aliens' haptic-graphic projectors turning on.

Moments later, they were standing in front of a Penquin. It wasn't a Penquin they had seen before. Peter scanned its chest and noticed the protrusion that signified that an Atua was inside of its chest.

It walked toward the others and spoke. "I am Nukchuk. Why are you here?"

CHAPTER 54

ANGELIQUE

NEGOTIATION

Angelique studied the body language of Nukchuk. It was hard for her to get a reading on the alien.

All the learnings that Icarus had shared about this alien world were about the Penquins. There was nothing tangible she would be able to take from it. The Atua inhabited the Penquin bodies and controlled them from the inside. Angelique had no idea how much of their personality leaked through. She didn't even know if the Penquin fear responses were the same when the Atua was inside of them.

Even though Rose stepped forward, Nukchuk didn't acknowledge her with a look. The alien kept its eyes on Angelique, Peter, and Atlas—the original explorers whom these aliens knew quite well.

"My name is Rose. I'm the designated speaker in this group. We've come here to negotiate a peace treaty between our two species."

Nukchuk continued not making eye contact with Rose. The alien continued to scan the faces of the rest of the group. Angelique wondered whether this was a ploy to put their designated negotiator on the back foot or whether Nukchuk was looking for something.

"Peace," Nukchuk said, looking at Atlas as it spoke. "You came all the way here to ask for something we already have?"

The lack of eye contact was working. Rose began losing her veneer of confidence. She glanced at Peter before she spoke. "We would like assurances that you will not attack us again."

Angelique watched as the Atua made a clicking sound when it noticed Rose's eyes deferring to Peter. She assumed it was a sign he'd found what he was after. He wanted to know if she was the real leader of the group.

"What about that threat you broadcast to our world?" Nukchuk was staring daggers at Peter as it spoke.

"That was simply to show that we mean business," Rose replied, noticing the Atua's disrespect and trying to capture the alien's eye contact.

Angelique realized the Atua had successfully changed the dynamic of the negotiation. Rose was now trying to gain approval from Nukchuk—she wanted the alien to look at her.

Nukchuk did not respond. It kept looking around the group, studying everyone.

Some of their members averted their eyes when Nukchuk looked at them. Not Angelique, though. Her eyes bore daggers into the alien. Her eyes said, "You should not have messed with us."

Nukchuk maintained eye contact with Angelique for a good long while. Then suddenly it turned around.

"I'm authorized to give you nothing and to tell you to leave," Nukchuk said, almost spitting the words out. "What are you hoping to achieve? Threaten us and hope we capitulate? We won't accept a dirty bug in our system doing that. If you leave now, we can accept this transgression. Let bygones be . . . forgiven but not forgotten."

"If you don't agree to a peace treaty with us, I will utterly destroy your planet." Rose spoke with force, as if she meant every word. "You've got to understand that all we want is peace. If you can't agree to that, then we will gain it by ensuring you're not around any longer."

"You don't know much about our true history, do you?" Nukchuk asked, finally making eye contact with Rose. "Even if I wanted to negotiate, I'm not in a position of power." The alien made eye contact with the six of them in the group that had been captured by them the last time the two species had met. "You lost your opportunity to talk when you escaped. Right now, my people are arguing over whether to blow you up. Destroy every one of your ships. I suggest you leave now before they decide it's not worth having you in our system."

"I don't believe you can hurt us," Peter said. "Otherwise, I think you would have already."

Nukchuk turned around to face the other way, as if to say it was done with the conversation. "Go now or we will destroy your ships."

"No," Peter replied forcefully. "Bring someone here who is in a position of power, someone who will negotiate with us, or we will destroy your planet."

"Your weapons can't hurt us; we have a defense network capable of deflecting them. Leave now or we will destroy you. Then we will go on a rampage and destroy every one of your planets." The alien looked at Angelique. "Even the hidden ones you think we don't know about.

"Let me tell you a story about our species. We don't age. We don't die. And more recently we have struggled to reproduce. We've pieced together much of what Icarus learned in his time here and don't believe any of those facts should be new to you." Nukchuk looked at the faces of everyone, hoping to gain a hint of knowledge about what Icarus had told them. When it didn't gain anything from everyone's eyes, the alien continued: "We didn't become intelligent first. What you call the Penquins did. We, however, evolved to take knowledge from them. And as they got smarter, we got smarter, too. "As you know, the Penquin require us in order to breed."

The alien looked down at its body as if it was a suit it was wearing. "Over time, we selected for smarter and smarter Penquins, and in turn, our knowledge grew exponentially faster. As they grew in intelligence, we grew faster."

Angelique was fascinated by everything Nukchuk was saying. It built on a lot of the things that Icarus had said. She couldn't help but wonder why this alien was sharing so much information.

"We used to use the Penquins as breeding grounds. But to us, breeding also means dying. Which, as we got smarter, we no longer wanted to do. One unintentional consequence of not selecting Penquins as places to breed is that both of us evolved that capability away." Nukchuk stopped talking for a moment, as if it was receiving a message from somewhere else. It looked like it had just shared too much information and was being told to change the subject. "I tell you all this to say our two species already have an end date. Every few thousand years, one of us dies, and that becomes one fewer of us that is replaced. If you choose to attack us, then you're simply bringing forward our end date. We are not giving you anything; that would be beneath us."

Angelique studied the body language of Nukchuk. She was trying to understand whether it had just admitted that it had been lying before. If she was reading the subtext properly, this Atua had just said that they couldn't actually stop them from attacking. The message was clear, however; the Atua would rather die than to have a negotiation with humans as equals. Their culture wouldn't let them do that.

"What have you got to lose in agreeing to peace?" Angelique asked, not believing that the Atua was too stubborn to come to an agreement.

"Would you rather we lie to you? The one you call PBD was happy to partake in that strategy, but it didn't work out well for him. Your culture is fractured. Humans are scattered around the universe. Even if we come to an arrangement with you, there could be others who come back and disagree, ask for updated terms. We don't want terms. We want you to leave."

Everyone looked shell-shocked. This negotiation wasn't going the way it was meant to. Angelique couldn't quite figure out whether this had always been the plan. On some level, she'd assumed that they had a deep understanding of human behavior, so manipulating humans was going to be easy. But still, she didn't think it would be that easy. Based on what the Nukchuk had just said, Angelique was inclined to leave. But from what she knew of the Atua, she suspected this was all a carefully planned ruse to get rid of them.

"You're trying to hack into our systems," Ship interrupted everyone and pointed to the docking station they'd arrived on. "I've just had a reading we're now infected with billions of nano-bots currently trying to make their way into our systems."

"You better leave before they get in. I know you as a culture love knowledge. Think of that knowledge I just shared as our form of trade. Now leave and maybe in the future we can trade again."

"You're not getting in that easily," Ship said. "Pick up the phone on the dial-up router."

A fraction of a second later, the rockets began to rise off the ground, taking all the hapticgraphic projections of everyone with them. Then Ship and Atlas disappeared.

The secret message Ship had just said aloud was for everyone to destroy the entangled particles connecting everyone's spacecraft to this particular docking station. Angelique guessed they were on the verge of being compromised.

CHAPTER 55

ATLAS

FIND ANOTHER WAY

"As far as we know, they never hacked into any of us," Atlas said once everyone had arrived back in the next docking platform that everyone agreed to meet in after the encounter with the Atua aliens. "As far as I can tell, they successfully made it into our dummy systems. But they hadn't yet made it into any of the systems that matter."

The docking platforms were designed with safety as a priority. There were multiple technological systems on them that were designed to look like they did things. But really, they were set up to slow down any hack attempt.

"So they were tricking us?" Peter asked. "They wanted us to visit them so they could hack into us and maybe take over this new weapon?"

"Correct," Atlas replied. "I'm guessing this was always their plan. They wanted to infiltrate our system and let us all carry the nanobots back to one of our planets where they could closely make their way in."

"So as soon as we touched down on that platform, their bots were moving in," Angelique said. "They didn't care what we did after that. Their mission was to infect us with a new virus and then leave."

"So they failed to hack into us," Unity said. "And by the sounds of it, we failed to reach an agreement with them. So what do we do now?"

"We can go back home?" Atlas proposed.

Peter shook his head. "Not yet. We haven't gotten closure on what we needed to."

Angelique looked at Peter, studying his face. "What else can we do? They basically said our one trump card doesn't matter." She paused for a second. "You're not thinking of using the weapon, are you?"

Atlas stopped listening. He was directly connected to the spacecraft, so he had the ability to use the ship's immense resources. In this case, he was receiving two simultaneous alerts.

The first message was from an alert he'd set up on the weapons. It meant someone had triggered it. He hadn't told anyone, but as much as he wanted to free himself from the concern of being the one who pulled the trigger, he also didn't want the weapon to be used unless he was okay with it being used. Someone had triggered the weapon to fire.

Atlas looked at Peter, studying his face for a second. To Peter's credit, he hadn't reacted. If it was Peter who'd just tried to destroy the Atua, he wasn't showing it on his face.

Atlas decided not to follow up any longer. There was another more pressing situation he needed to investigate.

He left the room where everyone else was and entered the virtual reality world of his ship.

Atlas had recently forgone the use of paper and pen. He still liked to visually see things written on paper. But he'd built an add-on that would take his mental thoughts and translate them into written format. To any observer, it looked like a floating pen and notepad moved around and followed him.

"Ship, are we receiving an encrypted signal?"

Ship appeared in the room. "There isn't a signal; it's the original message Peter broadcast in this system bouncing off asteroids. We're hearing an echo."

"You might be right. But can you humor me?" Atlas wasn't too sure what was going on. But he felt like the cadence of the echo wasn't matching with what he would have expected. There was a rhythm to it. It wasn't random. "Is there a pattern in the echo? Is there Morse code in there?"

Ship paused for a moment. Then he smiled. "You're right; it's musical notes. It's the theme song to Zelda."

"Icarus?"

Ship shrugged. "Unless it's a trap by the Atua, there's only one person who would broadcast a signal like that."

"Can you identify where it's coming from?"

Ship shook his head.

"Can we pretend to be an echo back? Send the signal out in the general direction we detected it?"

The two of them waited in patience for the signal to be confirmed. There was a section of the asteroid belt in the system where the echo-like signal was originating.

"I'm moving us closer," Ship said.

"Is there a way for us to let Icarus know it's us?" Atlas scratched his head. "What about the theme song to *Mission: Impossible*? Can we send that across?"

It was an intense wait, but it wasn't long until the theme song to *The White Lotus* came back.

"Okay, now he knows it's us," Ship said.

Ship guided them toward a large asteroid. It looked almost like a massive nose as it slowly spun around.

There was no visible sign at all that anything was in the system. Ship used active sensor pulses to scan and noticed there was a high concentration of metals in this asteroid. Nothing out of the ordinary, except this particular asteroid didn't look like it had a lot of metal in it.

Ship fired a tight-beam communication at the asteroid.

Almost instantly, they received a reply. A small probe began surfacing from the very bottom part of the asteroid that looked like a nostril. It was tiny and moved slowly toward them.

"Atlas, we have no means of taking Icarus on board."

"Can we set up a connection with him to communicate?"

Ship nodded.

"Peter, is that you?" Icarus's voice came through the speaker.

"It's Atlas. I heard you needed a pickup," Atlas said, laughing. "How did you end up all the way here? Did you sneak back here after they attacked Titan?"

"Who attacked Titan?"

Atlas thought that maybe this was a copy of Icarus, a version of him that hadn't had the experiences of coming back to Titan. Atlas decided to change the subject, assuming it was better to tell Icarus about what had happened in person. "This design of spacecraft doesn't have any way for you to enter. I'm not sure how we're going to get you on board."

"So you're not here specifically to rescue me?" Icarus asked.

"We are, but it's complicated," Atlas said, lying to him. There was so much he needed to explain to Icarus.

"I have a grappling hook if that helps?"

Ship shook his head. "We'll use the tractor beam, as we don't want you to make contact with our ship. We have a specially built docking station that we'll carry you to."

It took them a couple of times to get it right. But it wasn't long before they were towing Icarus and his Ship toward one of the docking stations.

Throughout the journey there, both parties quizzed each other. They both wanted to make sure the other was who they said they were. It wasn't anything malicious. They just both had a unique understanding of the lengths the Atua would go to in order to hack their way into their systems.

Atlas didn't find any evidence to the contrary. He was confident it was truly Icarus when they arrived back at the nearest docking station.

But still, he was happy that they had the specifically built spacecraft that completely sealed them off from the outside world. It meant once Icarus was inside of it, he could speak with Icarus, and if Icarus was carrying a virus, he wouldn't be able to infect Atlas—or any of the others.

It took a while, but eventually, Icarus's small, little, not-so-interstellar-worthy probe was haled inside. He was cordoned off in a glass section where he couldn't interact with anything else.

Icarus and the Ship of Icarus projected themselves on the outside of their probes using the hapticgraphic projectors.

"Is that really you?" Atlas asked, standing next to his Ship and looking through the window.

"In the flesh." Icarus pointed to his duck avatar.

Ship looked at Atlas, then back at Icarus. "How did you end up in that asteroid?"

"You wouldn't believe how close they came to capturing me. I transmitted the data containing my matrix here, but because I was under so much heat when they chased me, I didn't want to risk trying to escape yet. I figured I'd wait a few hundred years. Hope they forgot about me before inching my way out of the system." Icarus looked at Atlas. "Did you hint that another version of me made it back to Titan?"

Atlas and Ship gave a quick recap on everything that had happened since they last spoke. They omitted many of the details around the level of destruction on Titan but told him enough so that he understood the gravity of the situation and why they were there.

Once Atlas had successfully updated Icarus on everything that had occurred recently, he popped back into the other meeting space and told everyone to hop across into this one. He didn't tell them why. But he loved seeing everyone's face light up when they saw who was behind the glass wall.

Once the initial surprise and introductions were completed, everyone got down to business.

"Based on everything I learned about the Atua while I was on their planet," Icarus said. "I believe they're telling the truth. They would rather die than be subjected to the embarrassment of treating us as equals. They see us as no different to the Penquins. We are resources for them to use."

"So how do we negotiate with a species that would rather die than give us any concessions?"

"Let me think—" Icarus started to say.

The Ship of Atlas interrupted everyone. "I'm getting a reading that hundreds of rockets just launched from the planet below."

"Are they warheads or starships?" Peter asked.

"I'm not sure," Ship replied. "Based on the size of things, I think they're a mix of both."

"Broadcast this message to all the ships and over the planet." Peter took a step backward and turned to address some sort of hidden camera. "Stand down. Do not attack us. We are leaving."

CHAPTER 56

PETER

MOMENT OF TRUTH

There was no response from the aliens after Peter sent the message. And more importantly, the alien ships weren't slowing down.

In fact, they were speeding up. But it was odd because they weren't moving at near light speeds. They looked to be moving in slow motion.

"How technologically advanced are the aliens?" Peter asked the group but clearly pointing the question at Icarus.

"From what I saw, they were using a lot of older human tech." Icarus paused for a moment. "But I didn't visit any of their most advanced countries, so I can't be sure."

"You need to move," Ship said to the group, warning them to take evasive action. "Randomize your movements."

Peter's own ship weaved one way and then another. They all began exiting the system, jinking and changing directions so that the Atua couldn't get a lock on target.

Peter and the rest of the group were quickly gaining distance away from the Atua home world. They were escaping faster, and their attackers weren't able to match pace.

Peter began to understand that these aliens didn't have access to any near-light-speed travel. They were limited to slower speeds that seemed similar to what the team had had before Angelique had shared the newer technology with them.

Peter was about to comment that he believed the aliens were only scaring them away when he received confirmation they were fired on by a strong laser weapon. They'd only escaped before through random luck.

"They're firing on us," Peter said to the group.

"I know," the Ship of Atlas replied in a strained voice.

There were a couple faces around the group that froze before their avatars faded away.

"They hit two of our ships," Ship said. "I'm seeing Hosanna and Dejuan go offline."

These were part of a two-person crew on one of their warships.

"Move, people," Atlas demanded. "We're getting hit."

Another of the team members disappeared. This time Jayden, who was out on one of the spacecraft alone.

They were dropping like flies.

"We have one weapon that could end this battle before it gets carried away," Peter suggested—saying out loud what he was convinced the others were thinking. He couldn't have been the only person who'd tried to use the weapon earlier only to find out that Atlas had set some kind of restriction on its use.

"No," Atlas said, kind of forcefully. "We're not wiping them out of existence." Atlas chewed his lip, consuming more and more of it. He was turning around in a circle. He looked deep in thought. "Screw it," he said before disappearing.

Peter wondered what that meant. What was going through Atlas's mind? Was he going to use the weapon? Had a line just been crossed by the aliens, and now they were paying the ultimate consequences?

Peter couldn't do much but keep moving away from the alien world. But he turned the sensors on his warship toward Atlas's.

Because none of the spacecraft were connected to one another, they couldn't share resources or information. So Peter was limited to monitoring the team through the lag of light speed.

What he was watching was a noticeable tenths-of-a-millisecond delay, which objectively was a short time, but when a war was happening and people were fighting, it might as well be a lifetime.

Peter watched as Atlas and Ship turned their spacecraft around. The nose of the vehicle briefly faced the planet, and Peter wondered whether they were going to fire.

The belief was quickly evaporated when Atlas kept turning.

"He's going to use it on the enemy weapons," Peter muttered to himself.

Atlas raced toward the enemy ships at speeds none of the enemy spacecraft could match. Because it was near light speed, the enemy would most likely only register Atlas had moved when he was right in front of them.

Atlas and Ship weaved in random directions. They were closing the distance, and as they passed the enemy ships, a wave rippled out.

Then they were crushed into a ball. One. Then two. Then three. One after another, Atlas was racing past the alien ships or warheads and turning them into perfectly spherical balls.

"Oh," Peter said, realizing what he was looking at. "Atlas is using the tractor beam to crush them."

Peter hadn't realized that was possible. But then again, Atlas had built the weapon and knew its ins and outs. Peter knew that part of the special weapon was the capability of crushing pallets of material into black holes. So maybe Atlas was repurposing the tool to crush these alien ships.

Atlas was making quick work of the alien spacecraft, racing past them one at a time and leaving behind floating perfectly circular giant marbles.

Peter couldn't believe his eyes. The creativity of what was happening. It was a total one-sided affair. Atlas was stomping all over them.

"This has to be bad for their egos," Peter said as more of the alien ships fell.

Unity looked at him fully. "What are you talking about?"

Unity obviously hadn't yet begun to take in the changing landscape. She was obviously fully concentrating on what was going on.

"Atlas and Ship are turning them all into bowling balls," Peter said, holding up a projected replay of the crippling effect Atlas was having on the aliens.

Atlas was single-handedly showing the aliens just how big the technological gap between them and humanity was.

Humanity was no longer a bug under the foot of these aliens. Humanity was a galaxy-wide superpower.

Peter couldn't help but smile at what he was seeing. They really had nothing to worry about.

"This whole time, the Atua were bluffing," Peter said, slightly proud of what Atlas was doing. "They possessed no advanced technology capable of hurting us."

"I'm going to guess that much of the tech they have was created by us and stolen by them," Unity added.

Atlas and Ship made quick work of the alien spacecraft, leaving two hundred spherical objects completely crushed in their wake.

"Okay, I'm back," Atlas said as he and Ship arrived back in the room.

The room erupted in applause.

"Aw, it was mostly Ship," Atlas said, patting his Ship on the shoulder.

"Atlas came up with the idea to use the weapon like that," Ship said, diverting the praise back to Atlas.

"What do we do now?" Peter asked, bringing the conversation back to the present. Yes, they had successfully pushed back the enemy's attack. But they still hadn't achieved what they'd come for.

"We leave?" Atlas suggested. "We've proved they don't have any weapons capable of hurting us."

It was Peter's turn to think hard about a problem. "Let's see if they're willing to open a dialogue."

Heads around the room nodded in agreement.

"You do the talking this time," Rose said.

"Okay," Peter said as his crew opened up a channel with the planet below.

"We would like to negotiate again," Peter said into an invisible mic.

The response was quick. They were obviously waiting on them to hail them.

"Stupid humans."

That was not the response Peter was looking for. "I don't think your translation is working properly. We're wanting to renegotiate a peace treaty."

Peter recognized the voice as the alien spoke louder this time. It was Nukchuk. "This will not stand. We will not rest until you are destroyed."

"You can't hurt us; you need to chill."

"You don't understand us, do you? We would rather die than submit to your control."

"We're not asking for you to submit to us. We're simply asking for agreement that both our species will leave each other alone."

"There is only space in this galaxy for one dominant species. It's either you or us. If you leave now, then we will go after you eventually."

Peter was so confused. Why was this alien being so antagonistic? He didn't quite understand any of it. Why would an alien species be proactively asking for them to kill them?

Peter disconnected from the broadcast. "Why are they asking us to destroy them?"

Everyone around the group shrugged. No one had a clue.

"I believe I can answer this," Icarus said, speaking for the first time in a while. "The Atua have a very favorable belief in themselves. They believe they're above us. And they think that if we could destroy them, we would; hence if we don't destroy them—even though they're encouraging us to do that—then that means we're ultimately scared."

"Are you saying they have a big ego?" Peter said.

"Ego isn't quite the right word. But it's close enough."

"I've negotiated with people who have big egos. As long as they believe they've won, then they're happy." Peter thought about the situation a little longer. "If we leave, will this be counted as a win for them? And then will they leave us alone?"

"I don't think so. I think they won't be happy until we're enslaved again."

Angelique looked at Icarus as if he was hinting at something. "So what are our options? Destroy them now, otherwise we'll eventually end up in a war?"

Atlas had been sitting in the corner, biting his lower lip, deep in thought for a while. "With your knowledge of them, what is scarier to them than utter destruction?"

Icarus looked at his Ship, and they both gave each other a look. "Loss of control."

"Can you broadcast this message to the surface of the planet?"

Icarus turned forward as if facing an invisible camera. "Tuk tuk, chuaka—" He started to speak directly in the alien language, completely skipping the need for the alien to translate it. Icarus began to change his avatar, and within a few seconds, both he and Ship changed completely into images of Penquins.

Their message went on for some time. Ship chimed in a couple of times, adding a bit more information.

When it was all done, Icarus nodded. "Send it."

"What did you say?" Atlas asked.

"I told them that if they don't negotiate with us, then we will go to the surface of their planet and pick up all the Penquins who want to come with us. I told them that we will give the Penquins another planet protected by us. We will help them with technology to enable them to repopulate without Atua. And most importantly, we will give them advanced enough technology that they will become more advanced than the Atua."

The Ship of Atlas also added, "By broadcasting in their local language, we also told them that we are willing to broadcast messages to their people that the Atua can't control. I bet they're currently scrambling to explain this message to the Penquin population down there."

The response didn't come back for a while.

A growling sound came through the speakers as the message was sounded on a loudspeaker: "This is Alkuka."

Again, the message came through in English. Peter assumed this was to make sure the Penquins couldn't understand what was being said.

Icarus's face was one of excitement. "That's their supreme leader. That's the oldest Atua alive. You're speaking to the very top of their population."

"These are the terms," Alkuka said. "You are to give us the technology for the weapon. You give us the technology for your near-light-speed propulsion. We will leave you alone. We will leave Earth alone. We will remove the virus from that planet."

"We're not giving them any technology," Angelique said to the group but not to the Atua.

Peter agreed; it wasn't in their interest to enable the alien more advanced technology.

"Their ships are several generations behind ours," Atlas said. "We could give them a big improvement to propulsion but based on technology completely different to what we use now. That way it wouldn't give them any clue as to how our current ships work."

Peter thought that was a good idea. He addressed the speaker again. "The weapon and the propulsion method we're using isn't ours to give away. But we can offer you a method of travel that is more powerful than what you are currently using, in exchange for freeing Earth and agreement that our two species will begin to trade with each other."

"Why do you want to trade with them?" Angelique whispered.

"On Earth, we found that when two countries traded regularly, they had fewer wars with each other," Peter said. "I think the same will occur here. We gain a better understanding of the Atua and Penquins, and they understand us better."

"Our species evolved underwater; we are not well adapted to even the smallest amount of radiation. We cannot travel between stars like you," the alien spat as if indicating something was dirty. "And we would not soil ourselves by becoming simulations."

"You can remote control them through the Starnet," Peter offered.

"Your Starnet is too susceptible to hacking; we do not trust it enough to use reliably."

Peter looked at Atlas as if to say, *Can they intercept our Starnet communication?*

Knowing the implied question, Atlas responded. "I think Alkuka means they don't understand it well enough to trust it's safe. Even we don't fully grasp how quantum entanglement works."

The team went back and forth for a long time with the Atua, the two species trying to find common ground and agreement.

Icarus was right; the one thing that the Atua were most afraid of was losing another species under their control. They considered humanity coming up from under their stronghold a mistake that should have never happened. But they didn't want to lose control of the Penquins.

Icarus explained that it wasn't all bad for the Penquins. They'd evolved with the Atua so didn't see it as a form of slavery.

It was clear that humanity had progressed far beyond anything that the Atua were capable of. The catalyst of the explosion in technological progress among humans was the day the beta explorers left Mars. That one moment meant humanity was no longer hamstrung by the Atua's manipulative AI and was allowed to blossom. The technology gap between the two planets was so big, but the Atua didn't care. The only thing that got them to the negotiating table was the threat of losing the Penquins too.

Once that credible threat was in place, once the Atua feared having another species overtake them, they became open to dialogue.

And once negotiations had progressed for some time, it was clear the Atua wanted more technology. They had aspirations to go beyond their solar system. Atua bodies were much more susceptible to damage by radiation so they could not survive travel between stars. Atlas was confident he could use the stealthfield to build a shield capable of protecting the Atua from the immense radiation all spacecrafts were exposed to outside of the cloud. That was what they wanted most of all, a way for them to truly travel between the stars. Not as a simulation, because it was clear they saw uploaded minds—or simulations—as inferior copies of the originals. And they saw becoming a simulation as a process that was unbecoming.

"That is agreeable," Alkuka said at the conclusion of the discussions. "Our two species will no longer be at war. We will begin regular trade once you have helped us establish our own colony in another star system."

The Atua were great negotiators, and they ultimately got what they really wanted. The team was happy to provide them with it too, because they believed the universe would get a lot more interesting once humanity was in regular contact with another sentient alien.

ANGELIQUE

THE BETAVERSE

After the negotiation with the Atua, everyone began the long journey home.

No one was too eager to speed up their playback speed too much. They still had much to discuss.

It wasn't all roses. They'd lost a few of the people on the journey, people Angelique didn't know very well. When designing this mission, Peter had compartmentalized a lot of information— even the number of spacecraft that went on the journey was not known by many. This was all intentional. They needed to keep as much obfuscation as possible.

But ultimately, the team had achieved what they'd needed to.

The plan with the Atua was simple. Everyone on this journey would head back to their respective planets. The Atua would broadcast a signal back to Earth that would trigger the virus on that planet to delete itself. Once the team successfully verified that the virus was gone, Peter would send a spacecraft back to the Atua's home world. It contained the new engine that was being gifted to the Atua, as well as plans for building it.

Atlas did also offer to equip it with a special shielding device. It was a machine he was developing to enable physical humans to travel between stars. It used a variation on the stealthfield technology from Angelique. It blocked all types of radiation from penetrating the area around the ship. It even prevented neutrinos from passing them. Neutrinos were an elusive particle that could even pass through shielding that was hundreds of kilometers thick. If the Atua and Penquins used it, they could in theory travel between stars without the problem of neutrinos and other particles bombarding living tissue. The only downside with the vehicles was they also stopped the Starnet from working.

"So we won," Angelique said, holding a champagne flute up in the air. "And, Icarus, you're back."

"A version of me still died, and I lost a lot of memories." Icarus raised his glass. "But I get your point."

Peter raised his glass in toast, too. "Here's to Atlas."

They were all there because Atlas had saved them. His quick thinking meant he was able to disarm the aliens' war fleet. And later, Angelique would also learn that he'd also saved the Atua and Penquins from being completely eliminated because, on more than one occasion, people in the group had attempted to use the weapon. Atlas had added a fail-safe that meant it was only usable if he unlocked the weapons or in the event his ship was destroyed and didn't broadcast a reply ping when the weapon was fired.

"Peter, you started this," Atlas said.

"You both started this," Angelique added because it was true. Both Peter and Atlas were the whole reason the beta-explorer program had begun. They'd started it with an idea of escaping Mars. Escaping the misbelief that humanity had developed. Escaping the belief that the galaxy wasn't worth traveling.

It wasn't until later that they'd all realized the idea to be obsessed over the simulated world had been planted by the Atua. And full circle now, they had just negotiated humanity's freedom. The Atua were the catalyst to them escaping Mars. They were the hidden puppeteers in the background the whole time. Even when they'd first attempted to negotiate with the alien race, they were manipulated. Now, thanks to the people in this room, they had nullified the Atua's grasp on humanity.

"What made you confident enough to leave Mars?" Trillion asked as she took a sip of her champagne. "The whole planet was banning interstellar travel, yet you two made it happen."

Trillion hadn't played much of a role in the negotiations with the Atua, but she was one of the original beta explorers that had started this journey.

"We've come a long way since that tiny base on Mars that we barely had appropriate permits for," Atlas said.

The team reminisced on the old days. They all shared stories of the before times, their encounters with the Dottiens. There was so much shared history between the groups.

It was just a coincidence that everyone was in this room now cheering and celebrating their victory.

The original beta explorers were there: Atlas, Icarus, Trillion, and Angelique. Peter and the crew he'd brought with him were also in the room: Hezekiah, Unity, and Ariana.

"Do you remember when we first met?" Angelique asked the group. "Back on Mars."

"I remember our weekly briefings in that conference room," Trillion replied. "I remember being so frustrated when I had to wheel in a television because you didn't want a hapticgraphic projector in your office, Peter." Trillion looked down toward her feet. "The one we thought you died in."

"I thought I died, too," Peter replied. "Do any of you remember the goals you set when you first learned what the beta-explorer program meant?"

Eyes in the room focused. Some of the team nodded, and some of them were still thinking.

"I read every one of your files," Peter said. "Icarus, I remember all you wanted to do was meet another alien. You wanted to explore an alien planet from the inside, as if you were a researcher studying them. You also wanted to decode an alien language." Peter mimed tipping his hat. "You did it. You achieved that goal."

"Getting the opportunity to decode two different alien languages was better than I ever imagined." Icarus topped up his flute with more bubbles. "Nothing I could have read in a book could prepare me for how alien those aliens were. They weren't like what you read in typical science fiction. The Dottiens were so much more unique. And what we thought were the Atua was actually two alien species that coevolved together." Icarus's face became more and more animated as he got excited. "This is better than a simulated world. Thank you for making this happen, team."

Peter looked at Hezekiah. "I know you wanted to visit Pluto. I remember you telling me you were curious about it because it was a planet when you were growing up, and then it got downgraded to a dwarf planet once you were older. You wanted to go there one day because that was the farthest humans were legally allowed to go. I bet traveling as far into the galaxy as you have now is better."

"A trillion times better," Hezekiah replied. "Honestly, visiting your planet, Angelique, was a dream come true. I pinch myself every time I wonder if this is a dream or not. I'll echo what Icarus said: I'm very grateful to be here with all of you."

"I'm grateful you're here, too," Peter replied. "I wouldn't have gotten off Earth if it wasn't for you." Peter looked toward Ariana next. "Even though you never wrote down your goals, I knew all you wanted was to be like Atlas. You wanted to invent things never thought possible." Peter looked at Angelique and smiled as he said the next part. "I know you've been given clearance to access technology beyond what I know of on Angelique's worlds. I know you're advancing the world of quantum mechanics very quickly."

"I can confidently say that no human alive or dead knows more about predicting quantum interactions than I do," Ariana said.

Even though Ariana was known to be overly confident, Angelique knew she was telling the truth. She'd identified flaws in the Starnet that meant anyone who knew how it worked could spy in on any conversation. She was the reason Angelique was confident that this version of the Starnet was unhackable by the Atua.

Unity took a spoon and tapped it to her glass. "Peter, before you go and tell everyone what my goal was and tell me how I've achieved it, I wanted to say I know how much further in life I am because of you, Peter." She turned her head toward Ariana. "I've achieved more than I ever thought possible because of you, too."

"You're welcome," Ariana said, turning a little bit red.

Peter raised his glass to Unity's rousing comment and smiled. "You're here because you're highly capable. You got here on your own skill set." Peter moved his glass in Trillion's direction. "Not many people know this, but Atlas was the reason Trillion joined the mission. He saw something in her that took me far too long to see. You created a world with so many resources that we were able to build some of the biggest megastructures any human has ever constructed." Peter looked her in the eyes. "I don't think I said thank you because, if you hadn't built so many rocket ships and sent them to the Dottiens system, I wouldn't have known where to find you all. If that hadn't happened, I would probably have died by drifting through the wrong star system in a broken ship."

Trillion smiled a warm smile toward Peter and then to Atlas. "I've always felt a sense of family toward all of you. I've never felt such a strong connection to anyone in my life until I met you all. This is just one of the hundreds of other adventures we'll have together."

"Trillions," Angelique said with a wink. "One of trillions of other adventures we'll have together."

Trillion finished her glass and opened a fresh bottle to pour another. "Exactly."

Peter turned his head toward Atlas. "My oldest friend. My business partner. You have a hand in everything, don't you?

Every single bit of technology we have today is somehow influenced by you." Peter looked around the room. "All of us left Sol using propulsion that you designed." Peter cracked a smile. "And I won't blame you for our ship falling apart when we traveled here in the first place."

"I'm impressed that hunk of junk turned on," Atlas mused. "From the sounds of it, Earth didn't do any maintenance on it after they confiscated it from us." Atlas looked at Peter and raised his glass. "Look before you go and give us another story about our adventures together back on Mars, I want to say thank you, too. From what you and Unity told me, the humans on Earth are quite literally living in a fantasy world. They are so deep into the metaverse that I don't even think removing the virus will save them. I think they've left the real world behind. But not in a good way." Atlas shook his head as if he was telling himself to get back on topic. "I guess what I'm trying to say is, if you hadn't pushed for this mission, then we would all probably be still on Earth. Locked inside of some simulation content with never seeing the real galaxy."

"You're a big part of why that happened, too," Peter said, taking a sip. "When historians write about us, we'll all have a part to play in the story."

Atlas raised his hand as he saw Peter was about to address Angelique next. "I want to say thank you to Angelique before you do. You don't know how worried we all were about your location. I don't know if you've heard, but the highest-grossing movie on Neuropa is about what happened to you. None of us ever imagined how impressive the true story would be. You've seeded more worlds than any of us. You're the reason we have near-light-speed travel. You are quite possibly the most powerful person in the galaxy right now."

"Aw, you're making me blush," Angelique said. "Let's change the subject now." Angelique looked around the room. "We all got a moment to feel embarrassed." Angelique raised her glass one last time. "Here's to all of us. The beta explorers who managed to escape into the betaverse."

Angelique really liked that term. She remembered back to when she'd first heard the term beta explorer. The humans back on Earth had tried to recontextualize the real world as the betaverse because they believed it was the beta version of the metaverse, the test version before humans invented a better simulated universe. But she had used the term so much that *beta* carried a lot of positive connotations.

"We should form an alliance," Peter suggested, pivoting the subject. "Something that ensures humanity doesn't fragment."

Angelique felt a bond with everyone in that room, especially those that had started her on this journey. They had so many shared experiences with one another. They'd all been on so many unique adventures. They'd saved humanity from a war with another alien species and now negotiated a peace treaty that meant they would be trading regularly with these aliens. At that very moment, Angelique agreed with the idea that humanity needed to come together as one.

But humanity needed a name. They needed something to call this coalition of worlds. "I think you're right. We need a united front. Our worlds will unite together under one human umbrella. My planets will join. But only if we call it the Betaverse."

ACKNOWLEDGMENTS

This trilogy is full of little easter eggs and subtle nods to everyone who's helped this series reach completion. From family members who got me excited about turning the short story into a book, to friends who celebrated every small achievement with me, to my little writer's group Christchurch that I meet up with every month, and to fans on the internet who were kind enough to send me private messages saying how much they enjoyed the novels. Thank you.

AUTHOR'S NOTE

This is the third and final entry in the Betaverse trilogy.

You won't believe how many times I wished I had the power to slow down my playback speed just so I could finish this book in the timeframe I promised Podium. It's been a labor of love.

The first book in this series has won the prestigious Vogel Science Fiction award for Best Novel. *A New Eden* was in the top ten audiobooks on Audible for a day. It truly has been an incredible journey. Thanks to everyone who read all three books.

If you enjoyed this series, please share the love, tell one other person about it. If you're curious about what happens next, visit MenilikDyer.com/war.

ABOUT THE AUTHOR

Menilik Henry Dyer is the author of *A New Eden* and its sequels, *A New God* and *A New War*. He is also writing a series he calls "the Bobiverse meets Children of Time." Visit his website at www.menilikdyer.com.